Marlboro Blues

T.L. Rotkiewicz

Rocklynn Press
Windsor, CT.

MARLBORO BLUES

Copyright © 2013 by T.L. Rotkiewicz

Rocklynn Press
P.O. Box 562
Windsor, CT. 06095

rocklynn75@gmail.com

Cover by Lynn Lepko
Lettering by Robert Arnow

For those who inspired me and continue to do so.
Dare to dream the possibilities.

Chapter 1

Oxford, England, March 1987

In the quaint suburb of Oxford is a townhouse cottage. Inside, a man with sandy blond hair and roguish good looks, jams a Camel cigarette into his mouth. While looking in the mirror, the smoke billows out as he cranes his neck to see he has his entire outfit ready. The gentleman is Edward Brockton, a photographer who wound up finding love while on assignment in New York seven years earlier. Ed lives with his girlfriend, a British singer named, Evelyn Winthrop. She too is of fair hair, lighter than Ed's. Evelyn has a distinguishable presence.

Evelyn sits in the bedroom. She quickly applies a wine hued lipgloss to her full lips. She checks to make sure her black mascara doesn't show any flaws or a curled eyelash out of place. Her pool blue eyes are her most fetching trait. They are the eyes that of a newborn, bright and full, wondrous with excitement and curiosity. A small sound whisks her away from getting ready for a dinner party. Evelyn dashes over to the window and peeks out the drapes. Beyond the balcony and across the street is a woman who walks with a stroller carrying a little girl, holding a doll. The girl catches sight of the woman looking through the window. Their eyes meet as if to have that connection. Without the mother seeing, Evelyn gives a wave and brightened smile. The little girl does the same. For a moment, Evelyn feels great joy. Yet, her beauty and happiness hide her inner core that of an empty, lonely feeling that she could not provide. She turns to look at the photo of herself and Ed from their second year together. That was 1982 and they were both content and in love. The picture depicts their great warmth for each other. Martha's Vineyard provided the perfect setting with the full sunshine beaming upon the patio, which was their summer home. She hadn't seen it in such a long time in person. A lot had changed since those five years. Evelyn no longer simply wished for Ed, but an extension as well. She had set her sights on starting a family two years earlier; figuring four years with her mate was enough. Knowing full well she was no spring chicken, Evelyn made many attempts figuring out her cycle and when she would be the most fertile. Time and time again, she would bring home pregnancy tests. Each one heartbreakingly turned out negative. Ed suggested two doctors he knew and each one sadly told her she was unable to have children of her own. Ed had finally thought adopting was the best way to go, but Evelyn felt it was wrong. If she couldn't bare any Brockton children, then it wasn't meant to be. This eventually would take its toll on both of them.

Evelyn stares at the picture when Ed calls out "Evelyn? Are you ready yet?" Ed scrambles from the bathroom, back to the bedroom calling out in his gruff worn voice that sounds as though he's had several packs of cigarettes a day. He sees her and she looks up.

"Yes, Darling. I'm just about ready."

"Good." Ed rushes out of the room and runs down the stairs.

Just then, a long black car pulls up into the driveway. The driver beeps the horn. Ed looks out the small window adjacent to the front door. He grabs a wool-striped scarf from the closet and runs back upstairs.

With his Camel dangling between his lips, he says, "Christ! We're gonna be late!"

Evelyn steps out of the bedroom, blindly placing earrings on while watching her frazzled boyfriend search for things.

Ed then says, "Mac just pulled up. Are you ready?"

"Of course I'm ready," Evelyn says in her deep voice.

Ed replies. "You know, now that Phyllis and Allistair have their little boy, we probably won't be staying for long."

"I almost forgot that we were going to Al and Phyl's tonight."

Ed says in a concerned fashion, "Are you sure you'll be okay? The last time when you saw little Paul, you damn near fell apart in front of them."

Evelyn takes Ed's chin into her hand. "I'll be fine. I wasn't feeling well that day."

"That's all?"

"That's all. Come now. We must be going. You know how Mac doesn't like to wait."

Evelyn grabs her coat. Both she and Ed exit the front door.

In the evening, the moon glows outside of Ed and Evelyn's bedroom window, revealing their forms lying on the bed. Ed is firmly tucked in, purring with a good night's sleep. Evelyn lies awake softly crying to herself from the thoughts spinning in her head. It was nights like these that kept her up for hours. The hollowness within her body had overtaken any happiness she was feeling. Their visit to see Allistair and Phyllis was of no help. Her eyes turn to the soft snore churning out of Ed, lying there with no thoughts or worries. Evelyn wanted to know why Ed grew insensitive to her needs. He dismissed all of her feelings even when she was hurting badly. She knew this was tearing them apart. Their love life was virtually non-existent. Ed was still very much attracted to Evelyn, but there wasn't much feeling as there once had been, even though Ed wasn't too passionate of a man. The lacking of having a family only brought out the worst in spirit for both of them. Evelyn sinks to the pillow and turns the opposite of Ed. She tries to erase those bad feelings and instead thinks of what she can use as lyrical material for her next album.

***

On a Monday morning, the rain pitter-patters against the window. Evelyn sits next to an end table, smoking a Camel. She begins thinking of music that had inspired her from the past. Peggy Lee's, "Black Coffee" spins on a turntable. Peggy had such pose, such dignity in which the way she sang. She was sultry, not brash or sweet. It was her voice that carried

Evelyn through some lonely hours. Peggy, Dinah Washington, Nina Simone, Billie Holiday and Ella Fitzgerald influenced Evelyn's jazz style heavily. Her voice though had grown raspy and dark in tone. It was definitely lived in and gritty, ravaged by cigarettes and some hard living. No longer had she been able to pull off the voice of an angel. Surprisingly, she started out as a soprano. Evelyn had been through much in her life. Forty years of life. Her pain and hurt she put forth into song. The lyrics reflected that of anger, jealousy, and sometimes an outcry of hatred for the opposite sex. She garnered a good-sized audience from her angst-ridden music. It seemed as though her fans felt they could relate to her pain. She was their hero, somebody who understood the fragile human condition. No sweet songs of happiness, just bare bones pain.

It was this kind of music she missed. She had thrown herself into the arms of the jazz world for six years. Evelyn had hoped to appease Ed with her change. A change of music would mean a change in lifestyle. At least that's what her boyfriend thought. The punk scene was home for her. Jazz was lovely but it was an experiment with another type of music, something to stretch her horizons with and make her more versatile. Only now, she grew more restless. She wanted a piece of her past back, the one that made her comfortable. The one that made her angry and create her best music.

Evelyn watches the rain pelt the window. She takes a drag on the cigarette before walking to the far end of the hall. There, she opens the door. The singer flicks on the light switch revealing what's inside. Her sanctuary is full of images of what she had been to her present state. It was a little piece of serenity for her. A piano sits near the wall of photos of herself at different stages of her career. A sprightly teenager's face beams, surrounded by flaxen blonde hair in one of the frames. Evelyn looks at it, and then sits at the piano where her fingers bare down on the keys. She hums low, trying to find the right key to match her voice. Picking up a notebook from the floor, she turns the pages. The singer looks at what's written. There are lyrics for a song that had plagued her for a better half of the year. Words that could only be induced by her mind, painfully squeezed out. Some artists would say songs are like children. They give life, the labor of trying to get it out, and watching it eventually graduate and get on the radio. There would be those disappointments due to a picky A&R manager not liking it or the record company balking because of its length. How is one to ever let go of something they so strongly believe in? How do you choose which child graduates and which one doesn't? Or if not aborted, then possibly a soundtrack or better yet a compilation as a bonus track for a *Greatest Hits* package. Evelyn wasn't happy to sacrifice her latest album, *Hero's Requiem* to the corporate barking dogs. It was fragile. Neither bouncy nor upbeat, the song spoke of being something a person is not. To stop pretending and kill it off. It was Evelyn's outcry of the changes she had been through. The time had come for her to shed her cape and bare her feelings. The lyrics though weren't meshing together properly with the arrangement.

Evelyn writes a few lines while puffing on the cigarette. The page gets torn out, rippling down the spiral binding and curled into a ball. It gets tossed on the floor, tumbling against a stack of cassette tapes. She looks down at the pile. There are black, analog, uncased, unlabeled tapes piled as if ready for the garbage can. Soulless fluff that couldn't come close to what she wanted or what she desired to hear. Nothing gave her goose bumps. Nothing made her smile. £250,000 worth of work in one studio alone, thousands more at other studios and rehearsal halls. Odd mixes thrown together in a ray of hope. None. It just seemed like it would never be done. This project would have to be put to rest soon, as funds were drying up fast. Strangely, Evelyn knew which tape was which. By instinct, she could pick up on which one had a certain part of a song on it. On a shelf sits an audio deck player. She grabs one of the tapes and puts it in. Holding the Camel between her fingers, her brows furrow with disdain. It was a mix of the jazz version of her title track. Quickly, she presses the eject button. She couldn't have done it fast enough. The tape gets flung into the trash can with a resounding thud.

"Shit." She utters. "A pile of worthless shit."

Evelyn rubs between the bridge of her nose while looking down. She hears the front door shut. Ed was back home. She closes the notebook, abandoning the piano to greet him.

Ed peels away his wet raincoat, placing it on a hanger in the closet. He fluffs his hair just as a streak of lightening marks the sky.

"It's bad out there." He tells her from a murky squint.

Pushing back his hair, he looks at her.

She responds to his glance. "Would you like me to make you some coffee or tea?"

"Tea will be fine. Absolutely miserable out there." He repeats.

"Yes. I know. Let's go in the kitchen."

She soon disappears through the swinging door to the next room. There she prepares a cup and saucer.

"How did it go? Did you get the job?" She asks.

"No. They said they didn't need a field photographer. I showed them my portfolio and they said my stuff was too outdoorsy. Whatever the hell that's supposed to mean."

Evelyn places a pot of water on the stove. "Well, maybe they just don't see it. You're known for your out...exterior shots."

"You were going to say, outside." Ed says back as he lights a Camel with a small silver engraved lighter bearing the initials *E.B.* "It just really gets me. They want things a certain way."

Evelyn pours the boiling liquid into the cup, delicately dipping a tea bag. She agrees enthusiastically. "That's the way I feel about my music!"

Ed says in a monotone sort of way, "Not the same."

Her similarity; shot down.

He carefully sips at the hot tea. "Not the same at all. Your music is easier for you. Put a few notes together, toss in some instruments, and boom! A song."

She shakes her head in disbelief. "It's not like that at all. Why, it's very painful." "Yeah." Ed replies in a gruff tone, unwavering in nonchalance and arrogance.

Evelyn closes her eyes. There seemed no use in explaining more about her music.

He snorts out, "Next thing you're going to tell me is that it's akin to labor pains which I may remind you, you have never felt."

With mouth gaping in disdain, Evelyn leaves the kitchen.

***

On a fairly warm if not cloudy afternoon, Evelyn looks out the window. She had plans on going to the park but decided to forgo those. Ed was out of the house. He would return within a few hours to pick her up for a gallery party. It would give her enough time to get ready. She sees a car go by. Right away, a spark goes off in her head. Evelyn exits the room.

She heads through a side entrance beyond the dining room where she opens the door that leads to the garage. Originally fit for two cars, it had been redone with an extended bay for three. Two for her. One for him. She steps around the midnight blue colored 1980 Austin Rover Maxi. It had a few minor scratches and scrapes. One dent was when she had trouble with it. She kicked in the door, leaving a small concave mark on it. She hated that car when she first saw it. She despised it being there instead of Baby Blue. Now that was a car!

It was a 1967 Aston Martin GT. A record company was after her to sign with them and she was wooed into switching labels when they presented her with the brand new light blue car. It had beautiful beige seats, a matching steering wheel. The sound it would make when she started it up! Smooth traction. Best of all, it made her look good! She could go around town with her black Italian sunglasses on catching the cool breeze with the convertible top down. People would stop and stare from the sidewalk of Carnaby Street in downtown London. She was a somebody! For nearly fifteen years, she had 'Baby Blue' as her prized possession. It was a very dependable car and she loved it so. No rust, not a dent nor a ding. Just a beautiful silk-looking light blue as the Moore skies on a sunny day. Nothing lasts forever though. Once Ed had moved in, he began eyeing it in a disturbing manner. Ed hated anything fancy or rock star related. To him, Baby Blue was like an eyesore. It stuck out like a sore thumb in the quiet Oxford neighborhood.

One day in early September of '81, something happened to Baby Blue. She thinks of when Ed wanted her to see something in the garage, which he seemed awfully proud of. Ed in his entire varsity styled good looks had the grin of an impish child waiting for his mother to see his latest accomplishment. He led her in and she gasped with horror. Baby Blue was gone. In its place was a dark blue economy sized four door. Its aerodynamics if it had any, was mostly that of a hatchback. An unwelcome sight from the beauty of the convertible she had owned. With a big smile, he eyed her.

She uttered beneath her breath, "Where is my car?"

"Do you like it?"

"What did you do with my car?"

"Isn't she a beauty? I got her for a bargain. Okay, so she's considered used. Boy, but at Benton's she was practically screaming, 'Pick me! Pick me!"

He gave a hoarse laugh.

With lips drawn down from the atrocity, she yelled out, "It's bloody ugly! What is that thing?"

"It's last year's model. An Austin Rover Maxi."

Ed became surprised and hurt by her reaction. "I let you keep the other one! Come on! That car was almost fifteen years old. What did you want? You can't get parts for it anymore." Was his rebuttal, which she quickly rebuffed.

"How can you do this to me? I loved that car! That car got me a deal with Anlan Records."

"It's just a car. You trade them in when they get old. No big deal."

Enraged, she shouted at him. "No big deal? You bloody prick! You got rid of my fucking car! And all you can say is, 'No big deal?' I guess it wouldn't be much of a big deal if I wrapped my hands around your throat and crushed your larynx with my own bare hands?" She looked at him. "How could you?"

"Look. I even got a load of cash back from the trade in!"

He handed her a large wad of bills.

She threw them down.

"I want it back! I want Baby Blue back!"

"You can't! It got sold right when I was making the trade."

Evelyn seized a breath. Looking back at the bills, she flung them in Ed Brockton's face. Then she ran back inside the house, crying uncontrollably.

Those are the fond memories she had of first seeing the Austin Rover Maxi.

She steps around it from the back. Still it seemed like such an ugly car even though she had been driving it for six years. On the other side is a hidden automobile underneath a white sheet. Baby Blue was gone but her other car was here to stay. She glides a hand over the soft covering. Biting lightly on her bottom lip, she feels she has to see it again. It was time. With no hesitation, she pulls the billowy material away, watching it slide from her newer precious auto. An all white 1978 Alfa Romeo Spider Veloce.

With its deep red interior plush seats and convertible features, it rode like a dream. Evelyn had purchased it herself from the money that had poured in from her first major hit album in the spring of '78. It was a car she used as luxury since she no longer had the Aston Martin. Evelyn took it out only when Ed would be out of town. There was that temptation. She fishes in her pocket. Pulling out a set of keys, she unlocks the door. Getting in, she rests her head against the front seat.

Sweet luxury!

***

Racing down the stairs is Ed, with Evelyn closely following behind.

"Why must everything be my fault?" She laments.

"You don't make things easy." Ed replies while pulling out his lighter. He lights up a Camel in a flash.

"I know what the doctors have told me. But maybe we should consider adoption."

Ed takes the cigarette out of his mouth, giving her a glance as if to say, "Huh?" He squints his eyes trying to find the clarity from her proposition. "Are you serious?" Ed says back with sharpness to his gruff phrasing. He grins. She remains unmoved. "You are serious. Evelyn, honey, weren't you the one telling me if you couldn't have any then it was not meant to be?"

"I know and I've started to have a change of heart. It wouldn't be that bad. Neither of us is getting any younger."

"Say we did have a kid...bought of course. They go on to graduate in eighteen years and shortly after they would have to take care of us folks. I'd be nearly seventy and senile by then."

"You already think like that and you're not even fifty yet."

Ed sees she won't let up. "What about the money it costs? I'm not talking about how much it would be to get a child. You have to consider the cost of what that baby would need. What with the care costs, and hospital bills if they should get sick. Did you ever think of that? Diapers are a fortune alone."

Evelyn reassures him. "We can always cut costs by using cloth diapers instead."

"Yeah? And who would stay home with the baby? We're both out of the house a lot."

"I would. When they would get older, I would bring them with me. It's not as though I'm in the studio all year long."

"Oh no? What would you call it last year where you hopped on a plane and I wouldn't see you for weeks at a time?"

"Darling, that was last year. I certainly wouldn't do that now. I'm not selfish."

"You're not? What do you think you're doing now? You want a child without thinking of anything important! How much did you spend on the last studio?"

Sheepishly she answers. "Enough."

He puts a hand to his ear while the other holds the lit cigarette. "How much?"

She says reluctantly, "Ten."

"Ten thou?"

Quietly she mutters. "Yes. And you're calling me selfish? I think you are by being utterly pigheaded about this!" She raises her voice to a distressed level.

Ed turns in shock after taking a drag.

With the smoke still coming out of his mouth, he answers her with a grunt. "What? Me? Pigheaded? Listen to you. 'I want a child. I don't care what anybody else thinks. Money is no object.' Listen; why not just take the advice of Dr. Hawthorne and Watkins? And your own advice of, 'If I can't have any naturally, then it wasn't meant to be.' Kids just aren't meant to be for us."

Evelyn looks at him straight in the eyes. "You don't want any."

"Evelyn, we just simply can't have any. You can't reproduce. Remember? And adoption is so costly."

With a straightforward glare, she speaks with authority. "I want a third opinion."

Her dead-serious tone makes him turn quickly with the slow motion action of taking out the cigarette from his mouth.

***

Riding along the M40, Ed drives with a Camel dangling from his lips. Evelyn looks out the window. With a sullen and worn expression, she blinks. The cool breeze from the lowered window flips up her hair, sending it every which way.

Ed pulls over along the motorway to study a map. "Let's see. If we go past Milton Keynes, we can catch the M1. Then that will take us all the way up to Leeds and..." Ed turns his head towards his girlfriend. "You're still not talking to me."

Evelyn closes her eyes in defiance.

Just before leaving the house, they had a big fight about their relationship. She had suggested they needed counseling. He refused and turned it around to make it seem as though once again it was her problem. Ed begins folding the map.

"Hey. I apologized already."

No response.

"Are you listening to me?"

Still no answer.

He looks to the side and zooms back onto the motorway, mumbling to himself.

Evelyn continues to take in the scenery.

Up in the Moors, Ed stretches out the legs of his tripod while Evelyn sits on the hill contemplating her life with him.

He cackles with delight. "Yep. Let's see if Ormsby Publishing can get a better shot than this."

He oversees the lavender skies with billowy green vistas below. A light breeze blows bringing about the voices of bleating sheep from the farms nearby. A flock of grouse spring forward into the sky. Evelyn looks up. Ed looks up for only a moment while switching the aperture on his camera. He readies his lens the way a skilled hunter would look through his periscope for a clear aim. With a slight air of bemusement, Evelyn tries to make herself interested in what her boyfriend is doing. Curlews scream from afar alerting Ed.

The only thing that screamed louder than birds to Evelyn was the thoughts running rampant through her mind. She could only think of two things, her music and the feeling of a relationship slowly disintegrating. Her latest argument with the photographer was only one of a few within a week's time. It was becoming more and more evident that a break from each other would be needed. She watches as Ed snaps away.

"It's not working." Evelyn tells her manager, Ben Voorhaun.

The two sit in what looks like a cold sterile waiting room. Beyond the door, loud thumping is heard with some bass guitar filling in parts. Evelyn drinks a cup of coffee while her manager explains with his German tinged accent.

"If it's not working, why not let it go? You can afford to drop the one song."

"But Ben darling, that's the title of the album. *Hero's Requiem.*"

The sound of drumsticks hits either the wall or door. Both look over. Two men are heard yelling right after that. Evelyn goes to investigate.

Inside, she finds her drummer, Clayton arguing with the new bassist, Stefan.

Clayton shouts out, "I don't have to take orders from you, you half pint wanker! You've been here for only five days and already you're telling me how to do my business. Go join a cover band. That's what you're worthy of!"

"All I said was, I think you're doing it wrong. Your timing is all wrong." Stefan says back.

Off to the side, guitarist, Chris minds his own business while keyboardist, Jake doodles on the keyboard.

"What is going on here?" Evelyn asks. "I'm in the next room over and I hear this commotion going on. Clayton's sticks are on the floor near my feet. Why is that?"

"This bloody no-talent doesn't know the progression of the song. It's, *La Ta Ta De Da.*" Clayton replies in disgust.

"If you listened to what she said instead of getting all hotheaded about it, you would hear it's, *La Te Da Da.*" Stefan corrects him with pride.

The singer drops her head down and shakes her head in anguish. "It's wrong. Both of you are wrong. It goes, *La Ta De Da Dahhhh.* Separate and draw out the last dah. You have to hold down the note longer on the keyboard and let it ring out on both the bass and guitar naturally. Don't stop it. I know you're all stressed out over this too."

Chris looks up. "Can I say something?" He checks to make sure everybody pays attention to him. "Evelyn, we've done the song two or three dozen times. Each time hasn't been right for you. We don't know what else to do. We've probably tried every combination and it's not happening. We've changed strings, Stefan and me. And Jake over there switches keys from D to G. We just don't get it."

"We bloody will get it if it takes us all night!" Evelyn retorts.

Ben takes a seat next to the wall as he watches the sessions unfold.

Evelyn walks up to the microphone. "Now, Clay? You take it with the cymbal."

"Which one?" He asks.

"The ride. Stefan starts the whole thing. Clay comes in after. Then Jake. Chris adds guitar over the keyboards. Draw it out all together then I'll come in with the words. Ready? Go."

Stefan begins the pounding bass beat. Clayton begins the pattern on the ride cymbal and bass drum. Evelyn turns to look at them.

Above the rhythm section, she shouts out. "Remember! *La Ta De Da Dahhh.*"

Jake begins his keyboard part, followed by Chris strumming lightly to the accompaniment. Evelyn goes to the microphone. She begins to sing in her deep, sometimes strained approach.

Come to your senses you're a foolish old man.
You run...
She looks back at Clayton with concern.

...So fast, as fast as you can.
No need...

"Hold it. Hold it. Stop. Stop. Stop. Clayton you're drumming is overpowering my vocals. I can't hear myself. Chris, I can barely hear you." Evelyn states.

Chris tells her. "You said you wanted me and Jake to blend."

"I know, but darling, I can't hear you. All I hear are drums and bass. I can't sing louder. The song is not to be played with a sort of bombastic fury. It's soft and subtle."

Ben asks. "Is that what happened in Paris? You said the players were too loud."

Clayton asks, "What is it? Do you want me to ghost note it? Then it'll be too soft and Stefan will be bleeding with bass. Is that what you want? Why not just have you and Stefan since nobody else seems to count?"

Frustrated, the singer ruffles her hair. "You do count. All of you. We have to find a way of everything balancing without all of you feeling as though getting your toes stepped on."

Ben gets up. "Evelyn. Can I talk to you outside?"

She turns around to see him with a beckoning finger.

They walk back into the corridor lounge.

Ben warns her. "You're overworking them. Look. Let the song go for now."

"But maybe it's not them. Maybe it's the production or possibly even the mixing."

"You're grasping at straws, Evelyn. This song is not meant to be. Not for this album. You're already way behind the schedule of what you first told the record company. You've spent thousands of dollars and you're just flushing money down the toilet. Even the last producer you worked with, Adam Cory said you would never get the effects you want for Requiem, because no studio can facilitate it."

"Ben, he said that because I didn't want his sound all over my record. If I had let him have it his way, it would have sounded like a Phil Spector production. The man wanted to add a tuba on my song! I didn't want that. Cory is very good at what he does but it's not my style."

"Maybe you should just go back to the jazz sound you had before this."

"It wouldn't sound right either. I've tried countless arrangements and none have even come close to what I'm looking for."

Yelling is heard once again. The door to the rehearsal room flies open. Clayton yells. "I quit!" He turns to look back at the door. "That little bugger is drivin' me up a bloody wall! 'You play too loud.' That little shit!

Telling me, I play too loud. And you...you defend him! I'm done. I'll go find a better bunch to work with. Ones that have backbone."

He grabs his jacket and shoves his drumsticks into a knapsack. Clayton walks out of the lounge past Ben and Evelyn. The heavy door behind them slams shut. Evelyn looks at her manager.

Slowly she says, "I guess maybe you're right. That song can wait."

Chapter 2

While Ed is away snapping pictures for his latest assignment, Evelyn slips out of the house. She needed her own retreat. Ed never liked the places she would hang out at and that was fine by her. She didn't care much at all for the bars and taverns he would frequent. That sort of riffraff was not meant for a woman of her stature. She was supposed to be a lady. That's what Ed thought of her as. She preferred the small nightclubs where she could be herself. That's where friends who felt the slow burnout of punk and new wave went to for some glimmer of the past. The Green Light offered some hope.

Evelyn steps inside the small nightclub. She gasps in aghast at the vision of much-loathed '80s Synth Pop. On the jukebox over in the corner is Howard Jones playing the latest drivel. What happened to the Green Light's welcoming sounds of The Ramones, Iggy Pop, Blondie, Patti Smith, The New York Dolls, Sex Pistols, Clash? Anything but the horrid sounds of a keyboard being wrecked with a MIDI and much abhorred drum machines! Right away, she sees the place transformed. The smell of hair spray fills the air. London youths dance to the music and seem to thoroughly enjoy themselves.

"No taste!" She thinks.

Then it occurs to her that it's their decade. No leather or funky iron-on t-shirts. Big pants replace slashed jeans for guys and spandex with leg warmers for girls. Designer jeans are all the rage. The top ranking designers from Jordache to Sassoon. Stonewashed wear, neon, all the tripe of the decade one could handle or stomach for that matter. The sports jackets guys wear are fashioned after the hip police show, *Miami Vice*. Skinny ties are another feature in black or metallic colors. Symmetrical patterns are everywhere. Whether they are the featured shape on a woman's jersey, earrings, or the odd cut outs on the wall. The bright lights flash from the colorful spectrum of spotlights. Evelyn waves a hand in front of her face from the ongoing stench of hair products in the air. She parks herself on a stool at the bar and pulls out a cigarette to light it with her own matching small silver lighter, like Ed's. Only this one has the letter's E.W. on it.

She finds a young gentleman sitting next to her. He's dressed yuppie style with a partial mullet.

Turning to her, he says, "Who's mum are you?"

Evelyn turns to him quickly, half jolted by the comment. Those were fighting words to a forty year old. A below the belt version of, "You're old. What do you want here?" She slyly eyes the young man and blows out a puff of smoke.

Evelyn thinks to herself, "Brash bugger you are." She says, "Ah. Don't you have homework to do or did you forget to clean the kitty litter box again?"

Confused, the youth says, "Why?"

With the air of confidence, she taps her cigarette into an ashtray. "Because you don't know shit."

The yuppie leaves quickly. Evelyn laughs to herself with gleeful hoarseness. She still had her wicked wit when needed.

Quickly she recognizes the bartender. "Kelly?"

The woman looks over with an airbrushed canvas face. She has two different colors in ghastly symmetrical patterns around her eyes. It gives off the look of pink and blue cellophane. Heavy slashes of rouge are applied to her cheeks in a China doll fashion. The jersey she wears is big and exposes a bare shoulder, while colorful jelly bracelets slide down to her wrists. Kelly pours drinks even though one could tell she wasn't fond of either the crowd or how she was looking that evening. Kelly looks at Evelyn.

Evelyn looks at her surprised as she asks, "What happened?"

Kelly replies in her heavy Scottish accent. "The manager wanted a change of pace. So, he said be trendy and we'll get more business. It's for Fridays and the weekend. Yuppies! I'm doin' overtime. Fookin' jellies! The boss wanted me to wear these."

Kelly lifts up one foot to show the singer her purple jelly shoes. "Ah, but I want me self a new guitar. Not cheap either! Me band wants to try and record when we get a good bit o' money." Kelly pours a cup of ginger ale when she eyes a few kids. "They come to hassle us. Thinkin' we're old to them. Christ! I'm thirty-eight, 'scuse me! Anyway, folks like you are lucky. You don't need a job like me, pourin' drinks or scrubbin' loos. You get to go to a nice clean studio." Kelly slides a drink to the left. She looks at Evelyn. "So, how's the recording going?"

Evelyn puffs on her Camel as she says, "I have quite a few demo tapes but no matter what studio I go to, I'm not happy with it. I thought it would be more jazz related but it doesn't sound like it. It's as if my voice doesn't want to go that way."

"Aye. Getting back to your roots?"

"I don't know. Ed wouldn't like that."

"Tell Ed to slog off! I don't know why you stay with that poor old sod." Kelly leans over the bar counter pointing a finger. "You need to do things for yourself. Music is sacred to you. You don't need Ed's approval. Take a chance! Roll the dice! See what you can get."

Evelyn nods. "Even if I wanted to, it hasn't been working. I've gone to so many studios already. Here, Montreaux, France, Los Angeles, New York, Chicago, Miami, West Germany. Aside from that, Hero's Requiem sounds like shit. Nobody can get anywhere close to what I want. I've spent a good amount of money on the time it's taken and the advance portion is just about dried up from all the travel. But it's still not right."

Kelly digs in back of the counter. She slaps down a copy of Billboard magazine. "Maybe you should try one more time...in New York. Look on page thirty-seven. You might reconsider once you read that. Hey, if I'm determined to wear jellies and get me guitar, then you must have it in you to finish the record."

Evelyn looks up at Kelly and takes the magazine while the smoke curls from the cigarette she holds.

At home, Evelyn surveys the pages of Billboard while munching on grapes. She had to admit that she didn't want to give up on her musical ideas. Why should Ed care about what kind of music she wanted to make? He felt jazz was safe; therefore he didn't have to worry about the lifestyle she once had. Still, it was her life. She wasn't happy with the results she had been getting for the past year and a half. Keeping busy with others' projects kept the money flowing steadily but was little comfort of her creativity and her record company. She was given a ten-year deal to make five albums. Three were already taken care of with little success. The fourth she wanted different.

Turning the page from thirty-six to thirty-seven, she finds what her friend Kelly mentioned earlier that night. She examines the article that reads,

From North York to New York -

Upon admittance to the studio oddly called, I.C.E. in New Paltz, NY, you know you won't be treated the same as the rest of the studios. For one, you won't get a receptionist asking what you want. Curator, Jim Zima, 34, who checks in on the studio has taken care of business since his father, Jack Zima died five years earlier. He left Jim with the business he loved. "There's approximately seven rooms available for guests to just move in while production is going on." Comfort is a factor.

Enter the wizards at the controls. At the helm of the three-piece production team is a savvy and charming individual. Jaime Weston, 43, a street-smart Canadian from North York is Mr. Cool, Calm, and Collective. When he wants something done musically, "It will get done. I push until it sounds right," Weston says with a sly smile. When asked about his many successes, he offers up, "Success is really based on interpretation by an individual. It depends on how the artist(s) feel about it in the end." Jaime Weston was trained in nearby Toronto, starting as an assistant engineer then moving to engineer over the years. Since the mid '70s, he's become a producer in his own right. "He was ambitious when I first met him," says Bob Whitfield, 45, a fellow record producer and longtime friend of Weston's. "I met him while studying as a sound engineer in Toronto. I grew up in Buffalo but there were no opportunities that fit what I was looking for, so I crossed the border. We're opposites. He's quiet and I'm rather outgoing." Dan Soren, 32, rounds out the three as the meticulous younger engineer who was born in Plattsburgh, New York. "I got slammed together with these two characters. Jaime is the leading man and Bobby is the supporting cast," Dan says.

They all live near the studio. So, they see plenty of each other and their families whenever.

If artists want to book time at I.C.E., they should plan on it several months in advance. Call Jim Zima for details.

"Hmm. Very interesting," Evelyn says to herself. "I'll definitely look into this more." As she munches on a grape, she nods. "Jaime Weston...charming? Very, very interesting."

The door to the house unlocks. Ed steps in with a Camel dangling out of his mouth and a tripod over his shoulder. Evelyn closes the large magazine.

He says, "Hi, honey."

Ed kisses her on the cheek. He places his tripod next to the couch where she sits. Taking off his jacket, he mentions, "I got that job for the magazine we talked about. I think the shots I got will knock the editor's socks off."

Evelyn watches Ed as he disappears into the kitchen. She could care less what he did. Instead, she looks back at the magazine. The idea of going back to New York begins to get stuck inside her head even more.

The next morning, Ed tosses a few rolls of film in a knapsack and rushes out of the house. Evelyn walks downstairs in her nightgown and fluffy white slippers. She watches Ed pull out of the driveway. Slipping into the kitchen with the Billboard magazine, she makes some coffee as she contemplates on whom to call first. Would it be the studio or her friend, Henry Winslow? She dials quickly then waits for someone to pick up.

A man's voice comes through the other end. "Hello?"

"Hello, Henry."

"Oh, hi, Evelyn."

"Did I wake you up?"

"Naw."

"The reason I'm calling is because I'm seriously thinking of going back to New York in the near future. You work at the newspaper around the area, right?"

"Mm hmm."

"Would you happen to know anything or any stories about a studio in New Paltz, called I.C.E.?"

"That's the next town over. I see one of the producers, Bobby, often enough. Karen and his wife, Andrea do the bake sales at the school together."

"That's lovely but do you know if the studio is any good?"

"I'd certainly like to hope so. They apparently have had a lot of success. They're all a great bunch of guys."

"That leads me to asking, do you know anything about the head producer, Jaime Weston?"

Henry hesitates. "Um, not too much. I don't see him half as much as Bobby. He doesn't come out of that studio too often."

"Oh. Well, it should be interesting meeting him and the rest."

"That I'm sure. Just remember, if I understand correctly, you have to call Jim first."

"Yes. I have all of that information already. I'll talk to you soon. Bye."

"Bye, Evelyn."

Evelyn puts the phone back down on the hook. Looking at the magazine, she flips to page thirty-seven.

Immediately, she dials the phone.

She says, "Hello? I'm looking for Jim Zima."

"This is," says the voice over the phone.

Evelyn replies, "Hello, sir? I'm looking to book time into I.C.E. I found this article in Billboard. There's a project I've been working on and every studio I've been to has disappointed me."

Jim says, "You're name is?"

"Oh, I'm sorry. It's Evelyn Winthrop."

"Okay, Ms. Winthrop. I'm going to give you the number."

Evelyn begins writing down the phone number on the magazine.

"Got it."

He says back to her, "If that doesn't work, call me back and I'll give you a different one. Okay?"

"Okay. Thank you very much, sir. Cheers and Goodbye."

Again, she puts in a call. The phone rings on the other end. Someone picks up.

"Hello, Bob Whitfield at your service. How may I direct you?"

"I'm looking to speak to somebody about I.C.E."

"Hold on. I'll connect you."

Evelyn looks at the page again.

"Hello, Bob Whitfield at your service. How may I direct you?"

"Hello, Bob... Oh, you're the one who..."

She's cut off again.

"Hold on. I'll connect you."

"What the hell?"

"Hello, Bob Whitfield at your service..."

Evelyn flares her nostrils until she hears a slight snicker.

"Hello? I'm looking to book time into I.C.E."

More snickering.

She states flatly, "And I won't take no for an answer."

"Even if I said we're booked until July?"

"That's fine. I'll take it."

"Who are you?"

"My name is Evelyn Winthrop and I..."

"Whoa. Back it up. *The* Evelyn Winthrop? *Kiss Kiss, Bang Bang*? *Ravaged Beauty*? *Childlike Sins*?"

"Um, yes."

"Well, why didn't you say so?"

"I couldn't get through you." She smiles back.

Her giddiness is abruptly stopped as Bob says, "I'm still not thoroughly convinced you're the real deal. We get phonies all the time. Tell me something that others don't know."

Evelyn sighs. She mumbles, "Impossible." She takes a moment to think it over. Then she pulls something out of her past. "Wait! Are you familiar with the front cover of *Childlike Sins*?"

"Mm hmm. The one with the two boys?"

"Well, we were supposed to get it done at my guitarist's place on 8th St. They moved it to the Bowery for greater effect. Still they used Jed Jackson's son and a neighbor's boy. The used matches were added when we used eight of them because they kept blowing out. So, Macy, the photographer put them in the shot." Evelyn then asks, "So?"

"How much time will you need?"

"I'd say probably a month."

"How about July fifth?"

"Fine by me. Oh, is Mr. Weston there?"

"Uh no. He's off jet setting in his private leer jet, sorry, Concorde, with a dozen pounds of caviar and sixteen cases of champagne."

Bob snickers.

Another voice says quietly, "Man, are you bad!"

Bob says to Evelyn, "What that really translates to is, Jaime's in L.A. doing work at a studio in Hollywood. He doesn't answer the phone, so you get to deal with me. Are you disappointed?"

"No." Evelyn soon finds herself giggling from the exchange of words with Bob Whitfield.

He goads her a little more by saying, "Oh, come on. You're a little disappointed I'm not Mr. Charisma."

"No. No. Not at all."

The other voice says, "Come on, man. Stop doin' that."

Evelyn hears Bob tell him, "Kiddo, don't you have something to do?"

Bob returns his attention back to Evelyn. "Sorry about that. Insubordinate engineer. He snickers.

Evelyn then says, "Well, I look forward to meeting you. Bye."

"The pleasure has been all mine. Bye, sweetie. See you then."

Once Evelyn hangs up the phone she says aloud, "That's not going to be a dull place. Mr. Whitfield, you just convinced me of that."

Then she thinks of the elusive Jaime Weston. He doesn't answer the phone normally? What kind of character was he? Would this studio fulfill her musical needs? Evelyn looks at the magazine again until it's time to fetch the freshly brewed coffee.

***

After a particularly grueling day, Evelyn arrives back home. Tossing her pocketbook on the couch, she notices that Ed is nowhere around. Then she hears a noise coming from upstairs. It's the rattling sound of a bag and thumping. She walks upstairs. The door is halfway open and what she sees confuses her. Ed is hunched down with a large black garbage bag. He rummages through her side of the closet.

She asks him. "What are you doing?" Evelyn manages to catch Ed tossing some of her old jerseys in the bag. She grabs at the plastic, pulling out a red and white striped shirt. In shock, she blurts out, "What are you doing with this?" Upon further investigation, she finds more. Her jaw drops. "My cut-off T-shirt of The Sex Pistols? Nobody touches my Johnny Rotten T! And my Ramones shirt!" She picks up the carelessly bunched shirts from the bag. "My God, Ed. What had you planned on doing with these?"

"I'm spring cleaning. You don't wear this stuff anymore."

"Like bloody hell I don't! I just don't wear them in front of you!"

Ed turns to look back. "For real?" He snickers.

"Don't laugh!" She barks back.

Ed starts to stand up in a confrontational manner. "You know this stuff is crap. What are you tryin' to do, keeping this shit in the house? Tryin' to get a ruse out of me?" He yanks out a Clash T-shirt, balling it up in his hand. His blue eyes glare at her as he talks with a condescending tone. With all of the drama of an actor in a theater, Ed unleashes on her. "This...this is your poison!"

"My past, right? You cannot erase it as much as you would like to! It's who I am! And who I was! Accept that, Ed!"

The photographer looks down with the glance of defeat back at the bag. Evelyn figures he'll see things her way. Instead, Ed takes the balled up shirt and throws it back in the bag, resuming to challenge her emotions. His eyes glide over like sharpened knives toward the closet. He grabs a black leather jacket. It's a beautiful biker styled garment adorned with pewter colored buttons on the cuffs, no studs or anything else. The silver zipper dangles back and forth as Ed hastily yanks it out by the hanger. Evelyn watches fearful while her beloved item gets held hostage. Stepping over the bag, she rushes over, grabbing a sleeve of the garment.

"Don't you dare!"

Ed grabs the shoulder of the opposite side.

She begs. "Let go! Ed, stop it! You know I love this jacket! I've had it since '76 and wore it on the back of an album."

This only makes Ed angrier. She had to mention one of those albums. Those damned punk albums.

He grits his teeth and tugs harder. "It probably doesn't even fit you anymore."

She pulls back tightening her grip on the sleeve. "Are you trying to say that I'm fat?"

"You don't need it."

"Bastard. Let go! Isn't it enough that you sold my car, you heartless prick?"

Ed stops tugging.

She yells out, "Why are you doing this? Just let me be!"

With a sudden jolt, Ed shoves the jacket at his frazzled girlfriend. She falls on the bed. Quickly she sits up. He tosses the bag with half-hearted effort onto the bed. The garments inside tumble out, revealing rock and punk T-shirts, among some striped less offensive wear. Ed leaves the room in a huff. Evelyn begins to cry as she drops onto the mattress hugging the garment.

***

"So, you're telling me there's no chance." Evelyn climbs off the tissue-padded bench. Dr. Johansen nods his head.

She pleads, "Isn't there something I could take?"

"I'm afraid not."

"I've never experienced cramping or an irregular period. So, what is wrong with me?"

"It's inside you. You'll have a normal cycle. Only it's your ovaries. Your eggs are stagnant. They won't move. They don't do anything. It's a form of infertility."

Evelyn looks at him with confusion. Dr. Johansen looks away for a moment out of guilt.

She asks, "What causes it? I mean, is it a result of my drug taking days?"

"It could be that or you were simply born that way."

Evelyn looks down attempting to make sense of her predicament. The doctor then suggests, "If you're serious about wanting a family, perhaps you should look into or at least consider contacting an adoption agency." A moment later he continues. "I'll send you the official results when I receive them."

Evelyn remains in shock. The only movement she can make is nod in acceptance of what she has finally learned.

After making her payment for the appointment, she leaves brokenhearted. Dr. Johansen watches and bites his bottom lip while shaking his head. He gives a deep sigh, and then returns to another patient.

Returning back to the house, Evelyn sees Ed fidgeting with a camera. She feels as though she's about to cry. Ed sees this and places his camera on the coffee table. "What's the matter, honey? Did Dr. Johansen give you any hope?"

Taking a gulp, Evelyn lets out a shaky gasp of, "No."

With thinly veiled compassion Ed says, "Damn. I was really hoping for different."

Tearfully, Evelyn tells him, "So was I. He said if I want a family, I should look into adoption." She throws her hands up, practically screaming in her raspy and pained voice, "What is wrong with me? What the bloody hell is wrong with me? I was born with a hollow body. Vacant! Empty space that can never be filled!" She walks to the stairs instead of running into his open arms for a consoling hug. Yelling out loud, she cries, "Do you know what that does to me? I'll never become a mother or a grandmother!"

"Aw, come on. It's not the end of the world, Evelyn!"

Evelyn then yells out, "I want to be left alone!"

The bedroom door slams upstairs.

Ed looks up at the room while Evelyn pouts. He walks to the kitchen and places a call. "Hi, I'd like to talk to Dr. Johansen."

After holding for a few minutes, Dr. Johansen answers. "This is Dr. Gerry Johansen. How may I help you?"

Cheerfully, the gruff voiced Ed says, "Gerry!"

Dr. Johansen hesitantly yet disappointed replies, "Ed. Um, hello."

"Just wanted to tell you that you did a great job."

"Tell me that if I don't lose my license."

"Naw! You don't have anything to worry about." Ed looks up towards the ceiling as he says, "She got the message. I think this subject is done with."

The doctor replies with, "Well, I hope everything goes well with the two of you no matter what, including this."

"Yeah. Hey! We're still on for Saturday's cricket tournament, right?"

Ed hears the sound of Evelyn walking down the stairs. "Hey, Ger? I gotta go. Cheers buddy."

Ed puts the phone back on the hook.

Evelyn walks into the kitchen. Right away, after wiping her eyes she says, "Ed, I'm sorry. I didn't mean to take it out on you. You've been supportive and you have every right to be angry with me. I'm angry with myself that if this is my fault then it's something I have to live with. God only knows I'm facing the consequences."

She gives him a hug for comfort. Ed turns his eyes away and grins to himself.

At night, the wind blows with a light breeze licking the curtains. Ed crawls on his hands and knees, measuring his prey like a mountain lion. Shoulders up and a sly grin he moves forward on the bed. Ed drops his shirt on the floor. He slides his hand under the sheet where he slowly picks it up and reveals a thin, pale leg. Lunging for the foot, he grabs it and goes for a kiss. Evelyn jumps, startled out of her skin, as she had been in a deep sleep. He sits up quickly.

She hears the sound of him unzipping his pants and blurts out, "Don't!"

Ignoring her outburst, he goes for a kiss against her knee. Quickly he slithers over her with a shadow. The lamp above the bed gets switched on.

It kills the mood.

"Stop it! Get off of me!" Evelyn shouts as she swats at him. Ed moves away from her. "Keep your pants on!" She exclaims. "What has gotten into you?" Evelyn says as she props her body up.

Ed looks at her with hungry eyes. He wasn't about to tell her he was glad that Dr. Johansen's third opinion finally would put the subject of babies to rest. It wasn't that he was feeling sorry for her or wanted to comfort her. He was feeling a sharp desire. Strangely, her disappointment made him want her all the more.

"Every time I look for some passion from you, you're quick to say, 'No.' Now you're all hot and horny as can be. Are you happy as to the result of today's test? Is that what you wanted?"

Gruffly, Ed replies in mock denial. "No! Of course not! I'm...I'm just as hurt by this as much as you. This would be mine too you know. But, does that mean we can't have fun as though to try for kids?"

"No! Don't even mention the word children! It's completely tasteless, rude, and inconsiderate of you to act this way especially after what I've been through. You know how much I wanted them." She gathers the sheet and leaves the bed. "I'll have none of it." Evelyn says coldly. As she leaves the room, spitefully she adds in, "Enjoy your own company, Edward."

Ed sits on the bed with no coverings. He puts his hands on his knees and blows out a breath.

***

Late into the month of March, Ed and Evelyn arrive back home from dinner. They head up the stairs into the bedroom. Ed grabs his pajamas while Evelyn talks.

"I was talking to a friend of mine a short time ago. And she said, 'Maybe it's the wrong type of music you're trying for.' Then I started thinking maybe it's the mix. I talked with Ben, and he was trying to tell me that perhaps I should leave it alone. But then my friend suggested I give it one more try."

Ed puts on his pajamas then slides his body under the blanket. He picks up his wire rimmed reading glasses off of the bedside set of drawers and a book. While she continues to talk, he goes about his business as though she has nothing of interest to say. She turns to look at him while unbuttoning her blouse. "You're not listening to me."

Ed puts the book down. "I am."

"Okay. Then what was it I just said?"

"Something about the music."

"Yes. If you bothered to listen, I was talking about my project."

"Oh yeah. *The Hero*."

Evelyn slips on her nightgown. "It's called, *Hero's Requiem* if you ever bothered to know."

"Oh, sorry." Ed replies with a hint of sarcasm. "Just get the thing done with."

"Do you know anything about recording because if you did, you wouldn't say that to me."

"No."

"No? Then who's asking you about production? I can imagine if you were to record an album. It would be shoddy at best."

After reading a few more lines, Ed rolls his eyes. "Listen, if I recorded a bunch of songs, monkeys could do the production better than any hotshot producer. Just press a few buttons. Stick in some effects and then you have an album."

"You would have shit." She tersely informs him. "You're an ignorant, pompous fool, darling, when it comes to recording. Wretched fool."

Evelyn pulls the blankets away, leaving him with none. She turns away from him as she snuggles deeply inside the covers. Ed looks at her with an oh-well expression. He shrugs his shoulders before removing his glasses and putting the book back on top of the drawer set. Ed leans over, switching off the lamp above the bed.

***

During April, Ed and Evelyn attend a photography gallery. Ed shows off a photo he had taken. Evelyn decides to step away from him, knowing he'll explain every nuance of the picture.

Ed calls out. "Rose! Jeff! Did you ever notice if you shift the light, it makes the flower look more dramatic?"

Indeed, Evelyn's thoughts ring true. Ed goes into photographer mode. It is the self-absorbed, pat-yourself-on-the-back attitude. The photo itself is a medium close up shot of a yellow exotic looking flower, which could just have been a daisy obscured in light and shadows. Evelyn knows the photo well. It was taken during their trip to Martha's Vineyard almost a year earlier. Ed would not let her forget. He blathered enough about it when they came back. A silly, stupid flower and he was proud as a peacock because of it. At least it made him happy. The three people laugh over a comment. Evelyn looks back at them.

Flute glasses of red wine get passed around in the room. Some feet away, Evelyn looks at photos under glass. Her reflection bounces off one as she looks at a picture of a dark tunnel. A little further away, Ed continues to hold court, laughing and talking with other patrons. He talks to a group of four, indulging them with more photo talk.

"Now this one is a real beauty. It's a music stand I got from my girlfriend's friend, Millie Grumbach's antique store. Probably one of a few normal friends Evelyn has. Notice the fine grain?"

The group of four lean forward.

One man says, "Ah, I see."

Ed roughly replies, "Yeah?"

He takes a glass of wine from the caterer passing them around.

Evelyn glances at another photo. Ed moves on in another direction, weaving between people. He then recognizes a couple.

"Hey, Billy! Marge!"

Evelyn perks up her ears as she notices them too.

Ed says to the couple, "How are you two doing?"

Billy replies. "We're doing fine but terribly busy."

Marge adds in. "The twins take up most of our time. I'm thinking of photographing them. It would be great to do so for a photo album."

Billy then asks Ed, "What about you and Evelyn? You still trying to have children?"

"Us? Nah! She got checked up again and the same thing happened. The doctor said she couldn't."

Marge says in a disappointed tone, "You must be devastated."

In a straightforward tone, Ed informs her. "Really, it's not that bad. I mean look what you have to live with, twins!"

Billy laughs slightly. Marge looks at her husband and Ed disapprovingly. At the same moment, Evelyn begins to walk towards the couple.

Then she hears Ed quip, "Besides, she won't have to worry about stretch marks or getting swollen in all of the good parts. You know? I just say, you can't, so you can't. No big deal."

Marge makes room for an infuriated Evelyn, who's jaw drops from the rude remarks made by her boyfriend. As he finishes his laugh, Evelyn flings her wine at him. He quickly feels the liquid cooling as it sticks to his T-shirt underneath his blue shirt.

She announces in a deep, ragged tone, "You insensitive prick! How could you? I have a picture for you. How's this, 'Image of a self important stain!'"

Evelyn nods then steps back, placing the glass down and rushing to get her coat. Mascara runs down her pale cheeks. Ed breathes out a strong sigh, bowing his head down. He is unable to say anything to guests who look at him. Evelyn walks out the door. Ed follows behind.

Once they return home, Evelyn walks in and tosses her coat in the closet. She wipes her eyes, seeing the gray smudges on the side of her index finger. Trouncing up the stairs, she squeezes the railing hard, wishing it were some part of Ed she would like to strangle. Ed walks in, placing his coat in the closet and picks hers up from the floor hanging it on the hanger next to his.

"I'm sorry, honey."

Flustered and hurt she turns quickly to him. Feeling scorned, she bitterly says, "You're not sorry for what you said. You're sorry because you got caught saying it."

"I was drunk and..."

"Bullshit!"

Ed looks at her a bit surprised by her outburst. He opens his mouth as if wanting to say something.

Huffily, she tells him, "If you were drunk, you would have made a fool of yourself. Only, you were stone cold sober and you made me look like a fool instead. How could you do such a thing like that? What? Does it give you perverse pleasure in mocking my condition? Would I be better off having a disease? How about a heart condition? 'Oh, she's got a bad ticker but she keeps on going.' Or how about some type of cancer? 'Her hair is falling out from chemo. Ha ha ha! Don't worry, luv, she can change wigs any fucking bloody time she wants!'"

Ed shouts out, "Stop it! You're being overly dramatic about this!"

"Overly dramatic? You're the one that's making me sound like the poster child for female infertility!"

Ed takes off his dark gray jacket and inspects the pink stain on his shirt. He begins unbuttoning it. Evelyn walks up the stairs more, almost reaching the top.

"It's one thing for you to make fun of my friends, which I would never do to you...but for you to be so insensitive is inexcusable!"

She trots upstairs, quickly running into the bedroom and slamming the door behind, that it shakes the ceiling fan downstairs in the living room. Ed removes the stained shirt. Then he sees the glaring pink spot on his white cotton T-shirt. It looks like it will need the bleach treatment too. He quickly takes it off. Flopping back his bangs, he looks up at the balcony above.

Placing a hand over his bare chest, Ed pleads. "Come on Evelyn! It was stupid what I said!"

Evelyn unlocks the door.

"Atta girl." He says with a smile, thinking all is forgiven.

Over the balcony, a pillow is tossed at him along with a crumpled blanket.

"Cheap bastard! Here!"

His pajamas fall down to the floor. She yells. "Sleep on the couch or the floor you pig!" With that, Evelyn slams the door once more.

Ed picks up the items, tossing the pillow and blanket on the couch while mumbling to himself. "Stupid ignorant slob."

He carries the shirt and undershirt through the kitchen door to go to the basement.

The following morning, Ed walks up the stairs clad in his blue and white striped pajamas. He sees that the door is wide open to the bedroom and the bed is unmade with a few freshly laid out garments. He hears the water running in the bathroom. Ed walks over to investigate. The door is about halfway open.

He enters to the sound of rushing water coming from the shower. Ed figures he can get ready while Evelyn is busy showering. He walks over to the sink across the way and pulls up his toothbrush from the holder. He starts to brush his teeth. When he looks up to see his reflection on the mirrored cabinet, he's not the only one staring back. Evelyn stands in back of him dripping wet and naked. Ed doesn't mind the view at all. Only, he won't touch her. Every time she had attempted to get him to join her in the shower or tub, he refused. His belief was that getting clean was not pleasure, but a necessity only meant for one at a time. Also, he feared shriveling up.

Ed continues to brush his teeth after getting his fill of seeing Evelyn's body. She remains in back of him. He rinses his mouth and then turns to her.

Evelyn says with concern, "You like the way I look don't you?"

He says back almost gleefully, "Of course."

"You would think I was hideous with stretch marks."

She draws imaginary lines across her belly with her fingertips.

Ed nods in disgust. "Aw, come on. Not this again!"

He rinses his toothbrush instead of paying attention to Evelyn. The buxom blonde steps up to him.

"You would consider pregnancy ugly, wouldn't you?"

She draws her finger under his chin urging him to look at her.

With his pale lips, he utters, "No."

Evelyn takes a step back and holds up her large breasts while saying, "I'd be a lactating fool! And this belly would be out to here."

Evelyn puts a hand several inches away from herself to illustrate the size. She continues. "I would not be pretty. I'd be waddling like a duck."

Ed barks back, "Quit it!"

He grabs her arm. She looks up into his eyes as though thinking he's about to kiss her. He says in an almost shaky tone, "You know you'd be beautiful whatever way."

Evelyn wrenches away from his grip. "That's not what you told Billy and Marge."

Ed looks down. "That...that I was just tryin' to rile up ol' Marge. She can be a real stick in the mud."

Evelyn turns and walks away. Ed lets out a silent sigh as his eyes feast on her nude, creamy flesh backside. She grabs her robe from the hook. Tossing it on and tying it she says, "Only, I'm not Marge," before stepping out of the bathroom.

***

Over the course of another two months, the bedroom had become a battlefield between Ed and Evelyn. Love was a tug of war. Chances are if Ed felt like having a little romance, Evelyn wasn't up to it. If Evelyn were to have the same thoughts, it would be Ed who would rebuff any advances. Clearly, things were getting worse between them.

Evelyn walks in the room with a dark red negligee on and matching boa. Any man wouldn't be able to resist the temptation before them, a woman with a voluptuous figure, full breasts, fuller lips and all. A man's dream! Not Ed's though. No amorous desires. Trying to get him in the mood for love had quickly grown into something less savory like going to the dentist. Every time either of the two had desired one another, children would somehow figure into the conversation, thus spoiling the mood. Ed felt the only reason Evelyn was in the mood simply became a motive to try and get pregnant. Even though they knew that wasn't going to happen.

Ed faces her way as his head rests against the pillow. He watches her slowly saunter over to him, tossing her boa. The fluffy red item crosses over his shoulder, lightly touching his chin, crawling to his mouth. There's nothing like eating those little feathery things.

"Poo!" Ed blows out.

The boa slips under his chin. Evelyn approaches him with her chest practically in his face. He stares right at the bountiful amount of cleavage.

Too much!

Ed didn't much feel like getting smothered by that ample chest.

He retorts. "I won't be able to breathe if you lean much closer."

Evelyn pulls away before she can even kiss him. She rolls her eyes and turns away for a moment. "Don't you love me anymore?"

"Of course I do. I just want to sleep."

"Oh, that's fine and all. When you're feeling good, you want me to jump up and satisfy you. But you won't do the same when it's me who wants some loving. Why is that?"

Ed leans up from the pillow. "If I can recall. You were feeling depressed when I wanted you."

"Are you talking about the same night when Dr. Johansen examined me? Darling, that was with good reason! I had just found out for the third time I couldn't have children."

"There you go again."

"There I go what?"

"You. Always having to bring up children."

"What...what do you want me to call them? Productions? Reproductions? Offspring? Kids? Spawn?"

"I want you to quit it!" Ed says in a harsh rasp.

Evelyn gets under the covers, rolling up the blanket to her chest and turning around. He flips over the opposite way, fluffing up his pillow.

It shouldn't have mattered much to Evelyn that Ed wouldn't want sex that night, or the night after that, or the night after that. He was non-sexual. He wasn't the kind of guy that would carry wanton desires. He was not a man of intense passion. Ed would satisfy her for all but five minutes. Foreplay or anything cute he wouldn't even think of. Evelyn could never think of cheating on him to satisfy her needs, longer than the few minutes he could give. She had grown accustomed to his kind of love for she felt she couldn't have anything better than that. Numb from his constant refusals, sex just wasn't fun to her anymore.

She shuts the light off, looking into the darkness. Less than a month before she would go back to New York. Maybe after that things would change...for better or worse.

***

Things had become so strained by the middle of June, unbearable for Evelyn. Maybe not so for Ed. Evelyn was having a hard time coping with his overprotectiveness and drama. A change was needed or she would go crazy. She felt loyal to Ed but was feeling vulnerable. Going to New York in a couple of weeks was making more and more sense to her.

Evelyn walks along the sidewalk leading to the glorious though stately Magdalen College and all of its picturesque beauty. She looks up to see the Bell Tower with the misty shade of blue provided in the sky. School was out, so the premises were left bare for boaters to tend to leisurely rides along the river. The whole area seemed serene. Lush green grass. The stone walls could provide the perfect texture for an artist's eye. Evelyn goes to stand at the Magdalen Bridge, a comfortable place where she would go to think. If her sanctuary at the house gave her the feeling of stability, then it was the outdoors of the bridge that gave her answers, which she would need. She looks to the sky as a confessional for her soul. The long, beige, lightweight coat she wears gets flipped with the teasing of the breeze. Down below she sees the boaters getting ready to take off. One looks up, smiles and waves. She does the same. The river's rippled waves move upstream. The image below is reminiscent to one of an oil painting, soft textured but pleasing to the eye. Beyond are the trees that line the outer edges with foliage dripping down; casting their reflection onto the green and copper toned shallow waters beneath. Evelyn watches as each boater disappears under the bridge, until it's just her and the empty river.

She closes her eyes, recalling the moments that had become so rocky for her relationship with Ed. The hands of time had made both uncomfortable. They felt age creeping up on them. She begins to think of how possibly foolish she was in putting pressure on Ed to have children. Three strikes and she was out. She had to put the idea of procreation on the back burner. Her music needed the attention. Nearly two years of the same thing. Studio after studio. So much money spent. One last try. Either this trip would break the relationship with Ed or make it stronger. She hoped for the latter.

All of the arguments come rushing to her. How she felt her feelings were shoved aside, dusted under a carpet like unwanted particles. She recalled telling Ed how she felt about his work. Her eyes get caught watching the ripples.

The voices echo as she remembers. "You want to know how I feel about your so-called artwork. Your photography?"

In a defiant tone, Ed barked back. "Yeah!"

"I'll tell you. I think some of the flowers must be miserable when you photograph them. Half the time they look like they've died in front of your camera. And you're so proud of them! You go on and on about that yellow flower you shot at Martha's Vineyard. I have news for you, Ed. I've seen better. You drag me out to some meadow across the other bloody side of the country to take pictures of sheep shit!"

The photographer's eyes widened with rage. "Sheep shit! That's what you think? Listen woman, do you know how much I get for that sheep shit you're groaning about? I got about £200 for those shots! You know what? The agency liked them so much that they want me to shoot for their winter catalog!"

Bitterly she told him, "Then do it by yourself because I'm not going!"

The door slammed after that.

Maybe she was too harsh with Ed sometimes. After what he had done for her, she was grateful but it was overlooked with the heated debates of late. If she had never met him, her motivation wouldn't have existed. Possibly, it could have come later or worse yet, she could have been found dead. They had met at a studio when she was strung out. She was addicted to heroin and cocaine often enough that he tried to put a stop to it by sending her away to a hospital. It was a scary experience. Patients who ranged from sane to Vietnam veterans who couldn't find their way back to reality from the horrors they saw. Their drug trips were of no help. Some people would go crazy; others would hold onto bed pillows and name them, treating them like pets. Drying out for her wasn't easy but what she saw made her straighten up quickly. She knew she could get better by her own sheer will. It would take time, but slowly she got her life back on track. Two months later, Ed moved into the house with her. He had become her unofficial caretaker and that grew into a relationship. But he had become fearful that she would go back to her old habits if she were to revisit her past in any manner. Now, it had become stifling.

That trip to New York was becoming more and more enticing. It's not that she even wanted to visit the city. Her music had dictated her feelings. It was her own obsession to see it get completed that would take her away for a month. It was causing a great rift to her tattered relationship with the man she had grown to love. She hated though that he was dismissive of her work. It was part of her and should have been respected but because she and Ed were such opposites, he never bothered to truly listen to her music or her opinion on such a subject.

The wind wisps down upon the coat again, attempting to get a peek underneath in a sly manner. She looks down again seeing her watery warped reflection below marred by a silhouette. Taking a deep cleansing breath, she closes her eyes once more. From thinking of Ed, other thoughts tug at her memory bank.

Kelly.

It stays fresh in her mind the chat at the Green Light she had from March.

"Tell Ed to slog off! I don't know why you stay with that poor old sod." Kelly told her. The memory makes Evelyn smile. The Scottish bartender was blunt and to the point. "You need to do things for yourself. Music is sacred to you." Again, Kelly was right. "Maybe you should try one more time...in New York. Look on page thirty-seven. You might reconsider once you read that. Hey, if I'm determined to wear jellies and get me guitar, then you must have it in you to finish the record. *Record.*" The word echoes deeply. The only thing she had on her mind.

The article she read grabbed her from the get-go. When reading about the head producer the line read, "I push until it sounds right. Success is really based on interpretation by an individual. It depends on how the artists feel about it in the end."

He didn't sound like a pushy guy. He could just get what the artist wanted. That was comforting, but maybe even this was too much of a challenge. Either way it intrigued her. Who was he? Who was this Jaime Weston fellow? The words follow up her thoughts of the descriptions that were bestowed on Mr. Weston. Words like, savvy, charming, street-smart, ambitious, quiet. And what about the guy he worked with, that engineer, Dan? He described working with Weston and that Whitfield producer as, "Jaime is the leading man and Bobby is the supporting cast."

Jaime.

It was a curious name in itself. She wondered what he possibly could look like. Could he be similar in looks to Ed? Was he completely different? What did he sound like? Was he married?

"You're a little disappointed I'm not Mr. Charisma." Bobby Whitfield cracked with slight mock disappointment that he wasn't the one grabbing attention.

Then it occurs to her that she and Ed would normally take off for their summer retreat in Boston, visit Cape Cod and Martha's Vineyard for two weeks or so. This couldn't wait though. It might be a disappointment to him, but she had to think of herself for once. Not what made him happy or what she would try and convince herself was right.

She stands a little more upward from leaning over the bridge, a little more straight and stoic.

Take charge!

Her reflection appears more vivid with a smile appearing on her face. No more taking herself for granted. There was more to life than the bright green grass, small rivers that danced under boat bellies. More than what was beyond Magdalen's majestic reaches. More than what England had to offer. More than what Ed Brockton's small mindedness could bare. Time to conquer America!

New York, here I come!

Evelyn looks up at the sky for a kind of confirmation. The brightness beams down upon her. Yes! Yes, that's what she waited for. She smiles widely at the answer.

Walking away, she heads back down to the sidewalk where she sees a woman with a stroller. She looks over, seeing a little boy peeking up at her with all of the happiness and sunshine in his eyes. Light strawberry blonde hair is nearly in his eyes.

Evelyn asks, "How old is he?"

The woman replies. "Oh, he's two and a half. An absolute joy."

Evelyn smiles down at him. He tends to a bottle he holds, drinking from it heartily.

The singer says with her voice deepened, "That's so sweet. Thank you."

With that interaction, Evelyn walks away with a little bounce to her step. Running into a person with a child had no effect on her as it might have a few short months earlier. She was content and excited for her journey to New York.

Evelyn disappears down the sidewalk, humming to herself.

***

Ed steps into the living room with a drink in his hand. There he finds Evelyn on a chair, looking at the Billboard magazine. He looks at the wall in back of her, studying the poster print of a daffodil he took while in Cape Cod.

"Hmm."

Evelyn looks up in thought. "Ed?" She says.

Ed remains in deep concentration of the picture. He then realizes she called his name. Blinking back, he says, "I'm sorry. What was it you were saying?"

Evelyn asks him, "Do you love me?"

He looks at her with brows furrowed. "Of course I do."

"Why don't you ever show it?"

Ed sees the pity in her eyes. In a more caring tone he says, "I do." He stoops down to her level in the chair. "Come on, baby. You know I love you."

"Yes." She answers in deep and regretful tone, eying the floor.

Getting up, she puts her hands on his shoulders. He stands up. Her hands fall away. She reaches for his sides and takes his hand to touch her face. He immediately pulls away, leaving her disappointed. Instead, he gives her a big bear hug. She lets out a gasp from being tightly squeezed. While he holds her, he looks at the large framed photo on the wall. Evelyn looks over his arm, at the magazine's open page about I.C.E.

***

"What are you doing?" Ed asks Evelyn as he sees two open slate blue colored suitcases. He watches her. Squinting while the Camel is in his mouth he says, "We don't take off for Boston until mid July. Are you that excited to go this time?"

Evelyn leans her body in the closet. She stops to look over at Ed standing next to the bed. "That's not what I'm getting ready for."

"It's not?"

"No. I thought I told you already."

Ed looks down at her defiantly, crossing his arms. "Remind me."

"About my trip back to New York. I told you..."

Ed cuts her off. "Uh-uh. You never mentioned anything to me about a trip to New York."

Evelyn goes back to rummaging through the closet hoping to avoid the conversation.

He then asks, "When had you planned on telling me?"

She answers back, "It slipped my mind."

Ed puts his cigarette out in the ashtray on the bureau. "It slipped your mind. Evelyn, you know we go every July to Boston. The ride to

Martha's Vineyard and the view from Cape Cod has always been your favorite. Or did that slip your mind too? So, why would you want to go to New York? You'll be back by the fifteenth. Right? The sixteenth is when we leave. I have the reservations taken care of already."

Evelyn releases a blouse from the hanger, tossing it on the bed. She throws a pair of dress pants at the bed. Ed catches them instead.

She informs him, "I'm taking off on the fifth."

"But you'll be back in a week or two after that, right?"

With an obstinate expression towards Ed's pathetic whining, she says, "I'm staying about a month."

"A month?" He gasps back. "What...what for?"

"I have work to do."

"Work? In July? What kind of work could that be?"

Evelyn tosses more items, and then begins folding them as she sits on the bed.

"*Hero's Requiem*."

"That song, still?"

She shakes her head. "No. The whole thing. The whole project. An album's worth."

Ed looks at her, unable to believe. "I thought you were done with that. Isn't that the same project you had been working on over the past year and a half?"

Evelyn places some folded garments into the suitcase.

She says, "Yes, and it is two years now. Not a year and a half."

"Didn't you tell me when you got back from West Germany you were done with that? Didn't you tell your manager that too?"

"Initially, I thought I was done with it, but then I listened back and it doesn't sound right. My voice doesn't seem to fit the style of the music. It doesn't want to. The words don't convey that impression."

Ed mutters. "Jazz is jazz."

"I'm not talking about jazz. I'm thinking more of when my voice was edgier."

"You're talking about the music you made when you were a gutter rat? That's what this is really about. That's why you want to go back to New York."

"No. No. Not like that. I don't want to be the same person as when you first met me. I'm talking about music."

Ed looks at Evelyn with doubt and unwillingness to compromise.

"The studio I'll be recording at isn't even in Manhattan. It's up near where Henry Winslow lives."

With a serious expression Ed asks, "Did he put you up to this?"

Evelyn rolls her eyes and gets up from the bed. "No, luv. Henry did not put me up to this. Why are you acting so suspicious of me? This is not the first time I'm going somewhere to record, darling."

"I just don't like the idea. Why can't you just leave the recordings alone the way they are?"

In a growing frustrated tone Evelyn says, "Why should it matter? I don't bother you when you need to take pictures in Ireland or Scotland. I think I have every right to make a living out of my career and make my own decisions. I wish you would support what I do in any way I see fit to record." She places a hand over her heart for emphasis. Looking down, she adds in more solemnly, "Look, I don't want to argue about this. There is nothing to argue about because there is nothing to fear. The faster I get this done, the quicker I can have a normal life."

Evelyn puts her hand under Ed's chin. "That is what you want, right?"

Ed begrudgingly says, "Yeah."

"Aside from that, we need some time apart from each other. We've been getting on each other's nerves lately. I don't want to see that happen, as I'm sure you don't either. This is the last one. I promise you."

Ed takes a moment to think before nodding again in agreement. "All right. Do what you need to do."

Ed gets up from the bed and walks away rather contemplative. Evelyn walks over to the bureau, picking out a Camel from the pack. She lights it with her lighter, letting out a stream of smoke from her mouth. She looks in the large rectangle mirror. She finds her thoughts in a cross of uncertainty and curiosity. Evelyn was uncertain about her life with Ed, yet she was strongly curious about what awaited her in the next seven days.

She continues to pack her suitcases.

***

Evelyn's destination is less than twenty-four hours away. In America, they would be celebrating Independence Day, but in England, it would be like any other average day. The singer prepares for her trip. She turns on the lamp on the bureau to the dimmest setting. Since informing Ed of her planned trip, he remained bitter that she was leaving at a time they should have been thinking of their visit to Boston.

She looks at the bureau, figuring on what other little items she needs to bring. Her eyes glance over at a photo of her and Ed smiling. She had her hand under his chin as if to lift it. His squinty blue eyes showed glee along with a big smile on his face. She smiles at the picture, remembering the good times. Then she finds Ed's cufflinks, which partially obscure a small compact mirror. A bottle of lip-gloss gets tossed into the heavyweight travel bag. She looks all around her to see if she's forgotten anything of importance. Slowly she counts on her fingers whatever needs counting. Stopping to stare ahead, she freezes her position. The large rectangle mirror picks up on her reflection from the side. Evelyn walks out of the room to the next one over. She checks the bathroom. All of the essentials had been cleaned out. Her eyes widen as a thought pops in her mind.

"Oh my God! How can I forget?"

Evelyn runs down the stairs into her sanctuary. Quickly she tosses in about two dozen tapes into a small black bag, which by the end of gathering, bulges. Looking around, she knew she wouldn't see her beloved room for a whole month. She takes in the sight of the piano and all of the pictures surrounding the room, along with her valued record collection. Returning upstairs once again, she goes to the bedroom. Evelyn walks over to the closet, taking her black leather jacket off of the hanger and tossing it on. She walks over to the bed where Ed is fast asleep, curled under the covers.

Very quietly, she approaches, giving her sleeping boyfriend a kiss on the forehead and whispers. "Goodbye, darling."

She shuts off the light and carries her bag down the stairs. Her two large suitcases wait at the bottom of the steps. Briefly, she goes inside the kitchen to match the time with her watch. 4:48 AM. There would be enough time until she caught her flight at 6:10.

Beaming headlights shine through the side window next to the front door. Evelyn looks over. Her ride had arrived. She pulls along her luggage as a man gets out of the car. He helps her at the front entrance picking up both suitcases. Evelyn hauls her travel bag in one hand. The door closes to the house. The car in the driveway pulls away. They drive off.

Nearly an hour later, the car pulls up to the doorway of Heathrow Airport. Evelyn emerges from the car. The man takes out the suitcases, leaving them on the curb. He gets back in the car. She leans in.

"Tell Millie I said goodbye."

"All right." The man replies.

"Bye."

He drives away. Evelyn walks in and receives help from an airport assistant. While there, she gets her baggage and passport checked, along with having to go through metal detectors. Evelyn looks at the itinerary running on the screen. *6:10 AM. New York.* No delays. The singer takes a seat in the waiting area of British Airways. Not fully aware that she's staring at her travel bag, Evelyn picks it up to remove the notebook she has inside. Picking out a pen, the singer analyzes her lyrics.

Over the loud speaker comes a voice. "Flight 1450 to Normandy is now boarding. Flight 128 to New York will be boarding shortly."

Evelyn looks up, alerted by the flight number called out.

Time to go!

The waiting area fills up quickly with other future passengers.

Aboard the plane, Evelyn looks at the growing morning sky turn from a dark hazy blue to light and vibrant. Evelyn was used to flying in and out of Heathrow. It had been her practical existence for two years. This was no different, although her excitement was starting to wane. She just wasn't sure if even I.C.E. Studios could fulfill her musical needs. It was a flip-flop of emotions she felt since first finding out about them. A voice comes over the loudspeaker to break her thoughts.

"We will be arriving at J.F.K. Airport in seven hours and twenty-five minutes. Please enjoy your flight and thank you for flying British Airways. Be sure to buckle your seats and we ask that you turn off all electronic devices at this time. Thank you."

Evelyn looks around, as everyone grows quieter. Since it was still early, she would try to get some shut-eye.

Nearly seven hours later, the plane would be flying over Canada due to the air stream westward. Evelyn looks down, as if she could pinpoint exact towns from that high of a distance away. Ah, Canada! That producer, Jaime Weston was from there. Chances were the plane wouldn't be going near Toronto or the enclave of North York, but more likely, they were over Nova Scotia and Québec. A smile creeps onto her lips at the thought. Evelyn already feels giddy. Her reflection shows up on the small window she looks out of. Again, she finds herself feeling a little drowsy.

Must rest up before getting to the studio or New York for that matter.

Not too much time later, Evelyn opens her eyes as the pilot talks again. His voice booms through the entire plane. Passengers blink from awakening. Heads once sidled next to their companions arise to greet the warm airspace above Albany.

"Good morning again. We will be arriving shortly at J.F.K. Airport. The time in New York is now 9:43 AM Eastern. Please buckle up as we finish our journey and we ask that you turn off all electronics at this time until we land. Thank you again and we hope you will choose us as your flight again."

While the plane descends to one thousand feet, things become more defined and clear. Evelyn smiles broadly at the sight of the grand landscaped line of skyscrapers. The majestic Twin Towers that make up the World Trade Center, the Empire State Building, the beautiful art deco point of the Chrysler Building and the others less notable but all the more important in creating the menagerie of Manhattan. The brightness of the sun bounces onto various windows.

Oh, New York! How I love you!

The passengers leave the plane in an orderly fashion, taking out their carry-on luggage from the overhead compartments and bidding adieu to the flight crew. Evelyn steps out from the terminal, turning around in a circle. Something was very comforting about New York. It felt like home in some ways. It practically had been throughout the late '70s for her.

She goes over to the rentals to pick up a car. Ben Voorhaun was picking up the tab. Evelyn checks out the car she would call hers temporarily, a dark red Toyota Camry. Determined to stay inconspicuous to others, she liked the idea of an average car. She could have gotten a Lincoln but that Toyota would satisfy her. Checking the time, she notices that it's still early. Probably too early to drive up to the studio. Oh, what to do? The singer looks in the direction of the metropolitan.

The Camry drives toward the city thereafter. It was the simple temptation. Evelyn needed to feel New York in her blood again. A good shot of it would do. Better than heroin or a snort of coke. High on life. High on happiness was the best replacement from those years gone by.

Ah! The Brooklyn Bridge in all of its masterful glory up ahead!

She smiles while taking in the sight. Heading into the city, she pulls into a parking garage, then greets the Manhattan morning. Such a release to be out of London and away from Ed.

Manhattan!

Evelyn feels the sudden rush of giddiness. Knowing the city, she looks up at the sky. A bright blue beckons her to take to the streets and have fun. Eat! Shop! Be merry! The singer strolls down along 5th Ave. Saks with its noticeable windows filled with beautiful and pricey gowns gleam with sequins and beads. F.A.O. Schwartz, the children's haven of toys. Thematic with oversized teddy bears and rocking horses. Men dressed up as toy soldiers outside to greet the line of people resembling the Christmas season. Evelyn thinks to herself. If she had children, this would be the store she would let them loose in. Feeling a bit daring herself, since nobody's around she decides to try out the piano mat that is simulated to sound like a real one. Evelyn giggles as she steps on the keys under her feet.

Walking along Broadway, she sees the Coca-Cola sign in lit fashion. The peep show windows seem a little less intimidating during the morning even though the street had been sleazy all the time for the past decade or so. A man holding a boom box turns up the sound urging a crowd to clap along. In front of them is a black youth who break dances, spinning on his back on the bare sidewalk. Crowd goers toss change into a box. Evelyn watches in amazement and pulls out some change herself.

The city, so alive! New York! Further down she walks. The smell of hot dogs and roasted peanuts get caught with the breeze between the buildings. Steam pours out of the manhole covers. A brisk bit of warm air ventilates from the subways passing by underneath. A little past 6th Ave. are crowds of people starting off their day. Evelyn stops off at a small café. Again she checks the time; 11:58. Stopping in to grab a biscotti biscuit and coffee she continues her travels.

Again, she carries on. Ahead is the Manhattan Library with two stone lions perched on the small pillars. Only steps ahead are another hot dog stand. There must have been a hundred or so around the city alone. She marvels at the wonders. Funny enough she hadn't even reached her old stomping grounds in Greenwich Village, the Bowery, and Chinatown. Men are dressed in dark suits with ties and crisp dry-cleaned shirts in July. Women scurry in their high heels from one street corner to the next.

A bus carrying commuters stops at the corner of a street, squealing to a stop. Several dozen people walk out. Evelyn begins to walk among the throng of commuters. A blond haired man eyes her curiously. He wears a dark tan suit and brown striped tie. The man lowers his Wayfarer sunglasses to the end of his nose.

"Oh shit! No way!" He says with quiet amazement.

Evelyn walks a little further ahead.

The man catches up with her. His ponytail takes to the wind as he quickens his pace between people. "Evelyn!" He calls out.

Evelyn turns around. Had somebody recognized her? She continues to walk.

"Ms. Winthrop!" The voice calls out again.

She stops. The man catches up with her. He stops, half out of breath, half simply excited. "It really is you!" The man says in a rough voice tinged with Southern Californian surfer. He yanks off his sunglasses. "I used to go to your shows at the CBGB before I became a working stiff. Oh, man. This is totally awesome! I've followed your career since I was a kid. You had like, the most radical drummer. What was it you called him one time? The Charlie Watts of punk drumming?"

"Ah, Nucci. Yes. I did call him that."

"Dude, he had like the most solid groove going. Does he still drum?"

"Oh yes. He's around Italy. That's where he's from."

"I'm a drummer myself. Like I said, I went to see you whenever I could with my brother. When I turned twenty-one, that's all I wanted to do was go and see shows and copy licks off the masters. My brother and I started this band called, Kinstroke. I sell computers now. Commodores. Needed a real job 'cause I couldn't quite make the big time. I still play gigs, though. But, this is totally awesome meeting you."

They walk together to where a hot dog stand is.

"Oh man, I just... This is so incredibly cool. Would you mind signing something for me?" He checks his pockets. "Man, I left my pad at the office. Shit!" The man looks at the hot dog stand. He goes to pick out a napkin. "Okay, I've got something.

Quickly he asks the vendor, "Dude? Got a pen?"

The vendor picks out a pen from within the stand.

"Thanks."

Evelyn looks around just as confused as what to write on. She sees the abandoned storefront window and places the napkin against it.

"Who should I make it out to?"

"Toby. That would be me."

Evelyn signs the napkin.

Toby says, "I had a girlfriend who was so jealous of you because that's all I listened to at that time and she wanted to play Frisbee with the records. I told her to hit the bricks. I was like, 'Dude, nobody messes with Evelyn!' So, what brings you to New York? Are you like, playing at the CB?"

"Um, no. Actually, I'm on my way to record upstate."

Toby almost chokes. "You're recording? Awesome! I'll be the first in line to get your new album. I think they all rock, even the jazz stuff."

"You're kind but you can be honest."

"Well, okay, I didn't like it half as much as the other stuff you had done in the '70s. Is this going to be another jazz album?"

"Really? No. I'm trying to get that same feeling I wrote the others that you speak of."

"Totally awesome!"

He pulls out the rubber band from his hair, revealing a long poodle hairdo. Toby exclaims, "Ah, that feels better." He checks his watch. "Gotta go to work, but it was an honor to finally meet you."

"Goodbye, Toby!" Evelyn yells out.

Toby says, "See you around, Evelyn." He grins and dons his sunglasses, taking off among the crowd.

Past noon, Evelyn shops at Macys on 34th St. Again, another wonderful window display greets passersby. She visits the many fanciful shops along the way. The sea of yellow taxicabs spread out along the Avenue Of Americas. Evelyn sees if she can hail one down. Sure enough, a cab pulls over. She stuffs her shopping bags in with her and announces to the cab driver noticed to be Hakim Ahkbehn, who doesn't seem to know too much English,

"Broadway and First."

He smiles at her from the rearview mirror. "British, right?"

While Evelyn situates her bags, she looks back up. "Why, yes."

"Ah! I knew. I knew. Dee accent."

Well, that was sweet. He recognized where she was from.

The scenery goes flying by as the cab sandwiches between various other cars and trucks. The meter runs every so often. Driving past streets, some grungy, some clean, it becomes more and more familiar to her as the taxi rounds the corner onto Broadway again. First Street! Ah, Greenwich Village. He drops her off. She pays. Hakim speeds off in hopes of finding the next passenger.

Evelyn looks around. Nothing much had changed since then. Houston St. Bleecker was the ever-vigilant eye of the bohemian hub. Cafe Wha? Still brimming with good food and vibes. Odd boutiques line the streets. Everything is so vibrant. Colors splashed about on buildings with funky print. She stops off at another café. Green and blue lights give off a warm glow as she sips on espresso. She was going to get enough coffee in her system. That way she wouldn't get tired while driving up to New Paltz.

Several hours into her journey through the city, she goes to a pizza shop and gorges down on the deli delight.

Off to the Bowery.

The time draws near for her to leave. Foregoing anymore Manhattan destinations, she catches a cab back to midtown where she picks up the Camry and starts off. The city eventually disappears in the background as Evelyn drives further away, past the Bronx. On I-87, the New York State Thruway, she pulls over to look at a map. Exit 16 is what she would need to look for. Evelyn begins to notice that the exits are spread far apart from each other, at least fifteen to twenty minutes from the next. Exit 15 is Newburgh. Further along, she finds her destination of Exit 16, New Paltz.

Following the directions both Robert Whitfield and her friend, Henry Winslow, had told her she hopes only for the best that they know what they're talking about.

She follows the fork in the road and takes a left.

Chapter 3

At about 5 PM., Evelyn pulls into the long driveway of the studio. The Camry makes its way over the gravelly, unfinished pavement. There is no marquee or advertising in front, only a small black mailbox with the numbers *319* on it. As she nears the building, she sees the large unassuming structure. It didn't look like a studio, but rather a large dark brown house or teaching facility as one might find on campus of a university. Evelyn was used to fanciful, small studios with obvious signs outside or ones squirreled away within several floors of a business building in the form of a suite. I.C.E. was definitely going to be a different experience for the singer.

She pulls up, discovering three cars parked already. The first is a jet-black 1984 BMW 318i that Evelyn immediately admires. In back of it is a gray station wagon, about a 1981 or 1982 model with a small soccer ball dangling from the rearview mirror. Then, an aged light blue Volkswagen Bug is parked in back of the line of three. Evelyn's rented Camry crawls to the front, joining the BMW to the left side. She gets out of the car and takes a better look at the car next to her.

While walking over to the trunk she looks at the other two cars, noticing all have New York state license plates. Unlocking the trunk, she pulls out the two heavy suitcases, plopping them on the gravel. Unable to wheel them, she thinks, "Why on earth would such an expensive studio not pave the parking area?" Instead, she tugs the two items off the ground one at a time until she reaches the door. Her hands become too numb for anymore carrying. She wondered how she would handle walking upstairs as she had read about the studio being two floors.

Tired and exhausted, the jet-lagged singer raps at the door. A click is heard. A tall man with dark curly frazzled hair and an angular face gives a lopsided grin. He wears a baseball jersey with red sleeves and dark blue jeans. His darkened eyes look at her.

"Yes?" He replies to seeing the stranger."

"I'm here to see either Jaime Weston or Robert Whitfield."

He squints as if trying to remember who she was or what she was doing there. Suddenly, she realizes she didn't introduce herself yet.

"Oh. Silly me! I'm sorry." Evelyn puts her hand to her forehead. "I'm Evelyn Winthrop. I called you back in March about setting some time for me and my project."

"Well, I'm the guy who was a pain in the ass to you over the phone when you called to make your reservations. Bob Whitfield. But, I much rather prefer to be called, Bobby."

Bobby leads a hand inside. "Please, come in!"

Evelyn smiles as she grabs the two suitcases on both sides of her.

Bobby stops her. "What do you say I'll take one and you can take the other?" He picks up a suitcase.

Evelyn looks all around.

On the right side of the wall is a framed list of the various artists that have passed through the studio to record. On the left is a plaque baring Jaime Weston's name next to the words, *Producer of the Year*. That was impressive. The light above gives off a warm glow to the rust colored carpet below. Several doors surround the lobby-cum-foyer. Only there is no reception area to be seen which makes it peculiarly odd knowing it's a recording studio. Just before they head up the wooden staircase, voices are heard coming from one of the rooms nearby.

One man says in a low voice, "He said, 'You're not exactly what I expected. I thought you might look different.' I told him, 'What did you expect? Me to wear feathers?'" He chuckles warmly.

A second man with a higher tone says, "You told him that?"

"Yeah. I know the guy doesn't keep up with the times, but really... Is he living in the seventeen or eighteen hundreds?"

"Either that or he watches too many Westerns. But, you did get the job?"

"Yeah. I got the job."

Evelyn listens to the voices for a moment. There was something about the first person she heard. She liked his tone.

Bobby turns to her, noticing her preoccupation.

He smiles. "Don't worry. You'll get to meet the other guys. Let's get your stuff up the stairs first." Bobby walks up the steps followed by Evelyn. He says to her, "I give everybody a hard time over the phone. It sifts out the pests and bullshitters from the honest ones."

They reach the top of the steps.

"Ah! Here we are!" Bobby puts the suitcases down in front of the first of four doors on the right. Evelyn looks across, noticing there are four others on the left side. She thinks back to the article she read back in March. It said there were seven available rooms. What about the eighth? Bobby opens the door with a key. He wheels in her two pieces of luggage and hands her two keys. Pointing to one, he says, "This one is for your room and the other one is for the front door. Now, don't lose either one of these."

"Oh, I won't."

"If you need anything, you'll know where to find us. See you later." Bobby leaves the room, heading back downstairs.

Evelyn closes the door behind her, resting her back against it. She was still curious about that voice. Taking in the sight of the guest room akin to a hotel room, the singer looks around at her new surroundings. Evelyn slips off her shoes to feel the soft texture of the gray-green colored carpet under bare feet. She steps inside the bathroom. Turning on the light, she finds everything a soft gray, from the tile to the bathtub. A tiny kitchenette is in the next area of the room, complete with small table and microwave. Instead of unpacking, Evelyn plops down on the bed with the turned up gray and green blanket underneath. She untucks it from the mattress and snugly fits her body under the coolness of fresh sheets and the blanket. Moving herself in the center of the bed, she lets out a yawn. She waves her hands and feet under the covers as though to make snow angels. Slowly she stops, as exhaustion overcomes her.

Opening her eyes, she awakens to the sight of a small table with an alarm clock that reads 8:04 PM. She rubs her eyes and thinks aloud to herself. "One more chance. Then I'm done with this project." She then suddenly remembers telling Ed earlier the previous night she would call him once she arrived at the studio. It was too late to do that with the five-hour difference in time zones. She figured she would call him the next day.

Now, it was time to meet the other guys.

Evelyn makes herself proper and puts her shoes back on before heading for the staircase a few feet away. She slows down her pace as she hears the voices come from the same room as before. Music is also heard. Listening further, Evelyn leans for a better listen.

"Leave that one out." A voice says. The same one she first heard before her nap that intrigued her. It sounded to her like an American tone but an odd accent with the pronunciation differently, unlike what she was used to hearing. It was a man with a rather deep yet hypnotic resonance, mixed with a smoky and romantic tone. Who could that be? She steps closer. Bobby becomes alerted by the sound outside of the room he's in. He almost runs right into Evelyn.

"Ah, so you've finally decided to come and join us."

"Yes. I'm sorry about not coming down earlier. I fell asleep."

Bobby laughs back, "No need to apologize. Come on. I'll introduce you."

Evelyn follows him inside the room.

The producer says, "This is the control room. And beyond that window is the recording room or booth...what have you." He turns to the two gentlemen sitting at the controls. "Fellas, this is the lovely lady I was talking to you about."

Evelyn bows her head down from bashfulness. *Lovely* had never been a word she thought best described her. She raises her head, getting caught completely off-guard by the vision of the gentleman sitting at the end.

Bobby announces, "Evelyn Winthrop, this is Dan Soren our faithful and trusty engineer, a quickly successful one at that. Probably the only one who'll get a Grammy nod among the three of us."

Dan gets up. With a physique that's similar to Ed, Dan is friendly. He is a bit taller than Bobby who looked to be under six feet. Soren has smooth dark blond hair and blue eyes that narrow when he smiles with very thin lips. His body is thin with a tight blue-gray jersey over blue jeans.

Bobby adds in. "We sometimes refer to him as, 'The gentle giant.'"

Dan gives a look to Bobby. He leans over slightly to shake Evelyn's hand. Softly he says, "Glad to meet you."

It wasn't the same voice that intrigued her. Her eyes curiously meet the glance of the man at the end, who slowly gives a smile. Bobby turns to Evelyn with a hand out. The gentleman stands up. He is taller than Bobby, yet slightly shorter than Dan. With her jaw slightly open, the singer stares at him with wonderment.

Bobby then says, "This my dear is the one and only...Jaime Weston."

Evelyn thinks to herself.

So, this is the elusive and charismatic one!

Mr. Weston is most definitely a sight to behold. He is the definition of tall, dark, and handsome. His hair is dark chocolate brown, wavy, longish and ruffled but not unkempt. The tone of his complexion is slightly tanner than the other two. There are the darker slender lips. He wears a fully buttoned white shirt over black pants. A dark jacket is slung over the chair. Jaime's eyes are hidden under black-rimmed oval shaped sunglasses. She can only see her reflection hazily through the dark smoky quartz colored lenses. He then removes his sunglasses, revealing a pair of heavy-lidded brown eyes. Evelyn finds herself staring into them while he gives a gracious warm smile.

He says, "Hi, Evelyn. Pleasure to meet you."

That voice!

The one that she was intrigued by! Jaime shakes her hand. She looks down noticing he has large hands and long graceful fingers like a guitarist or bassist. The singer almost feels as if she has seen him before in her lifetime but not recently. There is a certain familiarity about him. He looks at her almost in the same manner. Could their paths have crossed sometime before? Evelyn can't get over the fact that he is Jaime Weston. The voice! The looks! Those eyes! She definitely wanted to know more about him.

After a few minutes of meeting, Jaime asks Dan, "What time do you have?"

The engineer looks at his watch. "Eight sixteen."

"I have to be somewhere by nine." The producer puts his dark suit jacket on as he gets up to leave. He says to Bobby, "Give Evelyn a tour of the place so she can get familiar with it."

He looks at Evelyn for a moment then walks to the front door. Upon opening it, he sees that something is wrong. Jaime bows his head down and returns to the control room. He strides back in quickly.

"Dan, can you please move your car? Your boat is blocking me in again."

Dan says back, "Yeah, but Bobby's in back of me."

Evelyn looks at the men, realizing the black BMW belongs to Jaime. She then makes the distinction of his accent being Canadian.

She offers up, "If you would like, I can move mine. It would probably make it easier since I'm parked next to you and there's nobody in back of me."

Jaime smiles. "Thank you." He turns to the others. "See that? Our guest has more consideration than you two."

Evelyn walks to the door. Jaime opens it for her. They walk outside.

As Evelyn turns on her brake lights, Dan says to Bobby, "I think this might be interesting having her here."

"Why's that?"

Dan begins to walk away as he says, "Just a gut feeling I have."

A short time afterwards, Bobby leads Evelyn on a tour of the studio.

She asks, "So, tell me Bobby, how did I.C.E. get its name?"

He tells her, "It was a mistake made by the owner, Jack Zima. The man had horrible handwriting but it was supposed to be called, I.R.E., which stood for International Recording Experiments. This place used to be an engineering school but it never took off. So, Jack bought it for pennies. The guy drank a lot and signed over the papers, as I.C.E. Nobody can be sure if he did it on purpose or he was blitzed out of his mind. I.C.E. has no meaning. It just stuck. His son, Jimmy is a good kid. He took over once his dad kicked the bucket. Yeah, the poor son of a bitch had liver failure at the age of fifty-nine. What a way to go." Bobby shakes his head in disgust. He then eyes Evelyn. "Okay, so you know the upstairs is devoted to the guests quarters. You saw the control room, demo room, mixing suite, computer programming stuff." Then he remembers. "Ah! Downstairs! Of course! How could I forget? Come on." Bobby shows her a small stairway close to the one leading upstairs. They make their way down the steps. The producer turns on the light. The sight of one big room with a maroon carpet and a matching empty drum riser greets Evelyn.

"This is where we fit whole bands. There's a dark window in back to the side. See? That's another control room. There's a small kitchen in the next room over." Bobby looks around. He sees a recorder sitting on the floor. "This thing is one of Jaime's seven pride and joys. It's a recorder he's had since the beginning of the decade. He swears by it." Bobby places the item inside the control room. When he steps out, Evelyn's mind is preoccupied.

"What is he?" She asks.

"Who? Jaime? He's a workaholic."

"I heard the word heritage attached plenty and his own mentioning of feathers."

"Oh, that. He's half Mohawk. It's American Indian. I still don't know what the other half is. His mom's a sweetheart though. That's where he gets his Indian roots. Both her and her sister live near Rochester. I don't know anything about his father. He's never said anything about him and I leave it alone. Is that what you wanted to know?"

"There's something about him." Evelyn says aloud.

"He's not easy to get along with. I still have a hard time trying to figure him out."

Bobby turns to her with the thought that Dan was right in his assessment about Evelyn. She wanted to know about Weston in ways perhaps even he might be surprised at. Indeed, it would be interesting having her around.

***

Evelyn says over the phone, "Ed, darling. Please don't worry. A month will pass by before you know it."

Ed grumbles back. "I know, but I miss you already."

She says back. "Don't even think about it. The more you do, it will eat you up. Darling, go out with your friends. Have a good time."

"I don't know if I can do that."

A little agitated, Evelyn tells him, "Do it for me. Say '*Hello*' to Mac for me. He's always willing to do things with you. Call him up and see what he wants to do."

Ed grumbles again. "It's not the same."

"Darling, I'm trying to help you any way I can."

"Hop on a plane and come back home."

Evelyn rolls her eyes and slaps her hand against her thigh. She says with exasperation, "You *know* I can't do that!" With a quick breath, she calms down. "Look darling, I have to go and do some recording. Please. I beg of you. *Please* don't worry. I love you. Kissy, kissy." She puckers her lips twice.

Over the phone, he does the same then says, "Goodbye, honey."

She places the phone back down and goes for her suitcase. There she rummages through. Then it strikes her that she should look in her carry-on bag. On top of everything else is a black sack.

There they are.

She opens it up as though talking to whoever resides in there.

"We're going to do this one more time. If it doesn't work then we'll simply retire all of you."

She gets up and heads for the kitchen to search for something to eat.

Just below her guest room, Jaime is on the phone in an office.

Henry Winslow tells him. "Hey, do you know what time of the year it is?"

"Yeah. It's summer. I just had a birthday."

"No. No. Something else. Hint. Me."

"You?"

"Yeah."

"Um..." Jaime tries to think.

Henry says, "Have you forgotten? Next month it'll mark my ninth year knowing you."

"Jeez, already? Henry, you're going to make me feel old." The producer laughs back.

Henry informs him. "You know, you were a no-show at my wedding."

So was Evelyn, but he wouldn't let Jaime know that. He promised Evelyn he would never tell anybody else that he knew her or was friends with her for a little over a decade, especially a producer. He gathers his thoughts and continues to talk to his friend. "So, you know when you finally decide to get married I might not show up at your wedding."

Jaime laughs back. "I'll remember that."

Bobby enters. He picks up some papers. Looking over his shoulder he steps in front of Jaime. "Who's that?" Bobby mouths.

Jaime looks up. "Henry."

He returns to the conversation when Henry talks. "You know, we'll have to celebrate when the time comes next month. You, Karen, and me. Hey, bring Bobby and Andrea along."

"Mm hmm. Listen, I think Bobby wants to say a few things to you. I'll talk to you later."

Jaime hands the phone to Bobby who nods.

"Hey, Henry. How's it goin', man?"

The head producer walks out of the office with a smile. He was off to do some work and see what Evelyn had for recording sessions.

Fifteen minutes later, Bobby and Jaime stand inside the demo room talking. Evelyn walks in, carrying a black cloth sack. She places it on the table in front of them.

Bobby says to his friend with a little bit of excitement. "This should be fun."

Jaime says back, "Mm hmm."

He takes a sip of coffee in a white Styrofoam cup. Closing his eyes, he swarms the dark liquid by shaking it slightly. He goes for another sip. Evelyn dumps the bag. A flood of uncased black cassette tapes drops onto the table with a clatter. Bobby's jaw drops as he stares down. Jaime, with the cup up to his mouth still looks at the table. His glance slowly focuses on Bobby who stands next to him. Both men look at each other. Jaime still holds the cup all the while concealing his jaw dropped expression. He pulls it away, slowly taking in a large swallow. His eyes stay transfixed to the sight of all those tapes.

He picks up a cassette tape and flips it over. Bobby does the same then picks up another one. He does this a few times.

With a dead serious voice, Bobby announces. "These are all unlabeled."

Evelyn answers him back. "I know. There are parts on each tape."

"Parts?" Bobby asks. He studies Jaime's expression. "Evelyn, what is it that you want us to do? Do you mean to tell me that these aren't even full vocal tracks?"

"No. They are."

"How about the music portion? You told us just before you went to go get these that you went through a dozen or so studios. So, where are the results from those sessions?"

"I threw those away."

Jaime stands by looking at her. Bobby seems to be the only one who's willing to question their latest client.

"You threw those away." He mumbles as he steps away. "This is unbelievable."

She defends her decision. "I figured they were useless."

Jaime takes another sip of coffee.

"It would have been nice to go by something." Bobby laments.

Feeling as though she's been forced into a corner, she answers back. "The article said you were the best around, that you understood what an artist was looking for. You would push to get it right. I didn't write that. And yes, I went to many studios and producers. They wanted their sound on my record. I'll tell you right now that it did not sound the way I wanted it to. So, the next time your services are lauded and applauded, you can correct them and tell those publications differently."

She turns to Bobby while folding her arms. Looking at the table full of tapes, she picks up the bag in preparation of putting them back. "I was hoping for this to be the last chance for this project but I'll watch out what comes recommended next time I want to record." She looks up. "Next time I won't believe them." Disgusted, she begins to pick up a few tapes. "Even if it is Billboard."

Jaime says, "We'll do it."

Evelyn looks down as she sees a large hand over hers on the table. Bobby turns back to face Jaime.

"We will?" He asks.

Jaime responds. "Yeah. We'll do it."

Jaime Weston was one who always liked a good challenge. That's why he was in the business. His reputation was on the line and he didn't want anybody questioning his good name. Jaime's confidence was well intact and he couldn't resist a pretty lady's request. Besides, it might not be *that* bad and it would give him more time to learn about her. His curiosity about the singer was piqued simply by the notion he had seen her before.

Evelyn's gaze falls upon the six foot Weston. She felt comforted by his low voice. The way he sort of rescued her from doubt was rather debonair. Those warm dark seductive eyes that exuded confidence and hidden sensuality. He smiled at her as she felt her hand under his. There was no doubt Evelyn was starting to feel something for the charismatic record producer.

Slowly she smiles back, careful not to show too much excitement. She was afraid it would look like she was acting as if being a spoiled child getting her way.

Calmly she tells him. "Thank you." She then asks. "What happened to Dan?"

Jaime replies. "He got the day off. It's his wife's birthday. He'll be back tomorrow." The main producer looks at Bobby then back at Evelyn. "Let's get to work."

Jaime picks up a tape and walks away.

Evelyn has it in the back of her mind, wondering if Weston himself has a wife. She's sure he does.

Thereafter, the three resume in checking out the tapes in the mixing room.

Evelyn explains. "This one as much as I like the keyboards and bass, it's not needed. The other tape didn't work with it."

Bobby mumbles. "We'll never know what that was."

They put on another tape. This is bass and drums alone. Bobby finds himself tapping to the infectious beat. Jaime chuckles at his enthusiasm.

"I see potential with this one." Bobby excitedly says.

Evelyn laughs back roughly. They listen to another. This one is a vocal track. Jaime thoroughly enjoys what he hears. Bobby sees that Jaime is completely immersed in the sound of her voice.

Past eight o'clock, the producers have since listened to about twelve to fifteen tapes. Evelyn has since gone to her room for sleep. Bobby lets out a yawn.

"You're not tired, are you?" Jaime asks.

"No. That just slipped."

Jaime gets up. Clearly, he already has some ideas for the tracks on his mind. Slowly he tells Bobby, "I'm going to go downstairs and grab a beer out of the fridge. Are you staying up here?"

"I'll be down in a few minutes."

Downstairs in the kitchen, Bobby shakes his head as he holds onto the back of an empty seat. Jaime sits at the table with a bottle of beer and a slight smile.

"How are we ever going to get this project done?" Bobby worriedly asks.

Jaime says back calmly, "We'll do it."

"Winthrop dumped about two dozen tapes upstairs on the table."

"So?"

"So? Is that all you can say? Jaime, we're talking about bits and pieces for most of it."

"She said she had confidence in us. So, let's show her."

"Man, you seriously have got to check your ego. You fly pretty high with these projects and I know you get excited but this is..."

Jaime finishes the sentence. "A challenge. I know."

"Usually, we get *some kind* of help on these things. But these are *parts*. A drum track here. A bass line there. Some guitar pieces. Keyboards in clusters."

Jaime sips his beer calmly while Bobby walks around him.

"What we do have is her voice."

"What good is that?"

"Her vocals somewhat match the key of the notes to the pieces." Jaime squints trying to remember something, then snaps his fingers at the same time. "What was that song? That song she was talking about? The one where she said she was desperately trying to figure out but couldn't?"

"Hero's Requiem?"

"That's the one!" The head producer's voice gets slightly higher. "Her voice is very low, so... It needs something. She said that everybody else was trying echo effects but it muddied her delivery. Some even used their trademark sound that was annoying to her at times. Something..."

He begins humming Evelyn's vocals.

He asks Bobby. "What do you hear?"

"When you do it?"

"Yeah."

"With your voice it's a bit deep but somewhere along the lines of more rhythm."

"Okay. Fair enough." Jaime smiles back. "But what goes with it?"

"Bass."

"Right. Still, it's not enough. You can't just move up a bass track and that's it. There's got to be something else. There's a piece missing." Jaime puts his index finger to his lips while thinking. He lowers his gaze trying to come up with an answer.

Then Bobby suggests, "We can make it a little trashier. Although, she wanted this to be a jazz album at first. I do know the style of her past music."

Jaime swivels his head to Bobby. "That's it." He points his index finger up as if it's the statement or suggestion he was looking for. "How about..." Jaime stands up and looks around. "Um..." He turns to Bobby while rolling up his sleeves slightly. Reaching up to the cupboard above the stove, he pulls out a pan and takes out a fork from the utensil drawer near it. Jaime says, "You tell me." He hits the pan with the fork.

Bobby shakes his head. "Not quite."

Jaime picks up the bottle to have another sip. Then it hits him. He blinks for a moment. "Trashier, right?"

"Yeah. Although, maybe it wasn't a good..."

"No. No. That's perfect." Jaime says in a deeper tone. "Get one of the recorders." Bobby dashes out of the kitchen. The producer starts to say, "Grab a drumstick while..." Then he lowers the volume of his voice to a quieter pitch. "Never mind. I'll do it."

In the meantime, Jaime continues to hum out the tune to "Hero's Requiem." Trying to keep the right key, he thinks of more to do with the song. Bobby returns with a small recorder. Jaime then strides out of the room for a moment.

Bobby looks at the recorder and quietly mutters. "What are you up to?"

Jaime then returns, holding a drumstick and puts on a light weight black jacket.

"Grab your jacket. We're going outside."

Bobby repeats but with question. "Outside?"

Jaime walks to the back door, unlocking it. Bobby follows right behind him.

"What are you up to?"

"Trash."

"What?"

"That's what we're going to use." Jaime fishes in his pocket for a Marlboro. He pulls out a matchbook and strikes a match. He surrounds himself among the burning glow, giving his face an orange tinted appearance for a moment. He shakes out the match. Walking over to the trash cans in back, he talks to himself. "Hopefully they're empty."

Bobby calls out. "Watch out for those raccoons, man. Those critters are rabid."

Jaime puts the cigarette in his mouth. "We don't have raccoons here."

"Among all of these woods you don't think so?"

"No." Jaime picks up a can by the handle and places it down closer to the dim light above the back entrance. "Put the recorder about four feet away."

"Isn't that too far?"

"Don't worry. It'll pick up the sound. I know what I'm doing."

They hear the sound of crickets.

Annoyed, Bobby announces. "Damn. We have to contend with crickets."

Still with the Marlboro between his lips, Jaime sets up the trash can and pulls out the drumstick from his jacket pocket. He strains to look up, partly squinting, as he's unsure of what the night brings them. There comes the sound he's not thrilled of hearing. Lightly he puffs away.

Jaime says, "Fuckin' owls."

He throws one hand up. Bobby begins laughing. Jaime takes the cigarette out of his mouth, flicking out ashes for the moment. "We're going to have to work with Mother Nature in general. Hopefully we won't get any hooting on tape."

Bobby cracks up laughing. He sees his friend with the drumstick. "You're going to wake up the neighbors."

"We don't have neighbors, Bobby. They're at least half a mile away."

"Exactly my point."

Jaime shakes his head. "You worry too much. Just turn on the recorder when I give you the signal."

"What's that?"

Jaime points to Bobby. Bobby nods in agreement. The producer puts the cigarette back in his mouth. A moment later, he points to Bobby who presses on record. Wham! A harsh deliberate stroke is made by the stick onto the trash can. The lower trashy sound fills the back area of the studio. Jaime gets a decent quarter note beat going. Bobby stoops next to the small recorder smiling.

In her guest room, Evelyn becomes alerted by the banging sound. She scampers down the stairs. Opening the door to the room all the way in back of the studio, she looks out the window and sees the two guys. Jaime in particular is outside whapping away at a trash can. Very peculiar! What was that Bobby Whitfield doing sitting there watching him? She can't see the little recorder in front of him. Weird as it looks, Evelyn finds herself peeking to study the two. It was going to be very interesting to see how the music would work out aside from Jaime Weston and Bobby Whitfield's odd habits. She steps away from the window slightly confused but increasingly attracted to the head producer. He was definitely eccentric.

Jaime finishes the beat and points to Bobby once again. Bobby presses the recorder off.

Jaime takes the Marlboro out of his mouth and says, "Perfect." He smiles at Bobby. Dragging the trash can back, he calls out. "Do you remember what you did with those bats that time?"

"Yeah. I fed it through the mixer and remixed it about eight times. Maybe ten. Are you telling me you want a mix of this?"

Jaime walks back and flicks away the remains of the cigarette. "Yes. If we feed it through and get a muddied sound, it'll be better. Lower than a crash cymbal but have a droning effect in the background enough that it *sounds* like drums but it won't mess up the main bass line."

"You already know what the bass line will be?"

"Yeah. It's the second tape we heard. We'll just try and see what we can get out of that. There were some good parts that I distinctly heard."

They walk back inside the studio.

"What time is it?" Jaime asks.

Bobby checks his watch. "What?? It's ten thirteen already? Andrea is not going to be happy about this."

"She knows you're working."

"Still, it's late."

"Let's try to figure this out while it's fresh in our minds."

Bobby corrects him. "You mean *your* mind."

Jaime removes his jacket and walks into the recording room with Bobby following him. He pulls out the keyboard off to the side of the large empty room. "The only instrument that I have any clue on what the hell to do with is a piano. So, with the keyboard, um, it's going to be a little different. You've played in a couple of bands. Why don't you work out a line on the guitar that's sitting inside the control booth? What we're trying to do is duplicate the bass sound... Wait a minute." The producer places the recorder on the empty drum riser and presses rewind. The tape stops. He pushes *play*. On goes the sound of the trash can. "I'm going to try and get the sound of the bass on the keyboard. Then you add little flourishes of guitar to overlap over the rhythm. What we have to do is play it with subtleties. It's a song that doesn't need too much melody as her voice carries it through. That's the main thing you're supposed to hear. I think that's where everybody else was going wrong with this track. They were constantly layering it and diluting her voice. You leave the bare essence *alone*. Or if you're going to have other instruments, you let them stay but take a backseat. It doesn't *need* bullshit dumped on it."

Jaime presses a key at the low end of the keyboard. He begins to figure out the specific pattern. Bobby holds the guitar while listening. His fingers pick the right time to chime in. Both men close their eyes as they let the sound take them away. Just with two people and the help of the recorded trash can beat, stands the sound that's both bare and complimentary. "Hero's Requiem," a long-standing musical thorn in Evelyn Winthrop's side. The cornerstone to the verge of a comeback.

Jaime stops playing. He says, "We're dealing with a song that is very *dark*. It's the death of this hero in her words. Do you feel the sense of droning or dragging? Sort of like a toll bell?"

"Now that you mention it, I do. That loping bass line that we heard earlier in the day would be good."

"That's the one I was talking about."

"I definitely see potential in this." Bobby begins to smile back. "So, we should keep the drum beat under the layers. Very lightly. I'm thinking of like the sound of banging on a water pipe in a room with the door closed."

Jaime stands up. Excitedly he says, "Then let's do it."

Bobby hesitates then suggests. "Tomorrow. 'Cause I've gotta go home now. It's nearly eleven. But seriously I'll be thinking of that song tonight."

He goes to the control room and puts the guitar back. Jaime says back with slight disappointment. "All right. Go on."

"'Night."

"Yep. Goodnight Bobby."

Bobby runs upstairs to grab his jacket and heads out the door. Jaime walks up the steps and heads into the mixing room, closing the door. He places the tape on the table. In a contemplative position, he looks at it just before jamming it into a player hooked up like a patient on an IV drip. Moving up the levels, the sound of the pounded on trash can comes alive. Only, it's a little too sharp as the equipment picks up on the higher resonance than the small recorder downstairs. Softly he says to himself. "Okay." His fingers move down the treble knob. The bright green lights stretch across the board with each strike of the can. Flicking on the mute button, the sound goes muffled. Other knobs get turned and buttons get pushed on. A small orange square lights up. Jaime strokes back his hair as he studies the mixing console. Scooting the swivel chair over to the computer linked to the board, he begins arduously punching in the keys while the sound propagates through the system. More buttons are pushed. Quickly he shoves a disk into the disk drive. Again, he moves over to the mixing board, studying the sound.

Well past midnight, he's still rocking in the swivel chair trying to achieve the right sound. Finally, he calls it a night by ejecting the disk out of the computer before turning it off. The buttons on the console go dark. The row of green lights retracts similarly to measuring tape. Jaime stands up, slightly stretching. Then he plops the disk on the table before shutting off the main light in the room.

In the morning hours, Dan Soren has returned to the studio.

Bobby immediately asks. "Did Vicki have a good birthday?"

"Yeah. I have to thank you and Andrea for taking care of the boys while we went out."

"Ah, they were no trouble at all. They're well behaved kids as it is. I got back late, so Andrea did all the work."

Jaime who sits at the mixing board says, "Sorry to interrupt the homecoming but we really need to nail this track down."

He hears the sound of Evelyn walking down the stairs as he looks up. In a much deeper tone Jaime states, "She's coming."

She walks in. "I'm sorry to tell you this but I have to go somewhere."

Jaime looks at her. "Okay." He nods.

"I should be back around three."

Bobby adds in. "That'll be fine."

"Great!" I'll see you later."

Jaime gives a tight-lipped smile as he waves. Evelyn disappears from the room out the front door of the studio.

Jaime orders Bobby. "Check to make sure the coast is clear."

Bobby calls out from the lobby. "She's gone!"

Jaime pulls out the tape and loads up the computer.

Dan asks out of curiosity. "What did I miss yesterday?"

Bobby lets out a laugh.

Jaime announces as he punches in some keys. "Everything."

Bobby puts an arm around Dan. "Well, dear boy. You missed the unveiling of about thirty unlabeled, unmarked, uncased cassettes which we are to match."

"That's what she has?"

"Not only that, but bits and pieces of instrumental tracks."

In her defense, Jaime tells Dan. "She has the vocal tracks. That's all we need." Waiting for a sound grid to appear he says, "I got a little further with "Hero's Requiem" last night. Yeah. You see if you change the keyboard layer just a little, you'll discover it matches with the bass line."

Across town, Evelyn talks with Henry Winslow. He puts a hand to his hair, which is light brown though lightly graying at the temples. With his other hand free, he holds a cigar. His small squinty eyes keep watch of her.

"Sounds like you have a real dilemma on your hands. But what I don't understand is, why should he care about what kind of music you're making? It's not like he's a musician himself. You know?"

Evelyn responds while holding a lit Camel. "Ed is very concerned because he has a dreadful fear that I'll go back to my old ways if I record the stuff I used to."

Henry holds out his hands. "What does that have anything to do with how you are now? I don't get it?"

"He thinks that I'll go back to the gutter if I pursue the punk scene again along with my old habits."

Henry puffs on the cigar. "Jesus, Evelyn! He's nuttier than a fruitcake! Doesn't he trust you? I thought that's what relationships were based on. Pardon me for being naive. Have you ever suggested counseling?"

"Tried it."

"And?"

"And he'll have no part in being analyzed. Our love life is dried up. Not that he was ever concerned about that part. We have argued more than talked lately. I think we're done with."

She looks at Henry as she blows out a puff of smoke.

***

The following evening, Bobby, Dan, Jaime, and Evelyn sit at the table in the kitchen over pizza and beer.

Bobby informs them. "These are turning into some very *interesting* sessions." He muses over a pizza crust.

Jaime asks. "How is that?"

"Just that it's a different experience. I would say it's akin to Mr. Potato Head."

Jaime immediately laughs back.

Evelyn sees he's thoroughly amused by Bobby's explanation, not knowing what Mr. Potato Head is.

Bobby says back while trying to be serious. "Now wait. Think about it. The songs are interchangeable."

Dan, who rubs his belly, groans. "Man, why do you have to mention potatoes after we *just* filled up on pizza?"

Jaime chuckles warmly, shaking his head.

Bobby turns his head to Dan, tossing the crust into the empty box. "Dummy, I was making a *comparison*. You know how you can change the parts of a Mr. Potato Head doll? You can do the same with Evelyn's arrangements. Instead of keyboards, you can add in guitar in its place. Bass for a low chord on a guitar, vice versa. So on and so forth."

Dan slowly says back. "Oh. I see."

Bobby sips his beer. He grins at Evelyn. "I'll bet you can't *wait* to leave here."

Evelyn darts her eyes toward Jaime for a second. Leaving couldn't be further from the truth. She was enjoying herself thoroughly.

Abruptly she says, "No."

"Aw. Be honest. We'll be fodder for your evening chats with your husband when you get back home. You'll tell your kids of how weird *I* was."

"No." She shakes her head while picking up a bottle of beer.

Bobby knew he was giving her a hard time and trying to be funny at the same time.

"You would...*if* I were married."

"Divorced." Dan says matter-of-factly.

"No. I've never *been* married."

Jaime looks up from being lost in thought. Evelyn smiles back.

Bobby inquirers. "Any kids?"

"No. I wish that I could."

Dan adds in, "If you were with the right guy."

"It's not that simple." Evelyn advises in a low more melancholy tone. Lightly tapping the bottle with her fingers she looks down. Sheepishly she grins. "I can't have any."

Bobby and Dan give each other a look of guilt.

Dan slowly says, "Sorry to hear that."

Evelyn sees Dan's expression along with Bobby being very quiet. Reassuringly, she tells the two. "It's all right. I've gotten past it. I've gone to see a few doctors and the last one explained it to me. My insides are like a hollow pumpkin, only there are two seeds and they're just stuck to the bottom. My eggs... They *exist* but they don't do anything. Just sit there. One doctor told me it was a form of female sterility. So, even if I'm to be with someone...nothing will happen." She laughs back covering up the hurt she truly feels inside. "I'm useless for breeding purposes."

Dan eyes Bobby uneasily. Overwhelmed with a feeling of getting sick, Bobby pushes his bottle away. Jaime remains silently looking down.

Dan takes a peek at his watch. "Uh-oh. It's time for me to go."

Quickly he gets up to leave the kitchen.

Bobby stands up too. He tells Jaime and Evelyn. "I'll be on my way too. I think I had too much pizza." He pats his stomach. "Gotta break out the pink stuff when I get home."

Moment's later, Bobby and Dan put on their jackets.

Dan says, "Now *that* was *sad*."

Bobby admits. "I should have never said anything. Me and my big fat mouth."

"Jeez, a pumpkin...a hollow pumpkin. I can't imagine what it must be like for her." Dan shakes his head with uneasiness. "You know, I couldn't imagine a life without my boys. It's just... I'm gonna give Jake and Josh a big hug tonight."

"Yeah. I think I'm gonna take Becky out bowling real soon." Bobby heads for the lobby. He turns back. "Danny? I guess the things we take for granted are the richest."

"Yeah."

"Good night."

"Good night, Bobby."

Bobby opens the door and leaves. Dan follows him only minutes later, turning to look back.

***

"Turn up the bass a little bit." Jaime orders Dan.

The engineer turns a knob.

Bobby suggests. "How about softening the keyboard more?"

Jaime adds in, "Yeah. Bring out the drums so you can hear them underneath the layers. They need to be more up front."

They listen to what they have. A creeping smile appears on Jaime's face.

Bobby smiles. "I *definitely* like it."

The head producer eyes Bobby incredulously. "You didn't think this song had a chance."

Bobby hesitantly replies. "Well... That was *before*. When we had nothing but vocals and a trash can."

Jaime chuckles back. "It *still* amazes me how something can come out of nothing."

Bobby shakes his head with disbelief and admiration. "My friend, *you* amaze me."

In the control room, Evelyn attempts to figure out what she wants. She jots down instruments that she hears in her head. The arrangement had to be just right. Shaking her head, she erases something. Her stomach begins to growl. Already past noon, she hadn't eaten a bite. The excitement was building up. It was so much so that food wasn't even on her mind.

Bobby enters the room. "How is it going?"

"This is very tough even for myself." She laughs back. "No wonder so many studios could not get the sound I was looking for. I can't either! I don't know how you ever do this."

"That's Jaime Weston for you. He somehow figures out things others don't think about. I don't know? Maybe he has another sense? He hates bragging about projects. So, maybe that keeps him on even ground. When I try to figure it out... Jesus, after twenty-four years of doing this stuff, I just get frustrated."

The doorbell rings.

Bobby leaves the room, rushing to the lobby. He goes to open the door.

A man stands with a tripod and camera bag, wearing a dark green T-shirt and blue jeans.

Bobby states emphatically. "What's this about?"

The man says back. "I'm here to take pictures. Pat Beaumont."

Pat sticks his hand out for a handshake.

"Bobby Whitfield. So, why today?" Bobby squints while shaking hands with Pat.

"You guys stay in the studio so much that you lose track of what day it is."

"What? I know it's somewhere towards the middle of July. That's for *Billboard* though. Who do you represent?"

"*Billboard*." Pat smiles. "We're set for the ninth."

"And?"

"And, today *is* the ninth."

Evelyn peeks her head outside the door.

Pat continues. "You or someone told us that the singer, Evelyn Winthrop, Ms. *Ravaged Beauty*, *Childlike Sins*, so on and so forth herself was recording here in July. Isn't that right?"

"Yes. I just completely forgot. Brain fart." Bobby grins sheepishly. His eyes meet Evelyn's.

The door to the mixing room opens. Jaime and Dan check to see what's going on.

Jaime mentions. "We saw the light flash on in the room. Who was at the door?"

Pat introduces himself. "I'm from *Billboard*. The name is Pat Beaumont."

Jaime holds out a hand. He places a lit Marlboro in his mouth. "Jaime Weston. The pleasure is all mine." He takes the cigarette out of his mouth. "What brings you here...Pat?"

"Heard you had Evelyn Winthrop at the studio."

Bobby interrupts. "That was me."

Jaime turns to him.

Bobby eyes him back. "You know, one of those things."

Jaime replies as the smoke appears out of his mouth. "Mm hmm."

The head producer walks back inside the mixing room while the others await his answer. He comes back with no cigarette in sight. "Well, let's do it." He says with a smile. Bobby walks over to Evelyn. He explains to her while Pat sets up his tripod. Jaime and Dan watch him. Jaime's eyes swing over to Bobby and Evelyn in particular. She catches his glance. It was the look of a man up to something. In response, she giggles.

Pat asks. "Where would you like to do this?"

Jaime answers back. "In here will be fine."

Bobby offers up. "Downstairs might be better. It's roomier."

Dan pipes in. "He has a point."

They head down the stairs. Bobby turns on the light switch. Pat resets his tripod. Dan gets into place. Bobby goes over to stand next to him. Jaime, then Evelyn follows.

Pat suggests. "Ah. Perhaps Evelyn, you should get between the two producers."

Evelyn takes on the suggestion by sandwiching herself between Bobby and Jaime. Looking through the viewfinder Pat then says, "Let's get a warm feeling between all four of you."

Dan puts his arm around Bobby's shoulder. Bobby has his hand lightly draped over Evelyn's shoulder. Jaime glances to his lower right. He pays full attention to the camera but his right hand has a mind of its own. His long fingers creep along her back. She feels the soft sensation. Her eyes close. He must have hit the perfect spot. Jaime notices with his advance that she doesn't try to move away from his touch. The singer makes no motion of refusal. He makes his way to her right side against her waistline. She takes a quick look at Bobby and Dan. They weren't paying any attention. Her left arm slides in back of the six foot Weston. Lightly, her hand glides up to the middle of his back. She smiles at the camera. The production team does the same. A flash from the camera goes off. They switch positions for another picture. Bobby and Dan remain in the same pose. Jaime slides his hand over her shoulder. Evelyn brings hers around his side. She feels the side of his rib cage through the shirt he wears. A smile appears on her face again. Jaime gives a content smile to the camera. The bright light pops again. Bobby blinks with hysterical expressions of exaggeration. Dan turns away, laughing madly.

During later hours, Evelyn goes over pieces of music with the production team. She sips on Corona. Dan gives a concerned look her way.

Bobby asks her abruptly. "Did you finally eat?"

Evelyn hesitates. "No."

"You're having beer on an empty stomach?"

Dan says, "*Not* a good idea."

She replies with a quizzical expression. "How come?"

Bobby turns his swivel chair to face her. "Because sweetie, it'll hit you like a ton of bricks. That shit is strong if you don't watch out."

While Dan watches over the computer monitor, he answers. "Yeah. Especially if you haven't eaten."

Jaime looks at the two men sitting next him and Evelyn. "Are you finished interrogating her?" He scolds. "Can we please get some work done?"

Bobby throws his hands up. Evelyn takes another gulp of beer.

She informs Bobby and Dan. "I've had beer before. That includes on an empty stomach."

Dan snickers back to Bobby. "Probably the weak stuff."

Bobby tells him quietly. "This is the Mexican brew. She's asking for trouble."

Jaime darts his widened eyes with the glare of watching over two young mischievous boys. He drops his pencil on the desk. Bobby takes in his friend's aggravated stare. He feels as though he's stuck without a defense. With defeat, Bobby slinks back to analyzing tracks.

He mumbles. "If she wants it that way. Don't blame me if something happens to her. I was just tryin' to warn her."

Jaime flares his nostrils, swinging his eyes at Bobby for the second time. Bobby goes silent. Jaime and Evelyn talk over plans for one of her songs. Bobby and Dan exchange looks. Evelyn finishes her Corona, looking at them as if blatantly flaunting the last sip. She was going to show them. Nobody was going to tell her when to eat. Evelyn simply wasn't hungry. Her nerves had grown jittery around the attractive head producer and she was excited about the sessions. Food? It didn't seem to matter to her throughout the whole day. She had the photo session on her mind though. Jaime sure was the flirty type. His fingers crawling up her back the way they did. Such an enticing touch!

Before long, it's time for both Bobby and Dan to leave. Evelyn stands up to fetch another tape. Only, she feels lightheaded. The wooziness makes her stumble. Where were those tapes? Where was that table?

The table is no more than ten feet away from where they sit, possibly less. She holds her head as she blindly walks over to get a tape. Looking behind, Evelyn checks to make sure nobody watches her struggle. She didn't want to prove Bobby and Dan that they were right. Blinking, the singer feels a growing sense of sluggishness akin to her feet being tied down to weights while running in a pool. Their voices seemed so distant. Everything was morphing into a swirl. She takes hold of the table for support. Nobody was to know how she was feeling. Safely she makes her way back to the seat...without the tape.

Jaime asks her. "Got it?" He then sees she's leaning her head back. Quietly he assures her. "I'll get one."

Bobby shrugs his shoulders to Dan. Getting up to get his jacket, he looks back at Evelyn. She just needed a couple of minutes to get her second wind. At least that's what she believed.

Dan looks at her. Nodding his head, he heads out the door. "Goodnight guys!" He calls out. Bobby fetches both his and Dan's jacket. They leave quickly as they sense something might happen to prove them right.

Bobby advises. "Let's get out of here before she spews."

Evelyn looks in back of her. Bobby and Dan didn't know anything about her. She could hold her liquor. No denial. Just confidence. Her eyes are about to shut for a mere minute when Jaime stands up quickly.

He lets her know why he's abrupt. "Bathroom break. I'll be right back."

The producer leaves the room.

The singer figures it's the perfect time for her to get rejuvenated. A minute to herself at last! A minute to relax. She massages her temples. It was working. Now all she would have to do is stand up. Already she's feeling much better. Cheap beer. Strong beer. No difference. They all affected her the same way. She would grab another tape on the table while he was away.

Evelyn goes to stand up.

Jaime walks back in the mixing room. He couldn't be sure if he heard a noise while away or not. He sees not one but two empty seats. Where was Evelyn? Maybe she went upstairs? Or perhaps she was downstairs? He begins to head for his seat. Then he hears the sound of light snoring. A couple steps away, he finds the singer. Her hair, fanned out. One arm situated under her head in place of a pillow.

"Shit." He mumbles.

Propping his hand to his forehead he looks down. Quickly he runs a hand through his hair. Something had to be done. He thinks for a moment. Good thing Bobby and Dan weren't there. Jaime takes a large sigh as he kneels down next to her. "Evelyn?" He asks in a husky whisper. She makes no movement in response. He rolls her over. Quietly he says to himself. "Here goes nothing." Jaime picks up the limp Evelyn, hoisting her over his shoulder. In a blur among sleep, the singer opens her eyes slightly. She partially sees the lobby of the studio getting further away. Evelyn feels the sensation of levitation. It's all a dream to her though, an illusion brought on by exhaustion and hunger. She lets out a light moan. He looks over to his right, taking notice that she stirred for a second.

At last, he reaches the top step. He flips on the light switch to the hallway. The producer opens her door as it was left unlocked. Jaime walks over to the bed gently placing her down on the mattress. Carefully he pulls the covers over her. Turning on the lamp on the table, it creates a warm glow. She wiggles under the covers trying to change her position. He watches her with a smile on his face. Again, her eyes begin to flutter open. In a blurred state, she sees a face. The eyes warm and dark as night. Her hand lifts to his cheek. Jaime feels drawn to the singer. Slowly, he leans closer to her. Evelyn's lips are plump and soft...kissably soft. His black eyelashes flutter with hesitation to close, inching closer. With hardly any space between them, he feels her hand fall away. He opens his eyes. She's asleep once more. The producer edges away, shutting off the light.

Chapter 4

Early the next morning, Evelyn talks to her friend, Liz on the phone. She cradles a cup of water. A Camel burns in the ashtray.

"You know, I woke up this morning and I don't even know how I walked up the stairs last night. I didn't have a bite to eat at all... No. It almost felt as though I were carried up. The last thing? Um, the last thing I remember is talking with one of the producers. Yes, darling. There are actually two of them. The head producer...oh, he's stunning. Listen to me! I sound like a giddy schoolgirl. No. Ed doesn't know about any of it. You know him. He would *completely* lose it! I know what he would say." Evelyn tightens her already deepened voice imitating Ed. "What's goin' on over there? Are you doin' orgies and God knows what? Eat dammit! That's what you have a mouth and stomach for." Immediately she laughs hoarsely. "Liz, I *swear* that is what he would say." She switches, placing the cup on the table and picking up the cigarette. "Mm hmm. Right. Yes. Mm. Aside from that, I'm fine. I'm on my fourth cup of water. Yes. I've learned my lesson. Yes. Food is important."

For a minute, the singer is distracted by the rumbling sound of footsteps down the stairs underneath. She returns to speaking while letting out a ring of smoke for her own amusement.

"I know they're doing something. I keep hearing someone running up and down the second set of stairs underneath."

Liz asks her a question, which brings a smile to Evelyn's face.

"Him? What do you mean? What I said? Oh, well! Yes! He's a real flirt. He put his arm around me while we were all getting our picture taken.

No. No. It's the *way* he did it. I know. Yes. How is Marco? Oh, that's wonderful. I know."

Evelyn looks at the clock on the small table. The time reads 9:56 AM. "I didn't realize what time it was. I have to go. I'm expected downstairs. Yes. I'll talk to you again very soon. Really, it should be in early August. That's what I hope too. Okay, give Marco a kiss for me. Goodbye darling."

The production crew remains squirreled away in the mixing room. Evelyn steps up to the door.

She hears Bobby exclaim, "Got it!"

Jaime tells the other two. "Now all we have to do is..."

A knock comes at the door.

Evelyn announces, "May I have the tapes with the vocal tracks to "Tomorrow's Child" and "Little Miss Independent?"

The door opens enough for a hand to appear. In an animated way, it reaches to feel hers. A long finger grazes the palm of her hand. She stifles a smile. The hand disappears. It reappears with two tapes. Her hand takes the tapes. She fondles the pinky. The fingers wiggle away. They vanish behind the door, which shuts quickly.

Hour after hour, Evelyn remains alone. Bobby dashes down the stairs. She darts her eyes to the room. Evelyn learned her lesson about not eating. Her fingers squish down on the fresh elongated roll of a tasty sub sandwich. While the guys were busy being ensconced in the room upstairs, Evelyn was going to eat in peace. She sits in the kitchen. Thankfully, a deli wasn't too far away from the studio. The smell of food must have lured Bobby in.

"Mm. What's that?"

She responds with a full mouth. "Fthub." Smiling, she puts her finger up for him to wait a moment.

He says, "Sub?"

Evelyn nods enthusiastically with agreement.

"Well, enjoy. You know...if you can't finish that for any reason..."

"I *can* and I *will*." She shoots back.

Bobby dashes up the stairs.

She opens the notebook she had brought with her. Why couldn't she figure out certain aspects of the songs? The lyrics seemed fine. Turning the page, she finds the words for "Hero's Requiem." Her first reaction is to tear it out. It was too frustrating to bear. *Requiem*. Yeah. It was death all right. The song was basically dead. Only a miracle could save the track. Flipping back a page she decides to study what she has for, "Little Miss Independent." Nearly finished with her sandwich, Evelyn hears footsteps again. She pops open a can of soda. Letting the tiny bubbles fizz down her throat, Evelyn leans her head back.

Dan walks in. "We need your opinion on something."

"Right now?"

"Yeah. Come on!"

Bobby begins to head down the stairs.

Dan says to Evelyn. "Go to the mixing room. I'll be there in a few minutes. Tell Jaime that."

Evelyn runs up.

Dan then addresses Bobby on a step. "And what are you doing?"

"I just need a little snack."

"Now? We're gonna check out the track and see what she thinks of it."

Bobby sees the almost finished sub unattended.

Dan views Bobby's glance from the doorway. "No. No, you're not. Tell me you're not going to do that? Wait until you get home. We only have fifteen or twenty minutes tops."

With a devilish smile, Bobby takes out a knife from the utensil drawer. He goes back to the table analyzing the sub's bitten areas. Carefully he cuts away at it.

Dan disgustedly remarks. "Man, what are you doin'?"

Bobby tells him. "She won't be back for it. Not once she listens to what we have for her."

"You are a vulture! You must have been one in your previous life."

Bobby chomps away gleefully. Dan walks away disgusted. Bobby finishes the sub. He cleans up the table, throwing away the remnants he cut off.

In the mixing room, Dan returns.

Jaime asks, "Where's Bobby?"

"He's coming." Dan vouches.

Bobby rushes in.

Jaime asks testily. "Where have you been? You've got ten minutes left with me. Any longer and your wives are going to take it out on me."

Bobby replies with the hint of a smile. "Yours must be really understanding."

Jaime smiles back. "Funny. Very funny."

Evelyn couldn't quite understand. Jaime was married? Why was he flirting so heavily with her?

Dan laughs back.

In a deep and defeated tone, Jaime offers. "Okay. Let's just do this." Evelyn watches him. "Now, we need to know if there's anything more we have to do with this track. Are you ready?" He asks

Evelyn replies. "Mm hmm."

Jaime darts his eyes to Bobby and Dan just before he presses play. Evelyn listens to the subtle resonance of a dragging cymbal. Then comes the lilting strings of a guitar. The rhythm sounded like a church bell rung at a memorial service. Her voice then cuts through with the arrangement playing lightly in the background.

Come to your senses you're a foolish old man.
You run so fast, as fast as you can.
No need to bother leaping buildings in a single bound.
Stay home with me 'cause I want you around.

Throw your tattered cape to the floor.
You know you won't need it no more.
Heroes are for winners, bad guys are for losers.

Wondering if there's room left for choosers.

Evelyn has her hand clasped over her mouth. She draws in a breath. Jaime looks at her fragile blue glassy eyes. She holds back tears. The head producer glances at Bobby and Dan with a creeping smile. They smile back. Evelyn wipes back tears with the back of her hand. The song finishes. She tries to recompose herself.

"I'm sorry. I don't usually break down and cry because of a song. It's just that... I mean it... I..." She rubs her forehead not knowing how to properly tell them how she feels. "I'm speechless!" She sputters.

Bobby says, "It's the first track we worked on since you came here. Jaime insisted on it."

Evelyn looks over at Jaime. His head is bowed down. Underneath, he has a huge boyish grin with top teeth protruding through, biting down lightly on his bottom lip with shyness. Evelyn's eyes widen at him with amazement. He begins to pick up his head. Right then it strikes her.

Bobby continues. "We worked on that until we hunted it down."

Evelyn pays no attention to either the secondary producer or engineer, only Jaime. Cupid had struck her badly. Her eyes meet his. It must have hit him the same way. He gives her the look of a shy schoolboy discovering a pretty girl. Only, the pretty girl was in the form of a forty-year-old British singer. Jaime looks back down.

She informs them all. "I love the drums!"

With a crooked smile, Jaime responds. "There are no drums."

She corrects herself. "Well, I mean cymbals."

Bobby tells her, "No cymbals."

Evelyn asks out of confusion. "What then? Obviously there is some percussion going on."

Jaime answers. "Trash can."

Bobby adds in matter-of-factly. "It was his idea. Drums wouldn't sound good at all. We wanted something that would fit into the dark mood the song creates. So, we initially took the bass line from tape 3. Overlapped that with guitar. Then added in the light wash of keyboards."

"Who were the studio musicians? I must thank them." She says excitedly.

Bobby replies with a sheepish grin. "You're looking at them."

Jaime adds in. "No session players. Bobby's on guitar and I'm on keyboards. Danny helped us put it together. So, do you like it?"

"Like it? I *love* it! I can't believe you made "Hero's Requiem" sound so...*alive*! I was downstairs before thinking nothing would ever come of the track." She thinks of something on the spur of the moment. "Listen, I need a favor from all of you."

Dan asks, "What's that?"

"I want all three of you to turn around."

Bobby raises his brows with curiosity. "Oh, and do you have a surprise for us?"

They turn around facing their backs to her.

"Okay. You can turn around now."

Bobby says, "So?"

"I was checking to see if any of you had wings."

Jaime gives her a confused expression.

She says, "I did it because I must be looking at three angels."

Jaime bows his head down again, this time chuckling.

Dan walks over to her with arms outstretched. He gives her a hug.

Bobby looks down. "That's probably the sweetest compliment I've ever heard."

Dan reminds him. "We have to go but really...thanks." He smiles.

"No. Thank you for doing what I thought was the impossible." She corrects him.

Jaime slips out of the room. Bobby grins to her. He and Dan leave.

They call out at the same time. " 'Night!"

Evelyn giggles while standing alone in the room. Now she wants to talk some more with the head producer. She notices though that he has disappeared. She walks out of the room. The light is left on in the control room. That's where he must have gone off. With a hankering for coffee, Evelyn goes to the office where she makes a fresh pot. Once she's done, she carries her cup over to the control room. There she hears some noise. She walks in. He looks up. Immediately he grows nervous around her but tries not to show it. Looking down at the control panel, he informs her.

"Bobby left everything on in here. I don't know if he stepped in this room any other time."

The singer looks over at the counter top in back of her.

"I would truly like to thank you for helping me with that track," Evelyn says as she takes a seat on the edge of the counter.

Cradling her cup of coffee, she waits to hear what the music producer has to say. He turns off all of the controls until the red, orange, and green lights of all sorts fade to black.

Jaime turns around to Evelyn and says warmly, "No problem."

His seriousness is betrayed by the slightest smile. She continues to gaze around the room uttering with surprise, "So many studios, producers and engineers I've been through. All of them said it wouldn't come out right, but I knew better." Evelyn places her hand over her heart to emphasize her belief. Her low tone breaks into a hoarse squeal as she says, "I was *passionate* about getting it done. Everywhere I had been...Los Angeles, Chicago, Miami, Switzerland, West Germany...all of them said it would be impossible to get what I was looking for. I come here and you just do it. How is that so?"

Her eyes lock onto Jaime as he looks down in attempt to avoid the gaze he's going to connect with, but can't avoid completely. He finds rolling up his sleeves will be a good distraction for a moment. Evelyn takes notice at his arms and the fact that he doesn't even wear a watch; he's simply devoid of any type of jewelry. The only accent he possesses is the brown hair that is displayed to his wrists.

Choosing his words carefully, the producer replies with, "It's just that I sort of knew...what...you were looking for."

Jaime finally glances at Evelyn when he notices she's already looking at him intently. He smiles at her and right then Evelyn feels a rush through her body that shuts off all of her confidence and she's left feeling like a puddle. With slight apprehension, the singer tries to get back some of the lost feeling she had and musters up the courage to say, "Are you doing anything now? I mean did you want to go out and celebrate? You did an excellent job on "Hero's Requiem" and I just thought that perhaps...perhaps you wouldn't mind."

Jaime eye's the floor in an almost shy manner and smiles. She proves to be a strong persuader but not strong enough for the producer who can't seem to take up her invitation. Evelyn continues with massive apprehension and a slight bit of worry as she questions his status.

"Unless, I've bothered you, and your wife wouldn't be very happy about it, then I can completely understand. I wouldn't want you to get the wrong impression or suggestion even." Uneasily she adds in, "You never said anything like Bobby and Dan did, so I figured you were."

He looks back up. Jaime picks up a pack of Marlboro's sitting next to the main control desk and fishes out a cigarette. Holding it steady, he takes the book of matches he has in his shirt pocket and within a flash, lights the end of the cigarette.

Taking a puff of smoke, he interjects with, "I'm not married. I just don't really celebrate the work I do. It's my job and I don't want people thinking I have an ego after completing an accomplishment."

At this point, Evelyn feels like shrinking to the size of an ant. There goes her confidence. She walks to the open door, then turns around to see he is busy taking out tapes, and labels the one that has freshly been removed from the machine.

Evelyn makes one more attempt, hoping he'll agree to her suggestion. "Rain check?"

Jaime turns slightly while labeling. With arched brows and a sly look, he takes the Marlboro between his fingers and says, "Maybe."

Evelyn begins to head out the door when he addresses her. "Evelyn...." He walks straight up to the singer, taking her completely off-guard.

"What?" She replies.

He looks at her, then says, "Nothing." Edging away, he shakes his head.

It would have been so easy for her to simply kiss him, but she refrains from doing anything she might regret, and walks out of the room. She calls out, "Good night!"

He says back to her, "Night."

With that, she walks up the staircase and retires to her room.

With the cigarette dangling from his mouth, Jaime looks up at the stairway with a slight smile. He lets out a puff before returning to the darkened room.

Meanwhile, Evelyn sits in her room and gets ready for bed.

She says to herself, "He is something else," while continuing to mouth the words, "Not married."

She closes her eyes and picks up the tape Jaime had presented her with.

The more time Evelyn had spent with the tall, dark, and handsome producer, the less she thought of Ed. Jaime had simply intrigued her to the point she could completely lose her senses and do something irrational. She knew that she herself was not married, but Ed was the closest thing to a husband she ever felt she could have. Jaime on the other hand was something else. There was an unnerving sense that he was quite shy, although somehow deeply passionate. Evelyn changes into her sleeping attire, a light pink camisole over matching pants. She climbs into bed and pulls out her small lighter which she lights a cigarette with. Taking a deep breath and exhaling quickly, she says quietly to herself, "God, he is gorgeous." Evelyn looks at the tape while a smile creeps across her face. She puts it on the bedside table and takes the ashtray right next to it, putting out the unfinished cigarette. Then she turns off the lamp that sits on the same table and places her lighter next to it. Tucking herself in, she closes her eyes.

A distance away, the sound of somebody either wailing or singing can be heard. This alerts Evelyn to sit up and check outside the window. Getting on her knees, she leans up against the window, unknowing where the sound is actually coming from. There are a lot of trees around the area and it could be a number of things. The owls would hang around all night, or some other particular creatures. Only this wailing or humming sounded more human than anything. There are no noises outside. She closes the window and tries to fluff her pillow. Again, the humming is heard. Evelyn nods her head and wonders where the sound is coming from. Nobody else was around. As far as she knew, she was the only guest that Bobby had told her about. He, Jaime, and all of the rest had gone home for the evening.

Off in another room down the hall, the humming can lightly be heard. In a darkened guest room, the turntable spins a Willie Dixon record. A pair of dark eyes peers from within the shadows. "I Can't Quit You Baby" is heard as the eyes close with contentment. Cigarette smoke seeps through the light cracks from the window off to one side. The humming continues but grows softer as the music comes to an end. Two fingers gently pull the needle away from the spinning vinyl, resting it on the arm of the turntable.

Evelyn peeks out the door of her room, but hears no more than mere silence. She closes the door and returns to the bed, where once again she tucks herself in until falling asleep.

The next morning, Evelyn is seated across from Henry who inhales the smoke from a cigar. She wanted to know more about Jaime Weston.

"Who is he?" She asks her longtime friend.

Henry replies tersely to her. "He's a hermit. That's what. Do you ever see him around here? I know I don't."

"Well, I realize he doesn't get out much."

"That's an understatement." He chuckles back. "To understand this guy, is something else. He wears tinted sunglasses...at night. He doesn't want others to know about him. As it is, he doesn't like to get very close to people. He keeps to himself quite a bit."

Evelyn inquiries, "What about women?"

Henry shakes his head and says, "What women? The only thing that studio ever really sees are guys in bands, very few women. Bobby tells me the ladies they have record are quite young. Other than that, I don't know much about Weston's love life. I've seen him enough to understand he's very much a loner."

Evelyn starts to smile.

Henry catches her reaction and sits back while holding his cigar and putting it back in his mouth. He angles his eyes to her in perplexity. "You're not telling me you have a thing for this guy, are you? What about Ed? I know you told me a few days ago when you first arrived that things were not looking good for you and him."

Evelyn says back, "Well, that's true. We just don't get along as we had before."

Henry grumbles back, "You never did." He looks at the menu.

Evelyn leans over the table. "Can I tell you something?"

"Shoot for it kiddo."

"In regards to Jaime. He is something else, hermit or not."

Henry peeks past the menu to see Evelyn is on Cloud Nine in her thoughts of the record producer.

Her deep tone runs into gleeful appraisal. "He's absolutely gorgeous!"

A waiter comes by and asks if either Henry or Evelyn is ready to order. Both order eggs with toast and coffee. They hand over the menus back to the waiter and he soon disappears into the morning crowd. Hungry patrons at the patio restaurant can hear the clanking of dishes and forks.

Henry looks at Evelyn with disbelief. "The problem with you is that you have raging hormones. Don't you think you should try to patch things up with Ed? The guy's been with you for seven years. My wife and I have been together for eight. I couldn't just give up on her or my son like that."

Evelyn looks down at the table. "Henry, I'm really unhappy. Our life just isn't the same anymore. It's as if the spark was simply put out like that."

Henry tries to sympathize with her. "This is all stemming from you wanting kids?"

"Mostly, and he doesn't understand me."

"Like I've said before, Evelyn, why not adopt?"

She shakes her head quickly and responds with, "We talked and argued about it. When I changed my mind and thought of adopting, he didn't want anything to do with it. He started questioning me on how long I stay home, making me sound like a workaholic. I told him that this project needed a lot of attention. It still didn't fly with him. He didn't like the idea of me bringing a child to the studio. A complete mess, Henry. He's unresponsive in bed. The only time he would want me is if I was feeling down. I can't be sure if that was because he felt sorry for me or wanted to take advantage of my weakened state. It doesn't matter though. It's not like I can have any...anyway."

***

Evelyn stands in the enclosed studio space of the recording room. With headphones on, she grows restless with anticipation while slightly swiveling her whole body. She puckers her lips making sure they aren't too dry when she sings. Her fingers lightly graze the microphone boom stand in front of her.

On the other side of the glass window is the control room. Bobby, Dan, and Jaime sit looking over charts. Dan nods.

Bobby presses a button, leaning over into the small microphone speaker that attaches to the recording room. "Okay. Evelyn? Can you hear me?"

"Yes." She answers back.

Bobby continues. "We're gonna take the song up to the third line and see where that goes because that wasn't good. The copy you gave us."

Jaime leans over toward Bobby with Dan in between.

He instructs the other producer. "Tell her to bring her voice up one octave."

Dan says, "Her voice is very limited."

Jaime responds with, "I know that. Still, it might work."

Bobby presses the button down and asks Evelyn, "Do you think you can push your vocals up one octave higher than you originally did?"

She hesitates for a moment. "I don't know. My range is pretty short."

Jaime rises from where he's sitting. Turning to Bobby, he gestures for him to get up as well.

"Switch." Jaime states.

Bobby says back in a tone that's not too happy, "What? I can handle it."

Jaime puts his arm out with his thumb pointed back the other way to the right.

"Oh man!" Bobby mumbles disapprovingly.

Jaime tells him back in a low almost mocking tone, "Yeah. Yeah. Come on."

Bobby goes to take the producer's place while Jaime takes on the main controls.

Bobby asks, "Why do I take this from you?"

The head producer says back dryly, "Because who else would put up with you?"

Dan begins laughing. He turns to meet the eyes of Jaime. They both laugh. Bobby shrugs. Evelyn watches the interaction. With a noticeable smile, Jaime looks at Evelyn. He clears his throat and presses down the button to talk to Evelyn.

"I think if you go one octave higher, we'll be able to get a better mix with the instrumental track. Do you think you could do that?" Jaime remained persuasive and convincing when he wanted something. "I want to see if there's something that can be pulled out and amazing at the same time. I'm convinced if you have the absolute *passion*. Don't even think about it. Let it out with your voice."

Evelyn thinks for a moment then nods in agreement. "Okay." She answers.

Jaime says to Bobby and Dan, "Let's roll."

Dan flips up a dial, watching a bank of green lights climb up. Bobby pushes the button for the tape to turn. Once everything is in place, Evelyn takes her place waiting for the signal. Jaime puts on his tinted, oval sunglasses, and one finger up before pointing to her. Closing her eyes, she thinks of what the producer told her moments ago. She closes her eyes and presses the headphones closer to her ears while stepping up to the microphone.

So many times, you played the strong willed one.
Things aren't always as they seem, or so it goes.
Had the guts to tell but feelings could never show.
Now it's time to let you know.

Little Miss Independent
Never needing no one (or so it seems)
Trying to live her life as some beauty queen.
Telling off others without a sound.
Deafened noise with no one around.

She thought she found true love.
Knowing her, words that didn't come out.
Now she's watching her future walk away
Let him slip away and it only goes to show.

Jaime puts his hand up for her to stop. The music abruptly ends. Evelyn looks at him. Bobby stops the tape. Her eyes scan the expressions of the three men in the next room over. Jaime puts a hand through his hair and does the same with the other.

"Whoa! That was it."

A smile grows on his face. She's relieved by what she sees.

Jaime returns to the speaker. "That's what I was talking about. You really hit the nail on the head."

Evelyn says back, "Should I do the rest?"

"Knowing the way this sounds, I'd say, yes. You should. It sounds much better than the original."

Evelyn smiles quickly while adjusting her headphones.

Bobby cues up the tape again. Dan looks at the switchboard. Jaime turns a few knobs. He puts up his hand, and then points back to her. Evelyn goes back to where she left off. The three men settle back. Jaime leans over the main console. Through his sunglasses, he watches her intently. He starts to realize his strong attraction to her. His thoughts dawn on his refusal to take her up on that invitation to dinner. Not that he didn't want to, just that he was a bit nervous around her. It would be easy to take that rain check she mentioned. After all, Evelyn was residing upstairs in the guest quarters. Under thin lips, the corners of his mouth grow further apart with a smile approaching. He contently keeps his eyes on the singer through the control room window. Bobby and Dan simply watch her and every now and then pay close attention to the lit up console board. Not Jaime though. His eyes are strictly on Evelyn. He peers up, lowering the sunglasses to his nose. The tinted dark view leaves him unsatisfied. What Evelyn doesn't notice is that he scans her small though voluptuous figure. She wasn't skinny as a rail but she was just right in all areas. Her features intrigued him to no end. Evelyn had a look about her that fresh-faced school girls had. When she would smile, it was contagious. She looked sweet and innocent but then again there could be something more she was hiding. Jaime then feels a warm sensation throughout his body, like somebody turned up the thermostat. He undoes the first button of his shirt. In the next room over, Evelyn finishes the song. Bobby goes to turn off the revolving tape. Jaime and Dan lower the levels. She gives a big smile. Bobby gives her the thumbs up. Dan smiles. Jaime stands with arms folded and a slight smirk on his face.

Evelyn dashes out of their sight after removing the headphones. She enters the control room. Quickly, she brushes by Jaime who lets her by. He glances at her backside while allowing her through.

Bobby says immediately, "You did great."

With excitement, Evelyn rushes over to Jaime, who is busy unwrapping the cellophane from a fresh pack of Marlboros. She places a hand on his black-sleeved arm, oblivious to knowing what she's doing to him in the inside. She looks up at his face and says, "You were right. One octave higher."

He feels her hand squeeze his arm a little. With a sly smile, he tells her, "You know you're good."

Right at that moment Evelyn feels warmness through her body. She would have to look up into his eyes obscured by tinted lenses. Evelyn simply would have loved to reach up and kiss the tall and handsome producer. Instead, she settles on a small gaze, hoping to see his eyes through the sunglasses. If only he would take those damn things off! Evelyn steps away from him. He walks over to the back of the room and lights up a Marlboro with a match.

She announces to all with excitement, "What's next?"

Dan says, "Now? Now we go home."

Confused she asks, "Isn't it early?"

Dan tells her, "Not early enough for my wife. I'm sure I missed dinner."

"You can always stick a TV dinner in the oven." Bobby teases.

Dan turns to Bobby. "I've already done that. Listen, when the kids are eating better than their dad, something isn't right. Like I said, I'm out of here. I'll see you tomorrow."

All three wish him a good night. After a few minutes, Bobby tells Jaime and Evelyn he's leaving too. The secondary producer heads out the door, leaving the final two people in the small room. Evelyn turns to look at Jaime.

Figuring it's useless in getting the producer to do anything, she says, "Well, I guess I'll be going back to my room now. And you?"

"I'll be fine. I have some things I have to finish before I leave."

Evelyn begins to leave when she feels herself being held back. Jaime holds her arm gently but firmly. He pulls off his sunglasses with the other hand.

They stare at each other.

The singer smiles sweetly. "Okay. Then... Goodnight."

He lets go and gives her a tight lipped smile before uttering, "Yep."

She disappears from the control room. He looks up to wait for the sound of her going up the stairs. Once he's satisfied, Jaime smiles to himself.

Upstairs, Evelyn stands inside her room thinking. She knew he was holding back his feelings. What was with him grabbing her arm like that? Why didn't he just do whatever he was thinking? She would have been happy. Removing her shoes, she feels the soft carpet below bare feet. Looking at the phone on the table further away, she contemplates calling Ed. She felt herself feeling less and less for him since her stay at the studio. As much as she was attracted to Jaime, she was still glad to distance herself away from any man. There was no need to jump into another relationship. Already she was wondering how to end it with Ed. Sitting down on the bed, she reaches for the receiver. Before punching in the numbers, her mind wanders to the time zone. Calculating in her head the five hours apart, she figures that it's too late to call. She longed for company though. All of her good friends were in England too. So, it was out of the question to chat with any one of them. Henry was probably at work since he took that dreadful night shift some months ago. If she dared talk about the record producer she had eyes on, he would treat her like she was crazy. Staying up in the guest quarters of I.C.E. Studios was getting dull. Being alone, even worse.

Down the hall in a room further away, the turntable is turned on. A record is pulled out of its sleeve and placed gently on the flat surface to spin. Two long fingers place the needle on the groove of the vinyl disc and the rumbling of drums starts up among the crackling. The well-furnished room is softly lit. The light illuminates while smoke billows from a corner of the room. Dark tinted oval sunglasses are placed on a small table. B.B. King sings with authoritative pain while wailing away on Lucille's strings.

Evelyn looks in the mirror to see the reflection of her pool blue eyes. She wonders what she should do. Not feeling tired; she plops down on the black leather chair that swallows her body. Taking off her earrings, she slips them onto the small table to the right side. Evelyn puts her head back and sighs. Only, there is that subtle sound within the studio again. She figures that everyone has gone home already. The clock reads 9:17 PM.

Who would be left? Evelyn rubs her eyes and looks at the door. Maybe she should finally investigate and find out her fellow company.

Quietly she tiptoes out of her room, to walk down the long hallway. It sounds like music, but where it comes from, she has no idea. Down the blackened hallway, there is a sliver of light coming from beneath the last door on the left. The music becomes louder. The melding of "The Thrill Is Gone," a marriage of music between B.B. King and Lucille fills the air. The thrill is gone. Evelyn could definitely define her relationship with Ed that way. There was nothing left between them.

Moving over to the door, she hesitates but gives a light knock. There is no answer, but the door slightly becomes ajar. Evelyn slowly slides her hand, attempting to open it. She peeks inside and sees that nobody is around. Lucille is wailing away on the turntable and the light is on, but nobody home. How odd? Somebody had to be within the artists quarters upstairs beside herself. Curiosity gets the best of her as she enters the room. She looks to the adjacent wall and views the paintings. One is a soft oil painting of Appaloosas running through a mist of water. Another is a colorful pastel picture of a feather. She stands back to get a full view of it, and bumps into the bottom of a bedpost with her heel. She turns to look and sees a gray zigzagged Navajo blanket neatly covering the bed. Evelyn takes a step back and bumps into something else again. She turns around and discovers exactly who has been occupying the room. He comes into her view. "Jaime! I had no idea you were still here." Quickly she makes up an excuse. "I was in need of headphones. The wire broke on mine."

Her deepened British tone can't hide the nervousness in her voice. He narrows his eyes on her while sucking on the Marlboro. She feels his stare, yet she can't quite tell what he's thinking. She takes a look at him and immediately becomes intrigued, as it could be many things about him that she is attracted to. Those exotic looks he had due to his Native roots for one thing. It could simply be the way he treated her or that mysterious aura he carried. Jaime is certainly a man of mystery, wearing the black shirt. The first button is undone with the slightest bit of brown hair showing underneath. Snug black jeans fit him nicely over his tall, slender figure.

He says, "Sure," in a deep smoky voice.

Quietly she walks over to the turntable and picks up a pair of headphones. Slowly he saunters over to the other side of the room, still watching her. She looks back up. His stance is very direct as he watches her every move. He holds the cigarette between his fingers. Taking the headphones, she walks up to him. Standing on her tiptoes, she stretches her 5'4" frame to kiss the six-footer. Then she heads for the door but something stops her from leaving. She turns around and sees he's still staring at her. This brings a smile to her full lips.

His reply to her reaction is, "What?"

Evelyn says to him as she sees that he has one hand in his pocket, "What do you have in there?"

He lets the smoke from his Marlboro unfurl into the air as he says in a deep voice, "Nothing. I'm naked."

She walks up to him and tosses the headphones onto a small table. "Not if I can't get you that way first."

This gets his attention as he quickly puts his cigarette out in the small ashtray nearby. Pulling her by the forearms towards him, he whispers. "Wanna bet?"

She closes her eyes at the feel of his warm breath against her ear. His voice is sheer ecstasy. Evelyn places a hand on his chest and lightly rubs the loose-fitting cotton blend shirt he wears. For a moment, the producer looks in her eyes. He leans over, fluttering his lids closed to kiss her. It's a refreshing strong kiss at that. She could taste the obvious difference in brand of Marlboro from her usual Camel. The feeling of his mouth against hers only entices her more. He notices her unflinching stare and goes for it again. Smack! The kiss to jump-start her passion, long since locked away. A sensation she longed to feel. Evelyn's eyes move down his shirt. Just what did that body look like under there? Her heart begins to pound faster as she decides it's time to undo the second button. Her fingers fumble to undo the third while she's at it. He doesn't stop her. The fourth comes undone. She pulls away, looking him over. His shirt is now unbuttoned enough to reveal the lightly matted brown hair underneath that reaches from just below his throat, down his chest. He pulls her by the forearm and starts kissing her wildly, letting his own fingers creep up to unbutton her blouse. He holds her back, noticing no undergarment underneath. She lightly runs her fingers down his chest. He breathes a little faster as Evelyn undoes the final buttons.

He manages to say very softly, "Evy."

She stops.

Nobody had ever called her Evy before and she liked it, especially coming from him. This only makes her want him more. She lets her hands slide up to his shoulders, opens his shirt widely and kisses down along his chest. He pulls at her blouse and yanks it to her shoulders. Jaime forces her head up as he passionately kisses her neck. His other hand runs down to fondle her breasts. The feeling makes her shudder, but she slides her hand down to the waistline of his jeans where he doesn't wear a belt. Evelyn tries to tug at the button but his hand reaches hers in an effort to stop her. They are both almost halfway undressed. Their eyes meet as if wondering should they go further.

Jaime says to her in his low cigarette worn voice, "I haven't done this in a *long* time."

Her reply is equally as deep. "Do you want me to stop?"

With a smile that's so endearing, he says slyly, "No."

They continue kissing. She lowers the zipper. Jaime pulls at her blouse.

Soon the needle on the turntable lifts, and on the floor is a pile of black and white garments.

Over on the bed, movement underneath occupies the blanket. Jaime's shadow hovers over Evelyn. He nuzzles up to her neck and strongly kisses her from her chin down to her neck. His hand runs down the side of her left breast. She breathes heavy. Reciprocating, Evelyn runs her fingers down his chest. He grabs her fingers away with his hand and forces hers to the pillow. With her other hand free, Evelyn strokes back his hair.

Within time, his hair becomes slickened back from both the heat and her fingers running through it. Their bodies against one another perspire from passion. He holds her tightly, giving in to his desires.

Evelyn's fingers bear down on his shoulders. "Oh God! Jaime!" She cries out.

Her heart pounds strongly, body quaking with delight.

Then the phone rings.

He slides his tongue into her mouth. She breathes sharply. He tries to completely keep his concentration but the ringing becomes unbearable. Closing his eyes, he goes for it again, but still nothing. Giving a heavy breath, he lets up. Jaime looks down at her.

In a heavy tone he tells her, "Well, this is embarrassing. I can't fuck to this."

The ringing goes off again. He closes his eyes in anguish.

"Fuck it." He says.

Regaining his composure, Jaime slides to one side of the bed and answers the phone. He says in a mock sleepy tone, "Hello?"

"Did I wake you up?"

It's Henry on the other end. He sure had a way of calling at odd times.

"No. I'm just tired."

That's not what he really wanted to tell Henry. Evelyn lies on the other side with a smile on her face. They would continue their business after, but right now, she would just close her eyes. Jaime looks to the other side and sees that his blonde companion has already drifted off, or so he thought.

Henry continues with, "Could you make it down to the cafe tomorrow morning? I'll be there around nine."

"You called me this late to ask me that?"

"It's only ten o' clock. You're usually up still."

Jaime closes his eyes in disgust. He breathes heavy silently.

"I know, but I've had a rather busy schedule lately and tomorrow is no different."

"Anything exciting going on over there?"

The producer grins back. "No."

"All right then, I'll let you have your beauty sleep."

Jaime gives a tight-lipped smile as he says, "All right. Bye."

He then hangs up.

Over on the other end, Henry does the same, but smiles and says to himself, "Yep. Goodnight Jaime...and Evelyn."

Jaime slides over and puts his hand next to Evelyn's shoulder. She's fallen asleep. Sliding back to his right side, he sinks to the pillow and stares at the ceiling while listening to the crickets coming from outside. It was nice of Henry to call but how was he to know the lovemaking session he was interrupting?

Still restless, Jaime doesn't want to wake up Evelyn. He picks up a couple of objects. Then he sits up, moving over to the center of the bed. Taking a deep breath, he inserts a Marlboro in his mouth and holds a matchbook. One strike. It does nothing. Second. Still nothing. Even lighting a damn cigarette doesn't work. Clearly, it wasn't his night. Evelyn quietly sits up. She moves over in back of him. He takes a deep breath. She places her arm around his shoulder. He puts his head back for a moment. Her fingers lightly graze against his chest. She appears to have known exactly what he wanted. With the right hand, she flicks on her small silver engraved lighter. The orange glow illuminates him. He leans over to her offering with the cigarette still in his mouth.

In a low voice she asks, "Which do you rather see burn? Me, or that cigarette?"

He narrows a glance and takes the Marlboro out of his mouth. Jaime looks down giving a soft chuckle. He passes the matchbook and cigarette for her to put on the nightstand.

With a beckoning finger, Jaime says softly, "Come here."

Evelyn slides her body in front of him. He slides back, allowing her more room, then leans to kiss her. She leans more. He pulls at her. She feels her thigh against his knee. Evelyn puts her hands on his chest and lets her nails lightly scrape down. He grasps her back with his right hand. Quietly chuckling, they fall back.

Looking down at him, Evelyn sits up. Jaime looks up, his hands land on her sides. He takes her lead to sit up, then feels her legs tightly straddle him. She takes his face into her hands and kisses him. Then, her hands move down to his shoulders. He kisses under her chin, down her neck. She situates herself over him more. He shuts his eyes to the sensation. She feels his whole body tense up, before moving in synch with her. He releases a labored breath and low moan. Evelyn kisses his lower lip. Her hands run up and down his chest. She slides her head down in an effort to kiss his throat. Jaime leans his head back and closes his eyes. He feels the sensation of her mouth, and the rhythmic motion of her body against his own. His hands slide up her back.

"More." She says in a breathless whisper.

Her hands remain spread over his chest, with the pounding heartbeat underneath.

Jaime looks her in the eyes to communicate his acknowledgment without words.

Evelyn leans to kiss him hard. He responds the same way, only more forceful. She tries again. He wraps his arms around her for a tight embrace, kissing her all over. Getting her hands free, she wraps them over his shoulders. Glancing down for a split second, he adjusts his tensed body, changing his thrust tempo to harder and faster. His long fingers sink to the small of her back, tightening his hold on her. She lets out a moan and grabs onto his shoulders, her back arches. He squeezes his eyes shut, gritting his teeth. A final gasp, and she relaxes her body. Her hands loosen from his back. He exhales a long breath with a deep moan. Still holding her, his fingers lightly tap on her back in an indication he's about to change positions. She removes herself and her sore calf muscles. Jaime falls back to the pillow, with her over him.

Both are hot and perspire from passion. Evelyn takes her hand underneath his chin and urges him to look at her. She says, "Burnt?"

Immediately, he starts chuckling softly.

Afterwards, Evelyn rests her head on Jaime's shoulder. He has his head propped against the pillow. Her hand lightly runs down his chest.

She asks him. "So, do you stay here all the time?"

"Only when I'm working on a specific project that needs a lot of attention. If it should happen, I can simply go downstairs and work on it. Do you have any ideas at the moment you would like to share?" He smiles.

"No, but I do need lots of attention." She answers back suggestively.

Jaime takes her hand, gently kissing her fingers. Then he peculiarly looks at something. He lifts her hand and asks, "What is that?"

"What's what?"

"That thing...on your hand."

"Oh, that? It's just a tattoo of a small bird. I got it done when I was terribly young and drunk."

"How do you feel now?"

"Stone...cold...sober." She answers slowly.

Jaime reaches over to kiss her. She takes his face into her hands and kisses him back stronger. Her arms reach over his shoulders. Taking her in his arms, they roll over. Evelyn looks up at him. She takes the opportunity to run her hands down his chest, feeling her way around flesh and hair. He lowers himself, and then starts kissing her neck. His hands roam around her ample breasts. She reaches to run her hands through his pushed back hair. Quickly, he runs a hand down underneath the blanket. She feels her left thigh pulled away. He cradles his body against hers. Evelyn's body stiffens. Her eyes close at the sound of his voice.

In a husky, breathy tone, he tells her, "I want to take you to the highest mountain." He gives her long, deep kisses.

She manages to softly whisper, "Yes." Reaching to wrap her arms around his back, her wrists get caught by his hands, one at a time. Fingers get entwined on the pillow. Evelyn gives in to the producer's rhythmic desires. Every tempo change sends a shockwave of sensations throughout her body. "Oh God! That feels wonderful! Yes! Don't stop!" She pleads.

Both breathe heavy until they each feel a deep explosion within. Jaime lets out a sizable moan before collapsing onto her in extreme exhaustion.

Again, they roll over and she rests her head on his chest. She props up to him and says, "You are amazing."

Evelyn strokes back a few strands of hair from falling over his brows. He looks at her attentively. She runs her hand down his sweat soaked chest. He looks down and places an arm just above her waist, gently stroking the soft skin. With his other hand, he strokes back her hair. Evelyn desperately wants to say something but can't find the words. Instead, she slides her head down against his shoulder. He continues to stroke her hair, tenderly kissing the top of her head. She eventually doses off with a smile across lips of contentment.

Only moments later she whispers, "I love you."

Jaime's eyes dart over to her. He stops stroking her hair. Maybe she was dreaming? Whatever, it makes him think. In the darkness of night, Jaime stares at the ceiling wondering about the meaning. Had Evelyn fallen for him that quickly? Of course there was more that he didn't know.

Morning arrives. Evelyn lays sleeping on the left. Jaime faces the same way with his right arm draped over her side. Slowly he opens his eyes to the brightness that greets him and props himself up. He exhales a deep breath, and then looks over at his sleeping blonde companion. Jaime closes his eyes. He runs a hand through his now dry hair, and rubs his heavy lids from sleep. Again, he turns to look at Evelyn before getting up and slipping back into his black denim jeans. Walking over to the closet, he puts on a beige shirt without buttoning it and rolls up the cuffs. He thinks of the last words she said before drifting off to sleep. Evelyn yawns, and then continues to lie peacefully. He looks over, then back at the closet where he pulls out a striped shirt and lays it on the bed. Jaime steps away into the bathroom just as Evelyn begins to open her eyes.

She smiles to herself and whispers, "That was grand."

Her eyes move down the blanket where she sees the shirt draped over the right side of the bed. She then realizes that he left it for her to borrow. Slowly she gets up, tosses on the shirt and buttons it up. It reaches to her knees and the sleeves go past her fingers. She reaches for her lighter on the nightstand and flicks it on saying to herself, "Ed, you were never *that* good."

She wanders over to see that the turntable was not shut off from the previous night. Evelyn turns off the power and rests the needle in its proper place. Returning to the bed, Evelyn looks up to see that Jaime has arrived back in the room. He pushes back his hair and then realizes that Evelyn is awake. She stares at him coyly. He looks at her, almost wanting to say something but doesn't. He goes over to the adjacent kitchen to sit down at the small table. She decides to join him on the opposite side. Jaime pulls out a Marlboro and inserts it in his mouth. Evelyn leans over with her lighter and flicks it on. Peering at her cautiously, he lowers the tip of it to the flame. Would she try to proposition him again with her offering? He leans back and eases out a breath of smoke while closing his eyes. Evelyn pulls out a Marlboro and lights it quickly, perching it between her fingers. Letting out a puff of smoke, she immediately launches into conversation with glee.

"You were *incredible* last night. Truly wonderful, darling. I don't think I can ever remember a night like that."

Jaime closes his eyes tightly with anguish.

She informs him. "Mark my words, I've had some good partners but none like you."

Jaime lets out a deep breath and holds his cigarette in a manner that Bette Davis would be proud of.

He responds cautiously. "Can we keep this to ourselves?"

"Of course darling! I wouldn't want it any other way. Our little secret." All the while, she's smiling and continues. "And what did *you* think of last night?"

Coolly he says, "It happened."

Her smile cancels. "I know that silly, but really what did you think of it?

Jaime states flatly, "I'm not the type to love 'em and leave 'em."

"Is that what you think I am?"

He takes another long drag of his cigarette.

This upsets her a little. "You know, I usually don't confuse sex with love, but apparently you have." Evelyn pushes away from the table and gets up. Disgusted she says, "I guess you are like all of the other arrogant bastards out there."

She snuffs out her cigarette in the ashtray and walks over to gather her pile of clothing from the floor.

Jaime watches her and utters, "Damn it."

He puts his Marlboro in the ashtray. She makes her way to the door. Just before she can open it, he has his hand on the knob, forcing her to stay. She turns around to face him.

As if to apologize for upsetting her, he says in a serious tone, "One more thing."

He pins her against the door and gives her a lengthy succulent kiss. She drops her belongings and puts her hand on his chest. He pulls away quickly. Evelyn's eyes go wide in shock. Once again, she picks up her garments and opens the door. After leaving, she closes her eyes and hugs her clothes tightly with a big smile.

On the other side, Jaime leans against the door and chuckles softly while buttoning up his shirt. He says to himself, "God. What a night."

Evelyn rushes down the wooden steps, trying to tuck in her black blouse, which she changed into rather than the obvious men's striped shirt Jaime had let her borrow.

She comes in and announces, "Sorry, I'm late. I overslept."

Bobby, Dan, and Jaime look at her unsympathetically. Jaime was not going to vouch for her tardiness, nor was he going to take the blame. He looks up at her, and then checks the charts of her track listing. Picking up a pencil, he points to the written chart.

"Let's try Track 5 and see what we end up with."

Right away, the producer is unsatisfied with what he hears. Evelyn sits next to Bobby and sees that there is something obviously wrong. Jaime says, "It's not right. Dan, move up the keyboards one level."

Bobby looks over at Jaime and says, "If you do that, you'll drown out the guitar."

The producer lets out a big sigh while peering at the three people sitting next to him.

"Fine. Move the guitar track up."

Bobby scratches his head, saying, "Um, then you'll have a tiny rhythm section. Why not just leave it alone?"

Jaime looks over at Bobby again, then darts his eyes to the control panel. "Let's try Track 7."

Dan slowly pushes up the level, attempting to even out the sound.

Again, Jaime is not happy with what he hears. He avoids making any eye contact with Evelyn in the meantime. His sight bounces from the control panel to Bobby or Dan, sometimes both but never Evelyn Winthrop. She had gotten to him badly. Her words of '*I love you*' left the producer's mind and concentration in disarray. As it was, he figured it was a one-nighter, but he knew it was great at the same time. Only his own feelings kept him back.

The producer shakes his head again. "There's not enough bass in the beginning."

Evelyn says, "There isn't supposed to be *any* bass in the beginning whatsoever."

Jaime drops the pencil down. He asks, "What are we supposed to do with it then?" A slight agitation creeps in his voice.

She says back huffily, "Just leave it alone. Nothing needs to be done with it. It's been done already."

With a glance down at the sheet of paper with lyrics, Jaime asks, "Who wrote these? They sound awful."

Evelyn leans over with distress and embarrassment, snatching away the paper from his hands. "Don't you know *anything* about songwriting?" Darting her eyes back at him, she answers disapprovingly. "Obviously you don't and I say *tough* to that!"

Bobby watches with his cheeks puffed, and then blows out a sigh.

Dan frowns.

Bobby mutters. "The honeymoon is over."

Pushing back his hair in front, Jaime gives a tight-lipped smile before saying, "Okay. Go to Track 8." Dan pushes up all the levels once more. Jaime shakes his head. "Dump it and do it all over again. It sounds like shit."

Bobby turns quickly to Jaime with exasperation, "What? That's the second best track we've worked on!"

The head producer looks down for a moment. Agitation turns into an uncomfortable gaze Evelyn's way.

Dan has had enough and stands up. No more pussyfooting for the disgusted engineer. "If anything is wrong Jaime, it's in your head. What's with you, man? Ever since you came down here, you've been seriously carrying this bad mood and treating all of us like shit. What gives you the right? We're trying to do our job by getting this lady's record done and you're copping an attitude. What? Next thing you're going to say is that "Hero's Requiem" doesn't sound right either. Why not? You only spent four days and countless hours working on it!" Bobby looks at Dan who continues to speak his mind. "Let's just add in some horns. Huh? Maybe just maybe we can add in a tambourine!"

Jaime glares at Dan.

Bobby blurts out quietly. "Shut up, Danny."

He can see his friend growing enraged rather quickly.

Dan adds in, "We can use a flying V guitar for the bridge portion."

Jaime then suggests with a bitter tone. "How about you don't know a flying fuck about sound?"

Dan shuts his mouth and swallows hard. Bobby and Evelyn say nothing, only glance at the embittered producer.

Evelyn says quickly as she looks at the flustered producer, "I think I know what it is." All three pay close attention to her. Immediately, Jaime looks down and breathes with growing fury. Would she tell Bobby and Dan what happened between her and him? She says calmly, "It is burn out. I see the way he stays here and works the controls long after you two are gone. He does it alone. It's no wonder he has little sleep."

The last thing Jaime needs is anybody's sympathy. He mumbles while rubbing between the bridge of his nose. "This is bullshit." Shaking his head quickly, he tosses the pencil down and gets up in a huff. The producer grabs his sunglasses quickly. Jaime gives them all a disgusted look before leaving. He yells out, "Ah, it's fucked! Take the whole fuckin' day off!"

The door slams behind him. Evelyn looks at Bobby and Dan.

Just outside of the control room in a small equipment room, Jaime says, "Shit!" He grabs his jacket, tosses it on with one shirttail hanging. Once outdoors, he shuts the door quickly and jams on his sunglasses. In second's time, he grabs out a cigarette from his jacket pocket and strikes a match from his matchbook. He lights it in a flash, blows out a curl of smoke. In an unnerved tone, he utters, "Son of a bitch." He gets in his car and leaves among a cloud of swirling dust.

Inside the control room, everyone remains quiet until Bobby announces to the other two people in the room. "That went well." He says with raised brows.

Dan picks up a pair of headphones, saying, "Let's see if we can figure out these tracks on our own."

Evelyn turns to look at the door. Bobby sees her concern. He says to her, "Ah, don't mind him. He'll be fine. He's been cooped up here for a little too long. We all can overwork ourselves too much."

Dan eyes the door. "Yeah. Or he got up on the wrong side of the bed."

Evelyn's eyes dart to the engineer without him seeing her reaction.

So much for her wonderful evening with Jaime Weston.

A half an hour later after the head producer has left the studio in a testy mood, he's seated across from Henry at a trendy little cafe across town. Henry is a little surprised at his friend's appearance. Usually, Jaime was extremely tidy and neat in public. Today, his shirt is partly untucked and a couple of buttons are undone under a thin black jacket. He wears his usual sunglasses.

Henry asks, "What happened to you, my friend?"

Jaime runs a hand through his hair. "Rough night."

Henry squints. "I see."

The producer puts the palm of his hand to his forehead. A few strands of hair lightly fall over his brows once he removes it. He exhales quickly. An older lady dressed with an apron takes Henry and Jaime's order.

Jaime says, "Coffee. Black."

Henry tells the waitress, "I'll take a coffee too. Make mine with cream and sugar."

She repeats the order. "Two coffees. One black. One cream and sugar. Coming up."

The waitress disappears within the crowd.

Jaime sits in a contemplative manner.

Henry asks, "So, what's goin' on with you?"

Jaime pulls off his sunglasses, prompting a table of four women nearby to approve and fan themselves with their menus. He turns quickly to see them giggle. Returning back to what he was saying, Jaime places his eyewear off to the side.

"I did something and I'm not proud of my attitude. After all, I have nobody to blame but myself." He stops to think for a moment. "I left the studio in a rather, um, bad mood. I don't know what else to call it." Jaime shrugs. Looking at Henry, he chooses his words carefully. "*You* on the other hand have an odd sense of timing. Not that I don't appreciate talking with you. Just that...last night was a little difficult to get to the phone."

"Yeah. That'll happen when you're trying to sleep."

Jaime says with a slowly creeping smile, "Under the circumstances I can't really say I was sleeping."

Looking down at the gray granite surface of the table, Jaime lets out a sigh.

Out of curiosity and believing to know what's bothering his friend, Henry guesses as to what really happened. "Studio overtime?"

Jaime shakes his head. "No."

Henry then decides the jig is up and says flatly, "Company."

The producer's eyes dart up. His friend knows that he has hit the nail on the head. Jaime lowers his sights to the table again before looking Henry in the eyes and admits in a lower than normal tone. "Yeah."

Henry's brows go up as he replies with curiosity. "Oh?"

Two cups of hot coffee are placed on the table in front of the men.

The waitress says, "Here you go gentlemen. Two coffees. One black and one cream and sugar. If you want to order anymore just call out, Charlotte, when you see me walk by."

Jaime and Henry agree at the same time. She disappears again. Gently stirring the dark liquid, Jaime launches into his tale about the previous evening.

"I don't know...well...it started out innocent enough. Then it escalated. She was different than the others I've been with. It...it was as if it was meant to happen. The emotions were built up until they exploded." Jaime lets out a small smile while recounting his time with Evelyn. "I'm not in my twenties anymore. I'm sure she's not either but she *sure* made me feel that way.

Henry tells the preoccupied forty-four year old, "I think I'm beginning to understand."

"We're not talking about something very quick or wham-bam-thank-you-Ma'am." Jaime lets out a laugh. "It was *passionate* and *meaningful*. The way it's supposed to be. Jeez. We must have been at it, I don't know... three times at least."

Henry almost loses his sip of coffee. He saves it by swallowing hard. "Holy shit, Jaime! Where did you get the energy?"

Jaime chuckles back, "I don't know."

Henry then gives him the look of suspicion or as if to interrogate him. "Are we talking about the use of vitamins here or possibly meditation?"

"No."

"Did you go up to the Catskills and get spiritual advisement from some monks? I heard they do some strange things up there."

Jaime laughs back. "No. None of that."

"I'm just wondering, so you can give an old guy like me pointers. Karen might thank you. I know I would!"

Jaime nods in agreement. "Mm hmm. Well, like I said it just happened that way. There was nothing different. No enhancements. It was just *us*."

He throws his hands out for greater emphasis. Then he turns his attention to the small isle way as he takes out a cigarette. The waitress who had waited on them, heads in their direction.

Jaime manages to catch her on time as he summons her over. "Excuse me, Charlotte? Can I have an ashtray?"

She replies back, "Sure thing."

She steps away and the table of adoring women calls her over.

In the meantime, Jaime grabs out a book of matches.

He begins to tell Henry, "I've got to say, she..."

Henry looks at the table with the women. Charlotte returns with an ashtray. Giving her a quick glance, Jaime is slightly shocked. "Wish the service could be that fast everywhere." He places the Marlboro in his mouth.

Charlotte replies. "Oh, this is actually courtesy of the table over there."

She points. Jaime turns in the direction of her finger. Slowly, his sight focuses on the four women as he removes the cigarette from his mouth. With a tight-lipped smile, he catches the eye of a brunette that giggles with glee. He gives a small wave.

Henry laughs back. "Ah, The Weston Appreciation Society!"

Jaime gives a glance to his buddy.

Back to the conversation, Jaime puts the cigarette back in his mouth and lights it.

He says to Henry, "She wore me out. I barely had enough energy to do anything." He looks down. "I did take out some frustration at the guys in the studio."

Henry inquires, "Bobby and Dan?"

Jaime repeats sheepishly, "Yeah. Bobby, Dan...and her."

"A guest? Or a musician?"

"More like a singer. Apparently, Bobby was more familiar with her work 'cause I don't think I've ever heard of her." With all of his fingers,

Jaime steadies the cigarette for a puff of smoke. "She said, 'I love you.'" His eyes look up at Henry while his head is lowered. Confused, he asks, "Why? Why would she say that? I mean, it was one...*one* night only."

Knowing exactly who Jaime's female company was and hearing Evelyn pouring her heart out during their conversations of how she was miserable, he's able to surmise. "Maybe there's something going on with her. Some people need to feel something that they're not getting elsewhere."

"The strange thing about this time is that I *do* have feelings for her to a point it could be long term. Ya know?" Jaime releases the smoke as he continues, "I saw her before."

He shakes his hand slightly with the Marlboro perched between two fingers.

Surprised, Henry asks, "Where?"

"At a gallery about ten years ago. A little before I met you."

"Did you tell her this?"

"No. I don't know if she would even remember that."

Henry reminds his friend, "Obviously you do."

Jaime smiles back, repeating deeply, "I do. She was something back then too."

***

Evelyn sits in the control room, munching on M&Ms. Bobby picks up her notebook and takes particular interest in the title he reads "Chasing The Dragon."

She notices his preoccupied state. "Oh, that's a song I had written three years ago. My band and I tried to repeatedly play it, but my voice wouldn't go deep enough. "I even tried smoking a pack a day for two weeks."

Bobby looks over the lyrics. "Pretty deep stuff." He thinks for a moment. "Kind of reminds me of Andi. Really interesting and powerful words. Oh, uh, Andi's my wife. She went through a rough time with addiction for a couple of years. This really hits home. What goes on with someone in that situation. Of course, I was no help." He turns his attention back to Evelyn. "I'm sorry sweetie. What did you say before?"

Evelyn says, "Oh, I was mentioning how my voice wouldn't go as low as I'd like. I tried smoking a pack a day for two weeks. It didn't work."

Bobby points to a line. "Ooh. That right there is a particularly sad line."

She looks over. "Which one?"

"The one where it says, 'Catch a hit on Sunday from a former boyfriend's wife.' I can't imagine the desperation that poor soul in the song would go through. That *is* pretty desperate."

"Yes. It was." She looks down. "To understand desperation is to live it. In '74, I was hanging around a record store in London a former boyfriend of mine ran. He was newly married. I was twenty-seven at the time. She was twenty-one. Lovely girl. On Sundays she would mind the shop, and her and I would go into the basement and shoot up heroin. A year later, I heard she had offed herself from a rooftop. She suffered a miscarriage three months before that."

Bobby turns his head, shaking it. "Oh jeez, Evelyn. I'm so sorry. That is awful."

Evelyn answers with, "So you see why this song has to sound just right."

He puts his hands to hips. "Yeah. You're not going to get the sound you want from destroying your lungs either." Bobby nods back. "I know what it needs."

"You do?" She asks.

"Let me see." Bobby goes through the tapes piled on the counter. "What did we label that as? Wait. I think…" He picks one up. "I believe it was *5-Rhythm*. Yes. That's it. The bass with drums."

Evelyn breaks into a smile from his enthusiasm.

He says, "We were going to use it for "Hero's Requiem," and obviously we didn't."

"How will I get my voice to sound the way I want?"

"Sleep on it." Bobby says quickly. "It's getting late, as it is. Just get some rest. I know what to do with this. When you get up, the first thing you're going to do is barely get ready. Don't take forever in getting prim and proper. Don't eat a bite. Don't even think of a café. Don't gargle water or even drink it. Nothing. Come down here to the main studio room and we'll take it from there." He puts his finger at her. "You have to trust me on this."

Hesitantly yet with understanding, Evelyn nods her head in agreement. "Okay." She picks out an M&M, and then pops it in her mouth.

The clock in the lobby reads 9:18 AM as Evelyn rushes down the stairs. Turning the corner, she looks outside. The BMW is nowhere to be found. She thinks better of it, and continues to walk towards the main studio room. Bobby turns around.

"There she is. There's Sleeping Beauty." He looks at her.

Evelyn's appearance is that of groggy and no makeup. Her hair is wispy from not being combed, eyes with a half-awake gaze. She rubs her stomach.

Bobby smiles at her. "Tell me, how do you feel?"

"I feel tired and famished." She says in a low tone.

"And your voice is just right. Now, I can't promise you'll sound like Lauren Bacall, but it's close."

"Yippee." She says dryly.

Dan walks in. He looks at Evelyn.

"A little worse for wear."

"We're doing a session, Danny. So glad you could join us." Bobby grins.

"That's nice, but where's Jaime?"

"Screw him. I'm doing this one. He can join in later."

Evelyn drops the headphones to her neck as she listens.

Bobby says in an annoyed tone. "I can think of a good *J* name that would fit him right now."

Evelyn interrupts him. "But you work with him."

"Yeah, and I know he says things about me sometimes. With his attitude and the way he's been acting…" Bobby mumbles. "Crybaby." He shakes his head. "Never mind about him. Let me explain this to you. All right, the reason I put so many stipulations on you last night was to get the sound you're looking for. You see, Evelyn, your voice is at its deepest when you first wake up. It's dry from those six, seven, or eight hours of sleep you get. As the day wears on, your voice goes through stress, and you're not able to get that low timber you're looking for. I did this before." He calls out to the engineer. "Hey, Danny? You remember that artist we had about five years ago and he had a medium range?"

"Yeah. I can't remember his name, but he wanted it deeper than normal."

"Exactly." Bobby turns back to Evelyn. "I'm going to direct you on this. Okay? We're going to strive and get a feel out of you like it's 1978."

"*Ravaged Beauty*?" Evelyn asks.

"Yes."

"You're going to take the first stanza, the first four lines and drop that voice right there. Bomb it. Low. Then, you're going to rise as the action your singing gets more intense. The more you reveal, the more emotion you're going to put into it. You told me last night about what happened to you. What was her name?"

"Hannah."

"Think of singing it to her. What you feel. Is there anything you want to say to her? Do it like that. Sing it for Hannah. Make it heart wrenching. Damn that lifestyle to hell."

Evelyn looks down tight-lipped, preparing for her moment to sing.

Dan asks Bobby, "Think it'll work?"

"We'll see." Bobby readies the tape he had found the previous night, filled with a rhythm section.

Evelyn places the headphones on her head.

Bobby gives permission to proceed.

Don't want to snort it.
Don't want to inject it.

Don't want to take it on a spoon.
If I give in, I'll die too soon.

Scales. Shadows.
Beware of misery.
Scales. Shadows.
State of suffering.

Sleeping on the subway or lurching in an Alley.
Bite the Big Apple, burn out in San Fernando Valley.
Eating out of trash cans, the smorgasbord of life.
Catch a hit on Sunday, from a former boyfriend's wife.

Hate you when I'm clean.
Love you when I'm high.
There's nothing left to do, than sit on a curb and cry.
The reason I want to clip its tail.
To shed its skin of that hideous veil.

Slam the door on sister Cocaine, don't even let in Mary Jane.
Throw it all... Throw it all away in vain.
Feel yourself drawn, to the deepest depths of Hell.
Drive me under the devil's spell.

Out of the cracks, from within it will creep.
The claws will strangle until you sleep.
Salvation won't save you at dusk or dawn
The dragon will be victor when your mind is gone.

Bobby stops the tape.

"Wow." He nods his head. "I think you nailed that one. I'll add some tiny bits of guitar, and Jaime can do the keyboard part for some fullness." He turns to Dan. "What did you think, my squeaky-clean friend?"

Dan shakes his head. "Those are some sad lyrics."

Evelyn pulls off the headphones, wiping her eyes in pride.

"It's a bloody hard song to sing as well. Going low, and then high." She feels her stomach rumble. "If you excuse me, gentlemen, a croissant sandwich and coffee await at the diner. Ta-ta." She waves them goodbye, leaving the room.

***

The striped shirt lay draped over the arm of the black leather chair. Evelyn looks right at it. She was feeling guilty of what had happened between her and the producer she had slept with. Really, she felt guiltier for him. He was the one with mixed emotions. Jaime had bounced around from incredibly passionate, turned cold, followed by giving her a kiss before she had left, and then taking out his frustrations on the crew the next day. She couldn't convince herself it was something cheap and tawdry. It was love. Not sex.

She picks up the shirt, inspecting it. Smiling, she holds it as she steps out of her room. Walking to the end of the hall, voices are heard from downstairs. Evelyn darts her eyes. The door to Jaime's room was usually left unlocked but closed. Lightly she gives a tap. No answer. Her hand pushes against the door. A flood of light brightens the room. She drops the shirt on the right side of the bed, exactly where he had placed it for her when she awoke from their night together. The painting of Appaloosas grabs her attention. Beautiful, wild, and free. Could this be a representation of Jaime Weston himself? He was after all very attractive, wild with unharnessed passion and single.

Horses bring to her mind extreme romanticism. Images would abound of knights shown atop their trusty steed. Indians worshipped theirs whether for hunting or as a partner in warfare.

She smiles. Without letting herself escape daydream, she leaves. Closing the door the way she found it, she heads down the stairs.

Expecting to find all three guys in the control room, Evelyn takes a deep breath. She isn't so sure if she's ready to face him yet. The door is left wide open. Evelyn fishes for the car keys in her pocket. Bobby turns to the sound of soft jangling. The singer pops her head in. When she looks, Bobby and Dan are already eyeing her. Jaime's nowhere to be found.

Thankfully!

Bobby tells her. "Jaime will be back in a few minutes."

In an uninterested tone, she replies. "Uh-huh. Well, I'll be going out for a little while. I think I came up with something for one of the songs. I'll work on that later with you two. Okay? Bye."

Evelyn rushes out of the studio.

Dan looks at Bobby. "Us *two*? The last time I checked there were *three* of us. Man, talk about trouble in paradise!"

Bobby gives a glance at Dan. "There's nothing romantic going on between them. Work-wise, they're not seeing eye to eye. I think having only parts of songs is getting on Jaime's nerves finally."

Dan nods.

As Jaime had done the day before, Evelyn sits across from Henry. Unlike him, she's not flustered nor angered by anything. She lights a Camel. Releasing a puff, the singer talks with her friend.

"I had an incredible evening two nights ago."

Henry doesn't let on to what he knows already. Instead, he acts as if it's the first time he's hearing it.

He asks begrudgingly. "Okay, what did you do two nights ago?"

She takes a drag on the cigarette. "I did something I never thought I would do." A ring of smoke is blown. "I cheated on Ed."

Henry chokes back. "You what?" Leaning his head into his hand, Henry says, "Please tell me you won't reference one of our previous conversations."

"What do you mean, darling?"

"About *who* you cheated with."

"Oh, I think you know." She answers coyly.

Henry quickly tells her, "I don't think I want to know. Evelyn, why are you doing this to yourself? You have Ed back home."

"There's nothing there. Let me tell you. I believe Jaime is the best lover I have ever had. I felt incredibly comfortable with him. As if I had already known him for so many years. I don't know. Sort of the way a wife may feel about her husband. I guess you can say I felt like he...he was married to me. It wasn't even the act itself. It was the feelings that went into it. Love not sex. He is *extremely* passionate. With Ed, there's nothing. Maybe he had his moments in the beginning but none like this. It was fun in the beginning because it was new and I was off the drugs. My addictions took away any sense of sexual pleasure I might have had. So, yes, Ed was like a breath of fresh air. Although I believe anyone would have. I was so drug addled before then. I wouldn't have known who I was with or what we had done. I'm thankful Ed got me out of that, but that was then. You know Henry, I don't fancy myself as some sexual deviant or promiscuous type even. It's the opposite." Evelyn lets out a ring of smoke. She scrunches a napkin. Tossing it onto the empty plate in front of her, she looks down. "If anything, I have denied myself of feelings. Anything *remotely* close to passion I've learned to turn off. Believe me. I have tried to throw myself at Ed and just say, 'Take me!' He does *nothing*. He's the one that says, 'Not tonight honey.' Ed just rolls over or reads a book. I could wear nothing more than a little piece of nightwear and nothing would happen. Why I could even wrap myself in sandwich wrapping and he wouldn't react. Not even a little snack!"

Henry shakes his head in disbelief. "Have you ever thought that maybe he was having an affair before you? He won't touch you for nothing. Distant."

"No. Not Ed. He just doesn't like sex very much. I didn't either until..."

"Until two nights ago."

She replies while blissfully remembering. "Yes. To be touched in such a divine way. Oh, those hands! That mouth! Those seductive eyes! His voice! That body could..."

Henry puts up his hand. "Stop!"

"What?"

"I get the point."

"Was I going too far, darling?"

"Almost."

She taps ashes into the small ashtray off to the side of her. "I'm sorry for offending you but that's how he makes me *feel*. I have no regrets." Her enthusiasm starts to fade. "Or how I enjoyed it."

Henry notices her excitement dissipate. He adds in her thoughts. "But?"

"But I'm afraid that this has spoiled our working relationship. I don't know if it's possible for us to continue the sessions. I've avoided him since then. I'm unsure if it has hindered any of our progress. I don't want to quit but maybe it would be for the best."

"Instead of avoiding him, why not talk to him? See what he thinks or if he can separate professional from private."

Quietly she answers. "Yes. I suppose you're right."

Evelyn takes another drag from the cigarette.

Later on, she returns to the studio. Bobby and Dan help work out some tracks while Jaime is off in the mixing room. He steps inside the control room every so often to check how things are going. Neither he nor Evelyn speak to each other throughout the day. If anything, the main producer shows a tendency of distancing himself away from the singer more than she cares for. She finds herself frustrated by night's end. The whole thing seemed rather foolish to her. He was acting like a teenager regretting going all the way. It was funny to her that he didn't tell her to stop when she asked. He was only sorry and distant after the fact. She thinks for a moment.

Typical male!

In the morning hours, Ed can't stand waking up alone. Rather than enjoying hogging the bed all to himself, he feels neglected. Evelyn hadn't called him in a few days. Why hadn't she called more often? What was she doing there? He was sure there was more than recording. Ed's stomach churns as he thinks about the possibility of her going back to her old drug habits. New York City had a reputation. Drug dealers would hang around 42nd St. Sleazy shops and clubs would line 8th Ave. Hookers would crook out a finger, waiting for a pay day from an eager john. Ed lights up a Camel. As the smoke billows out of his mouth one thought startles him. Maybe Evelyn wanted to become one of those dirty girls.

Getting up from the bed, Ed surveys the top of bureaus in search of something. He mutters. "Where is that damn thing?"

Ed knew that Evelyn kept an address book somewhere in the bedroom. He had seen it before. Determined to find it, he begins searching through drawers. Inside one of the large oak drawers are shirts piled neatly into two columns. Ed carefully feels around and touches something underneath. His hand pulls up a manila envelope. He opens it and takes out the contents. He sees Evelyn's glowing face as he pulls out a thin stack of photographs. She looked so angelic and pure. Light and shadows danced around her, paying homage to her beauty. Evelyn had played up to the camera...Ed's camera. He felt they were images that represented his failure to compete with the A-list Rock photographers who made Evelyn look exquisite. Lynn Goldsmith, Annie Leibovitz, Bob Gruen, Norman Seeff, all who had captured Evelyn in ways Ed only dreamed of. In his mind, his pictures looked like that of someone shooting for a high school yearbook. Ed couldn't help it. He was used to capturing outdoor scenery and inanimate objects, not portraits. Surprisingly, Evelyn had kept each and every one of them. She wore her favorite black leather jacket with black fishnet stockings in a variety of playful poses.

Ed holds his cigarette in a contemplative manner. For a moment, he reflects on how he used to be with Evelyn. Then he shakes himself of his pleasant thoughts, tossing them aside to only think of his mission. That book. Ed slides the stack of pictures back into the protective custody of the envelope. He jams it back under the pile before closing the drawer. Ed continues to look through more drawers. Then he discovers one drawer he hadn't looked in. It was the one in the center of the oak chest, just below the large rectangle mirror. Quickly he sticks the Camel in his mouth as he opens the drawer. His hands dig under silk-like underwear. Tangled up bras in black, white, and beige get caught on each other or panties mingled in between. Ed finds a dark red piece of lingerie. Valentine's Day wear. Under it is the navy reptile-like surface of a small book.

"Ah!" Ed breathes.

He wipes away the garments from it. Lifting the item as though he's found a treasure, Ed smiles devilishly. He opens the book.

Inside are a list of names, phone numbers, and addresses. He flips through page after page. Demetrius Klemenis, Dee Davies, Simon Campbell, Dominique Bellamy, Murielle Bellamy-Santos, Gisele Bellamy, Thierry Verdeaux, Neil Broden, Nuncio 'Nucci' Nuccinelli, George Trin. All were musicians or background singers Evelyn knew. Ed barely even knew her agent in West Germany, Ben Voorhaun. Names of friends remained virtually unknown to the photographer. Heidi Roberts, Lee Chen, Victor Aldomovar, Henry & Karen Winslow, Elizabeth & Marco Rinalti, Phil & Mildred Grumbach. Ed only knew a handful of the names. Evelyn's best friend was Mildred. She hung around Elizabeth enough too. Then there was that one name that Ed strains to see, as Evelyn had scribbled it down. Kelly Gowan. Next to it was the name, *The Green Light* and its phone number. About halfway through the book, Ed realizes he never bothered knowing his girlfriend's associates or friends. The ones he knew were either from their frequent visits or brief passing. The other hundred or so were faceless names. He could care less who they were. Probably drug buddies, bohemians, Communists, and possibly rat-faced ex-boyfriends.

Ed groans at the sight of the name, Nuncio Nuccinelli.

In a deep guttural tone, he snickers. "Probably some past Italian Stallion lover."

How was he to know that 'Nucci' as he liked to be called was a fifty-eight year old session drummer that Evelyn's late father had known from the club days? Nuccinelli was far from being anyone's boyfriend. He had been happily married to the same woman for thirty-six years, raised seven children and his two oldest sons were successful percussionists as well. Ed could care less. He had that Nucci character all figured out. Just like the rest of them. Her Chinese friends he thought of as Communists. He never would believe the ones in her book either moved to or were born in America. Ed never knew back in the day while Evelyn was down on her luck she had help from kind folks in Chinatown of New York. When she had spent her money on dope or was trying to get straight and couldn't buy enough food because she needed it for rent, she got help. The Chinese families were eager to feed her and pull in some customers to the association of the rock star's name. Besides, she was hungry and thankful she didn't have to eat out of garbage cans.

Whoever any of these people were, Ed would have to pick and choose who he wanted to call by his own biased opinion and generalized intuition. He would start by her friends in England, then work his way down the list and pages.

His fingers begin dialing the phone on the end table next to the bed.

Bobby and Dan had decided to go out for dinner somewhere in town. They figured it would give Jaime and Evelyn some time alone. Both noticed the distance between the two. It was beginning to take its toll on the recording sessions. Opinions were needed but the singer and head producer were not on speaking terms. It was time to kiss and make up.

The door to the office remains open. Illumination is fully provided by two stand- up lamps on both sides of the gray and tan tweed couch. Evelyn walks in. There she finds Jaime lounging on the comfy couch. He's partly sunken in with his head leaning back and long legs stretched out with feet crossed. Jaime peers at her over the rims of his sunglasses. A murky cloud from the Marlboro in his mouth partly obscures his face.

She looks directly at him. "I figured you might be in here."

He says nothing other than sprawling one arm over the back of the couch. Evelyn notices he's wearing the striped shirt over black jeans.

"We really need to get this done. I think that's why Bobby and Dan went out. They notice. I'm...I'm not trying to act like nothing happened between us when we both know differently. It has put a strain on us working together. You do realize that?"

Without an answer, he calmly sucks on his cigarette.

She continues. "I know I may feel differently than you on this subject but I personally have no regrets to it happening. I do wish we could set our differences and emotions aside to finish what we started. I don't really want to stop recording *Hero's Requiem* but if I have to, I will. I have enough as filler material for another project or hits package. So, if you don't want to go any further with this project... I'll completely understand."

Evelyn turns her eyes not able to think of anything else to say. There is that uncomfortable pause. Still looking at her, he removes his sunglasses. Folding them, he slides the eyewear's arm against the second button of his shirt letting them freely stay. He uncrosses his feet and removes himself from the couch. The six-footer stands up. Evelyn takes a step back. He adjusts his belt while keeping a steady gaze on her. Still holding the cigarette, he puts the other hand through his hair.

"Evelyn." He finally says.

With that, he snuffs out the Marlboro in a black ashtray on the mahogany desk. Her eyes adjust. He had just said her name. There was either hope or failure in trying to reach out to the producer. Walking over to her very closely he says in a deeper than average tone, "Don't leave on the count of me. Do it only if you don't believe in this project anymore. What went on with us should not affect our progress with recording. I'm as much to blame for letting things get to the point that they are now. We can't turn back time, since the past is the past. Do you understand?" He asks with his hands out.

She agrees.

"It's not even the normal way I would romance a woman. I don't know what that's supposed to mean. I guess it could depend on each individual but this time was so..."

Evelyn thinks of what she wants to add in.

Spontaneous?

Just then, he's able to complete his sentence. "...Sudden."

Not the word she was thinking of.

"Normally, I'm responsible and more of a take charge kind of guy."

You certainly were that night and how!

"Like I said before and thinking of it now, it was a mistake. Don't think this is a daily occurrence between me and good looking singers."

He looks down at her with a slight smile.

Charming. Pour it on, handsome!

For a moment, Evelyn gets lost in his gaze.

His brows go up as he tells her, "It's not. This was just one of those things."

Sure.

"I hope we can put this behind us."

Liar.

They hear Bobby and Dan arrive back in the studio. Jaime looks up, a little caught off-guard. Their conversation would have to end.

He says quickly, "Thanks for giving me back the shirt."

She replies. "Well, it does fit you better than me."

For a moment, he looks down at her.

In a cool tone, she adds in, "I do know the difference between casual sex and love."

Jaime watches her walk out. He turns around with his head bowed down. He says, "I know too." Just outside the door, Evelyn has a creeping smile. She walks away gleeful. As the producer hears the chattering and laughter of the rest of the crew with Evelyn, he makes one more remark aloud to himself. "Evy, I do have feelings for you. That's how I know the difference." He smiles slightly while removing the sunglasses on his shirt. He then walks out of the office to join the rest.

Attempts at extracting information on Evelyn remained futile. Ed picks up the book and phone once again.

He grouses. "Someone has to know."

He dials as his fingers press down on the name, *Bellamy.*

A woman picks up the phone. "Ello?"

"Hello, is this Gisele or Dominique?"

"Gisele."

"I'm wondering if you've seen Evelyn lately? She went to..."

"Oh, Eveleen!"

He hears her call out, "Dominique! Eez Eveleen!"

Quickly he responds to her outburst. "No! No! I'm looking *for* Evelyn."

The other Bellamy sister lets out a squeal of joy.

"Eveleen?" Dominique asks over the phone.

Ed lets out a deep groan. "Aaaaaaaaah!" He slams down the phone. "Stupid French!"

He dials again. The ring tone gives way to a beep.

The voice at the other end speaks. "Hello, you have reached the office of Ben Voorhaun at Gizblüke Management. I'm not here right now but please leave a message and I will get back to you as soon as possible."

Another beep. Ed hangs up the phone. Pulling up his sleeve, he checks the time. 9:48 PM.

"One more call. The Green Light, sounds like something she would visit. Not far from here."

He dials one final time for the night.

"Hello? Green Light. Kelly speaking."

Ed hears her Scottish accent. Right away, he rolls his eyes. "Ah, just who I wanted to talk to. I don't know if you know me, as we haven't met. My girlfriend apparently knows you."

"Ooh? What's her name? Maybe I might know."

"Evelyn. She's a sing..."

"Ed? Is this Ed Brockton?" Kelly's tone changes to more serious.

Ed responds eagerly. "Yeah. So you do know her."

"Yes. I know of you too and so do me little sister, Sheila. What do you want?" She asks in a miffed tone.

"I'm wondering if you know anything about this trip Evelyn took to New York."

"It's for recording her album."

"That's all?"

"Are you accusing me of withholding information? Look, that's all I know. Why should I tell you any more? You treat her like trash. Any man who truly loves a woman wouldn't treat her so poorly as you do. Furthermore, you're pond scum by me book. You think you're Mr. High and Mighty. If I were to ever lay eyes on you, I'd spit in your face! You made me baby sister cry! Or do you remember? Arrogant sod. You made some rude remarks about her hair."

"Oh, was it the green haired gal?"

"Ah! So you do remember!"

Ed snickers. "She had it comin'."

"You're a lousy rat-bastard! It amazes me that a woman with such high class as Evelyn could wind up with raw sewage such as yourself. Your think tank is a toilet! You know if..."

Ed pulls away the phone while Kelly spews more derogatory comments his way. He mocks the angry bartender by putting one hand to his hip as though he were a pissed off woman, and also mouths the words, "Blah, blah, blah." He puts the phone back up to his ear to hear.

She yells. "Arsehole!"

Kelly hangs up. The phone goes dead.

He snorts back in anger. "Bitch!"

***

With his hand in back of his neck, Jaime walks downstairs. Bobby who is about to go in the room next to the control room looks up.

Jaime says to him, "Did someone turn up the thermostat? It's *hot*. I mean *really hot* in here!"

The producer lifts his blue buttoned up shirt, waving it in some effort to feel cooler. Already with the first two buttons undone, he undoes a third.

Bobby replies. "The air conditioning is busted."

Jaime says deeply, "That figures."

He sees Bobby dressed in a red and blue Hawaiian shirt, similarly attired with the first three buttons undone too.

They step inside the control room and immediately the humidity seems worse to both producers. As soon as Jaime pushes back his hair, he feels his shirt tighten up from sticking to his flesh underneath.

Bobby places a couple of Evelyn's demo tapes on the control room desk.

"Here's a couple more. What I hear on the first one is a great melody. Only, I don't know how we can use her voice."

Jaime says, "Let's listen to it." He rolls up his sleeves more and quickly undoes the fourth button. "Where is Evelyn?"

Bobby places a tape in the cassette deck. "She took off just as I was coming in." Jaime nods his head in an understanding fashion then airs his shirt again.

Evelyn sits at the kitchen table of Henry and Karen Winslow.

Karen offers. "Evelyn, would you like some ice tea? I just made a fresh pitcher."

"Sure."

As the willowy brunette pours the liquid into a glass, she says, "So, what about this guy you met?"

"Well, he's very different than the others. He's intensely shy. I met him at the studio."

"Maintenance guy?"

"No. His name is Jaime."

Karen raises her brows. "Weston?"

Evelyn takes a gulp of the refreshing cold liquid. She looks across the table with a growing smile.

Karen giggles back. "You're blushing. Oh my God. Are you serious? Jaime?"

"Mm hmm."

"Does this mean Ed's out of the picture?" Karen asks with excitement.

Evelyn hesitates with apprehension. "Um. No."

The brunette stiffens. "And *why* not? I say you should just let him off hard. That *bum*! He's given you a lot of pain and don't you deny that! There's no reason for him to treat you that way. You deserve better."

Evelyn sighs. "I know he can be cruel sometimes but I've been with him for seven years. It's not like he's ever been abusive to me. I've thought of leaving him, but... What if I don't find anyone later on, or if I do it won't last as long? I'm forty, infertile, and lonely."

Karen takes Evelyn's hand in a consoling manner. "Don't say that. Take a chance on Jaime. I've seen him enough times and we've talked some. He's really sweet but misunderstood because he is quiet."

Karen gets up and walks to the back door that's open to the screen. She looks out at the two boys playing in the backyard. Evelyn thinks while her friend attends to watching her son and his friend.

Karen calls out as she opens the door. "Evan! Honey, would you like some ice tea? Ask Kevin if he wants any!"

The two boys converse on the swing set. They nod to each other.

Inside the house, Evelyn questions Karen. "What if he doesn't feel the same way?"

Karen turns to her. "Well then, at least you took a chance. I wish you would move here. We would get to talk more often. I'm looking to possibly open a boutique shop. Thought you might be interested. You know, in case you wanted to do something different. I don't think anybody would find you out here and if they did, who cares!"

The two boys rush in. Evan lights up with a big smile. "Evelyn!" He says in his little voice.

Evelyn smiles back widely. She holds out her arms. "Evan!"

The seven year old rushes to her for a big hug. He looks up as she tenderly wipes away the hair that falls over his brows.

Evan asks, "Are you staying here?"

Karen quietly answers her son. "No, honey. She came here to visit though."

Evelyn says to Evan, "Since I'm here, why don't we go outside?"

Evan takes her hand quickly. "We're playing planes! Come on!"

"Are you the pilot?"

"Yep! Come on!"

Karen says, "Wait! Don't you want your tea?"

He says back, "Yeah!"

She fills a glass, then another. Both boys gulp down the liquid, smacking their lips. They take off for the back door. Evan grabs onto

Evelyn's hand and whisks her away, with Kevin who shouts out, "Thank you, Mrs. Winslow!"

Evan makes the sound of an airplane as they run off to the backyard. "Nyyyyyyyyrrrrrrrroooooooooooooom."

Karen nods with a smile. Henry walks in the kitchen. He smiles at his wife, giving her a kiss to the lips. She asks, "Did you rest well?"

Henry puts a hand through his graying hair. "Yeah, but it's quite hot today."

"What do you expect when it's in the upper nineties?"

Henry takes a look out the back door.

"Who's out there with Evan?"

"Oh, his little friend, Kevin. You know, Evelyn stopped by. She's out there with them. I'm telling you Henry, she's great with him. I wish she were around more often. It's just such a shame that she can't be a mother. You should have heard her, how she's so down on herself. Evelyn's great around kids."

Henry gathers a folder he's placed on the table.

Karen tells her husband, "I made some ice tea. Want any?"

"Yeah."

He flips through some papers.

She pours the tea in a glass while telling him, "Evelyn has discovered someone new in her life. And do you know who? Our dear friend, Jaime Weston."

"Ah yes."

Karen looks at Henry as she's rather surprised by his casual response. She takes a gulp of tea herself. "You know?"

"Yeah. They spent the night together already."

Karen's jaw drops. "You mean they already *slept together*? What? How do you know this?"

He says back in a confident manner. "They told me. Really, he told me then the next day, she told me."

"So, is it serious?"

"What I gathered from him is that he's pretty serious about her. She on the other hand, was smitten by him from the very start. She told me that she's not sure about staying with Ed." Henry checks the time on his watch. "I have to go run some errands, pick up something at the office supply store, and possibly drop by the studio."

Karen sits at the table muttering in disbelief. "Wow! Jaime and Evelyn, huh?"

Henry finishes his ice tea. He gives Karen another kiss as he gets up to leave. Turning to his wife, he reminds her with his index finger to his lips. "Shhhh. Remember honey, not a word."

Karen nods back. "I know."

At the studio, Jaime begins to pull out a pack of Marlboros. He feels for them but instead drops the pack on the table with anguish. It's too hot for him to even support his regular cigarette habit. Again, he airs out his shirt, undoing now the sixth button.

Bobby explains about the second track to Jaime. "This one has a harder edge."

"Mm hmm."

They listen to the instrumental. Jaime releases the seventh and final button of his shirt. He says while wiping back his damp hair, "You know how her voice sounds?"

"It's low."

"Right. Lift the bass, then it will match her vocal range easier."

Bobby changes the tuning. "Ah! Okay. That sounds much better."

Dan arrives in the studio. He heads inside the control room. Bobby and Jaime look at him.

Bobby says with a grin, "Tennis, Danny?"

Dan grimaces slightly while looking over the short-sleeved polo shirt with khaki shorts he wears. "What's wrong with what I'm wearing?"

Bobby answers. "Nothing. Just that you forgot the racket."

Jaime chuckles back.

Dan looks in his direction then realizes the dressed state the main producer is in. "What's goin' on with you? You're *way* more casual than us two. Usually, you're overly dressed. Instead, I find you with your shirt undone...like this."

Bobby gives an all-knowing glance.

Jaime turns his eyes to Dan. "Yeah, well it's not usually over seventy degrees in here. Weren't you supposed to call Jim when things like this happened?"

Defensively, Dan admits, "I didn't *know* because I wasn't the last to leave. When did it happen?"

Jaime answers back. "Last night or early this morning."

"You usually leave after me and if I'm not mistaken, you're staying upstairs."

Bobby interjects with, "Guys, lets just get this done. The quicker the better." He takes a piece of paper, folds it, and fans himself with the item.

On the other side of him, Jaime releases an unsteady sigh as he runs his hand down his wet chest. Taking one hand to the back of his neck, he feels his soaked hair underneath. His collar is now wet. He wipes the perspiration from above his upper lip. In front, he feels the sides of the blue material sticking worse. Nobody wanted to work on any tracks. Dan sits leaning his head against the back of the chair. Bobby continues to wave the paper while unbuttoning the fourth button, revealing some brown hair underneath. With an almost thoroughly soaked garment on, and the perspiration running quickly, Jaime opens his shirt to the widest amount, fully baring his chest. He stands up, looking down with hands on hips.

The producer shakes his head and says, "Well fellas, this is *not* going to work in our favor today."

Jaime picks up the pack of Marlboros along with his sunglasses and heads out of the control room.

Dan turns to Bobby. "What's he gonna do?"

Bobby gets up and stretches, then takes a peek outside the door. He senses something quickly. "I'll take a guess by saying something *drastic* in his case." Waiting a moment, Bobby says, "Yep." He retracts his head back into the control room." "It's something I almost feel like doing myself."

Outside in the driveway, Henry's dark green Mazda crawls to the side of Dan's station wagon. He gets out of the vehicle, sucking on a cigar.

Throwing his hands up in confusion he asks, "What happened to you?"

He looks at the now half undressed producer wearing light blue jeans and his trademark sunglasses. With his blue shirt close to his side, Jaime takes a cigarette and lights it with a match. When he's content, he relaxes his slender body. He lets the smoke from his Marlboro seep out of his mouth. His sunglasses show a hazy fog drift in an upward stream.

Jaime then replies to Henry. "The air conditioning went out."

Henry goes to sit next to his friend on the top step of the studio. "I'm just surprised to see you so...casual."

Jaime slowly turns to Henry. "I do have my limitations."

"So, how do you feel?"

Jaime takes a drag on the cigarette before answering. "Strangely comfortable." He chuckles at the thought. With a growing smile, the producer utters, "Yeah."

Henry asks, "Is Evelyn around?"

"No. She went out early this morning."

"Did you tell her anything we talked about?"

"No. As it is, I've tried to tell her it was a mistake, but she doesn't want to believe that."

"You're not convinced of that yourself."

"No."

Jaime pulls off his sunglasses, massaging the narrow bridge of his nose. He states flatly, "I don't think of it as a mistake. If it *was*, it sure didn't *feel* like one." He laughs for a moment. Jaime looks down at the shirt. Picking it up he says, "Here, feel this."

Henry lightly touches the curled up garment. "It's wet."

"That's from a half an hour only." The producer puts his sunglasses back on. "Christ. It's an oven in there." He places the garment a little further away from him. "It'll probably take the same amount to dry."

While sitting on the steps, Jaime begins to feel the effects of a stiffening back. He arches forward slightly, placing one hand behind his back. Finally, he decides to sit up a little more instead of being hunched over.

A candy apple red Chevy Camaro trudges through the unpaved driveway. Jaime glances up. Positioning his sunglasses down to peek above the rims, he sees the car coming.

"Oh no." He deeply groans.

Henry squints. "Say, isn't that..."

"God, not them. Not now." Jaime says back in an anguished tone.

The producer leans his head against his left hand, preparing himself for what they're going to say. He shakes his head.

Henry tells him, "Well, I'll go inside now and see how Bobby and Danny are doing."

Jaime utters, "Okay," as the smoke seeps out of his mouth. For a moment, he looks down at the small cement steps under his feet.

Two women, one red haired the other, blonde, look ahead in the windshield. Robert Palmer's, "I Didn't Mean To Turn You On" is blasting on the car stereo. The strawberry air freshener jangles under rough terrain.

The redhead tells her blonde passenger, "Do you see what I see?"

The blonde replies. "Is that him?"

"Oh my God." The redhead giggles back.

She stops the car further back from the other four. Both women step out of the Camaro.

Andrea Whitfield, attired in a tight blue shoulderless top appears with her frizzy, shoulder-length fiery red hair. Her slender hips are jammed into tight black Jordache jeans and little black sandals. She flips down her Ray Ban sunglasses.

Her partner in crime is none other than Vicki Soren, who dresses in a sleeveless pink blouse with denim cut-off shorts and white Nike sneakers. Vicki is more of a girl-next-door type. She's more subtle in her actions than Andrea and younger. She too wears sunglasses, dark to light in tint. Flat blonde strips of hair drape over her shoulders.

Andrea and Vicki walk up the pebble-encrusted driveway. Jaime steadies a glance at them through his dark tinted sunglasses. Andrea covers her mouth for a second before letting out a huge smile of shock. Vicki looks ahead stunned.

Andrea shouts from a few feet away. "I thought that was you! Only, something's missing."

Vicki calmly says in her Midwestern drawl, "Yeah. Like a shirt."

As Andrea nears Jaime, her jaw remains unhinged.

"Oh my God! Look at you!" She laughs again.

Vicki joins her for a laugh too.

Still holding the cigarette with two fingers and the thumb in his right hand, Jaime puts out his left hand with the mannerism to stop.

Deeply he tells them, "Ladies, be gentle."

Andrea pulls off her sunglasses, revealing dazzling green eyes while looking him over.

"My! My! My!"

She's quite taken by the sight of the half undressed record producer. Andrea nods in disbelief.

"In all of my fourteen years of knowing you, I had no *idea* you were so..." She almost feels a loss for words, "*So* attractive! I should have known better, what with your wardrobe of the past. "

Vicki says dryly, "More like hairy."

Andrea corrects Vicki quickly. "No. No. *That* is perfection. He *is*. Just unbelievable!"

Andrea addresses Jaime. "How do you stay in such great shape? Do you exercise?"

"No. Unless you consider racing from one room to another. Plus two flights of stairs in the studio."

The redhead smiles back in awe. "Stand up so I can see you better. This is a *very* rare moment."

He obligingly gets up from the steps. The smaller Andrea looks him over, nodding yet again. "You're two years younger than Bobby. So you're forty-three?"

"Really, I just turned forty-four about three weeks ago."

He smiles down at her. Andrea turns to Vicki then back to Jaime.

She then tells him, "Well, whatever! You look...totally awesome! Don't change a thing." Andrea nudges him slightly, grinning. Quietly she says in a suggestive tone, "So, is this what I missed nine years ago?"

Jaime goes back to sitting on the steps while chuckling. He couldn't be sure if he should be flattered or embarrassed by the lovely Andrea fawning over him. "Andi, " he answers in a deep voice.

Andrea asks, "So, why are you so casual today? Did you have a bet with my husband and lose?"

Vicki adds in, "The shirt on your back?"

Both women crack up laughing.

He says back with a hint of a smile, "No. It's just rather hot. Uncomfortably hot. The air conditioner went out this morning or late last night. Andi, you should check on Bobby. He forgot his hula skirt." He grins.

She immediately says back, "Oh, that Hawaiian shirt?"

"That's the one." Jaime takes a drag on the smaller cigarette.

Andrea holds up her index finger. "I have to tell you something."

She leans with her hand on his right shoulder. He leans to the right slightly. Andrea whispers into his ear something out of earshot that Vicki can't hear. Andrea then giggles and Jaime laughs back.

He says, "Whatever works for the two of you."

Vicki nods. "Kinky stuff."

Jaime turns to Vicki seeing that she doesn't say much, only makes brief comments.

He asks her, "So, what's the reason you two stopped by here besides merciless teasing?" He leans over tapping out some ashes from his cigarette.

Vicki answers. "Two reasons. One is that we came by to visit our long suffering husbands."

Jaime reacts instantly by stiffening.

Taken aback, he says incredulously, "*Suffering*? Bobby and Dan do not *suffer*. I know because that's *my* job. When your husbands go home each night, I'm the one who's still at the studio."

Andrea says, "We feel for you."

Vicki lets out a laugh.

Jaime says deeply, "Yeah. Sure you do." His tone changes an octave higher. "Now, what is the second reason you came by?"

Vicki replies. "We wanted to take out the new gal and show her around town. You know, the British gal."

Vicki removes her sunglasses, watching for a reaction by the producer.

He says back quickly, "She's not here. Evelyn is who you're talking about."

"Aw, too bad."

"I'll let her know that you stopped by though."

Jaime smiles at Andrea. He was always more comfortable with her than Vicki. He knew her a lot longer too. She smiles back. She knew his smile well. It was that boyish, mischievous grin that was self-assured and couldn't be broken over a flirting match, time and time again. She stands in front of him. He reaches to pull her hand with his. Vicki just shakes her head and folds her arms.

Jaime says to Andrea, "Andi, a little more off the top."

He was referring to her shoulder-baring top.

She eyes him deviously. "I'm a married woman."

The producer looks her over with a grin. Letting her hand go, she steps around him. In back, she wraps her arms around his shoulders and gives him a little squeeze of a hug. His hand holds her wrist.

She then concludes sweetly, "Jaime, you're a good sport."

She releases him.

Just before she walks inside, he calls out to her. "Go to your *suffering* husband. Flirt."

"Hey, I heard that! It takes one to know one!"

Both laugh. Andrea disappears into the studio.

Now, it's Vicki's turn.

She was the more serious and distant one who never wanted to flirt with anybody, even when Dan wasn't around. Jaime Weston on the other hand never overly impressed her. He did look good to her, but his personality was a major setback. Angling to her as they are left alone he says, "So, what's goin' on with you?" He gives a slow creeping smile. Vicki gives a crooked smile.

Boldly she says, "Danny told me there might be somebody new in your life."

His smile cancels as he becomes more serious. She puts her foot against the bottom step, very close to his shoe. He looks down for a minute. Jaime almost wants to peek over the rims of his only camouflage but decides not to.

Vicki remarks. "He thinks it's your new guest, Evelyn."

"You know Vicki, Danny's suspicious about everybody." Jaime eyes her. "Apparently, you are too."

"We just want to look out for your happiness. Me and Andi wouldn't mind a third party on our shopping excursions."

With a slight smile, he tells her, "There is *nobody*."

Vicki leans in closer to him. She folds her arms. "You're hidin'."

The producer looks at her in a surprised fashion.

The blonde continues. "I know your type. I know why you hide behind those sunglasses. You don't wear your feelings on the outside but inside you're vulnerable. The only way of telling what you're feelin' is through your eyes. Keepin' those dark sunglasses on is a way for you not to expose yourself. And I do mean figuratively."

Jaime knows full well she's right but he's not about to let her know that. He wore his privacy like a badge of honor. How dare she interrogate him and his sacred feelings? With possibly one or two more drags on the Marlboro, he sucks in. Releasing a breath of smoke he admits, "There is nobody new in my life at this time."

Vicki leans a little more toward him. "Take off those sunglasses and tell me that."

He inhales deeply. Alternating the cigarette from his right hand to his left, he pulls off the round shades placing them on the lap of his blue jeans. With the right hand completely free, he places it on the left side of his chest over his heart. He looks directly ahead.

The producer repeats his words to her. He says in a deeper than normal tone, "There is nobody new in my life at this time."

Vicki studies his dark eyes. Was it the whole truth he was telling? She gives a crooked smile again.

Jaime places his sunglasses back on and holds the cigarette with the right hand once again, freeing the left. Vicki snorts out a stream of air from her nostrils then shakes her head in disbelief. She walks up the stairs past him with nothing more to say. His eyes observe her as he turns his head to the right. The stub-sized cigarette gets one more drag from it. Jaime looks ahead. He snuffs out the remains from the Marlboro against the cement step. The producer couldn't be sure if the nervy Mrs. Soren was satisfied by his answer. Biting his bottom lip gently, Jaime removes his sunglasses once again. He strikes a finger across his chest and folds the arms of the sunglasses closed. He has to seriously wonder if his feelings for Evelyn are beginning to show. His gaze falls down upon the cement of the walkway.

Across the ocean, Ed sits at the kitchen table with a box of photos. He picks one up. The image is when he and Evelyn went to Cape Cod three summers ago. She was in a summer hat holding up a trout proudly. Picking up another, he smiles at the memory. This one showed Evelyn in a nightgown with slippers on. Her expression was of surprise since she didn't expect her picture to be taken so early in the morning. There were many photos of Evelyn. Ed begins placing the pictures on the table in columns of seven. He thinks of the sweet memories when he and Evelyn would watch the sun set on the beach. She always loved the reddening sun. It provided a magical time and feeling for her. The way the waves would lap up on the shore. He would chase her along the shoreline and draw her into his arms for a kiss.

His eyes look at the large cupboard near the basement steps. Ed walks over to it and opens the door. It creeks open, revealing all sorts of canned foods, tea bags, jars, containers, and boxes. He looks at the opposite side of the large oak door. A calendar turned to the page of July is shown. The image accompanying is of a quaint farmhouse among the sweeping ferns and tall grass. Ed's finger grazes the glossy page as he scans down, then across to July 21st. The date of the 16th has a star scrawled in the block. It had been five days since he and Evelyn were supposed to arrive in Boston on their summer getaway, just like they had the previous year, the year before that, and the years since 1980. There would be no photographs or memories from '87.

Ed closes the door and looks at the kitchen table plastered with images of his one true love...Evelyn Marie Winthrop. He walks up to the table, leaning his hands against the surface. Growing angrier by the minute at the past and what is now the present, he swipes his hand across the table. Most of the photos are moved from their spot. Some flitter to the floor like confetti. Others get grouped haphazardly on the table. Ed breathes uneasily of frustration. His hands grip the table. He bows his head and the blond bangs pull forward under the weight. The only sound accompanying Ed's tumultuous flustered breath is the low hum of the refrigerator motor.

Returning inside the studio, Jaime closes the door behind him. With his shirt tossed over his shoulder, he pulls off his sunglasses. He looks up to hear Vicki and Dan laugh.

Bobby is busy entertaining the ladies, doing a hula dance.

Andrea shouts out. "See! See! He does stuff like that when he wears that shirt!"

Vicki laughs loudly.

Jaime smiles to himself, and then steps in the control room to join the three. He leans against the doorframe. Realizing he has nothing to hang his sunglasses on, he simply holds them. The three look at him.

"Ah! Did you have a fun time sunbathing?" Bobby asks mischievously.

"Very cute." His friend replies rather dryly.

Andrea pipes up. "Indeed!"

This gives Vicki a good laugh. Jaime looks down at Andrea, knowing she's going to stick it to him as much as she can. She pivots on her toes, grinning like a schoolgirl. He starts to make an announcement with Andrea looking up at him.

"I really have to get something off my chest."

Andrea quickly retorts. "Oh no you don't!"

Vicki snorts back with laughter.

Jaime closes his eyes and breathes deep. Looking down at himself, he knows his appearance is creating great humor, although he makes no motion to cover up. He pushes back his hair. With the air of defeat, he nods. "Gee Andi, you sure know how to make a guy feel good."

Prompted to glance at the producer's hirsute chest, Andrea responds. "I certainly try."

Jaime pulls her against himself, laughing. "What are we going to do with you? Bobby?"

"Yeah, buddy?"

"How do you handle her?" Jaime asks with extreme curiosity.

Bobby looks at him. "You're doin' it."

Dan and Vicki laugh. Andrea holds onto her husband's best friend around his slender waist. Her fingers press against his belt.

"A real fire engine." Jaime grins down at Andrea's head.

Bobby answers back. "Where there's smoke, there's fire."

Andrea replies to the tight clinch Jaime has on her. "Oh, and you are definitely smokin'!" She laughs wholeheartedly. Jaime pulls her a little closer, enough so he can reach the top of her head easily. He gives her a quick kiss among her red haired scalp. Then he lets her go, while still chuckling. Vicki leaves the room, which nobody but Dan seems to notice.

Jaime asks Bobby, "Were you able to figure any of that stuff out we were talking about before?"

"No. I didn't want to ruin the equipment if it's that hot."

"There's a fan downstairs in the utility room."

"Okay. Then you go get it and we'll get some more of this mixed." Bobby thinks for a minute. "Wait. Did you get to that track I told you about? The one that needs keyboards?"

"No."

The two producers step outside of the control room, where they can talk privately.

Bobby's taken aback. "No? What are you waiting for? That's a really good song. You know what Andi went through."

"I know which track you're talking about. We all went through it."

"So, what's the hold-up? We've got Evelyn's vocals the way she wanted it. We got the drum and bass to correspond. I did the guitar part."

Jaime puts an assuring hand on his buddy's shoulder "Bobby, you worry too much. I'll get it done. Just give me some time with it. After all, you're the one who doesn't like to rush things." He gives a big smile and puts his sunglasses back on, before walking down the stairs.

Upstairs, Andrea asks, "Where's Vicki? She was here a minute ago."

The producer wanders into the kitchen where he finds Vicki. Once again, he folds the sunglasses. Without saying a word, he passes her by, opting to fetch a cold beer out of the refrigerator. She hears the pop and the spritz of the tab. His eyes swerve over to her. He meets her steady glance and angles down toward her. Vicki stares up at him. Jaime finds her gaze at him is more prying than friendly. He knows what she's thinking and she knows what he's thinking. Their conversation before was not the best subject to talk about. She started it. He ended it. Vicki had no business wondering about his life outside of the studio. Neither say anything. Jaime walks away. Vicki looks back down at the table.

Eventually, Andrea and Vicki leave. Neither Bobby nor Dan notices anything different between Jaime and Vicki. They were always quiet towards one another. Dan knew his wife wasn't the flirty type. Not at all like Andrea.

Jaime looks out the front door window on the side panel to see the Camaro disappear. Then another car appears.

He calls out to the other two. "Do you know anyone who owns a blue car?"

Bobby answers from within the control room. "No." Moments later he blurts out, "Uh-oh."

Jaime catches Bobby's worried tone. "Uh-oh, what?"

"What's the date?"

Dan answers him. "The twenty-first."

Sheepishly, Bobby tells them, "I think it might be someone to see us from a sound equipment magazine."

Jaime mumbles. "Great."

He puts on his sunglasses as he sees a woman approach the door. The doorbell rings and the producer answers it quickly. The small dark haired woman smiles wryly at the sight of the half undressed Weston. He smiles back at her.

At a café, two miles away, Evelyn munches on lunch and coffee. She pulls out her trusty spiral notebook. Examining the pages before it, she writes. She writes more than what she had before. Glancing out of the window, she smiles.

So much inspiration. It would seem her trip to New York and all the experiences she had in such a short time, were giving her the ability to think of new songs.

***

A light fog drifts along the small parking lot of Millie's Antiques in Kennington. A bell above the door rings. Mildred Grumbach is forty-four with shoulder length blonde hair. She's sensibly dressed. Her pensive blue-gray eyes are outlined in very thin strokes of black as she turns toward the door. She explains about a wooden chair to a couple and their young daughter. As she talks in a Lancashire tinged voice, her sight turns to Ed Brockton casually glancing at items. He flips over a tag that reads 18£ attached to a navy blue flowered vase. Mildred cautiously looks at him as she further explains about the item.

"It sounds like you have a beautiful rustic room this would fit in. I have a lamp that would match perfectly." Handling a lamp with a wooden base, the shop owner holds it up.

The female customer exclaims. "Oh, I love it! How much?"

"This is normally £20 but I'll give it to you for £15 with the chair."

The woman pulls out her pocketbook. "Great! I'll take them both! Can I make out a check?"

"Sure you can!"

The two women laugh.

The customer's husband looks at a desk. "I like this. It would look grand in the library." He looks at the tag. "£250"

"Oh, that's actually half off." Mildred tells the man.

In back, Ed snickers.

The little girl swings her legs while she sits on a chair. Mildred walks over to her. Clasping her hands on her legs, the owner smiles and leans over.

"You sweetie, have been very well behaved. Do you know what that deserves?"

The little girl asks. "What?"

"As soon as I get done with your Mummy and Daddy, I'll give you a little treat."

The girl gasps back. "Really?"

"Yes."

Mildred goes back to the couple. Before she says anything, she clasps her hands together.

The husband tells her, "We'll add the desk."

"Okay. *Great*! I'll just get you some help lifting that in your vehicle."

Mildred's eyes meet Ed's steady glance as she walks by. She goes into a back room.

In there, she finds her nineteen year-old son, Harris, who is visiting home during the summer from attending Columbia University in New York City. The tall, attractive, dark haired lad that he is, smiles at his mother. He has his feet up on a folding chair and watches the small TV set in front of him.

She says, "Honey, I need you to help out a customer move an item to his vehicle."

The light from the set flashes onto him as his brown eyes look up. "Sure thing, Mum."

"Oh, Harris before I forget, Ed is here."

He winces.

His mother advises him. "Don't say anything I wouldn't."

Harris gets up to stretch and yawn. "Don't worry Mum. I'll just ignore him." Harris smiles then walks into the showroom. He asks the husband, "Which one will it be? The desk?"

"Yes."

Harris says, "I'll take one side and you can take the other."

"Okay."

"Just tell me which car is yours."

The two pick up the desk slowly walking to the door. Mildred opens it for them. The wife finishes writing out her check.

After, she tells her daughter, "Almost done."

Ed looks at a chair near the little girl. His eyes swing over to Mildred.

The little girl makes the sound of a cat in her small voice. "Meeeow."

He gets closer to her. "Cute little kitty." Ed grins.

She stares at him. Her legs stop swinging. The man and Harris walk back in the store. The little girl lets out a nasty hiss. Her face scrunches. Again she hisses. Startled, Ed steps away. The woman turns quickly.

"Hannah! *Stop that*! You know better!"

Harris turns his head as he stifles a giggle. Mildred gives him a slight smile.

The woman's husband asks, "What did she do?"

"She hissed at that man."

"Hannah! All right young lady, no cartoons for you for *three* days!"

Hannah stiffens her body at Ed, all but ignoring her parents. The husband shakes his head while he picks up the chair his wife has just purchased. He brings it out to his car.

Mildred gives the woman her receipt. She begins to walk away. The woman apologizes to Ed quietly. Hannah hops off the chair, trailing behind her mother. Mildred opens up a glass jar containing a variety of candy sticks. She pulls out a cherry one and quietly hands it over to the little girl.

"Shhhh."

Mildred puts a hand on Hannah's shoulder.

The family walks out. Hannah turns around and waves to Mildred. Mildred smiles and waves back. Ed helps himself to a candy stick, sucking on it the same way he would a cigarette.

The storekeeper's brows furrow at the offensive man. "Those are for the children."

Harris watches his mother. Cautiously he walks around Ed and his mother to the back room again.

The younger Grumbach knew all too well the distaste both his mother and father had for their good friend's boyfriend. He took pride in watching the little girl hiss at Ed, and then get treated with candy for it. Had it been anyone else, his mother would have deemed them rude and undeserving but that wasn't the case. Not with Ed.

Ed takes out the stick. "Aw, Millie you can't tell me you don't like me that much that you spoil children with candy when they get rude with me?"

"No, Ed. I don't control others children."

"What will they learn by your example?" He asks in a perplexed tone.

"Perhaps not to trust people who act like Jekyll and Hyde in front of others."

"What a ya so sore about?"

"The way you treat others behind my friend's back."

"Come on Millie. You've always held a high opinion of me." He says with much sarcasm.

She turns quickly to him. "You're here for a reason. You're not here to shop. Make that...you're here to shop for *something* else." She squints with suspicion.

He comes out and tells her, "I wanna know what's goin' on with Evelyn."

"What is that supposed to mean?"

Ed leers at her from across the register counter top. "It means I want *answers*, damn it." He growls. Her eyes widen. "It means I want to *know* what the *real* story is in regards to her. She went to New York."

"Yes."

"She said it was for sessions."

"Yes."

"She's visiting some drug friends and wants to relive her glory gutter days with this album?"

"No."

"No? Then what's so important for her that she had to cancel our yearly trip to Boston?"

"Maybe she grew tired of your lovely little state of Massachusetts." Mildred smiles reassuringly. Ed's blue eyes slowly look at Mildred with the sense he's being mocked. "All she told me was that these sessions were important to her. I don't know if you know this but she's been trying to get this done for over a year, about two now. She said if it didn't work, she would throw away the project and start anew."

"That's all?"

"That is all." She repeats back.

Ed lurches away. As he walks, he holds out the candy stick while turning back to her. "Thanks for the candy." He says in a gruff tone full of taunting sarcasm. Sticking the candy stick between his teeth, he gives her a big smile. The door closes, triggering the bell above to chime.

Harris walks out from the back room. "I heard, Mum. He doesn't know she's in New Paltz?"

"No. We're going to leave it that way. Let him think whatever he wants. He comes to his own conclusions anyhow." Mildred watches Ed pull out of the parking lot. "I would have hissed at him myself."

***

A week later, Andrea and Vicki return to the studio. Andrea looks over a fully dressed Jaime. "What happened? It's not so hot anymore."

Vicki giggles. She says to Andrea, "You would just like to see him dressed that way again or more often."

"But of course! Encore! Encore! Woo hoo!"

With the slightest chuckle, Jaime puts a hand to his forehead rather embarrassed by the whole situation. "Oh God. You're not going to let me forget that." He closes his eyes and shakes his head. "It was just a matter of being too hot out."

Vicki says teasingly, "Now, he's going to be shy about it."

Andrea says to Jaime, You know you've got it goin' on. You *are* hot."

The producer bows his head down with a growing grin.

Vicki remarks. "And that shade of pink you're turning is lovely I might add."

Evelyn walks down the stairs.

Jaime turns to her. He says back with a smile to the two women, "Ladies, this is Evelyn Winthrop."

Andrea brightens up immediately at the sight of the British singer. "Hi, Evelyn! I'm Andrea, but everyone calls me Andi. Bobby's my husband."

She shakes her hand. Pointing to Vicki, she lets her introduce herself.

Vicki steps up as her soft oval face gives in to a big smile under dark mascara made eyes. She says, "Hi there, Evelyn. I'm Danny's wife, Vicki."

Evelyn shakes hands with her.

Andrea asks, "Are we ready to roll?"

Vicki replies as she looks at Jaime. "Yes."

Jaime turns to look at all three with a slight smile, then turns his attention to the singer. "Please go. Take those two with you." He eyes Andrea and Vicki.

Vicki announces, "That's our cue to leave."

Vicki and Evelyn step out. Andrea begins to leave when she feels a large hand on her shoulder.

Jaime leans toward her right ear. He quietly tells her, "Don't corrupt her too much."

Andrea breaks into a large smile then laughs. She goes to join the other two women.

The ladies take off in the Camaro, driving down the New York State Thruway. They stop off at various shops along the way and collect toll passes. Andrea and Vicki show Evelyn their favorite shopping place, the Outlets in Newburgh. There they buy kitchen utensils and L'eggs pantyhose packed in tan plastic eggs. Andrea checks out a clothing apparel store, going through racks of fanciful and glittery garments for possible evening attire. Vicki goes to a party shop to see what she can find for the twins birthday.

While Evelyn looks in an accessory store, she sees some long scarves. Something triggers her to look at them. She can't fully pinpoint her fascination with them. It wasn't as if she wore them herself.

Andrea steps up from behind. "Boy, does that take me back?"

Slightly startled, Evelyn turns her head. "Yes. It does."

Taking a break from shopping, the women stop off at a McDonalds where they feast on French fries and milkshakes.

As Andrea picks out a carton of fries, she says to Evelyn, "Like I told you this morning when I called, we were looking for you about a week ago." She sucks on the thick straw while examining down. Vicki munches on a fry held with the tips of her fingers. Andrea continues. "Well, what I didn't tell you was that it was so hot out that..."

Vicki interrupts, bemused. "Oh boy. Here we go again."

The redhead turns to look at her friend.

She says to Evelyn, "We got to see Jaime in a different way. I've known him for a while and he looked sensational that particular day."

Vicki adds in, "He didn't have a shirt on. Andi was practically salivating." She turns to Andrea. "What is with him never wearing jewelry? You would think with a chest like that, he would at least have some type of chain."

"Vic, he's not John Travolta. Ease off the *Saturday Night Fever* look. Jaime has always been the way he is. He has his own sense of style. Ooh, he had that Keith Richards thing goin' on about ten years ago. He's still hot. Besides that, I got him a watch three years ago for Christmas. Never wore it yet."

Vicki darts her eyes at Andrea. "Well, you were panting over him worse than Joey at dinner time." She says to Evelyn, "Joey is Bobby and Andrea's beagle."

Evelyn smiles. "Ah. I see."

Andrea laughs at something preoccupying her mind. She picks out a fry, thoroughly jamming it in her mouth. "I thought of something Bobby once asked me. He said, 'If I never existed or we never met, who would you want to be with? You can choose any guy.' So now I'm going to ask you two the same question."

Vicki says ever so nonchalantly, "I *know* who you would pick."

"And I know *your* answer. 'Nobody's better than Danny.'"

Vicki finishes taking a sip of her milkshake.

She laughs dryly, "Ha ha. Very funny. No."

Andrea takes a sip of milkshake while her eyes go wide. "What?"

"Remember, Danny doesn't exist."

"So, who other than Danny?"

Vicki bites the end of a fry. "Vince Geldini."

Andrea's jaw drops from shock. "Vince Geldini from that heavy metal band, Black Liberty?"

"Yep."

"The one with the blond palm tree for hair?"

"Hey! Under all that Aqua Net is a sweet guy. I had a *huge* crush on him."

Andrea giggles back. "One thing's for sure. You wouldn't miss Florida or California looking at that head!"

She and Evelyn start laughing.

Vicki says, "He's from my area. A good farm boy. His hair was a little shorter then."

"Oh? And did he look like a cute pineapple head in overalls?" Andrea laughs hysterically. Evelyn laughs roughly with her. Vicki smirks at them. Evelyn pulls out a Camel cigarette, which she lights with her lighter.

Vicki says, "Vince used to work for my uncle at the auto shop. He was sweet and until I met Danny, I wanted to marry him. I had dreams of our wedding day."

Vicki takes another fry out of the carton.

Evelyn studies the Camel in her hand. She attempts to hold it like she had seen Jaime do it on a normal basis. Andrea turns to her. She notices the manner with which her new friend clutches the item.

"I know how it's done. Ease up your ring finger and let your pinkie relax in mid air."

Evelyn tries it out. Vicki watches more seriously. Her suspicions about Evelyn and Jaime were beginning to show.

Andrea asks Evelyn, "How about you? Got anybody in mind you would trade in for even a night?"

Evelyn takes a drag on the cigarette. She thinks immediately of replacing Ed with Jaime but she wasn't about to reveal that. She says, "There are so many lovely men. That's a tough question." Evelyn looks up to the sky thinking of a name to make up. "Um, Glen Houghton. He's somebody I've admired. A very kind British gentleman who I met some time ago." Evelyn knew there was nobody in her life that existed with that name. The whole thing was a lie. A cover up to hide who she really wanted in her life besides the one night she spent with him. Vicki studies the singer's expression and mannerisms to see if there are any hidden signs. Evelyn catches Vicki's steady glance. She knew Danny's wife wasn't buying into her answer but that's all she could offer.

Andrea looks at Vicki, then Evelyn.

Vicki says to Andrea, "What about you? I *know* you're all hot for Jaime."

"That's true and what I've asked from the both of you almost really happened to me." She grits her teeth a little at the thought. "I haven't been able to say this until now. It's just us girls anyway."

Vicki asks carefully, "Was this with Jaime?"

Andrea takes a large sip. "Yes."

Vicki darts her eyes uncomfortably to Evelyn. "Maybe you shouldn't."

"I'm fine with it now." Andrea tells her.

Evelyn looks on with curiosity. She taps out a few ashes as she holds her cigarette the conventional way.

In strange astonishment of the memory, Andrea says aloud, "It was so stupid though!" She throws her hands up. For a moment, Andrea stays quiet while collecting her thoughts. "I can laugh about it now but before, it was a complete embarrassment. I know it was for him too."

She leans a little forward as she explains. "I told you I've known him for a while, fourteen years, really. He's a terrific friend to Bobby and me. Becky thinks of him as Uncle Jaime because he's known her since she was born. He's babysat for her countless times. The truth is, Jaime's great with kids. I would love to see him with his own. But anyway, in the mid to late '70s I was rebellious, a real hellion. I wasn't interested in being simply anybody's wife. There was a lot of fun goin' on and I felt like I was missing out on it. In '78 it all came to a head and became a real eye opener. I had just turned thirty and I wasn't done with my youth. Major ego trips. Bobby and Jaime were becoming these big time producers. I felt like I was hot shit because I was married to one of them. My role as a mother did not faze me in the least. Becky was almost three then but I didn't care. We were living in the Bronx at the time and Bobby would drive down to the studio in midtown Manhattan. So, he would either stay late to work or to find some drug dealer he knew. I was in bad shape. Got Jaime to come over and help watch over Becky. Only, neither of us was interested in looking after a toddler. We stayed in the basement of the house. I found Bobby's stash and we were snorting lines like you wouldn't believe off the card table. Mirrors. Razor blades. All of it! Jaime and I got blitzed out of our skulls on this stuff. We were feeling really good. I think he had a girlfriend at the time... although... He hung around with a lot of pretty ladies. He was thirty-four, dressed up and looked fantastic. The jacket, half undone shirt and a long scarf he was prone to wearing. Like I said before, the whole Keith Richards look. *Very* cool. Very sexy. Somehow, we made it up two flights of stairs. He tossed his scarf over me and pulled me to him. I wound up getting pinned against the wall near the bedroom door. Remember, the guy is much bigger than me and high. Both of us were. There was always something between us, but the drugs only magnified it. He's very choosy with his women, so I guess I was one of the lucky gals. He kissed me and, it's something I will never forget. Simply because I've never experienced a kiss like that before or since even with Bobby. It seemed pretty innocent at first but I took it a step further. This is a guy who is very quiet but very and I mean *very* passionate. It's the silent ones you have to watch out for. The loud mouths that brag are all hot air. Quiet ones are all action. Never believe otherwise. I know I won't. Then it just got a little crazy. I try to blur it out of my mind. He had his hand in my hair. Then things got heated fast. You know, it's one thing to get a kiss. But when you find yourself holding the ends of the belt belonging to your husband's best friend and you have been snorting up cocaine, things can become very surreal. That somehow woke me up to reality. I was so close to jeopardizing my marriage by sleeping with Bobby's best friend. I decided to get help. Even though there weren't many intervention programs at the time, I got spiritual guidance and took stock of my life. I know Jaime carried on being wild at least a year later or so, but it scared the shit out of him. He acted different around me after that, for a long time. Thankfully, we're still friends and put that behind us so much so that we can still tease each other."

Vicki stays quiet, twisting a fry between two fingers. Evelyn holds her cigarette, motionless.

Andrea says, "Well, whatever lucky woman gets their mitts on him are due for some toxic passion."

Evelyn turns her head from a zombie-like state.

Vicki shakes her head in disbelief. "I had no idea."

Andrea tells her. "How were you to know? I finally felt comfortable enough to tell you."

Evelyn thinks to herself of how she experienced that toxic passion already. Probably any woman would be jealous or get angry for what happened between Jaime and Andrea, but not Evelyn. She felt more respect for Andrea that she was able to put a stop to a mistake, one that Evelyn knew herself she wouldn't be able to help in the same situation. The singer had already taken it further than Andrea Whitfield. To think, Jaime had restraint and felt awful about what happened.

What a man!

Just knowing Jaime Weston had a conscience endeared her to him.

Before nightfall, Andrea and Vicki drop off Evelyn back at the studio. While in the car, the two women talk about what transpired earlier.

"I think it's her." Vicki tells Andrea.

Andrea keeps her concentration on the road ahead and the passing traffic.

"What's her?"

Vicki turns to Andrea at the wheel. "What you were talkin' about. How whatever lucky woman gets Jaime."

Flicking on the headlights, Andrea turns to Vicki for a brief moment. "You think it's who?"

"Evelyn."

"What makes you think that?"

"Danny told me there's something weird goin' on at the studio. He said that Jaime treats her more different than any other artist he's ever seen before." Vicki takes out a pack of gum from her purse. She sticks her hand out, offering to Andrea. "Wanna Juicy Fruit?"

"No, thank you."

Vicki unwraps the thin foil and curls the stick of gum in her mouth. Looking out of the passenger's side window, she mentions, "You know that Houghton guy she said she liked? I didn't buy it."

Andrea says, "I didn't expect either of you to answer that silly question honestly."

"She looked at me like I knew she wasn't bein' truthful."

"So? Were you?"

"Yep." Vicki slowly chews her gum.

Andrea utters, "Palm tree head."

Vicki looks out the window again. "What was with that whole cigarette holdin' thing? Did you not notice she was trying to hold it like *him*?"

"He holds a cigarette a very sexy and appealing way. That's all. I'm sure a lot of folks would love to look that cool."

Vicki shakes her head, not believing her friend's defense. "You know, last week when you were goin' ga-ga over Malibu Ken? You went in the studio and he and I had a little chat. I asked him point-blank if anything was goin' on between him and Evelyn."

"And did he confirm or deny it?"

"He went through this whole dramatic gesture. Took off his sunglasses, tryin' to look all proud. Puffed out his chest and put his hand over his heart like he was takin' an oath or pledging allegiance to the flag."

Andrea lets out a laugh. "What do you expect out of Jaime? You're barging in on his privacy! You should know by now he *hates* that. You're lucky he was even nice enough to answer you the way he did."

"Well, Andi, he sure *seemed* guilty."

Andrea looks at Vicki hopeless.

In the studio, Evelyn sits on the bed in her guest room. She begins thinking of the conversation between her, Andrea, and Vicki. The singer then realizes she could make friends easier with Bobby's wife. Vicki seemed too suspicious to her, much like the glances of her husband, Dan. Her eyes scan the bed as she fast-forwards the conversation in her mind. Toxic passion.

"Your love never goes out of fashion."

Evelyn scampers off the bed and goes through a drawer mixed with garments. She pulls out her green spiral notebook. Quickly, she writes them down.

Ah yes! Toxic Passion!

Then another thing preoccupies her mind instead of writing words. She thinks about the accessory store at the outlet center. Of how her fingers ran down a velvety blue-violet scarf, long in length with soft fringes at the ends. Why had that made her think of something oddly familiar? Then

Andrea's words pop into the space of the question mark to the puzzle in her mind.

"He was dressed up and looked fantastic...He tossed his scarf over me..."

Another thought creeps in and that was her reaction to meeting Jaime Weston. There was that curious feeling of seeing him before.

Evelyn turns her sight to a painting on the wall between the tiny kitchen and bathroom. It's a watercolor painting of flowers in a gray vase to match the grays in the room. Only, it wasn't the picture itself that Evelyn was interested in. It was the simple fact it was artwork. She closes her eyes while piecing the parts together.

Jaime. Scarf. Artwork.

"Could Jaime have been part of my past? Scarf? What's with that? Art."

She taps the pen against the opened notebook.

"Art. Artwork. Painting? Gallery?"

Evelyn's eyes open quickly. "Cosgrove! That's it!"

Shortly afterwards, Evelyn changes to her evening attire, a form fitting spaghetti strapped black nightgown. The thoughts run rampant through her mind. Andrea, Jaime, toxic passion.

Evening gives way to a very hot and humid night.

A warm rush runs through Evelyn's body. She reaches for the window, pulling it up higher. It's still stifling hot. The air remains stagnant. Pulling away her sticking gown, she tries to cool off her body. Stroking her hair back, her thoughts turn to the idea of a cool shower.

No. That wouldn't do. She had *him* on her mind.

It was two weeks since their night together. Evelyn takes out her trusty lighter and lights the last remaining Camel cigarette just to see the difference. Inhaling deeply, she pulls it away, attempting to hold it the way she had seen Jaime do it. The way Andrea Whitfield properly showed her. The thumb and index, middle, ring and pinkie up. Smiling to herself, she puts it out. Her brand was no longer sufficient to her needs or cravings.

Evelyn had quickly acquired the taste of Marlboro, unlike her Camel man. Ed. She lets the name roll within a final puff of smoke.

"Jaime."

She longed for his taste when he would kiss her. The slender lips that enticed her mouth. The touch of his long graceful fingers against her warm pale flesh. A head full of thick dark brown wavy hair that she could run her fingers through in the heat of passion. His chest, a mixture of hair and soft flesh that she found incredibly sexy and masculine. His sensual low voice that could send shivers up and down her spine even when he would speak in a husky whisper. Yet, little did she know that down the hall somebody else was having restless thoughts.

Jaime lies awake in the dark as he is propped against the post and smoking a Marlboro. Her words echo in his mind. He removes the cigarette from his mouth and studies it.

"Which do you rather see burn?"

He liked her style.

Somehow, she had gotten under his skin. Evelyn had a way with words. That was for sure. Jaime smiles to himself as the smoke unfurls from his cigarette. He was secretly longing for her but didn't have the guts to walk over to her room and sweep her off her feet. He could care less what anybody else thought or was suspicious of, particularly Dan or Vicki. Even by telling Evelyn that their one-nighter was a mistake, he knew he was only fooling himself of the truth.

He wanted her again.

There comes a knock at his door. He gets up to answer it. Evelyn stands leaning her hand against the doorframe, wearing her black nightgown. She looks him over. Between his fingers, he holds a lit cigarette. His hair is pushed back revealing the low hairline. He wears a light blue shirt completely unbuttoned, accompanied by a pair of navy denim jeans. He gives her an undaunted wild stare and a serious look on his thin lips that is so charming.

Evelyn says, "You're still awake."

Jaime replies in a deep tone. "Couldn't sleep."

Cautiously she tells him while closing the door, "I was thinking about the *other* night."

He looks at her then turns away for a brief moment, closing his eyes. With his back turned he tells her while feigning guilt. "It shouldn't have happened."

She walks over to face him, ignoring his words. "So, what are you going to do now? I mean, now that you are awake."

He says, "I don't know. Do you have any ideas?"

He gives her a sly look as he takes a drag from his Marlboro before putting it out.

She replies with, "I might."

Evelyn opens his shirt wider. Her index finger slides down the center of his hirsute chest as she says, "But only if you're up to it."

He grins and softly says back while looking down at the touch of her finger, "If I'm thinking what you're thinking, it would just get more hot."

Evelyn coos back. "It certainly would get hot." Leaning against him she whispers, "That wouldn't be such a bad thing, now would it?"

"I guess not." He answers while his eyes trail down her body.

He has his hands on her shoulders, tempted to let down the straps that hold up her sleeping attire. Then he feels her kisses down his chest and lifts his head. She stops and looks up into his dark eyes without saying anything. Her hand teasingly opens his shirt even wider.

He responds in a soft gravelly tone. "Oh, what you're thinking of is a reprise."

She whispers yet again, "This can be our little secret. Nobody has to know about this." Evelyn reaches and pulls at his collar, stealing small kisses from his mouth. With a breathier tone she says, "Tell me what you really feel like doing."

He says back to her, "You'll have to come closer."

She steps up, until her chest is pressed firmly against him.

Quickly he wraps his arms around her and leans down to kiss her. His long fingers make their way under her straps, dropping them over her shoulders. She runs her fingers through his hair, while her feet leave the floor. He kisses under her chin and makes his way down her bare shoulders. Her hands grab onto the back of his shirt as he moves his head from side to side in a deliberate motion while kissing her neck. He pushes down her gown. Evelyn leans her head back.

Toxic passion!

At the same moment in time, Ed is in the middle of talking to his friend. Mac is a man who is nattily dressed in a tailored suit over his much smaller frame compared to Ed's. His nose tends to be in the air most of the time.

"You know, Evelyn was starting to piss me off about having kids. Sometimes it was endless. There were days that if she saw a woman pushing a carriage, she would be flooded with tears. Can you believe that?"

"Women usually feel empty if they don't have children." Mac explains.

"Since when did you become a psychologist?" Ed asks in his gruff voice.

"It's just obvious. She's longing for what she can't have."

Ed tersely tells Mac, "*Used to*. I had her see a doctor."

"And what did they say?"

"Same thing I've been telling her all this time. That she's unable to have children. You know the story."

Mac picks up a saucer and takes a sip of tea.

"You know she'll go for a second opinion."

Ed takes a gulp of tea. "She already did."

"And?"

"And the second one told her the same thing."

"Oh my." Mac slowly says, "There's always a third..."

Ed interrupts him. "She's done that too. Same thing."

Mac puts down his cup and wants to hear more about this. "You mean to tell me that somehow three doctors were able to tell Evelyn that she couldn't have children. Not that *you* personally would have anything to do with her test results."

"I want to stay with her Mac, and if this is a way for me to hold onto a good thing then I'll damn well do it."

Ed brushes back his feathered hair out of frustration. "After seven years you wouldn't want to lose a woman like Evelyn either."

Mac looks at Ed like he's crazy.

Ed sees this and says, "What?"

Mac looks down at the coffee table for a moment and then looks up at Ed who is pacing the room relentlessly. "What if she were to fall for someone else? You said she went to New York. Anything can happen wh…"

Turning around, Ed cuts him off. "What? What if Evelyn were to have an affair? Is that what you're thinking?"

"Well, the thought did cross…"

"It's not going to happen," Ed growls.

Mac says, "Oh?"

"She would never have an affair behind my back. She doesn't have enough confidence and doesn't feel worthy enough. Trust me, Mac. That would never happen."

Back in New York, Evelyn and Jaime make love. He immediately kisses her with wild abandon, moving his mouth down along her neck, getting his fingers entangled within her hair. Moving down her chest, he plants more kisses along the way. As much as Evelyn was enjoying the feeling, it wasn't easy for her to forget what was back home in England waiting for her. Here she had desired the producer. And there he was. Giving her every ounce of passion, body glazed with sweat. By now, he was kissing her stomach, running a hand along her hips. In some ways, she was feeling a little guilty that she was getting immense pleasure. Then again, Ed had nothing to give. He was a complete zero in bed. She's reminded once more of who is with her and why she has enjoyed it so much. Jaime gives a soft kiss to her jaw, making his way up to her mouth. She takes in his kisses, which become slightly harder. Then a thought crosses her mind. Evelyn places her hand against his chest in an effort for him to stop.

He stops and asks in a heavy breath, "What?"

Evelyn points to the phone on the stand.

Jaime says with a slight smile, "It's disconnected."

He quickly grabs her, pressing his weight, kissing her mouth with heavy persistence. Evelyn presses her head against the pillow while her fingers grab his hair. He tenses. She shuts her eyes tightly.

"Oh God, Jaime!"

Again, he makes his way down her neck. Her hands dig through his slicked hair.

She suddenly stops. He looks at her, breathing hard. It is Dejá vu all over again, this time without the interruption of the phone. Seeing her expression, he releases her from his weight.

She sits up in the center of the bed. He sits up in back of her, wrapping his arms around her shoulders while his chin rests against the top of her shoulder. There was the feeling that the month she had been spending at the studio was flying by almost too fast.

Evelyn puts her hands against his and says, "I don't really want to go back in a couple of weeks."

"Evy." He pats her shoulders in a consoling manner.

"At least I always have something good to come back to."

He kisses the back of her neck and whispers ever so seductively, "Ten years feels like a lifetime."

Evelyn starts to turn her head as if she doesn't completely understand. He looks down at her.

He replies with, "Wilhelmina's."

"That was ten..."

She looks at him with surprise.

"That's how long I've been waiting."

With that, he kisses the side of her neck and his hands run down the sides of her body. She leans her head back as his large hands cup over her breasts.

He remembered!

Evelyn turns back around to face him. The slightest hint of a smile appears on his face. He holds her by the elbows leading her down.

Immediately he attacks her neck with passion, pressing his body against hers. With fingers stretched over his back, she lifts her body up from the feel of his sudden thrust. She quickly moves to the feeling.

Jaime asks her in a heavy raspy tone. "Any more...to say?"

His hands run down past her stomach under the sheets where she tenses. Evelyn stifles a breath.

"No. Just more."

He presses further against her, breathing hard and fast. Both feel the surge of ecstasy. A feeling Evelyn was growing accustomed too, rather than the lacking of any passion she got at home. Just as she opens her eyes, she closes them for another wave of sensations. Continuously he pleasures her until there's no more strength left in either of them.

Jaime rolls over and flops down on the pillow, breathing heavy. She pulls back a lock of hair from his forehead. His fingers run through her hair. She runs her hands down his shoulders to his chest. Once she's able and has regained composure, Evelyn kisses along his jawline and slides her mouth down along his throat. Her hands rest against his stomach as she eases her way down wet skin and matted chest hair.

He whispers to her, "Evy."

Without any words, Evelyn continues kissing his chest. Just to drive him crazier, she nips kisses to his nipples.

He leans his head back and gives a sound of exhilaration.

She goes further, kissing along a line of abdominal hair.

Jaime flutters his eyes closed, taking in every sensation.

Evelyn leans up against him, placing a hand under his chin. She then gives him a demanding kiss to the mouth.

Some time later, Evelyn rests her head against Jaime's shoulder. He sits propped up with a cigarette between his fingers.

She says to him, "It's been a long time since I've done anything like that to anyone."

He responds in a cool fashion. "It's been a long time since I've let anybody do that to me."

He raises his brows in a devilish manner.

Evelyn then says, "You know, I think you must be one of the best I've ever had."

Jaime takes a long drag on his Marlboro and looks at her for a moment.

She continues with, "You're a fine fuck."

Jaime nearly chokes when he takes the cigarette out of his mouth quickly, eliciting him to laugh and cough a few times.

Evelyn takes the Marlboro away from him for a moment.

"You all right?"

He still remains chuckling and replies back with a semi-surprised look on his face. "Well, I don't know if I would put it exactly in the same terms."

She hands the cigarette back to him when he's calmed down.

"You certainly have a way with words." He tells her as he leans his head back against the pillow while the smoke seeps out of his mouth.

Evelyn puts her hand against his damp chest. "So, about Wilhelmina's and this ten year thing."

"Oh, let me think." He squints at the memory. "It's '87 now, so it was '77. I'm trying to think of how it happened." He takes a swallow. "I was supposed to go to this club, but went with a strange woman I had just met at a bar on Bleecker. She brought me to this gallery. And it ended up being Wilhelmina... I can't remember her last name. It was something German I think."

"Weinderhof."

"Glad you remember. So, I went over there. It was a completely chaotic party. Martinis, champagne, weird German women who were going nuts over this...*artwork*. I was quite taken by the cabaret style of Germany, but it wasn't there. Not in that gallery. Not at that showing."

He puts the cigarette back in his mouth and lets it stay there.

Evelyn says, "What was there that you found instead?"

He replies with, "Weird shit. Some Dadaist paintings. Surreal. Very modern."

He lets out a curl of smoke.

"Then I was about to leave when I saw this woman. Blonde. She didn't look like she was having the best time either. I tried to follow her, but she disappeared. Then I got to meet her about three weeks ago."

Evelyn sits up in shock. The words slowly come out of her mouth. "I took a cab back to the hotel. I know I saw you then but didn't realize...you spotted me. I had read that you were the best producer around New York. Already I had been through two in the state. And I thought it was time for me to get out of England and give the project one more shot. Oh, Jaime. I never knew. I wish I had."

Evelyn thinks to herself, maybe she wouldn't have wound up with Ed.

He says back to her, "It was a long time ago."

She replies with, "But it's something you clearly remembered."

Jaime says nothing to her and instead gives her a serious glance before looking down to take another drag from the cigarette.

She was right about that.

For a few moments, they both remain quiet.

Evelyn looks at him. Oh, how that man could look so incredibly cool, yet hot at the same time. What comes between them is the cigarette he's been smoking. She finally grows tired of seeing it. Evelyn takes it out of his mouth, and inserts the Marlboro between her own lips. Her bold move intrigues him. Releasing a puff, she slides her body over towards the nightstand, snuffing out the remains in the ashtray. She says in a sultry tone, "Come to bed."

Jaime blinks back in a state of confusion. "Wh... Is this a trick question?" He gives a huge smile behind her back, chuckling warmly.

Evelyn stares at the nightstand, when she feels his hand around her small wrist. Gently he pulls her back, guiding her for a kiss. She gets lost in his dark eyes. Her hand is firmly pressed against his stomach, while her chest is against his. She feels the galloping heartbeat under her. Slowly, she leans up. His hand reaches down under the blanket. She gasps back. He feels her whole body tighten from his touch. Evelyn reaches down, picking up his hand from beneath the covers. Grasping the palm, she guides his wrist to touch her face. She runs the top of his hand over her parted lips, taking in the sensation of arm hair from his wrist. He pulls back his arm, over-powering her grasp. He takes the palm of her open hand, gently kissing fingers. Letting his mouth run down her palm, she lets her hand feel the contour of his jawline. Further, it travels past his neck, down the throat, to his chest. Her other hand reaches around the back of his neck, where she touches his damp hair. She looks back at his face to notice his eyes narrow a glance of the come-hither kind. His hand caresses the soft flesh of her fully exposed right side. He angles to her with a serious stare.

In a deep tone, he tells her, "Let's just fuck."

Evelyn breaks into a hoarse laugh. Looking directly at him, she sees his expression hasn't changed one bit. Her smile fades. Taking in his concentrated look, she leans against him for a kiss. He grabs a bunch of her hair, pressing his mouth against hers for a repeated kiss. She stifles a breath at the feel of a warm tongue. Breaking away from his hold, she leans up. He grasps her hand, pulling it towards him. Landing over his chest, he feels her galloping heartbeat join his. Again, he prods her mouth with his tongue. Evelyn gives in. Jaime sits up more to get a better grasp of her. They kiss each other hungrily. He gives a slight moan. She makes her way to his jawline, kissing along the contour. He lifts his head more. Her left hand reaches for the back of his damp hair, which is wet once more. Evelyn's right hand lands on his shoulder, sliding down a quickly perspiring body. As he feels her mouth run down, he feels an awkward surge that makes him sit up more and turn. She notices the immediate change. Before she can do anything about it, his hands run down both sides of her body. He leans all of his weight against her. Evelyn's head hits the pillow. Immediately, Jaime grabs a clump of her dampened hair, giving demanding kisses. She reaches, wanting to take hold of him. Instead, he captures both of her hands in a vice-like grip against the pillow. He kisses her relentlessly, enticing her body further. The July heat becomes nearly unbearable and so does his body temperature. His hand manages to partially flip back the blanket. Evelyn feels the air from the sheet lift briefly, before his whole body covers over hers. With knees locked, she knows he wants her again in every way. Under the sheets, he responds with a lingering hand.

"J…" She starts to say.

Her knees relax. Leaning her head back, his motion makes her move to an inaudible rhythm. Then her toes slide hard against the mattress. His breathing is sharp and heavy. She grabs the corner of a pillow with one hand, while the other reaches to feel for his rapid heartbeat, encountering hair and hot flesh. His deep moan makes Evelyn open her eyes. Jaime's hot breath against her ear, as his voice drops to a hushed whisper of "Evy," sends a surge through her body already taken physically. His mouth lingers over hers. She responds with parted lips, until he gives her one kiss before being overtaken by a quickened jolt from his body. She gives a hoarse gasp. He grasps the sheets with both hands tightly. A strained raspy groan leaves him just before his head hits the pillow next to her. He gives measured breaths that match the rhythm of his heartbeat.

She looks at him with awe.

Jaime's out like a light.

Evelyn smiles sweetly, facing him. She closes her eyes.

Darkness quickly gives way to light as morning arrives. Jaime lies on his stomach, face to the pillow. He lets out a deep muffled groan. Slowly, his lids flutter open. Again, he closes them, knowing that daylight is making its appearance. He rolls over frontward, rubbing one heavy lid after the other. Turning to lean over, he takes notice of the digital clock's red numbers, 7:43AM.

"Ah, fuck." He mutters under his breath. Pushing back his partly tousled mess of hair, he props himself up. He runs a hand down the center of his chest, noticing he's still slightly damp from sleeping on his stomach. Jaime then takes a deep breath, looking down at the mattress. Something is amiss though. He gathers the sheet a little more for his exposed back.

"Morning, sleepyhead." Evelyn says in a low tone.

Jaime has his eyes closed for a moment as he responds back. "Morning." Again, he looks at the sheet. Adjusting his vision, he rubs an eye before finally looking at her. What he sees, surprises him. His eyes widen for a moment.

Evelyn wears one of his shirts, a gray one this time, fully unbuttoned over black lace panties.

He grins back. "Dedicated follower of fashion I see."

"Oh. This?" She looks down. "I found it in the closet. I hope you don't mind."

Jaime shakes his head. "No." He looks around in concern. "What... What happened to the blanket?" With a slight smile on his face he asks, "Did things get that wild?"

Evelyn answers him. "No. It's right here on the floor." She says thoughtfully, "Your exact words were, 'Too fuckin' hot.'"

Tight-lipped he says back in a deep tone, "I did. It was."

He tugs the sheet around him, further gathering it. Looking up at her he asks, "What was that?"

Evelyn says, "It was fantastic."

"I know what we did. Was that a marathon?" He chuckles back, gathering the sheet closer to him. He situates himself towards the end of the bed, still rubbing his eyes.

Evelyn walks toward the bed, holding a mug. "I made some coffee."

He looks up, accepting her offer. Taking a sip, he immediately winces back, pushing the mug at her.

She asks, "Too hot?"

"Too sweet." He answers, nearly choking a breath. Turning away, Jaime shakes his head.

"How do you normally like it?"

He clears his throat. "Black."

Again, he tugs at the sheet, wrapping and folding it to his waist, until it's completely off the bed. He arches his back in stiffness.

Evelyn looks over. "You're quite limber."

"It takes its toll. I'm not as young as I used to be." He smiles back. "Last night was an exception."

Jaime rises to his feet, holding the remainder of sheets not keeping him in a waist-high cocoon. Evelyn steps up to him, eyes trailing the six-footer from head to toe. His tall slender physique makes her stifle a breath in awe.

She points to the sheets. "I really wouldn't mind."

Jaime puts a hand out for her to stop. Closing his eyes in anguish, he answers back. "Not in the daylight." He walks by her, avoiding any physical contact. Shuffling around, he goes from a drawer to the nearby closet, picking out fresh clothes.

"Ah, so you're shy." She surmises.

"I just don't like to… Not when there's company."

Evelyn thinks for a moment, folding her arms over partly exposed breasts. "I heard you weren't so shy the other day."

He turns to her, getting up with a small pile of clothes and the bundled sheets. "That was a necessity. Besides, it wasn't everything." Glancing back at the digital clock, he's aware of how much time he has to finish getting ready. He mumbles, "Shit. I'm not going to have enough time." Putting a hand to his hair, he proceeds towards the bathroom with some of the sheets trailing behind.

"Tease." She says, watching the door shut.

A second later it opens, with the entire sheet being tossed out.

Evelyn smiles back. "Wretched tease!"

Then she hears running water. Walking over, she picks up the sheet and puts it back on the bed. She goes over to the nightstand and picks out a cigarette from the pack. Realizing she left her lighter back in her own living quarters, she strikes a match from the nearby matchbook. Easing her head back, she releases a slow stream of smoke into the air. She looks back down, starting to button up the shirt. Glancing back up, her eyes take notice of an object ahead of her. She walks toward the turntable and picks up the round sunglasses. Evelyn grows curious. She gives a smile, wondering what Jaime's viewpoint is. Slipping them on, she notices they are a bit blurry. "Prescription." She says to herself. Stepping in front of the mirror, she can only see a tinted hazy reflection staring back at her. It makes her realize Ed never wore sunglasses when he first met her. He had seen her sharp and clear through his own eyes over the past seven years. Yet, he never could see her for who she was. Jaime on the other hand, from his limited view accepted her from the beginning, and gave her two wonderful nights. She takes off the sunglasses, placing them back next to the turntable. The feeling disturbs and confuses her at the same time as she sees her reflection with her own eyes. Sucking in a breath, she releases a breath of smoke.

The bathroom door opens. Jaime steps out, fluffing his hair. His white shirt is buttoned halfway. He rolls up the sleeves.

Evelyn leans against the wall. "I must say there is an element of adventure being in here with you."

Jaime pulls out a belt from a drawer. "Like I told you before, it's not like I make a habit of sleeping with attractive singers. As it is, I normally conduct affairs..." He stops to correct himself. "I normally choose to conduct *business* of a private nature at motels or hotels." Jaime does the fourth button of his shirt, and puts on shoes. He begins threading the belt through the loops. A shy smile spreads across his face. Blinking back at the realization of Evelyn's romanticism and thoughts, he offers up further. "I don't think making love in a studio can be called adventurous. Risky is more like it."

Evelyn steps up to him quickly. "So, you do admit it." She smiles in wonder.

His eyes widen at her sudden response. He smiles back. "What else would you call it?"

She stares at him, still holding the cigarette between her fingers. Turning away, she says, "You missed a loop."

Jaime says in a matter-of-fact tone as he fixes the belt. "Well, there are other more direct terms such as fu..." He's stopped by Evelyn's hand, before he can finish.

"Darling, you've used up all your fucks for this morning." She answers.

Her hand feels his growing smile underneath. She then walks away.

He remains confused in terminology and how not to offend her.

"What would you say it is when two people have a yin and yang effect on each other? When they share a part of their soul in the most intimate way and exchange..." Jaime suddenly becomes at a loss for words, carefully trying to spare her of any uncomfortable terms. He puts his hands out for greater emphasis.

Evelyn waves her hand. "Come. Come."

Jaime cracks up laughing, before he can finish tying his shoelaces. He shakes his head to her response. With raised brows, he says back, "That too." Clearing his throat, he walks by her, still softly chuckling. He checks the time on the clock. "They'll be here very soon. No later than eight-fifteen."

Evelyn reaches for the pack of Marlboros. She slips one out, inserts it in his mouth, and lights a match. He leans over for the offering. Nodding back in ease, he lets the smoke unfurl.

"Don't you ever wear a watch?" She asks out of curiosity.

Jaime tucks in his shirt more as he answers her. "Andi got me a watch about two years ago."

"Three." She corrects him.

The producer furrows his brows in puzzlement. He looks back up with the cigarette between his teeth. With a defensive look, he slowly removes the Marlboro from his mouth. "What else did she tell you?"

Evelyn looks up at him. She can tell he's not at all amused by her response of knowledge. It's a rather intimidating glance. "Nothing." She says back.

For a moment, Jaime doesn't know if he can fully believe her. A second later, he puts the cigarette back in his mouth, and nods in agreement. While doing the third button of his shirt, he becomes alerted by a sound. Looking up, he quickly puts a hand on Evelyn's shoulder. "That's Bobby. I know the sound of that Beetle. '60s nightmare on wheels." He angles to her, putting a thumb out as a signal for her to leave.

She looks at the door. Balling up her black nightgown, she races out into the hallway and shuts the door to her living quarters just as the front door unlocks.

Bobby puts a key back in his pocket.

Dan walks behind him, grousing. "You're gonna wake up half the neighborhood with that jalopy of yours."

Bobby says back, "You're the one with the muffler problem on that extended kid mobile. Compared to that, mine is luxury."

"Luxury? That BMW is luxury. Even the Camry. Yours is…awful!"

Later on the same morning, Bobby stands looking at the mixing console. Jaime and Evelyn watch nearby. Dan has stepped out to get breakfast. Bobby presses play on the tape deck. All three listen. Immediately, Bobby shakes his head in disagreement.

"See that? It needs more. It sounds too clean. The more I listen, the more I'm realizing that it's just everything."

Jaime asks, "What is it?"

Bobby turns to his friend. "Glad you asked. Remember, Frank Janns?"

"Fabulous Frankie?"

"Yeah. The guy who we considered a guru of producing? Remember how we used to meet him at Tim Hortons?"

"Yeah, but your wallet wasn't left so fabulous."

"That's true. Although, I learned a lot from him."

"He was a moocher."

"I can't call it mooching exactly."

"You were taking lessons from him for a price and I don't recall him exactly being a certified teacher."

Bobby looks at Evelyn.

He says, "Before we confuse the lady, it might help in explaining. Tim Hortons is a doughnut shop named after a hockey player. They're located all over Canada. Frankie was a guy who knew the music industry inside out. Especially production."

"For a price." Jaime adds in.

Bobby continues. "Well, I was studying to become an engineer in North York at the time. I wanted to learn some really cool stuff. Then Jaime and I were told about this guy." Bobby smiles at Jaime who returns the look along with a chuckle. "Jaime talked with Frankie only a few times."

"Hey, I wanted to save my money." Jaime retorts.

"I'll bet you never learned how to do some things though."

"What's that?"

"One of the times while you were away in New Hampshire with your mom and aunt, Frankie told me about something. You know how The Beatles paved the way for what we do? *Sgt. Pepper* plays like a bible for producers."

Jaime says with disbelief, "What? Did Frankie tell you he talked with George Martin?"

Bobby replies. "Actually, he told me he didn't have to."

Jaime smiles and nods his head saying deeply. "That figures."

Bobby sees Jaime's disbelief when he answers. "I asked Frankie and he said all he had to do was listen. I thought it sounded interesting, but then he said, 'Do you want to learn ahead of the game?' Of course, I thought The Beatles were geniuses. Frankie told me why some of the songs sound the way they do. It's pieces. Just pieces of music. Scraps. Like what we've been working on with Evelyn here. Previous audience tapes. Uh, guitar parts. It's a stew of arrangements thrown in to make this wonderful musical gumbo. So, I got this bright idea from probably the best meeting I ever had with Frankie and have carried it with me ever since. If there's anything that's Beatle-esque then it's due to my own influence. I saw a lot of potential on Evelyn's track, "Tomorrow's Child.""

Bobby sticks in the tape and presses play on the playback. "Now, there was a particularly great bass line over this already. I enhanced it by playing the exact same line with an acoustic guitar over it. Used one of Jaime's precious Derby recorders to get that sound, mixed it down to blend with the bass. Took a piano chord. Hit on that twice like right here. See?"

Evelyn says, "Oh my God."

Bobby grins. "That's not all. The drumming didn't sound right. Too generic. I thought of this thing that Frankie told me, about a 'reversal of fortune.' You take a particular track of an instrument and reverse it. I took the hi-hat and reversed it so it gives the song more body. It gives the listener a soundscape. No empty spaces. Sure it sounds a bit slurpy, but that's what comes with it. And I thought the horns needed something more, so I flipped those too. You would think with all of this, it would sound like a mess but if you put it together, it sounds cohesive. There you have a four track. Vocals, acoustic guitar and bass, keyboards, and backwards hi-hat and horns. The horns work if you climb the scale from the low key to the high key. At least I thought so for this song."

Evelyn says with wide-eyed astonishment, "That's incredible! Bobby, you're a genius! It's so amazing. I never knew horns could sound like that. This whole thing sounds like a Lennon arrangement! Brilliant!"

Bobby turns back to Jaime.

"See what you missed? Moocher, my ass. Frankie was fabulous after all."

Jaime groans in agreement. "Yeah."

"Okay, McCartney, let's see if you can top that!" Bobby challenges.

In the meantime, Ed tries to figure out any other angles in which he can get information on Evelyn. Already he had exhausted his means by her address book. That was useless. Maybe he could go to The Green Light to confront Kelly in person? She hated his guts. Or, there could be other ways. Perhaps a meeting with Mildred's better half might be in order for some time in the near future?

***

Jaime steps out of a coffee shop with a cup. Bobby pulls up in his VW Bug. A few people take second glances at the old relic the producer takes great pride driving around in. Bobby steps out.

Jaime asks, "Where's Evelyn?"

"She's back at the studio with Danny. They're trying to work out something."

Jaime tells him with glee. "You've got to check it out. I got someone who I think can help us."

"Who'd you get?"

"Emory Caldwell."

"Get out of here! No you didn't. You're bullshittin' me!"

"No. I'm not."

"You bastard. How did you manage that?"

"I called Morton's Music and talked with Don. I said, get me the next person who walks through the door. It just so happened to be, Emory. He's supposed to play at the Beacon Theater tomorrow night. When I met with him, I told him we were working with a singer named, Evelyn Winthrop. And he said, what an honor it would be. So, he apparently knew who she was, and was thrilled. Guess I'm the only one in the world who didn't. He asked me, 'When do we start?'" Jaime laughs.

"Where is he now?" Bobby quickly asks.

"On the way to the studio. As a matter of fact he might be there now."

"I'll be back there in just a few minutes. I'm gonna run in and get some espresso. Then we'll see what we can come up with."

Just before he gets back in his car, Jaime tells his friend, "Lennon, don't take too long." He laughs while putting his sunglasses on.

Bobby turns around slowly, remembering how he had teased Jaime. "*You...*" He responds.

The BMW leaves the parking lot.

Shortly afterwards, Evelyn is singing along with the sweet sound of a saxophone provided by Emory Caldwell. She gets immersed in the music that swells. The man in back of her; big, burly with a mountain man visage within small coal gray curls of a bushy beard and hair. Emory closes his eyes to the very feel of the notes he conjures. Jaime sits at a keyboard with a very big smile on his face, following the music. Bobby sits in awe of all that is going on. He moves his head occasionally in disbelief. When the last note has been drawn from Emory's sax and Jaime's final key has been struck, they come out of their spell. Evelyn opens her eyes. Emory excuses himself to use the bathroom.

Jaime looks at Bobby who says, "Unbelievable. The man can switch from a keyboard, to a sax or even a violin. That's just...*sick*. Man, that's not right. The man is a freakin' *genius*! He barely says a thing when you ask him of something. He just *does* it and understands it, then translates it beautifully."

"That's what makes him outstanding in this business."

"And you happened to get him."

Emory arrives back in the room, polishing his saxophone.

Bobby asks with enthusiasm. "So, you're playing at the Beacon?"

Emory gives a drawled out deep, "Yuuuuup," in his backwoods accent.

"Hmm. Gonna play several instruments?"

"Yuuuuup."

"You know, my wife is a really big fan of yours. Perhaps we might be able to get either some great seats or I can get her a backstage pass."

"Mm. Uhhhh. You'll have to talk to my manager about that."

Jaime asks, "I think that went quite well. Don't you?"

"Yuuuuup. Quite enjoyable with Ms. Winthrop."

Jaime nods his head in agreement; as he has nothing else he can say. Tight-lipped he looks at everybody.

Bobby thinks of something at the same moment. "We'll give this to Danny and see how we can work this in."

Emory packs in his saxophone and violin.

Evelyn says to the multi musical maestro, "It was a great joy having you work on my new album. I thank you sir, for the opportunity."

"Yuuuuup. Nooooo problem Ms. Winthrop. Nooooo problem at all. If you ever need someone to back you up on tour, your agent gets mine."

Evelyn looks at him shocked. "I will most definitely keep that in mind. Thank you so much again."

"Yuuuuup. Good day, gentlemen, and thank you, Jaime."

He walks past Jaime and Bobby, up the stairs. They hear the main door close. Jaime comments to Bobby.

"That was exciting. I do believe we have a keeper on our hands. You can't get much better than that. This is truly amazing what we've got with this project. Just unbelievable."

Bobby answers him back. "Yuuuuup."

Jaime bows his head down, laughing at the producer's dead-on impression of Emory Caldwell.

Chapter 5

Outside of an insurance building in central London, Phil Grumbach pulls out his keys from his jacket pocket. He jogs the key in the keyhole and looks up to see Ed Brockton standing before him. The breeze from the buildings blows his dark, collar length hair.

Ed says in a gruff though pleased tone. "Hello, Phil."

Phil keeps a steady glance with his dark gypsy-like eyes. His thick brows furrow. Ed takes out a Camel, lighting it then makes himself comfortable leaning against the side of Phil's car.

"Ed, what are you doing here? Isn't it a bit of distance?" Phil remarks in his nasally Liverpool accent.

Ed blows out a puff of smoke. "I was in town. Really, I came to see you. Figured you get out at this time."

Phil grumbles. "So nice of you to visit me."

Ed sighs. "Don't tell me you feel the same as Mildred?"

"We're one mutual admiration society family when it comes to you, Ed." He drops the key back in the pocket of his wool jacket. "I heard how a little girl hissed at you." Ed looks down and chuckles dismissing the embarrassment. "My son though it was quite hilarious. You have a way with kids."

"Yeah, well."

Phil asks. "You wanted to talk to me?"

"Yeah. It's about Evelyn."

Phil rolls his eyes. "Didn't you ask my wife about this?"

"Yeah. She told you?"

"Ed. Couples do talk. Maybe that's why you and Evelyn..."

"Hey. Hey! Hey!" Ed raises his voice.

Unknowingly, Phil hits a sore spot with the annoyed photographer.

"We're not like you!" Ed snarls back.

"Apparently not." Phil replies coolly.

Ed says, "I think you know where she is."

"Ed, don't be a foolish man. Everybody knows you suffer from paranoia when Evelyn's not around or under your thumb."

Ed's nostrils flare. He could tell the insurance man was being a wise-ass.

In a low almost growling tone Ed responds. "Listen to me you pigheaded Liverpudlian limey wanker." He puts up his index finger in an effort to intimidate.

Unfazed, Phil raises his brows. He remarks dryly. "I see you have picked up on British insults. I wasn't sure when you would get there. With your puny mind it's a wonder you have room enough to think."

Ed swarms his tongue in his mouth trying to keep his composure. His hand trembles slightly with the Camel still burning between his fingers. "Getting back to the subject at hand." Ed glares at Phil. "Why do I get the feeling you're hiding something?" He squints.

"I told you, you should learn to trust your mate. You have no right in disrupting others lives for the sheer purpose of selfishness." Phil pulls out the key again. "Good day!"

Ed steps in front before Phil can get the key in the lock.

The photographer growls back quietly yet firmly. "If I find out you or your wife have been lying to me..."

"Are you threatening me and my family?"

"Just stay out of my way."

Ed puts the cigarette in his mouth before walking away briskly.

Phil turns his head watching the man disappear. Unlocking the door, his eyes never leave Ed. Cautiously he gets in the car starting up the ignition. Phil knew Ed could be a nuisance. He could be cruel to any one of Evelyn's friends including the Grumbach's. Only this time it was different.

It was as if Ed sensed something that made him twice as insecure. He was on a serious mission. Trying to validate his feelings made Phil feel a little uncomfortable. He looks into the rearview mirror at the reflection of his own dark eyed stare. Thinking for a moment, the insurance man considers Ed almost on the verge of insanity. Phil shifts the gear into reverse as he pulls out of the parking lot.

***

"What I need from you is a little more attitude, like your stronger work. That attitude of 'I just don't give a damn.'" Bobby commands the singer over the microphone in the control room.

Evelyn replies. "Oh, you mean that *'Fuck all'* attitude?"

Bobby raises his brows.

Jaime chuckles back, "She has a way with words."

Bobby says back to her, "Yeah. That's the one."

Evelyn adjusts her headphones.

"I changed some of the lyrics as I didn't think the original sounded right."

"Well, I want to hear punk comin' out of you. This sad waste, done in by their own ego. That way the guitar fills will exact the passion with which you deliver and that drum beat can hook onto it."

Bobby rewinds the tape in the machine, playing back what they just heard. Both he and Jaime analyze it.

Bobby asks. "What does that guitar sound make you think of? What's the first thing that comes to your mind? The frenetic energy."

Jaime responds. "Ah. That would be the sound of traffic. Very hurried."

"Okay. That's what we're aiming for. Are you even familiar with any of Evelyn's past songs."

"Um, no. That's why I'm letting you take the controls on this one. Because you know."

He leans his curled hands underneath his chin while Bobby takes on the direction.

"'Angelic Waste.' Take three."

Bobby commands Evelyn who readies herself like a runner in a race.

"Go!"

Evelyn takes a deep breath as Bobby punches in the exact position of where the tape is stopped. He presses play.

I watch you as you sit down in a corner, have yourself a laugh.
Looking so beautiful, beautiful beyond compare.
I watch you stare, then look around.
The things around you that used to have life.
Now they're all gone, thrown out like yesterday's trash.

Angelic Waste.
Diminished beyond comprehension, diminished beyond repair.
Your life is such a mess. Your mind gone out and blitzed.
Snorted too much cocaine, done too much hash.
Now your mind is like looking at a mind numbing crash.

Freak out at every corner, watch the evening news.
Say to yourself why is this allowed to go on.
Over the balcony, you just want to jump.
Why am I.... why am I this joke? You ask.
Just found out that your fifteen minutes of fame is done.

Angelic Waste.
Diminished beyond comprehension, diminished beyond repair.
Your life is such a mess. Your mind gone out and blitzed.
Snorted too much cocaine, done too much hash.
Now your mind is like looking at a mind numbing crash.

On your hands and knees, helpless creature you are.
Once beautiful, but now porcelain with tears.

Treated ones badly, treated them cruel.
Now they laugh at you, the very fool.

Angelic Waste.
Diminished beyond comprehension, diminished beyond repair.
Your life is such a mess. Your mind gone out and blitzed.
Snorted too much cocaine, done too much hash.
Now your mind is like looking at a mind numbing crash.

Make me hate you.
Make me love you.
Make me feel sorry for you.

Angelic Waste.
Diminished beyond comprehension, diminished beyond repair.

Make me hate you.
Make me love you.
Make me feel sorry for you.

Your life is such a mess. Your mind gone out and blitzed.
Snorted too much cocaine, done too much hash.
Now your mind is like looking at a mind numbing crash.

Crashhhhhhhhhhhhhhhhhhhhhhh. Speed bump up ahead!
Oh, how Romeo bleeds!

Evelyn draws out her final words in a mocking, hissing tone, taking her stance of self-assurance against the microphone.

Bobby grins wildly like a joker holding all of the cards. "Oh yeah. Atta girl."

Jaime watches his friend's face light up.

With all the contentment in the world, Bobby says into the microphone. "That's it. That's what I was talking about. We can cross "Angelic Waste" off the list. That's a wrap!"

Ed turns his eyes up to the ceiling, trying to find answers. He glances at Mac who as usual, faithfully hangs on to every word he says.

Mac asks. "How has your search turned out?"

"So far, I've been hissed at, called an asshole, been made a joke and mocked. Funny thing is, I'm still not getting any answers from these people."

Mac looks at him peculiarly. He asks with a perplexed expression, "Who hissed at you? "

"Oh, some little brat at Millie's. You know what Mildred did? She gave this...this child candy for what she did. Can you believe that? She actually rewarded her. Then, two days ago I talked with her husband, Phil and he treated me like I was some mental case!"

"Are either of these two responsible for calling you something so coarse and vulgar?"

"No. That honor would be bestowed on some Scottish broad named Kelly. She works at the club that Evelyn goes to. I'm tellin' ya, Mac. She's got friends that are either stupid or don't understand English. I'll find out where she was once she gets back. We're talkin' about a week at the most. Then we'll get it all sorted out."

Ed tries to convince himself of that.

***

Dan puts on his jacket. Another day is done. This time it is the day next to the last for *Hero's Requiem*.

"We're just about done."

Bobby says, "We *are* done. We just have to check it for anything unnecessary. Tape hiss, bloops, blunders, stuff." He looks at Jaime. "One more day my friend."

"Yep." Jaime smiles back.

Evelyn looks at the tape rewinding.

Bobby places on his jacket. "Time to hit the road, Danny boy!" He turns to Jaime. "Did you get that little thing done with the song?"

Jaime closes his eyes, shaking his head. "No. I'll do it."

Bobby says, "All right. I'm counting on you," before walking out with Dan.

Bobby is heard from inside the control room. "Danny, so you said it's pot roast and potatoes tonight?"

"Yep. Andrea and Becky must be there by now."

"I'll meet you there, buddy."

Inside the small room, Jaime takes a match to the Marlboro he has just put in his mouth. His brows arch up as he hears the front door close. He says aloud, "Not everybody is as excited to revisit their past, Bobby."

Jaime turns to the singer who is preoccupied by the finished tape. "Evy, check to see that they're gone."

Evelyn doesn't verbally respond although she walks out of the room. He switches the rewound tape with one that is labeled *Blues*. Quickly, he adjusts a few knobs then presses play on the tape deck.

Evelyn walks back inside, to the sound of sweet guitar picking and stomping foot rhythm. John Lee Hooker sings in a doubled vocal delivery of "I'm In The Mood." Jaime Weston adds triple harmony. Evelyn doesn't see him at first. She looks at the reflection of the darkened control room window where she sees him behind her. She turns to see that he's sitting in back on the countertop delivering vocals in his deep voice, lower than Hooker's. Seductive yet playful, he looks right at Evelyn. She gets caught under his spell. Jaime knew how to get her attention. The blues had become the aphrodisiac of her soul. He had wooed her with it their first night together.

As she steps toward him, his lids lower. Still he sings with the music.

> *"Every time I see you baby, walkin' down the street.*
> *Know that I get a thrill baby from my head down to my toes.*
> *I'm in the mooood... I'm in the mood for love."*

She grins. "You sing beautifully. With a voice like that I can't understand why you don't do it more often."

He smiles at her while still carrying the song along.

"*Night time is the right time...*"

Evelyn says, "All right. What are you *really* up to?" She shuts off the tape. He puts the cigarette in his mouth, puffing away. She looks at him with a nod. The producer looks mighty good to her. His hair is fully slicked back and the gray jersey he wears clings nicely to his body. Evelyn notices she's pretty much even in height as the six-footer sits on the counter.

Easy access!

Jaime's eyes stay on hers. The singer closes her eyes for a second.

"You are a *terrible* flirt." She says in a deeper voice.

Evelyn gets caught up in being spellbound. It was the feeling of falling for him all over again. She would get adventurous, daring, and lose her senses amid passion. Vulnerability could take over if she looked in those deep dark eyes long enough.

Then it happens.

Evelyn smiles at him before turning serious. She asks. "Why is it...?" She can't think of what she wanted to say. Instead, her fingers pull out the Marlboro from his mouth. He welcomes it, sensing what's to come instead. Evelyn leans her hand against the countertop ledge right between his legs. As she holds the burning Marlboro, she leans closer to him. His eyes close at the feeling of her lips against his. A kiss is placed. She steps back, inserting the cigarette back between his lips.

Smiling, Evelyn begins to walk away then feels her arm held back. He holds her small wrist. Lightly he pulls her back towards him. He takes out the cigarette with his freed hand and asks in a seductive tone, "How about we cash in that rain check?"

She looks at him surprised. "I thought you said you didn't like to celebrate projects."

"Is the invitation still open?"

"Yes. I'm just wondering what made you change your mind."

"How about tomorrow? I know just the place."

Evelyn feels that he's dodging her questions.

He says quietly. "Change of heart."

Jaime remains holding her wrist. He puts out the cigarette in the ashtray next to him. He pulls at her until he can reach her elbows. Then he draws her to him that way. Being close enough to the producer, Evelyn places her hands on top of his shoulders.

She tells him in her deep tone, "Dinner and dessert?"

He grins back. "That all depends on how you think of dessert."

Slowly she leans closer and closer to his face. The producer has his hands on her sides, massaging them.

"You are trying to seduce me." She says with an all-knowing sense.

He breathes against her. "How am I doing?"

Slowly, in an almost sleepy tone she answers back. "Fine."

Close enough, he reaches to clasp his mouth against hers for a kiss. Wanting more, Evelyn tosses her arms around his neck, letting her fingers run through his hair.

Inside the living room, Ed walks over to the mantle where he picks up a small framed photo of him and Evelyn. It was an image of them both smiling. She had just gotten out of rehab. Her face was fresh as morning dew. Blonde fringed bangs hang over her big blue eyes. Ed stares at those eyes. He remembered them from a different time.

He thinks about the autumn of '79.

Ed was shooting pictures at a large industrial building in the West Village of Manhattan. He had just finished re-loading his camera during the shoot when he heard yelling in a nearby room. All of the assistants had finished for the day. They were putting props away. Ed squinted. The single voice he heard was harsh. Furrowing his brows, he left his camera over his neck. Walking through the darkened hall with various empty spaces, the voice became harsher and louder as he neared the room. Then he stood at the threshold of the entrance. It was another large studio space, empty in appearance, except for all of the photography equipment. Two people were consoling a dark haired woman. Her hand was on a Nikon camera. She mumbled between tears. In the far off end of the room was a middle-aged man in a suit raging with fury. He said, "I don't believe this. How many times do we have to go through the same thing? Look at you! You're a mess!" He hissed. The man stepped aside, revealing a crumpled up blonde lady sitting on the floor. In back of her were laser light effects shown on the screen. It looked to Ed like a bad traffic accident had taken place. The mourning, yelling, blaming, people at the scene. The man leaned over the lady and yelled, "I leave you alone for ten minutes." He pointed his fingers out like switchblades for greater emphasis. "Ten minutes. That was all. The first thing you do while Wendy is trying to get your picture is you run into the bathroom." The woman on the floor remained unmoving. She looked like a broken china doll, a marionette with strings tangled. Her eyes had deadness to them. Ruby red lips that were parted showed only small breaths. He picked up her arm, and slid back the sleeve to check for track marks. "You're nothing but a goddamn junkie, Winthrop. You're a junkie who's costing everybody time." Infuriated by no response, he slapped her left cheek to wake her up. "Come on!" Ed squinted to look further. He didn't like seeing a woman get slapped. The photographer felt it was only right to intervene and stop the madness. Something stopped him though. The man retracted his hand in such a way he was ready to strike her again. Without any facial movement, the woman's hand darted in front of her face in an immediate reflex. Slowly, her eyes swung to meet his. It was as if the slap had somehow awakened her from her drug-induced stupor. She writhed around in the agony of life. The man shook his head, looking at the poor, pitiful sight before him. He said, "Get the stylist. Make her have the sheep dog look. Nobody needs to see her eyes. Not like that." Wendy was dabbing her eyes, nodding at the advice given by the assistants. Ed watched as the man briefly looked at him as he exited the room.

That's how he remembered first seeing Evelyn Winthrop.

Vicki begins the arduous task of cleaning up the dining room table. The Whitfield's have since left. Dan helps her. He places dirty dishes in the dishwasher. Vicki puts some pots in the sink.

She asks her husband. "How many more days for Evelyn?"

"One."

Vicki turns to him. "That's all?"

"Yep. We're basically done recording. All that's left is to double-check everything. Make sure all of the tracks are up to her standards." As Dan loads up the dishwasher he says to himself, "I wonder how Jaime will handle it."

Vicki catches her husband in a daydreaming state.

"Who will handle what, honey?"

Dan shakes himself out of his thoughts. Vicki glances down while he's stooping down with some utensils bunched in his hand. "Oh, I'm just wondering how Jaime will take it when she leaves. I told you that I sensed something was going on between him and Evelyn. I still feel the same about it. It's just completely different the way he's treated her. You know we've had other women artists but..." He shrugs then pivots on his toes, angling up towards his wife.

"I know. Not because you told me before." Vicki says looking down.

"You do?"

"Yeah." She walks over to the refrigerator. "Wanna beer? Come on, hon. Have a beer with me." Vicki grabs two cans. Placing one on the kitchen table, she sits opening hers. Dan closes the dishwasher door just before joining her.

She reveals. "I talked to him already. Really, I talked with her too. I didn't ask her. I observed her though."

"When did you talk to him?" Dan asks out of curiosity.

He opens his can of beer.

She replies. "About two weeks ago. You remember when the air conditioner was busted at the studio."

"Can't forget."

"When Andi came in, I was talkin' to him outside. I asked him if there was anybody new in his life. I mentioned to him how you noticed he was actin' different around that Evelyn gal."

Dan gets up quickly, averting a telling glance from his wife. He winces. "Why did you tell him that? He's only going to take it out on me."

"Did he talk to you about it?"

"No. But I'm willing to bet he will."

"And I'm willing to bet he won't."

Vicki thinks about what Andrea told her and Evelyn, how she almost cheated on her husband with his best friend. Jaime had since never uttered a word about it to anyone.

Dan asks with questionable eyes. "How can you be so sure?"

" 'Cause, I know these things. He didn't talk to you about it already. Besides that, what do you think? Jaime's gonna fall apart without Evelyn around?" She taps the can against the tabletop. "Hon, he's not going to wilt."

Dan sighs while pushing back his hair. "I want to see him happy."

She gets up and walks over to Dan.

"I know you do. So do I." She reassures him.

"The thing is, I think they would be great for each other. She's close to his age. I mean, she can't have kids but at this point in their lives it probably wouldn't matter."

"I know. I know." Vicki rubs the back of his shoulders.

"Evelyn's a far cry better than those girls he picks up at the record company parties. Wish she didn't have to leave so soon."

Vicki takes a gulp of beer. "Well, hon. I guess only time will tell."

He picks up his can, uttering. "Yeah."

***

Evelyn, Bobby, Dan, and Jaime listen to the playback of *Hero's Requiem*. Bobby listens carefully for any blemishes on tape.

She squeals with excitement. "I love it! I can't wait to work this out live with my band!"

Dan asks, "What about the title track?"

"What about it?" She replies.

Bobby inquires. "Will you be having a trash can onstage with you?"

Jaime and Dan laugh.

"Oh, I can just see that now!" Dan exclaims.

With a hint of disappointment, Evelyn tells them. "I never thought about that."

Bobby puts a finger up. With seriousness he says, "Now, remember something. It can't be *any* trash can. It has to be of tin alloy."

Jaime and Dan laugh again.

Bobby's delivery, priceless.

Jaime looks at Evelyn with a huge smile. She begins laughing along with him and the engineer. She says between giggles. "I'll have to keep that in mind. But wouldn't a cymbal suffice?"

"No. No! It's not the same sound. You need the right color, tone. Evelyn, we're talking about *dynamics*." Bobby answers with seriousness.

If Bobby expected to be taken seriously, he wasn't. His quickness for causing hilarity was something still new to Evelyn. Bobby found the perfect victim to hook into. Jaime bows his head down, turning away from Bobby. Dan leans his head against the mixing console desk. His body quivers with giggles.

Jaime wipes his eyes.

Bobby breaks up the humored three. "Aside from that. Could I treat you to dinner, Ms. Winthrop? This of course would be with the lovely Mrs. Whitfield. And yes, Danny, you and Vicki are welcome to join us. Jaime, are you comin' along?"

"I have a lot of work to do. I have to plan something out with the next artist. Their manager wanted me to call him and it's sort of messy."

Bobby grins. "You're always busy." He turns to Evelyn again. "How about it, Ms. Winthrop?"

Evelyn opens her mouth as she turns her eyes to Jaime. "I would love to...but, I'm afraid I have plans already with some friends out of Manhattan. I hope I haven't spoiled anything."

Bobby pulls a face. "Nah! No trouble at all. It'll be the Whitfields and Sorens."

Dan adds in. "Again."

Bobby gives Evelyn a hug. "It was great working with you."

"Same here, Bobby." She turns to Dan. "You too, Dan. Danny."

He leans over giving her a big bear hug. "You take care."

Evelyn wipes her eyes. She couldn't be sure if the tears were from laughing so much, minutes earlier or from the fact her album was finished and sounded great. It could very well have been from the possible knowledge this was goodbye.

Bobby says in an abnormal low tone. "Well, we'll be seeing you."

He walks away quickly rubbing his eyes.

Dan nods, figuring he should get going. He smiles with thin lips partly grimacing,

"Bye."

Evelyn waves. Jaime stays tight-lipped while waving too.

Dan says back very quietly, "See you Monday."

She doesn't hear him as the door closes.

The two wait a few minutes. Jaime grabs his jacket off the chair.

Evelyn looks down. She says in a melancholy tone, "I kind of feel bad."

He answers back. "Don't. They'll survive without you. They always do this." The producer hands the singer her jacket on the table. "Are you ready?"

She puts on her jacket.

"Yes. Only, I'm not sure I'll have time for dessert. What with all of the packing and last minute errands I have to run."

Jaime lets out a soft chuckle. Walking to the main entrance, he opens the door for her.

They exit.

In the further reaches of New Paltz are the softly swaying oak trees caught in the warm breeze of the darkening sky. Light traffic moves along to the pace of a normal weeknight. Jaime and Evelyn walk along the sidewalk that winds through Main St.'s small shops and eateries. Dressed in a light blend black jacket, Jaime looks down at his female companion. Evelyn wraps her arm around his while her other hand gently grasps the same arm. She smiles happily. Nobody recognized her as the singer she was. The folks that walk by her and Jaime probably thought they were simply a couple. Evelyn feels her bond with the producer getting stronger. She feels comfortable enough to cling to him in public.

Evelyn looks up at Jaime admitting, "I think they're suspicious."

He says back, "Who?"

"Bobby and Dan. They would sometimes look at me oddly."

"Those guys *are* odd." Evelyn looks at him with a quizzical expression. "They're crazy enough to put up with the madness of the creative process...and put up with me." He chuckles back.

Evelyn lets go of his arm, preferring to stop in front of his path. She looks up while placing her hand on his arm again. "I'm crazy enough to put up with the madness of the creative process...and you." She leans up on her tiptoes. He leans down toward her. They connect for a kiss. Evelyn gives Jaime a firm hug with her arm wrapped around his back. Breathlessly with regret she says, "I don't want to leave. Not now."

He breathes into her hair with a soft tone. "Why go then?"

Backing away slightly, she says, "I have unfinished business at home. Besides, I can't just up and leave without anybody knowing." Evelyn knew full well that she had to do something about Ed. Maybe then she could get that done and return to New York for the new love in her life.

They continue their walk on Main St. Evelyn once again grasps Jaime's arm with both hands while leaning her head against him.

At a lovely though not overly opulent restaurant called Olivine's, the couple sit across from one another, under a web of tiny white lights.

Evelyn says, "You can't honestly be forty-three."

"Four." He corrects her.

She looks at him. "Forty-four?"

"Yep. As of July 2nd." Jaime puts the menu down. He turns the question over to her. "I won't even ask."

"Forty."

"Just forty?"

"Yes. Until November 28th."

He leans up, taken aback.

"You don't believe me?" She laughs.

"You could have fooled me." His tone grows deeper. "Actually, you did."

Evelyn giggles. "What did you think I was?"

"Maybe mid-thirties…tops."

"Oh, you need to put your glasses back on."

He chuckles, going back to take another look at the menu.

Evelyn says, "Ever since you said that you remembered seeing me at Cosgrove for Wilhelmina's showing, I can't help but wonder if I might have missed out on ten years with you."

Jaime looks up at her with a sense of absurdity and places the menu down.

He says flatly, "No."

A waiter steps up to their table. "Would you like to order a beverage?"

Jaime says back, "A bottle of wine would be good. Oh. Would you happen to know the year, while you're at it?"

"I'll check on that."

The waiter walks away.

Evelyn looks across at her dinner companion. "So, why wouldn't I have wanted all of this, then?"

He launches into his story. "About ten years ago, I wasn't the same person that I am today."

She says back, "Neither am I."

Jaime continues, "Not that I didn't have a lot of fun then, but I was pretty far out there. Truth be told, I was no angel. As a matter of fact I overindulged to the point of my own near demolition."

The waiter comes back holding a bottle of wine. Leaning over toward the producer he says, "Sir, it's from 1977."

Evelyn breaks into laughter while Jaime looks slightly unamused.

The waiter looks at Evelyn laughing. Confused he asks, "Will this be all right?"

Jaime looks at the bottle tight-lipped until he replies in a deeper voice. "Ten years is ten years. Yeah. It'll be fine."

Evelyn stifles her laughter as she orders her meal. Jaime gives the waiter his order.

The waiter disappears.

Jaime looks down at the table uttering deeply, "Shit. Unbelievable."

Evelyn picks up the bottle. "It's vintage, darling!"

He says back rather dryly, "By who's standard?" Moments later with a brief pause between them Jaime says, "Jeez, talk about coincidences." He laughs for a minute causing Evelyn to start giggling.

Jaime continues his story. "Success went to my head. When you get an opportunity to work with some major artists of the time, let alone being in the same room with them, it can change you. Add to that being told *constantly*, you're one of the best at what you do...plus the decadent dangers of the time. You put all of it together and you're in for a *major* disaster."

Evelyn says back understandingly, "Uh huh."

"Another thing is what you told me uh, last week." Jaime tries to find the way to tell Evelyn about their second night together. "How do I put this? Well, simply you said I was one of your...best."

Evelyn says back quickly, "Oh yes, *that*. I was serious about it. I meant it sincerely."

Feeling as though he's about to change five shades of pink, Jaime chuckles back from the flattering remark his female companion has reminded him of. "Well, that's what I'm talking about." He gets more serious. "If it was nine or ten years ago, I would not have made even one of your top ten. You would have been very disappointed. I would have been a complete waste. I had more hangovers than I did women. Too many people mistook how I appeared on the outside, but it must have been heartbreaking for them to find out I was an emotional wreck. That's why I say don't blame yourself for not meeting me back then."

Evelyn takes a sip of wine. She feels a very foreign sensation. It was something she thought she was feeling while back at the studio.

Jaime catches her wince and smiles back. "Not so vintage, huh?"

Confused, Evelyn says back, "I guess not. Maybe when I eat, it will go away."

A short time later while dining on salmon and fillet mignon, Evelyn explains her own past.

"I was a bit of a rebel ten years ago myself. My attitude towards anybody who didn't like me was, '*Fuck them.* They don't know me.' I had gotten into the whole punk scene. I was tossed into boarding school at an early age. When I got out, I went *crazy.* Someone found me singing at a club in London in '66. A friend of mine put me up to it as a dare. I discovered I liked it and eventually saw a growing paycheck for what I loved doing and ...that was it." Evelyn raises her brows. "I hung out at places like the CBGB here in New York, or The Whiskey and Roxy when I was in Los Angeles about eleven years ago. I didn't grow out of it until seven years ago. I'd like to go back but not with the same attitude I had when I was in my early thirties. The track Bobby helped me with, it was about what I went through in the mid '70s. He told me it was something his wife went through."

Jaime answers deeply. "Andi." Nodding back, he informs her. "Yeah. Decadent dangers and Andi. A nearly toxic combination." He closes his eyes in anguish for a moment. "Not a favorite time." He thinks for a moment. "I have to make a confession. One I'm not proud of. Have you ever made a mistake you nearly jeopardized your friendship for?"

Evelyn answers carefully. "I've made a lot of mistakes."

"I have one. Just one that embarrasses me when I think of it." He sits back in the chair and says deeply, "Jesus. Andi." Smiling at the thought, he says to her, "Andi is a dear friend of mine. I've known her for fourteen years. Her and I have this...*thing*. A lot of laughs and a lot of teasing. I had a lot of those decadent days. So did Andi. I don't know what it was, but we almost took our friendship to the peak of danger. One thing led to another and I took it a step further. I made a pass at her. The wife of my best friend and production partner. God. What was I thinking?" He says in astonishment. "We started to get hot and heavy and she stopped. I mean, she stopped *everything*. Got help. Took stock of her life. It was an incredible turn-around for her. I had a real hard time dealing with what happened... What *almost* happened. It took a little while for me to talk with her again. I tried to hide it from Bobby the best I could. I don't know if he ever knew."

Catching a bite of salmon on his fork, Jaime rests his gaze on Evelyn while changing the subject. "Let me ask you something. Are you content with this album?"

While he chews, she says back, "Why yes! Of course I am."

"Good. I just wanted to make sure."

"No. I truly love it."

They both smile at each other.

After dinner, the two return to the studio. Jaime unlocks the front door and turns on the dim light at the entrance. Evelyn walks in right behind him. As soon as he locks the door again, she seizes him against it. Under the low light, Jaime's brown eyes darken.

She asks, "How does one top a reprise?"

Jaime grins back before answering. "I don't know. Wouldn't hurt to find out."

Evelyn grabs the front of Jaime's white shirt under the jacket, giving it a pull. He's forced to lean toward her. Her mouth meets his for a soft, sweet, succulent kiss. Her fingers fumble with the top button of his shirt. She pops it open. Evelyn quickly goes for the second. Again, she kisses. Next, she wanted his jacket off. Her knee gets caught between the legs of his black dress pants. She presses her body against his. Forgetting about the jacket, she grabs at his hair, forcing him to lean over again for another kiss. He begins kissing her neck. Evelyn's hand travels up under his shirt. He stops, with the feel of her hand on his chest. Her leaving the next day weighs heavy on the producer's mind. It would be so easy for him to give her a third great night, but also the same fear she had their second night of passion. That would certainly break any spell of intimacy, the thought of losing her.

He backs away, pulling her hand out of his shirt. "This isn't right." In a deeper voice, he tells her, "I should let you get ready to go back…home."

Evelyn looks up into his eyes. "I can't talk you into dessert?" Rather than looking at her, his head is bowed down. Quietly she says, "You're right. I do have some packing to do tomorrow." He looks back at her with no words. Evelyn notices the look in his eyes. He may have said, no, but his body language proved different. "You sure you don't…" She stops herself. "Well, it's for the better. I'll bid you adieu and get some sleep." Approaching the stairs, she says, "If you change your mind, you know where I'll be." She ascends the steps.

Jaime's eyes meet the floor. As soon as he hears the door close, he looks up at the stairs. He shuts his eyes in anguish, knowing full well the torture in turning her down.

Evelyn was a tough refusal.

He comforts himself by pulling out a cigarette from his jacket pocket. Without lighting it, he leaves it dangling from between his lips. Walking up the stairs, he untucks his shirt. Tonight looked to be another night of listening to either Willie Dixon, B.B. King, Muddy Waters, or anyone who did the blues justice. He looks down at the sliver of light at the bottom of the guest room door. Pulling out a matchbook, he strikes a match. Staring directly at the door, the flame flickers between his fingers. Just before he can light the end of his Marlboro, he lets out a deep groan. "Aah." Shaking the match out, he removes the unlit cigarette from between his lips preferring to toss it back in his pocket. Eyeing down, he knocks lightly.

The door opens. His eyes meet hers.

Evelyn announces happily, "Ah! Dessert."

He steps in the room and closes the door behind him.

In the wee hours, a fully dressed Evelyn sits up on the bed. The intrusive feeling in her stomach returned. She touches it, unsure of the sensation. Looking over, she sees an equally dressed Jaime, asleep on his side. A smile crosses her lips while watching him. Evelyn gets up, careful not to wake the producer. She goes inside the bathroom and turns on the light. Again, she touches her stomach, hoping it will go away. The thoughts of her return to England invade her mind. Would she tell Ed right away she was finished with him? Would they have another argument? Would he make her feel guilty as he had so many other times, holding her past as his hostage?

Evelyn shuts the bathroom light off. Walking by the black leather chair, she looks at Jaime's jacket tossed on it. She picks up the garment, hugging it. The thoughts of only a few hours previous flood her memories.

Of how he had stepped into the guestroom and waited for her signal of wanting him. He tried to seduce her. His words were, "I couldn't pass up dessert."

She smiled back, unsure of what to reply. "I don't know."

Jaime thought she was playing hard to get. He was running very hot for her. The producer gently put a hand to her arm and answered her in a husky near-whisper. "All you have to do is say, 'Jaime, I want you too.'"

Evelyn could feel his breath close to her mouth. His hand had driven hers between his legs. He gave her one mouth-crushing kiss that made her fingers stretch in mid air. Immediately, her hand grabbed for his collar, moving down to undo the third button of his shirt.

Then came the one word from her.

"Yes."

That's all he needed.

Evelyn gave in to the feeling of his kisses. His hand slid over her right breast while kissing against her throat. She winced. A sharp stomach cramp jolted her body. Evelyn wanted him in the worst way, but there was a battle of tug-of-war raging deep inside. Every touch tantalized her senses.

She said breathlessly, "Take me now."

As he had managed to undo one button of her blouse, the interruption of tightness seized her. Her fingers hooked onto the fourth button of his shirt. He started kissing the open portion of her blouse. Both were breathing heavy. He leaned further against her. She put her head back, welcoming his wanton desires. There was another flurry of kisses to both sides of her neck. Again, he kissed her hard, his hands more demanding against the buttons of her shirt. She cringed, fighting the feeling that had interrupted her only moments earlier.

"I…I can't."

He caressed her back, his mouth against the contour of her jawline.

Evelyn moved in an awkward manner, wanting him, yet battling the cramps.

"Stop."

She pushed away from him. He was taken aback by her refusal.

Catching her breath, she said, "I just can't. It's not that I don't want to. It's me. I…" She was unable to say anymore. Dry of excuses. Looking into his eyes, she could see it was a big disappointment.

He turned away with his head bowed down. She let out a slight groan of pain that alerted him. Disappointment had given way to concern. Quietly he asked, "You okay?"

She nodded back, "Mm hmm."

Clearly though, her tightened expression told him differently.

He pushed away her hair. "Want me to stay?"

She gave a whimper.

Jaime gave her a warm embrace.

Evelyn stares at her sleeping companion, thinking of a ruined evening of passion.

Pesky cramps!

Oh, but he looked so beautiful, sleeping on his side.

Evelyn returns to the bed, where she lies next to him. He slowly opens his eyes to see her snuggle up. Jaime cuddles up to her, until he falls asleep once again.

Daybreak arrives.

Jaime shuts his eyes tight to the feel of sunlight. Rubbing his heavy lids, he leans up with one arm. On the side he was sleeping on, the dark hair drapes over, partly obscuring his forehead and right brow. He pushes it back. Looking at the empty side where she was, he then realizes today is the day before she would go back home.

Evelyn walks into one of the rooms and picks up her demo tapes among the clutter, she had first arrived with. She figures she'll pick up the master copy later on. She would finish packing then pick it up as one of the last items with full reassurance from Jaime.

Twenty-six hours left and she would be boarding a plane headed for London. Home. There remained a certainty she was proud of the work she had done for the latest project. I.C.E. fulfilled her needs where other studios couldn't. Going home seemed to be the worst of her problems. Would she tell Ed about her affair with the producer? How was one to explain after seven years, they wanted out of their relationship? Then it occurs to her that Ed might try to dissuade her from leaving. Oh, why couldn't he just go out and cheat on her instead! Whatever way, Evelyn was feeling wide open to vulnerability. A move back to New York. It would be a huge step to independence. Then again, Ed provided security. Jaime provided uncertainty. As far as she knew, it could have just been lust or loneliness for the both of them. They understood each other. She had her past in common with the producer; unlike Ed. Would Jaime want her in the long run though? If not, then where would she go? Jaime would probably repeat his romance with another singer, although, she couldn't quite convince herself of that. She smirks to herself as the tapes tumble into her bag.

Jaime was still in her bed as she was downstairs.

As she walks out of the room, there comes the sound of a door closing upstairs. Gathering her items in the bag, she's about to bring them out to her car.

Before placing a hand on the doorknob, his voice calls out. "Evy!"

Turning around at the sound of a flurry of footsteps, Evelyn sees the fully dressed producer rush towards her. She stops where she stands. Once he reaches the first level, he pulls out an item from his pocket.

He says, "I need to give you something before you leave." With his sleeves rolled up, his shirt is partly unbuttoned, and jacket undone from last night. He looks down at the tape and hands it to her. "It's the master analog we did for the sessions. You don't want to forget about that."

His eyes warm to a gaze on her. The flatness of his lips turns up a smile as he bows his head. Her finger reaches under his chin so he'll look right at her.

In her warmest, deep voice she says, "You're so sweet."

Her face rounds out brilliantly around her big smile. Evelyn lets out a cigarette stained laugh. Placing a hand warmly to his cheek she says, "You have been wonderful...in *every* way. This project was more than what I ever hoped for."

Jaime keeps his gaze on her. He mentions back with a slight chuckle, "You know it's going to be unusually quiet upstairs."

In a deep tone she says, "I know, but once I get things settled back in England, I'll be back. You'll see."

Evelyn reaches, giving him a kiss to the mouth. He cinches his arms around her back giving her a warm hug. She pulls away knowing she shouldn't show too much emotion. Looking him over again, the singer studies the producer's features knowing she may not see him again after the next day.

His hair remains a little messy. Evelyn can't figure if that was from her own fingers in the heat of passion, the previous evening, or simply from him sleeping on that side. In either case, he looked charming with it. Of course, she could never forget those dark eyes under a seductive shade of low lids. Then there was that body of his, slender grace. She takes another step back. Her insides are left feeling squishy again. He gave her the feeling of a teenager with a big crush.

"Well, I'll be packing and getting a few things for my trip home."

Jaime continues to watch her.

She says, "Okay?"

He nods then walks away.

Silently she mouths the words. "I love you."

Jaime walks into the control room, flicking a match to an unlit cigarette. His eyes move up, when he sees a tape sitting on the back countertop. He grabs it and places the item in the tape deck.

Turning the light on in the main studio, he looks directly at the keyboard in back. Evelyn's voice echoes with a heavy rhythm section from the speakers. Going back to the control room, he turns on all of the equipment just like he did the other million times. This time though, he doesn't have Bobby or Dan breathing down his back. It's just him and her voice.

Over the duration of the day, Evelyn prepares for home. Two suitcases are being filled fast. She drives to the pharmacy in town to pick up some extra items. Every once in a while that strange feeling bothers her. Only, she's not about to let it stand in her way of a six-hour flight back to London. Back to Ed. Feeling hungry on and off, Evelyn eats Chinese food, indulges in chocolate ice cream, and two lattés.

The lampposts begin to light up as the sun goes down. Evelyn gets into her rented Camry. She eyes the bag with the tapes, lights up a cigarette and puts in the master copy of her latest project. There she cranks it up. Now that sounds like music to her ears.

"Yes!" She smiles hugely to herself and laughs hoarsely.

Nine songs of pure greatness. The production was virtually flawless. Jaime Weston, Robert Whitfield, and Daniel Soren's magic touch worked wonders. It was closer to her rebellious voice styling to the projects of yore than her recent plunge into jazz. Evelyn was peeling away the musical repression she had placed on herself. Although punk was beginning to look like a joke saturated within a sense of commercialism, she still missed the possibilities of a return to glory years. She smiles to herself at the thought of everything that had gone on at I.C.E. While pulling into the unfinished driveway, she notices the black BMW is gone. Ejecting the tape, she thinks for a moment, tossing it in her bag. She was almost certain there were supposed to be ten tracks, not nine. Perhaps one didn't make it.

Evelyn steps out of the car.

Once she returns to her room, Evelyn packs her belongings and places a plane ticket on the table next to the bed. Since having dinner with the producer, Evelyn was feeling different. Those weird cramps and odd sensations had interrupted her in the heat of passion. It couldn't have been the wine, which made her feel that way. Her insides were acting up. Could it be her normal menstrual cycle? Was it going on the fritz? Was it the dreaded menopause? Was it due to the fact she had switched brands of cigarettes quickly, from Camel to Marlboro? She never remembered feeling the way she did now. It was as if her body had shut down for a moment then a power surge from deep within was awakening. What could it be? Being forty would have its burdens on the body but the strange sensation surprisingly had a calming effect on her. No need for aspirin.

Shaking her head at the thought, Evelyn walks inside the bathroom. Turning on the light switch, she examines her face in the mirror. There seemed to be no problems visually. She turns on the faucet and digs her hands in the rushing column of clear water. Placing her dripping hands over her face helps relieve some of the unusual warmness she had been experiencing. Evelyn grabs a cup by the sink and fills it with cold water. Taking a good long sip, she puts her head up letting the coolness overtake her system and get rid of that nagging feeling inside.

She goes back to the bed and looks at the small digital clock. It reads 9:47 PM. Without calculating the time, Evelyn picks up the phone receiver. Cradling it between her ear and shoulder, she punches in the dials quickly. The short blurting sound of the ringing begins.

After three times, she quietly says, "Come on. Come on."

Then the sound stops and somebody picks up.

"Millie? I'm sorry to wake you up. Yes. I'm at the studio... No. I'm feeling a little strange. I felt an odd cramping. Do you think it's menopause? It's...it's as if there's a buzzing sensation running around in my body. I don't know? I'm also quite sensitive in the chest. Maybe it's the start of a cold or something? Would you know? Well, I'll see how I feel tomorrow. I'm due to take the eleven forty flight and give it one last shot with Ed. I know. I know. Only, if this keeps up, I'll be staying here a little longer. Okay. I'll let you sleep. Goodnight, dear."

Evelyn puts the phone back down.

At the other end, Mildred sits up in bed as she slowly puts the phone back on the hook.

Phil pulls his face to the pillow. In his soft nasally tone he asks, "Who was that at this God forsaken hour?"

"Evelyn."

"What did she want?"

"She told me she was feeling odd sensations. Abnormal. The way she described it to me..." She thinks for a moment. Her husband tries to tuck himself under the blanket more. Mildred sits awake in the darkness pondering. "Phil? I didn't feel normal one time and it was similar. It was before I knew I was going to have Harris."

Sleepily, Phil pulls his face from the pillow and replies back. "It's impossible for *that*, so it must be a cold. She should check it out if it persists."

With that, he ends the conversation plopping his head back on the pillow.

Mildred remains awake, thinking.

Back in New Paltz, under the watchful glow of the moon Evelyn is asleep in bed. She thinks about one of her unpleasant talks with Ed. The time she had to follow him back into the kitchen enters her thoughts.

She had opened the swinging door in a huff.

"What's so bad about getting help or counseling about our problems? Other couples go through with it."

Ed reeled after taking a sip of soda. In a disturbed tone he said, "The difference is it's in *your* head. You don't *want* to do anything about it."

"We have problems. Being in bed with you is no picnic."

Ed looked at Evelyn with confusion. "*We?* I have no problem with my performance abilities. Maybe I just don't fit your style." Looking at her sternly, he could see he had hurt her feelings as her lips quivered. She took a deep swallow. Ed nodded slowly and reached to touch her hair. He said sheepishly, "I'm sorry. I didn't mean it that way." He put his arm over her shoulder and she recoiled from his touch, knowing that he wanted to kiss her.

In a quick breath she said, "Don't!"

From Ed's touch, Evelyn's thoughts skip to when she met the charismatic and charming Jaime Weston. Then she immediately thinks of the joy she had on the completion of the title track, "Hero's Requiem." She knew she had fallen hard for the head producer. Her thoughts turn to their first night together. She felt her head being tossed back in the throws of passion. He ran his long fingers through her hair, and then dropped one hand to reach for her side underneath an arm. He leaned up against her breathing gently into her hair.

Quickly, her thoughts run back to Ed yelling at her. Then it was back to Jaime and their walk to the restaurant only hours ago where she was holding his arm. Again, she thinks of Ed and how they once used to be close, laughing as they rode bicycles through the park with Big Ben in plain sight chiming in.

Then she digs deeper into her mind from a decade back. She was wandering around Cosgrove Gallery. Her latest boyfriend had dropped her off someplace in Greenwich Village while he went off to score his latest hit of heroin. As she walked around at the gallery, Evelyn's eyes caught sight of a man looking to be in his mid-thirties, dressed captivatingly in a slender leather jacket, rust brown shirt unbuttoned halfway and a long garnet colored scarf draped over his somewhat skinny shoulders. He was tall and strikingly handsome. His dark brown hair was shoulder length. She figured it wouldn't be any harm to approach him. Then a pretty auburn haired lady went to chat with him. That was the way she first saw Jaime Weston.

Like switching television stations with a remote control, she flips back to when she first met Ed Brockton.

It was October of 1979. The handsome husky blond was stooping down, trying to talk with her as she sit crumpled on the floor after a heroin fix. He asked her, "Why do you want to do this to yourself?"

Her eyes rolled his way, she could barely speak. Evelyn could tell the stranger felt sorry for her and wanted to see her get better.

A middle aged man in a suit walked into the room. "I want to tell you Winthrop, this was the last straw. As your manager, I quit. I don't work for garbage."

Ed stood up quickly, staring the man in the eyes and growled out, "How would you like it if somebody slapped you awake?"

"You be her babysitter. I'm done. Her funeral won't be on my hands." The man said, looking down at Evelyn before leaving the room.

Ed looked down at her out of pity.

Again, she flips back to Jaime and how he cuddled next to her the previous night out of concern for her. Something Ed would never do.

The flipping goes on from Ed to Jaime in second's time and continues again. They were so much the opposite, yet she cared for both of them in different ways. Like black and white or day and night, the two personalities had a hold on her. The feeling inside her never did go away. The sensation zips through her whole body. For a second there is a flash of darkness, then Ed's face comes in close range and yells.

"BOO!"

Evelyn catapults into a seated position from sleeping. Her eyes open wide as she gasps. Her right hand clutches her stomach while letting out an unsteady breath. Exhaling deeply, Evelyn covers her face with her hands then flops back down on the bed.

In the morning hours, Evelyn packs in her suitcase and pulls out her airline ticket waving it in front of her face. Something was wrong. She walks over to the mirror and feels hot and flushed. "I can't be sick. Not now." She dials the phone out of frustration. "Hello, Henry? I'm going to have to postpone my flight I think."

"Oh? Why is that?"

"I think I've come down with something."

"In the summer?"

"Um, yeah. It's taken me by surprise as well."

"What is it, a headache?"

"No. More like something I ate. I had some Chinese food last night, so that could be it. Although, I felt it as early as the night before."

"Want me to bring some chicken noodle soup over?"

"Heavens no! I can't even look at food! Do you know the closest doctor's office?"

"Yeah, there's one a little a ways from where you are."

"Okay. Do you have an address?"

"Sure."

She picks out a piece of paper and writes it down. "Okay. I've got it."

"Now, just make sure you take care of yourself. I'm sure he'll give you some medicine to calm your stomach down. That way you might still be able to catch your flight."

"I will take care of myself, Henry. You *are* a lifesaver. Bye."

She hangs up the phone, puts out her cigarette and makes her way out the door.

Once she arrives downstairs, she turns around to see Jaime leaning against the doorframe while lighting a Marlboro.

He says, "Leaving?"

"Um, no. Not yet. I have a few things I have to do."

"You know you won't be back."

"I will."

He nods then disappears into the room. She looks back. So badly, she wanted to stay but then what would she say to Ed? Evelyn closes the door as she walks over to the car.

At the doctor's office, Dr. Ruizel, an older gentleman with graying hair and spectacles, checks up Evelyn.

"So, Ms. Winthrop, what seems to be the case, since you seem to be in a hurry?"

"You see, I'm suppose to fly back tonight to England, but I wasn't feeling too well. I think I ate something."

"Have you eaten anything since then?"

"Oh, I can't bare to touch food. It just doesn't agree with me."

He touches her stomach.

"Tell me, ma'am. What are you feeling?"

"Cramps. Lots of little cramps. Oh, and a buzzing sensation. I've never felt it before. I did feel it last night though. I couldn't be sure if it was the wine I drank or the food. Food poisoning? I know that feeling. It happened in Montreaux. This time though...it's just different. It's at the very pit of my stomach. I feel like clock work. The gears are stuck. Perhaps early menopause?" She shrugs.

"Uh-huh. Okay, I'll run a couple of simple tests."

"Doctor? You think there's anything to be worried about?"

"No." Dr. Ruizel smiles slightly.

In the course of an hour, Evelyn has gone through three small tests. She quickly changes from a blue smock, back to her normal attire. Evelyn looks in a small compact mirror that she pulls out of her purse to apply lip gloss to. The doctor comes back. He holds a folder in his hand.

"I have your test results. They were very simple. All that was needed was one. You're not quite sick. Frankly, it's normal in your condition. You see, Ms. Winthrop, I understood completely what you were talking about as this is a common thing other ladies have experienced."

He hands her the beige folder. She finishes putting on her jacket and opens the item. Immediately her jaw practically drops.

"This is a joke, isn't it? A wretched joke." She says in an exasperated tone.

"No. It definitely wasn't something you ate, but it's in your stomach. I'm guessing this was unplanned."

Evelyn is in shock. She covers her mouth containing a very wide smile.

"Oh my God! I...I didn't think that... I mean, I was told that I couldn't..."

"Well then, either it's a miracle or somebody's been playing you for a fool."

Later on, she goes to a small cafe to meet up with Henry. She puts down her pocketbook and takes a seat across from him.

"You'll never believe this." She wears a huge grin on her face.

"What? You won the lottery? That will help your financial losses from the previous studios."

"No silly. It's better than that."

"I take it that you're feeling better and you can still hop on that flight."

"Yes. Very much, but no. I won't be going home yet." Evelyn says cheerfully."

"Did the doctor give you something to calm your stomach?"

"No. I didn't need anything."

He lights up a cigar.

"What then? Why won't you go back? Did you break up with Ed?"

"No. I'm really shocked about this...but..."

Henry takes a sip of coffee.

"Well, I won't be needing these for some time." She says as she tosses out a pack of cigarettes from her pocketbook.

Henry looks around with shock. "Wow! A complete turn around. No smoking for Evelyn Winthrop. Want me to announce it to the world?"

Again, Henry takes a sip then chuckles with a nod.

She says, "I'm pregnant."

Henry sputters out his coffee in a sudden choked spray. "*What the*...? You're joking, right?"

Evelyn remains still. She pushes the hair from blowing in her eyes.

"Oh boy, the shit is about to hit the fan. Ed?"

"I can't go back now."

Henry asks, "Does *he* know? Jaime, I'm assuming?"

"No. I won't tell him either."

"What? You won't tell him that you're carrying his kid. Evelyn, what has gotten into you?"

"I don't want to put him in a corner."

"So, you're not going to tell either Ed or Jaime? That's really considerate of you." Henry shakes his head. "Evelyn. Evelyn. Evelyn. Dear child. You're going to have some big problems. Someone's gonna find out, and it ain't through me."

She leans forward to talk softer to him. "I didn't even *think* I could have children. I gave up on the idea. Over and over again…three times I was told I couldn't, but look at me now."

"So, what are you going to do if that baby looks a lot more like Daddy?"

"I don't know. It shouldn't be *that* bad."

"I must be more nervous for you than you are for yourself. Or really of what Ed is gonna think about this. You *will* eventually go back to England sometime in your life, won't you? You can't hide from him."

"Yes. After the baby is born. I can't go back until I have this child. But I don't know where to go? I can't stay here. Do you know of a decent livable hotel? I'll even take one in the city."

Henry bites his bottom lip. "Nine months, huh?"

"About eight."

"Oh, well that makes a big difference," Henry answers in sarcasm. "One of my old girlfriends has a place in SoHo. Carol Mulligan is her name. She asked me a little while ago if I knew of anybody looking to have a roommate in the city. I'll give her a call as soon as I get back home and see if the invitation is still open."

"What if Ed tries to call you? You know he might. I'm sure he can find your number somewhere in the house." She asks partly worried.

"I'll tell him that you went off somewhere else and had more sessions elsewhere."

Evelyn relaxes her body from being tense. "Oh, thank you Henry! I honestly don't know what I'd do without you."

Henry looks down for a moment. "Well, thank me if Ed lets you live when you get back."

Later on, she arrives back at the studio. She sees his dark brown eyes within the shadows. Jaime makes eye contact with her. Then she trots up the stairs. He studies her while she makes her way up. He nods to himself and returns to the control room.

Suddenly, Jaime hears a thudding noise. He checks to see. Realizing Evelyn lugs her suitcases down the stairs, he's quick to help her.

They walk over to the maroon Camry. With the cigarette dangling out of his mouth, he places the piece of luggage down. Taking the Marlboro out, Jaime puts the suitcases in the trunk. Pulling an item out of his shirt pocket, he drops it in the suitcase. Evelyn tosses her pocketbook onto the passenger's side seat, closing the door.

Once they're done, she looks at him. It was the perfect time to tell Jaime she was going to have his child. There were different ways in which she could say it. How Evelyn would explain this happened though would be a whole story open to speculation. She remembered telling him, Dan, and Bobby that she couldn't have children at all. If she were to say anything, would he become suspicious and think differently of her? As though she had full intentions of getting pregnant and her sad little story was just a sham? But what would happen if she were to tell him right then and there? Would it be the end for her and Ed? Would she simply break it off with him and hope to have a life with the record producer she barely knew? What if he didn't want it? Then she would be completely lost and alone, burning her bridges with Ed without knowing how he might feel in helping to raise a baby. Tying Jaime down with something that wasn't planned gave her the feeling of entrapment. He wasn't ready to be a parent. Jaime was wild and free. Why should she be the one to saddle him with such a huge responsibility? Then she thinks some more.

The words flow to the speed of her thoughts.

"Jaime."

His glance stays focused on her.

"I just wanted to thank you again...truly for everything. You don't have to fear. I *will* be back as soon as I can. You'll see."

She stands on her tiptoes to give the six-foot producer a kiss. His lids flutter closed. He takes in the feel of her soft plump lips one more time. When he opens his eyes, she's already getting inside the car. She turns on the ignition, breaking into a smile.

"Goodbye, luv."

He throws her a kiss.

Evelyn backs out until she's able to make a K-turn then drives off among the dirt and loose gravel. He watches until the Camry disappears among the large spruce trees.

Gone.

Jaime and his BMW are the only things remaining in the long stretch of driveway to I.C.E. Studios.

Chapter 6

There is the lengthy drive from New Paltz down to Long Island to drop off the rented Camry at Hertz. Henry trails behind in his Mazda. The plan was for Evelyn to bring back the rental. Then she would join Henry in his car for the trek to SoHo for her temporary stay with Carol Mulligan.

As they head off on the Van Wyck Parkway, Henry asks Evelyn. "Has anything changed since earlier?"

"You mean, have I told Jaime? No."

Henry checks the rearview mirror as he switches lanes.

"He's going to find out. This won't be something you'll be able to hide for long."

"Like I told you earlier. I'm hoping this child looks like me."

"Blonde hair, blue eyes so you can pass the kid off as Ed's."

"Would that be so wrong to wish for that?"

"No. But be extra prepared in case the opposite happens."

"Well, the Winthrop family tree has always veered to that side; blonde hair and blue eyes. My father did. So did my grandfather and his mother."

"That's nice you have everything figured out. But what if he has stronger genetics?"

Evelyn settles back in the seat uneasily. "I never thought of that."

"Do you have a preference? Boy or girl?"

"Oh, I don't know. Ed would probably love to have a little boy around."

"As if you have a choice." Henry mumbles back. "Ed as a parent. That'll be the day." He turns to her, secretly wishing she would just tell Jaime. The thought of Edward Brockton as any kid's father makes his skin crawl. "So, besides Ed being the other guy in your life, is there any other reason why you don't want to tell Jaime?"

"It's not right for me to place such a responsibility on his shoulders when I full well know this is something I wanted. This isn't a case of me saying, 'You planted it. You pay for it.' I don't want to do that. He knows... At the time he *knew* I couldn't. I mean...I thought I couldn't have children."

"Exactly how many people have you told about your supposed infertility? Does it just come up in conversation? 'Pass the potatoes. I can't have children.' Or was it one of those intimate moments that you said it? Not that it's any of my business. I'm just trying to understand."

Evelyn responds cautiously. "I don't bring it up casually, darling. I only reveal it if somebody brings up the subject of children. Bobby and Dan brought it up one evening. Jaime was there with us. So he knew when they found out."

"Oh. I see."

"I had plans before finding out. I had thoughts of going out touring with this album. Calling my dearest friends, the Bellamy sisters and getting the band back together. I was going to settle things with Ed, once and for all. Then I would come back and hopefully start a new life here, in New York. Now everything has changed. I don't know what's next for me besides motherhood."

Evelyn brushes a hand through her hair. She looks off to the side. A green box is sticking out. She pulls at it. Her grim outlook is changed to joy when she discovers what the box contains.

"Oh! Club Crackers! How delightful!"

"I see your appetite has returned. Yeah. Evan snacks on them when we go out on road trips. You'll find a can in back. Sort of like an aerosol can. The kind you're not supposed to puncture."

Evelyn reaches in back. She finds an item. "Like a spray can? This one?" The singer produces a small can of processed cheese.

Henry looks back. "Yep. This one you can shake vigorously. Then squeeze it on."

"Fascinating!" Evelyn begins munching away. With a full mouth she says, "Vermy goo!"

"Evan calls it Space Cheese."

"Hmm?" She giggles back.

"He thinks of it like what astronauts eat in space. He saw a TV show where they eat foods out of tubes and stuff. Can't eat a big piece of steak 'cause it'll float around."

Evelyn laughs out loud.

He giggles back. "I'm serious!"

Looking out the passenger's side window she remarks to her friend. "So, tell me about Carol."

"Oh well. Um. Carol is a bit eccentric. I knew her before you. I was seeing her when she was an art student at Parsons. She was only about twenty at the time. It turned out she was more independent minded than what I ever imagined. At my age I thought of settling down with someone but that someone wasn't her. You might hear some folks call her *Pug*."

"Pug? Why on earth a name like that?"

"She actually likes it. She's told me before it differentiates her from other people. I think it's cruel but that's just me. It's a name she picked up before I even knew her. It's used because of her looks. She thinks she looks like a pug dog, others do too. I don't call her that. Some people I know don't call her that. She's just Carol to us."

They soon find themselves among a sea of yellow cabs. Henry pulls out from the traffic, zigzagging through various streets. Once they reach SoHo, Henry looks around.

"Damn! All of these lofts look the same. Tell me if you see one that looks artsy."

"Aren't they all?"

Henry sees one with what looks like a window mural.

"There we go. As you might be able to tell, I haven't been here in a little while."

He pulls up to the side of the street. Henry takes out Evelyn's two large suitcases. Each roll one into the building. They wait for the elevator nearby. Four names are labeled with their respective numbers.

Henry announces. "Mulligan C." The elevator rings and they get in. Now on the second floor, Henry rings the bell.

A woman's voice calls from inside. "Yes? Who is it?"

The door opens. Henry looks at Carol Mulligan. Evelyn walks up from behind.

"Henry!" Carol exclaims.

Now, Evelyn gets a hint as to why Carol is called Pug. Her facial features seem a little out of place. Mostly her nose looks to be a prominent feature, mushed into her face. Not a Barbara Streisand sized one but a nose that is considerably larger than the rest of her features. Dark arched brows loom over her brown eyes, which seem oddly beautiful and captivating. Her smile is tight with full lips. Dark wavy auburn hair hangs loosely framing her face. Carol's body is even a curious factor in her genetic make up. Standing above Evelyn a good six inches taller at 5'10", Carol has the shape of a model, almost waif-like. Her chest is tiny but she has the graceful legs of a deer. After allowing the two guests in, she walks into an open kitchen that resembles a part of the living room. Her stride is bohemian-like. Deliberate with a sense of purpose and the air of confidence.

Evelyn looks around the foreign surroundings. A turquoise colored couch sits in the middle of the loft with a magenta and yellow striped blanket draped over the side. A small bright rust hued pillow rests gently against the right corner. She turns her attention to a shelf with odd shaped sculptures. Those were just plain weird. Next to the large TV set is a Picasso influenced tapestry.

Carol and Henry talk in the kitchen. Evelyn goes to join them.

Carol turns her way. "So you're the lucky gal who gets to make the most gorgeous creature on the planet a daddy."

Evelyn breaks into a smile quickly.

"Carol Mulligan. Oddball extraordinaire."

The singer follows her lead. "Evelyn Winthrop. Producer of Weston offspring."

Both women laugh gleefully.

Henry looks at the two women, relieved they're getting along and bonding quickly.

Carol giggles back. "You don't have to worry about anything. I keep the refrigerator well stocked."

Henry remarks. "That's always good for an expectant mother."

The sculptress gives him a glance. She then gets serious. "I don't drink. I don't smoke. And I don't have any pets."

Henry asks, "What happened to that little Shih-Tzu?"

"Darla? She um, she went to Doggie Heaven during the spring. Viral infection."

"Sorry to hear that." He solemnly responds.

Carol snorts back. "That's life. I was feeling the effects after she was gone. I didn't think it would hit me that way but it did. So, I kind of wanted company. Less furry this time. Since you said it was temporary I figured I would give it a try."

Henry spots the time on the microwave. "Oh! I gotta go before Karen gets suspicious and begins drilling me for answers. You take care, kiddo. I'll be back to check on you." He says to Evelyn. "And *you...* Be good to her." He looks right at Carol.

"I will." The artist answers defensively.

Henry walks to the door. He jokes to her about something out of Evelyn's hearing range.

She responds quickly. "Kiss my ass, Henry." She smiles at him.

He gives her a small hug. "Bye."

Evelyn watches him leave. She calls out. "Goodbye, darling!"

The door closes.

Carol looks back at her new roommate. "I'll give you a tour of my humble abode very soon."

"That will be lovely." Evelyn says graciously.

"But first..." Carol begins to say just as Evelyn walks out of the kitchen.

The singer goes to sit down on the comfortable turquoise couch. She leans her head back and closes her eyes. When she opens them, she sees Carol striking a pose like she wants to eagerly ask her a question.

Among Carol's pug-like visage is a smile that creeps onto her lips. Without any further adieu, Carol launches into asking her new roommate anything she wishes.

"So?"

Evelyn repeats the remark. "So?"

"I want you to tell me all of the juicy details. How did you manage to land New York's premiere playboy producer?"

Evelyn responds confused. "What?"

"Jaime. I've known him for a little while. He's not around the city very much though. Yeah. Around these parts he's known as Hermit Weston. Yep. This guy is so quiet but..." Carol pauses. "Damn, he is so hot." Carol glances over to the kitchen. "Can I get you anything to drink? Um, coffee, tea, juice, uh, *milk*?" She nods her head and gestures her hand at approximately Evelyn's waist. Then she looks down.

Both women begin to laugh.

"I'll take tea, please." Evelyn giggles back.

"Okay."

Carol gets up from the couch and sifts through the cupboard. "I've got some of the Earl Gray stuff."

"That would be fine."

Carol wanders over to another cupboard and pulls out a pot, then finds a purple and red polka-dotted teakettle. She settles the tea bag into the hot water as she continues talking about Evelyn's liaison with the music producer. "Everybody, I mean all of my girlfriends who have met Jaime are captivated by him and confused at the same time. You know, each one is wondering if he'll find the perfect female companion...in them. It happened with me too. Although, I don't think he's into ugly ducklings who are brash and arrogant like myself." Carol tends to the two teacups in front of her and begins pouring the hot liquid while whatever comes to the top of her head. "Evelyn, do you want sugar or cream?"

"Sugar will do."

Carol continues on with, "Boy, he must have really liked you."

She enters the main room again and hands Evelyn the brightly colored teacup. "Careful, it's hot."

Evelyn looks at the cup peculiarly.

Carol sees this and offers up. "Artist's touch."

"I see."

"Anyway, what I can clearly suspect is, since you're a singer and he's a producer, then there's a lot of common ground. Things got a little heated. He helped you out with your record and…that's all it took."

Evelyn stirs her tea around with a spoon. "I don't know."

"Well, maybe it was just an old-fashioned one-night stand."

Attempting to find the words, Evelyn stops stirring which makes Carol look up from tending to her own cup of tea.

"I can't actually say that."

"What?" Carol's mouth starts to open with a thought crossing her mind, which she then blurts out, "Are you telling me you had seconds? Seriously?" Carol gives Evelyn a glare of wanting the truth. "Missy, you're going to have to tell me the whole truth and nothing but the truth. Now, you know it's just us girls here. Nothing will go further than this. I swear. Girl Scout's honor. Are you telling me this wasn't just once?"

"Well, as it so happens," is Evelyn's straightforward reply.

"Whoa! This changes the whole thing. You're telling me you and Weston... *Twice*?"

"It's hard to think of it that way."

"I mean the both of you. Like, was this two consecutive nights?"

"No. No. Not at all. It was an affair that occurred over time."

"Wait. Henry did say something about your boyfriend. So, you do have somebody already." Carol picks up her cup for a sip. "That must be awkward."

Evelyn goes through her pocketbook and produces a wallet. She hands Carol a small photograph. The artist inspects it.

"This is him?"

"Yes. That's Ed."

Carol grumbles, "I'd have an affair behind his back too. The question I have is, are you happy with him? Because, if you were, you wouldn't have slept with Jaime…twice, or with anyone else for that matter. How has he treated you, Ed that is?"

Evelyn bows her head down, eying the floor with no words.

Carol sheepishly answers with, "Oh, I'm sorry."

"No. No. It's okay." Evelyn gathers herself from falling apart. "He doesn't understand me. I wish he would. It would make things so much easier. We've always had problems. I met him when I was on skid row, undesirable to everyone, including myself. He saved me. He truly did. I know he doesn't get my career in music, but…I owe him."

Carol takes Evelyn's hand while saying, "You don't owe any man shit. If he's not treating you right, I'd tell him to hit the bricks. Nobody deserves to be treated like that."

"Carol, he's done so much for me. I probably would be dead had it not been for his intervention and caring."

"Caring? No, hon. That is mind control."

Evelyn says, "I admit, he did trade in my car."

"What kind was it?

"A '67 Aston Martin GT."

"For what instead?"

"An '80 Austin Maxi."

"I don't know what that is."

"It's a wretched looking little car. I can't forget how he hated my previous music, and tried to get rid of my late '70s collection of T-shirts."

Carol covers her face and shakes her head in disgust. "Let's change the subject. This Ed guy is making me sick." She licks her lips. "Um, so, like how did it happen the second time around?"

"I can't believe I'm telling you all of this."

"Don't worry, I can keep my big lips shut, honey. I'm just overly fascinated by this thing you have going on with the most complex music producer residing in all of New York."

Carol takes small sips of her tea while Evelyn explains further.

"The most interesting thing about all of this is, I remembered seeing him somewhere. I made the connection with an art gallery."

"Yeah. He'd hang around a few of them. I think Connigan? No. That's in Brooklyn. One that's close by. Cosgrove.

Evelyn points to Carol. "Yes. Exactly. Ten years ago I was there, and he was too. Even in a drug induced haze, I remembered him." She places the photo of Ed back in her wallet, tossing it back in her pocketbook. "Anyway, my second night. It was very hot out. I'm not completely sure if he was half awake but I will say, he looked quite fetching. I couldn't figure out since his shirt was undone if I had disturbed him in any way."

Carol's eyes widen as she chokes back a sip and lets her jaw hang on its hinges. "What??? You... He was dressed like that? Oh, you lucky, *lucky* woman you!" Carol grips her cup tightly as she listens some more.

Evelyn says, "It was just something in the air."

Carol leans in a little closer on the couch gripping her teacup like a small child would while listening to a good campfire story.

Curiosity sets in for the avant-garde artist. "He's what, about six feet?"

"Yes." Evelyn gives a smirk. "And he's gorgeous from head to toe."

She finishes off her tea then walks into the adjoining kitchen, leaving Carol with her jaw dropped.

***

A week later, while biting her bottom lip, Evelyn sits on the bed staring at the bright blue phone on the lime green end table. She contemplates making that one phone call. For now she would have to make up the perfect excuse. Would it convince Ed though? She dials the phone, holding her breath.

He answers. "Hello?"

"Hello, Ed." The singer says confidently.

"Honey!" Ed responds with excitement. "What...what happened? Somethin' wrong with flight reservations? You were supposed to be back a week ago. I could call and find out."

"That won't be necessary Ed." She says quietly.

Evelyn knew trying to tell Ed that she wasn't coming back for a little while would be difficult to explain.

With a hasty tone Ed says, "Did something happen at the studio?"

She thinks to herself.

Indeed something happened!

"No. No cause for worry."

"What then?"

"It's just that... It's just that I feel I need more time. I thought a lot about us and we need this time to find out what we really mean to each other."

He snuffs back. "Find out? I already know what you mean to me! Unless *you're* not sure. Is that the case? Huh?"

"Now I don't want you to get angry and I didn't call for a shouting match. God only knows how many we've had over the past year."

"Then tell me what in the Sam Hell is going on? Look. I know I haven't been exactly supportive with you lately and the whole kid situation. But we can talk about this when you get back tomorrow. Just hop on a plane and..."

"No! No. No. I know what you're trying to do! You want *me* to come back so we'll argue. I'll have nowhere to turn, so then I'll blame myself for whatever ill feelings I have. I *refuse* to do that again. I won't play the submissive wife or...or girlfriend in this case. This is the only way, Ed. The only way I know we won't go through the same things from the past."

"You want to be stubborn?"

"What I want are things to improve for us!"

"How can we do that with you across the ocean?"

She barks back. "You'll just have to take my word for it. I need this time!" Rolling her eyes, Evelyn changes her tone to tired assurance. "Please... Don't worry about me. I can take care of myself."

"Where are you?"

"I'll call you if and when I want to. You don't trust me."

"How can I? You won't even tell me where you are!"

"For once believe me." She pleads. "I must go now but please trust me. Goodbye, darling. We'll talk again in the near future. Kissy. Kissy."

Ed grumbles back. "Yeah. Yeah. Love you too."

She hangs up the phone.

Ed walks out of the kitchen. He grabs a magazine from the coffee table and throws it against the couch.

"Damn it!"

He plops down beside it as the pages drape over into a heap.

***

"I called that obstetrician you told me about." Evelyn calls out to Carol from the stairs. "I have an appointment in about an hour. You said it's on 8th St.?

"325. 8th."

"Okay. How did you know about this doctor? You didn't finish telling me after the phone rang."

"I know plenty of people who have gone to Dr. Soto. Nobody has complained about him yet. From what I've heard, he's very good with patients."

Evelyn nods. "Well, I'll be getting ready now."

She disappears up the stairs.

An hour later Evelyn is being checked up. Dr. Jose Soto tells her she can get up.

"Let's see. By my estimation, you are nine weeks pregnant. Is this your first child?"

"Yes."

He wheels his swivel chair to the desk, writing notes.

"Doctor? Is it possible that this was a fluke? I was told by three gynecologists I wasn't able to reproduce."

"A fluke? No. You said you missed two periods. That's normal in your condition. You'll be missing seven more."

"I know that. It's just... The others said it wouldn't affect my cycle. It's a form of infertility. Something about my eggs not moving. They sit inside and do nothing."

Dr. Soto raises his black brows. "Ah. I know what you're talking about. That is called F.O.B.S." He cleans his glasses.

"That's not what they called it." Evelyn says with assured confidence.

"Ms. Winthrop, as an obstetrician...trust me. It is F.O.B.S." He looks at her seriously from his black-rimmed glasses. "To bluntly put it, it's called "Full Of Bullshit. There is no reason I can find that you couldn't have a baby. Your temperature is just right. You have a monthly period. I can't find anything physically wrong with you. No sign of cysts or polyps. Ovaries are in fine working order. These so-called other doctors sound like hack jobs. Backseat medics. They make a joke of my profession. I *hate* that. Rest assured. You *can* reproduce, Ms. Winthrop. Are you even aware of how your system works?"

"Kind of."

"Okay. That baby growing inside is caused by your system or cycle. Those two eggs in your ovaries are moving about. You even sometimes may feel uncomfortable by about fourteen days since your last period. That's when the eggs are ready to be fertilized. If not, they simply get absorbed back into your system. They don't do *nothing*. This is probably the most absurd thing I have ever heard. How these doctors stay in business is beyond me. One egg will be fertilized if the time is right and your partner is able. Are you married?"

"No. The previous relationship was a boyfriend. But this was somebody new."

"What can I say other than *he* obviously had no problems. Had your last boyfriend been checked by his doctor?"

"Yes. He said he got a clean bill of health. It was the first time I had been with this new gentleman in my life. Completely unplanned."

"No form of protection or birth control?"

"None. I figured nothing would happen. I told him prior, that I couldn't have children. I guess that is what set the wheels in motion."

"Open invitation."

Evelyn looks down with a sense of guilt.

"I would investigate these three doctors that you were checked up by. Something just doesn't sound right."

After much debating, and a clean bill of health, Evelyn decides to call her friends in England to inform them of her joyous news. She picks up the phone. Waiting for the ring tone, she digs through her secondary suitcase, in search of her trusty notebook.

Mildred answers.

"Hello?"

"Millie, darling!"

"Evelyn! How are you? Phil told me you canceled plans to come back home. What happened? Hopefully nothing horrible. Did you leave Ed?"

Evelyn shakes her head while answering back. "No. It's the opposite. It's grand news. No. I'm not leaving Ed either."

Mildred's tone changes to disappoint. "Oh. I'm sorry to hear that. What is this grand news?"

"As it turns out, all three doctors were wrong."

"I'm sorry dear. I don't follow."

"You remember. How Ed and I wanted children."

"Yes."

"Well, before I was to leave New York, I had a check-up. I called you the night before and asked you…"

"…If I ever had experienced a certain feeling. Yes. I do remember that."

Evelyn says, "I'm expecting."

Mildred pauses on the other end. "You're…"

"Yes, Millie. I'm pregnant!"

Evelyn hears Mildred talking with her husband, uttering the word pregnant to him. Mildred asks her, "How far along are you?"

Thinking for a moment, Evelyn counts the months starting in July, then thinks of June. "Nearly four months."

"Does Ed know?"

"No. He wouldn't even be able to remember that lovely evening we had in June, shortly before I came here."

She then hears Mildred mumble. "I think I'm going to get sick."

"He will find out when I'm ready." Evelyn finds her notebook. She starts rummaging through her suitcase.

Mildred asks her, "Besides this lovely news, how did the recording go?"

"Oh, it went wonderful! I was able to get through the sessions. I came up with nine new songs. And..." She finds a lone tape at the bottom of the suitcase that reads *#5 – C.T.D.* The handwriting looks identical to her master tape's label. Reaching for the portable radio near the closet, she brings it closer to her. "And they sound incredible. Now, I have to send them to the London studio to get ready for a pr..." She puts the tape in and presses play. The first thing she hears is a thudding bass drum like a heartbeat, then the rising sound of a synthesizer, followed by her own deep voiced delivery. Her lips part at the discovery. She rubs her stomach. Dropping the phone, she wipes the tears from her eyes.

He didn't forget the track.

She fails to notice the tiny sound of her friend's questions.

"Evelyn? Evelyn? Are you there?"

***

"Why wouldn't I believe Ed?" Evelyn asks Carol all along as she paces the floor. "He told me there was nothing wrong with him. It was all me. I stopped thinking about it finally after the third doctor told me it was impossible. Possibly, from my drug use days. Then the first time I'm with Jaime, instantly I'm expecting my first child. It makes no sense!" She throws her hands up out of confusion.

Carol sprawls out on the sofa. She yawns, putting her hands behind her head. "He has *it* and Ed doesn't." She turns her head to Evelyn.

"I know that already."

"He definitely has *it*. He's got everything else. The looks. The charm. The talent. Now you've got his next generation, making them *very* lucky. That's all. Very simple. It's the Darwinian Effect. The strong ones live and the weak ones don't. Jaime goes on to reproduce and Ed doesn't."

Evelyn looks at Carol. "I suppose you're right." She sighs.

"You know I'm right. Would you prefer it be the opposite way around? From what you've told me, Ed sounds like a real creep."

The singer feels a bit remorseful for not telling the father-to-be. If only things weren't so complicated. For that matter, it was too bad Ed remained in the picture.

***

Carol and Evelyn watch TV. It's a Friday night in the city that never sleeps. Carol could care less. She has a date with Don Johnson and Philip Michael Thomas. *Miami Vice* is on and it's practically the only thing she ever watches. Evelyn feels the growing sensation of uneasiness in the pit of her stomach. Carol munches on potato chips while the soft glow from the TV set beams on her face. The crunching makes her roommate wince. Finally, the ickiness she was experiencing comes to a boil. She races up the stairs, shutting the bathroom door. Carol turns her head. Then she picks up a potato chip and munches on it.

Evelyn leans back against the tiled wall, sitting on the floor with the lid up on the toilet bowl. Morning sickness had befallen the singer. It was a feeling unlike any other. Like carsickness, getting stuck at every red light. The only difference is, it was ongoing. It could strike her morning, noon, and night. It knew no special hour or particular day. She couldn't take any antacid to remove or settle the feeling. It was there. The seed was growing. At the mercy of the toilet bowl, dictated by something so tiny she erupts into getting sick. Even the smell of clean water in the bowl sends her stomach into overdrive. She sits back against the wall, yanking a stream of toilet paper to her mouth.

Carol runs up the stairs. The sound of heavy coughing is heard. She knocks on the door.

Evelyn coughs back. "What?"

"Are you okay?"

The door opens. Carol looks at her roommate. Evelyn walks back to the far end of the bathroom settling herself across the toilet. She grabs more toilet paper.

Sniffling back with tear stained eyes she expresses. "Maybe there's a reason I never had any. I wasn't meant to. I just don't know if I can handle this." She chokes back while dabbing her eyes with the tissue. "I don't know how I'm ever going to live with this for another six and a half months."

Carol looks at her with a pained expression.

Exhausted and queasy, Evelyn says quietly, "Maybe I shouldn't. That way things could be so much easier for every..."

"Stop it! Do you hear yourself? You will be fine. Just think of what you went through to have it. Better yet, think of who's it is. It was meant to happen to you, and him. You know, not that I have first hand knowledge of this particular subject... You'll be very happy with the results. I can guarantee that. Other friends of mine who have had babies say the same negative stuff, but then they see that little angelic face, those tiny little hands and feet and their worries melt away." Carol sits next to Evelyn, cradling her shoulder. "You'll be perfectly fine. So will that little boy or girl you're carrying."

Across town, a black limousine pulls up to the curb outside of a nightclub called Purple Note on the west side of Central Park. The chauffeur opens the vehicle's door. Jaime Weston steps out followed by a dark haired, leggy beauty in a red dress. A couple of photographers flash their bulbs in their faces. The light bounces off of Jaime's sunglasses. A microphone is placed in front of him. He looks at the small man who put the object in his face.

The reporter asks, "What are you hoping for with Joseph Werner and Werner Records?"

Jaime turns to his female companion briefly. "Hoping for a good time. I have heard he usually puts on great parties and I wouldn't miss one like that for the world."

She smiles back at his response. They walk up the purple carpeted stairs with the grape colored awning above. Looking at the neon purple eighth note in the window, she remarks to the record producer.

"Ah! So, that's why it's called Purple Note."

He responds with a simple, "Mm hmm."

Jaime and his date walk into the club where Werner Records is throwing a gala fete with some of their artists playing live for the executives. President of the company, Joseph Werner and his wife, Joanne laugh with some people dressed in formal wear. One couple looks at Jaime who's not in a tuxedo or bow tie. It didn't matter to them he was attired in a black suit and fully buttoned white shirt over black dress pants. To them, he looked like a wannabe. The dark sunglasses reeked of smugness. Nobody was wearing sunglasses. Surely not in the evening! His female company was viewed as eye candy or something young and attractive to keep other women at bay. They notice there is no hand holding or sweet smile between the two. One man nudges his wife with self-assurance seeing neither Weston nor the lady wearing wedding rings.

Jaime and his guest sit in a booth with another couple.

The live band plays in the background. Nobody bothers to pay any attention to them. Everyone is busy talking amongst themselves or chatting with other executives. Glasses of champagne are passed around to the guests. Jaime turns to look at the live entertainment. Joseph Werner walks up to the table.

"Ah, Jaime Weston!"

Jaime stands up to shake his hand while Werner has his eye on the record producer's lovely date.

"What's your name, sweetheart?"

Jaime removes his sunglasses, opting to sit back down since the record president decided not to shake hands with him.

She introduces herself. "Regina Laughlin. I'm sort of interning as a receptionist at Ianese Records."

Joseph Werner says with enthusiasm, "Oh, Ianese! I've heard lots of good things about them. Ah, but I'm sure we might be able to get you into Werner with a possible pay hike and good benefits if everything works out. If you would like to join me and my wife over there, you're quite welcome."

Jaime looks down at the table.

Regina asks him. "Would you mind?"

He shrugs back. "No. Go right ahead."

She slides towards him. Jaime gets up, letting her through to leave. She says nothing else and doesn't even turn back. He watches her as she schmoozes with the record company president's wife. Jaime sits back down, taking a sip of champagne. He shakes his head. The only thing he can do now is watch the band on stage.

Joseph Werner says with a telling expression. "What can I say?"

Jaime looks up at him partly amused then back at the stage.

Werner asks, "So, you still producing with Bob Whitford?"

Jaime corrects him. "*Whitfield.* Yes I do."

The couple across from him asks. "What studio do you work out of?"

"I.C.E."

The wife says, "Is that around here?"

"No. Upstate."

"Oh. Buffalo or Albany?"

"New Paltz."

Werner adds in his own opinion as if Jaime wanted to hear it. The man only chased away his date for the evening. Then again if she were that star struck, she wasn't worth it. Regina only used him to reach for a higher plateau in the music industry. Joseph says, "You know you can do better. Why not reach for the stars? Here in Manhattan or other big cities like Chicago, Los Angeles, or even Nashville. You don't need to be making music in the woods. Come on Jaime. What do you have recording up there anyway? Skunks? Raccoons? Deer?"

Jaime turns his eyes down with a smirk. "We already tried out the city, which did not work for us. We have plenty of artists where we are. Don't you worry about that."

"Oh *sure*. You bring in old relics like Matt Hattinger and Evelyn Winthrop. Folks with their heyday in the past."

"They are n..."

"Seriously, you need to get with the times. Progressive rock and punk are so '70s. R&B is a surefire hit. Just look at Michael Jackson and Lionel Richie. Even Stevie Wonder. Ladies like Whitney Houston are getting in on the act. Selling like hotcakes. You need to be producing new and fresh talent."

"Hey. Hey. They are not relics. They happen to still be viable names in the industry making good music. These artists that you're putting down are the type of... Their music is what we like. They enjoy experimenting and so do we. I appreciate the gesture but we are not looking to get on any bandwagon just for popularity sake."

Joseph looks at him. He could tell the man was serious about music. Rather than saying more, he walks away. Jaime turns to look at him.

The party was pretty much done with. No date. Treated like a joke. His mistress was deemed a relic. The studio, made fun of. It was enough for him to tuck his tail between his legs, lick his wounds and leave. Not Jaime Weston though. He gets up and the band is done playing their first set. A handful of people clap. The singer removes his guitar strap just as Jaime approaches him.

The record producer begins explaining. "Have you got a record out yet?"

"We're lookin' around at studios."

Jaime pulls out a business card from his jacket pocket, along with a cigarette. Lighting it with a match, he shakes the musician's hand as he introduces himself. "Jaime Weston."

In a later time zone, Ed sits on the edge of the bed. A cigarette dangles from his mouth. He remains fully awake in the early morning hours. So what if he had an assignment later on that day? His priority was wondering about his beloved Evelyn. What was she doing? Why was she there? He starts to think of the many arguments they had before she left. It was all about children and her happiness.

Damn those baby thoughts.

Ed could never fathom himself changing diapers. He knew Evelyn couldn't have children so it should have put his mind at ease.

He goes through Evelyn's top drawer on the left side of the bureau. She kept all of her important letters and receipts in there. Finding an envelope sent by Dr. Brandon Hawthorne, he stares at it. He then closes the drawer and closes his eyes. Ed somehow felt the child issue wasn't done yet.

***

The phone rings at the Winslow residence. Henry picks it up. "Hello?"

Ed breathes back. "Henry. This is Ed Brockton."

"Hello, Edward." Henry tries to conceal that he's not too thrilled to hear from the man.

"*Ed* will do just fine. I'm trying to find out why Evelyn changed her mind about coming home a few weeks ago."

"Well, I don't get involved with friends lives."

"Yeah, right! And I'm the tooth fairy! Listen, Henry, I'm no moron. I know she talks to you. So, why not play it straight? You know and I know something's goin' on with Evelyn."

Henry hears the flicker of a lighter on the other end.

Ed exhales. "She said she needed the time away. This is after she told me recording would only take a month. It's nearly three and a half. So?"

"Ed, I don't know. Why not just believe her? Have you ever thought of letting her do what she wants without you being so suspicious all the time?"

Karen enters the kitchen. She looks at her husband. He exchanges a glance while waiting for Ed's response.

"I wouldn't have to be so suspicious if she were being truthful. We know that New York City ain't exactly the place for truth as it is known for slimy drug dealers, pimps, hookers, crime and every sin." He snickers for a moment. "Really, I just though of a great motto: New York City, the place where sins go to roost." Ed heartily laughs.

Henry asks. "Why would you think Evelyn's in the city?"

"Where else could she be?"

"Gee, Ed, there's a lot more in New York than just Manhattan."

Karen sputters back. "Ed? Gimmie that phone." Henry looks at his wife growing more furious with rage. "I'll tell him a thing or two." She attempts to reach for the phone. "Gimmie that phone."

Henry tells Ed, "Hold on for a second."

He covers the receiver with his hand.

Karen asks. "How did he get our number?"

"I don't know."

"He's asking about Evelyn. Isn't he?"

"Yes."

"Let me talk to him!"

"No. What good will that do? Calling the man every name in the book won't resolve anything. Okay?"

Karen stays quiet, pouting to herself.

Henry returns to his conversation with Ed. "Sorry about that Ed. You know the recording stuff sometimes takes a while to finish up."

Karen says aloud in hopes Ed hears. "Ed is a no class jerk!"

Henry closes his eyes trying to ignore his wife's comments. He continues what he was saying to Ed. "I wouldn't know exactly how *long* but you should know that yourself. It's not like this is the first time she's been away recording."

Again, Karen speaks out of turn and loudly. "I wouldn't be surprised if Evelyn left you!"

Henry rolls his eyes.

"She should have done it sooner!" His wife knowingly keeps talking. If her husband wouldn't let her have the phone then she intended on letting her voice be heard otherwise.

Henry breathes back with frustration into the phone. "Listen Ed. My wife is feeling a little under the weather so she's a bit cranky today. We'll continue this conversation at a later date. Bye."

He places the phone back on the hook.

"What? What? WHAT? *What* did you want? I *know* you don't like the guy. Guess what honey? I don't either! But yelling out, 'You're a jerk!' will only make the guy more infuriated than he already is."

"He has no right in calling us!"

"Yeah, but he got our number and knows that we're friends with his girlfriend."

Karen winces. "That's gross!"

"What? Me calling her his girlfriend? It's the truth, honey."

She puts her hands to her hips. "And what about Jaime?"

"What about him? He shouldn't be a part of this." Henry turns around to not face his wife as he mutters underneath his breath. "But he is now."

Karen emphasizes. "I just wish you would have let me talk to that ogre."

"Ah! See? You're doing it again."

"So where is Evelyn if she's not back in London?"

Henry tries to cover up the knowledge by feigning confusion. "I don't know."

"You do know. I can tell! You're generous with your friends. It's like you have some type of allegiance to them. Come on. How long have you known Evelyn?"

Henry quietly says, "Eleven years."

"Jaime?"

"Nine." He shakes his head. "Karen, you're reading too much into this."

"Is she sick?"

"No."

"Does she have financial problems?"

"No."

Henry begins to feel himself getting more annoyed with each passing question or guess.

She asks again. "Is it Jaime? Does he have somebody else in his life already?"

Her husband rolls his eyes as he begins to walk away from the kitchen. "What does it matter?"

She calls out defiantly. "Henry Charles Winslow don't you walk away from me!"

Both become frustrated towards each other.

"Now, I want to know, dammit!" Karen emphasizes by stomping her foot and folding her arms. "What are you hiding? She's my friend too! I felt just as bad when she couldn't make it to our wedding."

She raises her voice to the point Henry can't take it anymore. He reels around in a fit of anger.

"SHE'S PREGNANT!"

Karen begins to say, "How is it that..." She stops mid sentence as Henry recomposes himself. "Did you just say, *pregnant?*" Her eyes search his.

He nods with a tight-lipped response. "Yep."

"How...how did that happen?"

Henry says in a mocking tone. "Remember that night in Waikiki two months after we got married? We wound up conceiving Evan in..."

"I'm not asking how in *that* sense, dummy! How can that be? She couldn't have any. She and Ed were having serious problems because of it."

"Well, apparently she could. At least this time."

"This time?" Karen asks confused. Then it hits her. "Jaime?"

"She's close to three and a half months."

Karen's jaw drops as she gasps back in shock.

"He knows, right?"

"No."

"No? Why not?" She blinks. "He deserves to know."

"She doesn't want him to know. Something that's supposed to bring joy has turned into a catastrophe."

"Why is that? Did you put her up to this? How would you feel if I pulled a stunt like that? How would you like it if I never told you we had a son? You know and I know he would welcome the opportunity."

"Listen, Karen. It's different for us. We practically knew we wanted a child after we got married. For them it was completely unplanned. I know he wouldn't mind but Ed would bury her six feet in the ground if he knew."

"Why not let Jaime know? It's his child."

"I don't get involved in the private lives of my friends. This is something they need to find out on their own. Besides, he's doing fine."

Karen asks, "Where is she now?"

"She's staying at Carol's."

"Carol? You mean as in Carol Mulligan? Your ex-girlfriend?"

"Yeah."

"Why would you do a thing like that?"

"She needed somewhere to stay, away from Jaime and Ed. Carol said she was looking for a roommate. The city's not bad. She'll blend right in."

Karen sighs. "I still think it's wrong."

***

It's an early Saturday morning. Evelyn awakens to the sound of the soft muffled beat of a far off distant drum. She begins her walk down the stairs, tossing a hand through her hair. If there was one thing the singer could not stand, it was being awakened early in the morning when she wasn't pressed for time. Although, it was Carol's place. Things were made more complicated when Evelyn began experiencing the glories of morning sickness. At the moment, she was feeling fine but she had the hankering thirst for orange juice. Walking into the kitchen, she takes out the half-gallon carton. Then she finds a cup in the cupboard. The booming echoes louder as she guzzles down the beverage. It sounded as if it were nearby. Her eyes turn to the door towards the right side of the living room. She steps nearer. The sound changes from a beat to a full-blown tune. Slowly, Evelyn turns the doorknob and peeks. What she sees is Carol's partial backside swiveling and swaying. The singer cautiously takes a few steps down.

Carol moves around with a boom box perched on the shelf. Madonna's little girl voice on, "Like A Virgin" echoes throughout the basement. The sculptress, wearing a pink and green bikini top over her tiny chest with blue jeans, dances around the potter's wheel. She spins next to it the way a teenager would try to impress at a high school prom. Her tall lanky body moves from the wheel to the kiln next to the wall.

She lets out a breathy, "*Hey!*"

Evelyn watches and giggles.

Carol pinballs from a large table to the shelves where a few finished clay creations sit. She goes back, twirling to the potter's wheel where she pinches the ends of a bowl to smooth out the edges. Tossing her arms up, the sculptress moves to the frisky beat like a belly dancer charmed under the will of a snake.

"Touched for the very first time." Carol coos in a baby doll voice.

While moving around to and fro, her eyes catch a glimpse of Evelyn watching her.

Carol grows more serious as she goes to turn down the volume. She asks her roommate, "Did I wake you up?"

Evelyn replies. "No. The little one does plenty of that on their own."

"Aw. Morning sickness again?"

"It's off and on."

"Glad to know it's not me."

Evelyn leans against the wall with her arms folded. "Is this the way you always work?"

"Yeah."

Evelyn takes a seat on a magenta sofa chair at the end of the room. Carol rushes to take one item out of the kiln. It's a peculiar sculpture of pink tentacle-like branches with eyes painted on the ends. Carol smiles proudly at her latest creation. The song abruptly ends, segueing into the verbose splashy call letters of the pop station playing the tunes. Carol turns up the volume once again. The crescendo build up starts for the next song. It's the big power ballad structure that booms then quickly softens. At the very sound of lead singer, Steven Tyler's voice accompanied by drummer, Joey Kramer's snare click timing, Carol perks up her ears.

"Ooh! It's 'Angel!' "

Evelyn blinks out of confusion.

Waving her hands, Carol says, "I love this song! This is a perfect example of what I'm talking about."

She walks over a few steps to the potter's wheel. Pointing to the small bowl in the process of being made. She smiles at her roommate.

"Okay. A song like this is what makes me want to add something soft to the pieces like...um, little angel wings." Her eyes dart to the radio. "Ballads. Ballads of any type make me want to add emotion to them, or paint them pastel colors. You know, it's said that music is the soundtrack of our lives. I'm a firm believer in that. I let the music dictate the direction of what the object will be. If it's something heavier or has a faster beat, I tend to let it seep into a piece by giving it some attitude."

She puts out a hand to show Evelyn what she's talking about as far as her creations go.

"Put on some Zappa and the possibilities are endless. You just know you'll wind up with something special. Really good music can give you that ultimate high. Have you ever experienced something better than..." The sculptress stops herself, looks down at Evelyn's stomach. "I mean, have you ever listened to music in a different way? To borrow someone else's feelings and soul and apply it to your own work is gratifying. If I could be given five minutes with somebody who makes music that I love, I'd tell them how I applied it to a piece I made, no matter how weird it might look."

Evelyn thinks to herself. She never even thought of how music could influence others in their own career fields. It gave her a whole new perspective on what she did.

Carol continues with, "Do you know *why* music is so universal? It's because people can relate to it even though it's not the *exact* same experience as the songwriter. But, it's a reflection of what the listener experienced very similarly."

Evelyn says, "Hold on. I'll be right back."

She runs up the stairs. As Carol listens to the break of the song in progress, she begins thinking of embellishments to add onto the bowl.

"Hmm. Maybe it could use some gems in the pattern."

She places a paintbrush between her teeth, meticulously looking over the item. Again, she sings with the music.

"You're the reason I live. You're the reason I die. You're the reason I give, when I break down and cry... Don't need no reason why."

Evelyn runs back down the steps into the basement. She tosses two tapes to her roommate.

Carol asks as she catches the items close to her chest, "What are these?"

With a smile, Evelyn says, "See what you can do with them."

The sculptress reads one printed label. *Hero's Requiem.*

In a mischievous tone, Evelyn tells her. "It's *raw*." Then she laughs. "The other, there is only one track on it."

Carol turns to look at her with curiosity. "Raw you say? Hmm. Now you've piqued my curiosity dear lady."

Carol places the tape in the boom box cassette player. It starts.

The growing shock on the artist's face says it all. She exclaims. "Holy shit. This is you! It's your voice that I'm hearing!" Carol begins to bob her head and move to the rhythm of the music. "Wow!" She laughs. "I had no idea. I'm sorry I never listened to your music earlier. How many albums have you come out with?"

"I'd say twelve. You're listening to the thirteenth."

It finally occurs to Carol. "This is a demo tape? I've never heard a studio recording so...well, *raw*!"

She rushes over to Evelyn, giving her a big hug.

"Thank you. Thank you! I feel so honored. Nobody's ever let me listen to their demo. Oh, I promise I won't say anything about this."

"It's alright, Carol. I trust you."

The sculptress continues to listen while shaking her head in disbelief. "What? Is that a cymbal? It sounds different, not quite the usual."

"Trash can." Evelyn answers proudly.

"Really? Huh. How did that happen?"

"Jaime." The singer answers back.

***

Over at The Green Light, Kelly finishes preparations to opening the club's bar. She takes out a magazine called *Sound Off* from her light pink canvas bag.

The bartender says quietly, "Ooh, somethin' on I.C.E. Wonder if Evelyn knows about this?" She flips pages until she finds the article. "Ah! There it is!" Eagerly, Kelly reads it.

Four photos are shown, one of Jaime Weston, Bobby Whitfield, Dan Soren, and the studio itself.

Kelly marvels at the image of Jaime. "Ooh my! Isn't he a looker! Evelyn's quite lucky to be workin' with him."

Hot Music - by Jackie Donovan

More tales from the Innu/Irish little gal from Vancouver, Canada.

My travels have taken me to New York.

It's the second half of July that I'm sent to interview in upper New York two different subjects. One of which are the guys from a studio called, I.C.E in New Paltz, consisting of Jaime Weston (who is Canadian himself), Bob Whitfield, and Dan Soren. The other subject along my same travels is famed musician/producer/knob twiddler, Todd Rundgren. (Look for that story in the next issue).

The day I arrive is the worst time of the year for an interview. The heat is almost unbearable. A lot different than the cooler temperatures of Vancouver. I stop off at a coffee shop and ask what the temperature is and how I might be able to find I.C.E. Studios. A kind middle-aged man tells me it's ninety-six degrees and I can find I.C.E. about a half mile away. He says, 'You'll know it when you see it.'

I turn onto a road not knowing where I am, and then I see something. The gentleman gave me a number to go by. Only, where is it? Just as I turn my head, I see a red Chevy Camaro with two women back out of what looks to be a private road. I ask the driver, a beautiful redhead if the studio is nearby as I tell her I'm from Sound Off. She tells me that is where she just came from. I pull into the unpaved driveway, which seems a mile long. At last I find the unassuming large brown building.

I ring the doorbell and immediately a tall, thin, and very attractive man greets me. He looks to be maybe forty. Wearing round dark shades, light blue jeans, and a wicked grin, he looks me over. He says, "Hello," in only a very deep seductive voice. I can't figure out if he's either a pool boy or in-house artist. It's probably ten degrees hotter in the studio itself. Incredibly hot. The gentleman wears no shirt and absolutely no jewelry. Not even a watch. He's bare. Well, then again his only camouflage is a bit of brown chest hair. I shake his hand. Long fingers. I'm convinced he is a musician. About to ask him where I can find the production staff, he introduces himself. This is Jaime Weston, famed producer of many great albums. Okay. So, I'm left stupefied. Another gentleman wanders into the lobby to join us. This turns out to be another producer, Bob Whitfield. He's not as exposed as Weston, although he does wear a fairly open Hawaiian shirt over blue jeans. He apologizes for not remembering about my visit. I ask them about their receptionist. Jaime answers readily. "We don't have one." Whitfield adds in, "We do everything ourselves. We don't need to pay somebody to do work which we can handle. It's something we tried before."

Quickly, I'm led through the lobby to a room. Then I meet engineer, Dan Soren. Polo shirt, khaki shorts, sneakers make up his ensemble. Whitfield snickers back. "Tennis garb." Dan gives him a look. Right away they introduce me to what's inside the control room. Not at all what I'm expecting. Every piece of equipment is from no later than 1986. Bob expresses, "We use only Neumann mikes for everything. The best sound, bar none. They were moved from the studio we worked out of in Brooklyn in the late '70s. Control board is a Dimensia 3P80." Dan shows me the mixing room. The motherboard is hooked up to a computer proving they have some modern equipment. Dan tells me, "The mixing station we have now is a year old. It's the stuff that works for us." True. Although, the studio is full of outdated items. Jaime Weston soon takes over and leads me around the place.

I'm led to an office. Mahogany desk, couch, stand up lamps, record player off to one end of the room with two good-sized speakers. All around are plaques and quite a few record industry awards, along with some odd statuettes. He puts his hand out as though to introduce me to someone. I think, yes, it's an office. Jaime looks at me with a creeping smile on his thin lips. He guides me down a staircase in the middle of the main area. There's one large room to the right that could fit a whole band. Weston carries a curled up beige shirt as he tells me about his prized possession items. He tells me he wants to introduce me to his seven children. The man is almost gleeful. His fingers pull up a dark covering, exposing seven small recorders. Jaime says, "Here they are. 1980 issued Derby DRB57 recorders. If one breaks...God willing that ever happens, I'll have back up." Now I detect his Canadian pronunciation of some words that I should be familiar with. "Everyone has tried to sell me every multi-track recorder on the market, but I tell them I'm set. The albums that have been recorded at this studio or parts of have been recorded on one of these what I call,

Magnificent Seven. That's simply the way I think of them as. I could never give these up. Our latest artist we've used one of these for a song she had great difficulty with. And it came out great." I ask him if I might be able to have a listen to the track. He offers up hesitantly, "It's not fully complete. I don't know if she would appreciate it." Then he comes out and says, "We just don't do that. The artists put their faith in us and putting that out for others just isn't right. It's not right." He switches gears and talks about the heat, saying the air conditioner went out at the worst possible time. I look at him and he is quite hot. Both literally and figuratively. I tell him when he first greeted me at the door, I thought he was a pool boy. Jaime bows his head in a boyish fashion, thoroughly shy. He grins widely. "I don't normally dress this way. It's just too hot." I'm almost tempted to say that I don't mind the view at all. Weston unfolds the shirt draped over his shoulder. He puts it on.

Again, he leads me. This time we go outside in the backyard. There are a few outdoor chairs and a webbed chaise lounge, the kind you find at backyard picnics. I sit in a chair as he does. Finally, he removes his sunglasses to show a pair of beautiful sleepy brown eyes. Now I'm mesmerized. Yes, his shirt remains fully unbuttoned. It's the female hormone thing. Before we launch into more shoptalk, he lights up a cigarette with a match, then holds it a very sexy way with his fingers, very delicately. He says, "There is a reason why I showed you the office. It's what you saw in there, the awards. I know as do the rest of the guys that some folks or industry insiders don't find the way we do things as legit. Because we don't use what everyone else does, we get dismissed. Only, others don't realize that some artists still like an organic sound. Synthesizers and drum machines may be fine but we're not into that. If someone likes a certain part of...oh, say a guitar part, we'll make sure that stays untouched or blended without destroying it with layers. Overdubbing repeatedly can take away from that specific sound. Layer upon layer softens it to oblivion. We don't like doing that. We are about experimenting but in a very stripped down way. Our latest artist, Evelyn Winthrop, expressed to us she went through a lot of state-of-the-art studios but her album wasn't sounding right. A lot of the time an artist like her will say that. There are many great producers out there. I don't want to knock at them but some try to leave their sound on an artist's album that brings more attention to them. It's like saying, 'Since you came to us for help, we're going to make it known that we produced this for you.' Branding is what it is." He chuckles. "It's ego. Nothing more. I had my share of having one some time ago. A rather large one at that, but it was a personal thing. I never wanted it to show on the projects because I respected the artists. I don't buy it for one minute when someone says it's the way the studio sounds. Yes, the atmosphere can lend credence to a statement like that but it is the production where it comes from. You're trying very hard to make it sound like a previous album you produced before and then the cycle starts all over again. I'll probably get in trouble for saying that but I'm not concerned either. Call it whatever you want. We just want this to be the artists project, not our own."

I find myself more intrigued by what he's saying and organic sounding music in general.

He then says, "We're modern to a certain point because we have to. You always have to, but it doesn't have to be to a fault. We're not Todd Rundgren. Computers are fine. Only, we're not interested in making a computer generated album." How odd he mentions Rundgren, as he's my next subject to interview. Jaime tells me, "What you saw upstairs, we do perfectly fine with in regards to success. We play the same game, only using different rules. We're always booked. So, that must mean something. I'll probably do this (producing) when I turn old and gray, which I feel already." Looking at him, he doesn't look like he'll be getting gray hair anytime soon. I tell him, "You don't look it." He smiles hugely.

Once I'm finished talking with Jaime, who decides to rest his brain for a little while, it's back inside the studio I go. Bob wants to give me some insight. He says, "First, please by all means call me Bobby. 'Bob' is so formal. He leads me back into the control room. Immediately, he takes a seat and says, "I've been in this business since high school. Someone was really impressed with the work I'd done and took me to Toronto. I studied engineering there for several years and then met this kid, two years younger than myself and highly ambitious. We hit it off quickly, and formed this partnership. We managed to survive the whole '60s thing, what with the psychedelic era and those annoying swirling keyboards that everybody was hooked on. Everybody wanted to sound like Hendrix when it came to guitar. Then, luckily the '70s came around and everyone wanted to lighten up on the heavy sound. Jaime and I were ready to join the fray. Both of us had become producers in our own right, while having headquarters in Manhattan. We didn't realize that there was a lot of experimentation out in the regular world. That got in the way, especially for him. I got married and had a daughter. He'd pull a Houdini act, disappearing with some lovely record assistant or radio operations gal for days on end. We got some awards for various projects, but our resumes were pretty sparse during then. His suffered more than mine. When we were happy to get out of the '60s, we found ourselves even happier to get out of the '70s!" Bobby laughs. I ask Bobby how they got to where they are today. He answers with, "We wanted a clean slate. So, a move was needed. A friend of my wife's family said there was a place in New Paltz run by a guy named Jack Zima who was looking to do something with an engineering school. This building. Since we got a new location, Jaime and I put our heads together and he suggested we get artists nobody else wanted to touch. These would be the artists who really wanted something different in a sonic sort of way. A lot of progressive bands wanted our help and we were thrilled. He and I are what you call, 'sound junkies.' It's all about experimentation and getting that right sound. Building a sonic puzzle. So, that's our bread and butter. We've done business that way for seven years now and have had no complaints. It won't change. I won't change. I'm the same old Bobby Whitfield who can do a victory dance in a hula skirt.

I drive away with what went on fresh in my mind. A studio so refreshingly different. Equipment that could only be described as garage sale worthy turned into gold records and awards in the office as *transformed success. Producers for the artist not riding with them forcefully. It doesn't hurt having a half stripped down, handsome looking guy behind the controls, and a very funny partner who leaves some humorous visuals left to the mind.*

I'm off onto the New York State Thruway heading up to Woodstock next. I don't know if Todd Rundgren will be half as interesting.

Kelly's jaw drops. "Oh me God! Ooh! Lucky! Lucky! Lucky Lass! Evelyn, ooh. To be workin' with a stud like that. Aye!" She airs out her shirt quickly. "Whoee!"

The phone rings. She picks it up. "Hello? Green Light. Kelly speaking."

The voice at the other end is Evelyn's. "Kelly? Is that you?"

"Evelyn!"

"Darling, how are you?"

"I'm doin' fine. I haven't heard from you since you took off for New York."

"I know and I do apologize for not calling earlier."

"Are you still at that studio?"

"No. I got done with that in August."

"So, what are you still doing in New York three months later?"

"I called Ed and told him I needed extra time. Sort of like a trial separation."

"But why? Are you finally leavin' that bum?"

"No. I just need time to myself. Something came up."

"He called."

"Who? Ed?"

"Yeah. In July. He expected me to know everything and your exact whereabouts."

"Did you tell him?"

"I almost told him to go to hell but I called him an arsehole. Then I hung up on him."

A relieved Evelyn expresses her gratitude. "Oh, thank you. Thank you for not telling him."

Kelly looks at the magazine in awe.

"Evelyn, have you checked out the November issue of *Sound Off*? Ooh, you're lucky! He is a real beauty and that interviewer sounded like she was practically panting like a dog. I know I would too."

"What magazine is this?"

"*Sound Off*. The November issue. Do you get it?"

"I never even heard of it but I will look for it."

"It's a sound equipment magazine. That Jaime Weston fella... He just sounds so good. Ooh, and the description of him not wearing a shirt? Oh! That interviewer picked the best day. I'm sure his mate won't appreciate the attention he'll get for that though."

Evelyn smiles on the other end. She rubs her belly.

***

A white van makes its trek up the driveway of I.C.E. It stops next to Bobby Whitfield's light blue VW Bug. The door slides open. A large black man with a purple jacket on steps out. With the build of a linebacker, Carter 'Bear' Byron looks across in the van as Ginger Aldair exits. She pushes her wavy blonde hair back while looking at the studio. Her face is angelic and pale with Brooke Shield's charm. Bright and full of life, Ginger is undoubtedly spunky. Ready to have a good time. She laughs easily while the rest of her band come out of the vehicle. Ron, Jack, and Randy join her and Carter.

"Ron! Take a look at this!" Ginger points to the Volkswagen parked ahead of them.

Ron replies. "Hey! It's a hippie mobile, man!"

Ginger leans against Carter, laughing. The other band mates crack up too. They walk up the small cement steps. Carter rings the doorbell. Ginger announces to her crew. "Ding dong! Trick or treat!"

They laugh again as the door opens.

***

Evelyn sits on the couch watching TV. Since she is now into her fourth month of pregnancy, the cravings begin to kick in. Morning sickness has slowed down considerably. Lately she had acquired the taste for peanut butter and crackers. Not this time though. She draws a colorful plate to her with a large sub sandwich on it.

Heaven!

Grabbing a bag of potato chips next to her, she dumps the contents over the sandwich. Evelyn was living up life in style. Not the rebellious rock'n roll one either. She wears comfortable baggy clothes. No worries about makeup. Stuffing her face like a pig, she watches daytime fare on TV.

She pats her belly saying, "Cheers!"

As though toasting to herself, she pops open a can of Coke. She flips through channels with the touch of the remote. Her finger lifts off the button when she realizes *Sesame Street* is on. She breaks into giggles of the puppet antics.

Shortly thereafter, Carol returns. She spots her roommate slumped on the couch. Evelyn has her hand on her stomach. Potato chip crumbs are gathered between the creases of her loose fitting shirt. She leans upward opening her eyes and stretching. Carol walks in the kitchen.

"I bought some groceries while I was out. You said you wanted mint chocolate chip, butter pecan, or rocky road. Well, I got all three."

Evelyn gets up from the couch quickly to join her. "Ooh! How delightful!"

She picks out a spoon from the utensil drawer. While she opens all three boxes of ice cream, Carol watches her in shock. Her roommate scoops out big dollops of each. Then she takes out a knife and peels a banana, chopping slices from it. Carol's jaw drops. Making a face, she sees Evelyn taking a bite with glee.

The artist remarks, "You sure have some strange cravings."

Evelyn closes her eyes.

Euphoria!

Licking the spoon, she leaves the kitchen savoring the assortment of ice cream and chunks of banana.

***

In late October, Jaime and Ginger walk along the sidewalk towards the center of town. They had been getting along well over the past month. Taking in the sights, it's a familiar remembrance to the record producer. It was only a few months earlier he had dinner with another lovely lady.

Ginger clings to his arm, all smiles. She exclaims. "I've been having a great time at the studio."

"You have? That's always good to hear." He chuckles back.

"Best of all, I like being with you." Ginger looks up at him. "Halloween is in a few days. Ever go trick-or-treating before?"

"My mom took me out when I was young."

"Well, I like treats. No tricks." She throws her arms around him.

Jaime gives her a sly smile. "Oh? What kind of treats?"

"Kisses."

"Hershey?"

"No. The real ones." She says in a breathy tone while slowly inching her face close to his.

"Are you going to share?"

"Only if you want me to."

"I want you to."

She leans closer for a kiss.

"Mm." He opens his eyes. "You do taste sweet."

"There's more where that came from."

They kiss again.

She says. "The motel I'm stayin' at or your place?"

"Probably the motel."

"Oh, so you're the adventurous type."

He looks up to think about it. "I wouldn't call it adventurous."

They kiss some more. He pulls at her for a stronger sensation. She leans his head down for another lip lock.

He utters quietly. "Oh, Evy."

Ginger pulls away immediately. Startled just as much, Jaime opens his eyes. He sees her standing about a step back in a state of confusion. Her eyes scan his for an apology or anything for that matter. He's stuck for words. The only thing he can do is shrug. As if to say something, he opens his mouth. Nothing comes out. She could tell by his expression he wasn't about to apologize. She squints her eyes. Taking another step back, she turns around and walks away.

He calls out. "Ginger!"

She breaks into a trot then a run. The singer disappears into the darkness.

Jaime looks down.

Evelyn lies on the bed, reading a book. Suddenly she twitches from a very foreign feeling. Rubbing her stomach, the sensation makes her smile. She hops off the bed and runs to the room at the very end of the upstairs area. Knocking at Carol's door, she yells out, "Carol! Carol! "

Her roommate opens the door looking completely disheveled and sleepy. She rocks slightly when answering.

"What time is it? "

"It's um, one-thirty."

"Oh. What's up?"

"I think I felt the baby move. I can't be sure. It's a tiny fluttering sensation like little butterflies trying to get out. I can't believe it!"

"That's progress for you. Didn't I tell you once the morning sickness would disappear you would feel differently? Now. Good for you. Let me sleep. Good night."

Evelyn calmly answers her. "Goodnight, Carol."

She goes back to her room gleeful, still rubbing her stomach.

***

Carter Byron tunes up his bass. A deep twang echoes, making him cringe. "Ooh. That does not sound good." He looks over at Ron who readies his guitar. "Ron, give me a D."

Ron strikes a chord. Carter plucks at a bass string.

Closing his eyes, he listens for the tone. "Oh yeah."

Both begin a little jam.

Jaime walks in the room. Ron looks over and walks out. The record producer approaches the big man sitting in back of the recording room.

"Hey, Jaime. Need anything?" Carter asks in a friendly baritone voice.

"I'm wondering where Ginger is. We're supposed to get her in the booth upstairs and redo her vocals on something."

"She split."

"She what?"

"Gin took off about three o' clock this morning. Knocked on my door and left her vocal tracks the way they were. Said she didn't need anything changed." Carter sees Jaime's guilty expression. "Hey, man. You've still got us." Carter says in hopes of brightening the mood of the producer. He gets up. Jaime looks down at the floor with a smile. The big bass man stands on Jaime's right. He puts a reassuring arm around the producer's shoulder. "Ever been in love?" Carter asks bluntly.

"Yes." Jaime responds.

"Well, I'll tell you somethin' 'bout Ginger. She's always falling in love. Take it from me. I've seen her do it frequently. Only, she doesn't know if it's real. She's hoping to see if one sticks. So, don't feel too bad. She can tell when someone's taken."

Jaime doesn't correct him or say anything that might challenge the notion.

"Oh." Is all he can say.

Carter turns a knob on his bass. "She said, 'I should have known."

Jaime looks directly at Carter then down at the floor again.

***

Evelyn reads one of her first reviews as Carol tends to making sandwiches for lunch.

The title in the magazine reads:

A Hero's Welcome

Nine years ago, Evelyn Winthrop walked away from the rock world after setting the world on fire. Nobody knew when or if she would return. Over the past six years, she's immersed herself in the jazz world instead. Mostly working with the backdrop of clarinets, trombones, and saxophones. Sometimes providing softened vocals to soundtracks.

Winthrop has come a long way from the time she was discovered by Rufus McAvoy, giving her a deal with Anlan Records in '67. Then twenty years old, Evelyn was a fresh-faced British Barbie doll with long flaxen hair and the voice of a choirgirl. She changed over the years and so did her voice. Evidenced were the pictures of her smoking cigarettes. By the mid-'70s her voice transitioned from sweet soprano to brandy-infused. Her lyrics became more edgy in the 1976 release Kiss Kiss, Bang Bang. Working with guitarist/lyricist, Jed Jackson gave her new voice a chance to shine. He helped her craft songs and provided an indelible source of inspiration. Those songs came from experiences of growing up along the countryside of London, brought up to gain independence, and get thrown into a world of fame and fortune. That album became Winthrop's catalyst to creating her most well-known and critical favorite, Ravaged Beauty. It was 1978 and all the world was aglow with the war between disco and punk. Winthrop chose punk, not only from the times, but from those experiences. At the age of thirty-one, she embarked on doing something many women artists wouldn't want to do, go against the wishes of the record company. Evelyn crafted nine songs entirely credited to her. Jackson remained her guitar player and was only too happy to oblige in helping with the arrangements. Most of Ravaged Beauty's songs consisted of anger towards men, sexism, betrayal, and fear. "Pretty Pinks" delved into cleavage. While "Jack-Off Of All Trades" showed what her voice had become. A squeaky delivery, sometimes raspy, but full of emotion needed that ten years earlier she wouldn't have been able to. A bawdy tirade so brutal towards men and relationships, no radio station dare play it. A year later, she released Childlike Sins. On this outing, she only helped write five of the ten songs. Her voice had taken a heavy toll from a serious cocaine and heroin addiction. It did not hit the high-water mark as Ravaged Beauty had.

Now with those days behind her, and a much-needed sabbatical from the jazz world, Winthrop sounds more refreshed with her thirteenth record, Hero's Requiem. There are many pieces that sound experimental as she told Rolling Stone in January of last year. "This album is non effective for jazz. There needs to be more attitude. The lyrics reflect that." And how! Evelyn goes from her punk roots, "Just Let Me Be" and "Angelic Waste" to innocent and playful such as her younger days on "Little Miss Independent." Her voice has gotten deeper and her delivery is much more raspier. Returning to her best days of Ravaged Beauty comes the heartfelt and despair filled "Chasing The Dragon." An intro of rolling synthesizers and jabs of guitar over a heart-pounding rhythm section, completed with Winthrop's voice at its most worn and guttural tone. It's about addiction and the state of completion once it drives one "Into the devil's spell." Evelyn looks back on regret for most of the album, but along the way is that ray of hope. To find a happier existence. Not to play hero at every turn.

The production team of Jaime Weston and Bobby Whitfield, famed for their use of experimentation and organic music makings, is as much important as Winthrop herself. Odd percussion is evident and used effectively, studio tricks that other producers can learn by. The title track, 'Hero's Requiem' gives the feeling of death but within it's swirl of darkness is the soft churning of a trash can (provided by Weston), mixed to give the deep, rich quality which is needed. Instruments don't clash; they meld together in a very orchestrated manner. "Tomorrow's Child." An odd beat provided by Whitfield's reverse effect on high-hat, and saxophone by none other than a guest appearance by Emory Caldwell to fill in parts. It's very Beatle-esque and this whole album would probably be something George Martin wished he could have produced.

There is obvious chemistry between Winthrop and Weston & Whitfield that neither the artist nor production staff (including engineer, Dan Soren) ever outdoes each other. Their work shows passion yet effortless because all of the players know what is best for the music. Bravo and a hero's return welcome to Ms. Evelyn Winthrop.

Chapter 7

It's mid December, with a melting pot of people shuffling around the busy sidewalks and scampering through the streets with bags of future Christmas gifts. Manhattan is in all its wintry glory as Carol and Evelyn take in the beauty of the uptown portions of New York City. White lights shimmer and glow on trees along the streets against the pastel varied sky.

Dressed comfortably and snugly, Evelyn looks all around and exclaims to Carol. "It's beautiful!"

"Just imagine living here through all four seasons." Carol says back.

"It's really a beautiful city." Evelyn responds as she takes a seat on a wood bench.

"Well, I wouldn't take it that far. Some areas are a hell hole."

Evelyn looks at Carol in such a way that it makes the artist soften her outlook. "Then again, I'm not the one who's almost six months pregnant."

Evelyn smiles and rubs her growing belly.

Carol watches the traffic go by and suddenly remembers, "I need to go to the art store and get some supplies."

"Oh, that's fine by me."

Carol turns her attention away from the street, back to Evelyn.

"You know how they say pregnant women glow? Well, you're absolutely glowing now!"

"Really?" Evelyn says surprised.

"Don't ask me why I just noticed it, but you really are. Maybe it's the weather or something...I don't know?"

Evelyn giggles back, "Should we carry on?"

"Yeah."

The two women walk along 5th Ave.

A man's voice can be heard calling out. "Evelyn!"

Evelyn wheels around startled, afraid it's a journalist who has recognized her. She sees that the person waving to her is someone she recognizes and is put at ease.

"Evelyn!" The man calls out again.

He trots through the crowd and catches up with the women a few feet away. Carol's jaw flies open at the sight of him.

She asks her pregnant roommate. "Who is the blond stallion?"

Evelyn says, "You'll find out soon enough."

The gentleman stops in front of the ladies. His hair is a coifed blond tuft of perfection. With an angular pale face, he looks like a male model for GQ. His most beguiling and unusual traits are his two visibly different colored eyes. The left is brown while the other is blue. He says in a warm British tone, "Hello, Ms. Winthrop."

They exchange pleasantries with cheek kisses while Carol stands back.

"You do remember me, don't you? Edwin Muller?"

"Of course I do, Edwin," Evelyn says back.

He smiles with a big boyish grin. "I must say, you look smashing, darling..." His eyes run down Evelyn's figure. "Did you put on a little bit of weight?"

Assuredly, Evelyn tells Edwin, "It *is* the holiday season."

"Ah, that is so true. Also being in the studio so much destroys what little sense you have left from being cooped up. Ever since I've been working with Dominic Bauer, it's been truly insane. He wants to fiddle with so many mixes, it's enough to drive me up a bloody wall."

Carol listens to Edwin's voice and smiles to herself.

Edwin continues to talk with Evelyn. "So, my dear, I've heard things about you." Evelyn becomes a little more alert to what Edwin says. "Yes. I've heard that you hooked up with Jaime Weston."

Just then, Evelyn feels a tingling surge run through her body. How did Edwin know about that?

She outwardly says, "Yes."

"If I must say, he's a fantastic producer. You're completely in excellent hands and I'm sure the record will be a smash hit. I envy the man. He's top notch! Was he able to help you with that song that was becoming a pain?"

"Oh yes! I was amazed at that."

Edwin smiles back, "Very good."

A bus passes by, which distracts both Edwin and Evelyn. They turn their attention to Carol.

Evelyn does some introducing. "Edwin Muller is a music producer I've worked with Carol. He's much too modest for his own good."

Edwin laughs as he's about to put his hand out for a handshake. "Hello, ma'am."

Evelyn continues with, "Edwin, this is my roommate, Carol Mulligan."

Edwin's jaw drops. He says in a surprised tone, "*The* Carol Mulligan of Manhattan? *The* sculptress?"

Carol smiles back when shaking his hand in a firm grasp. "You mean, you know of me?"

Edwin breaks into a huge smile. "*Know you*? I'm a huge fan of yours. Your sculptures are all over my house and studio!"

He takes her hand and kisses it, honored to be in her presence. Carol turns to Evelyn with her jaw dropped. It's obvious to Evelyn that Edwin is fully impressed by Carol.

Edwin comments to Carol. "It's fabulous to meet you."

Carol says off the top of her head, "Well then, maybe we should have lunch sometime."

Edwin's eyes gaze into Carol's.

Contently he says, "I'd love to."

"I'm not doing anything on Tuesday."

"Great."

Carol shuffles through her purse and pulls out her business card. She hands it to him. He replies with a toothy smile. "Smashing!"

Once again, he turns his attention back to Evelyn.

"There's really something different about you, but for the life of me I can't figure it out." He checks the time on his watch. "Well, I have to go now. Some folks are waiting for me back at the studio. I'll see you later Evelyn. Carol? Tuesday."

He winks.

With that, he disappears among the crowd.

Carol says to Evelyn, "I think I just met Prince Charming." They continue to walk down 5th Avenue. Carol says, "Do you think he'll call me...seriously?"

"Knowing Edwin, I'd say, yes."

"What should I wear?"

Evelyn lets out a laugh.

They too disappear among the hustle and bustle of holiday dwellers.

***

Carol hosts her annual holiday party with a bunch of her art friends. None seem to know who Evelyn Winthrop is and she prefers it that way. Carol chats with her guests while Evelyn is upstairs. The doorbell rings. Carol hears it but is unable to reach the door with friends blocking the way and a large platter in her hands full of dips and chips.

She calls out to a guest. "Lisa! Can you get that?"

The guest opens the door.

Edwin Muller greets the woman with a smile. "Hello there. Is Carol here?"

Lisa responds quickly. "She's right there."

Carol places the platter on the oddly shaped coffee table and looks up just in time to see Edwin walking towards her. He tosses his tan trench coat on the couch and gives Carol a hug and a kiss on the cheek.

She exclaims. "I can't believe you were able to make it!"

"I wouldn't miss it for the world." He takes a look all around. "This place is smashing, darling."

"Oh, why thank you." Carol says in a charmed tone. She notices his coat on the couch. "I'll put that upstairs for you."

Carol takes the garment upstairs while Evelyn is heading down the stairs. She stops at the last step, looking around. Laughter and munching on snacks is heard throughout the loft. Some guests look her way. Evelyn remains glad nobody recognizes her. Then she bumps into Edwin. With a shocked expression, Evelyn can't avoid him.

He says to her, "Why hello, Evelyn." Looking down at her, his mouth curls around a smile of delight. "My dear, you're pregnant!" Edwin begins to laugh as he clutches a glass of eggnog.

Evelyn suspiciously looks around the room for a moment then grabs his arm and drags him to the open kitchen. Some onlookers watch or glance over their way. Carol walks back downstairs.

"So, are you unhappy about becoming a new mother?"

Evelyn hastily says, "No. The exact opposite. I brought you in here because I want you to keep your mouth shut around certain people."

"I wouldn't say anything." He tells her with assured confidence. "When did you decide to start a family?"

"I didn't exactly *decide* on a time."

"Oh?"

She says, "I don't want a word getting out about this, especially upstate. Better yet, you haven't seen me."

Confused, Edwin says, "Why would you be so..." He stops mid sentence when something crosses his mind. "When did you exactly go to I.C.E. to record?"

"July."

"When are you due?"

"Late March. Early April."

His eyes wander about with perplexity. "So, why would it concern you? I mean your mate, Ed must be..." He stops mid sentence again to make calculations.

In the living room, Carol talks with her friends. A curly haired blonde steps up to Carol. "Um, Carol, isn't that the guy you're interested in?" The woman points to Edwin discreetly.

"Yeah." Carol says back nonchalantly.

"It looks like he's talking with your roommate."

Carol shakes it off with, "Yeah. They have some unfinished business to discuss."

Back in the kitchen, Edwin takes a sip of eggnog. "I'm trying to figure this out." He takes yet another sip, then stares at her while his mouth is still to the glass. His eyes go wide. He alternates his glance between Evelyn's eyes and her stomach. He puts the glass down on the kitchen counter top. "You're telling me... You mean, this happened while you were at the studio? And not with Ed?"

Evelyn gives Edwin a look that lets him know he's right.

"Good Lord, Evelyn! Who would it be? Dan and Bobby are both happily married men." Right then his jaw practically drops when he comes to the conclusion, "You're not going to tell me Jaime?"

Evelyn rubs her stomach and looks up at Edwin with a slight smile. Edwin blinks a few times to let the new discovery sink in.

"No wonder you told me to keep my trap shut. He doesn't know, does he?"

Evelyn shakes her head.

"You don't have to worry. I won't say anything either."

Evelyn closes her eyes, calmly saying, "Thank you."

Edwin grabs the glass again and goes, "Mm." He pulls the glass away. "I just thought of something."

"What's that?"

Edwin narrows his glance to Evelyn's stomach. "I guess production was smashing?"

He breaks into a childlike grin before outwardly laughing.

Evelyn takes a towel by the sink and throws it at him.

From the living room, a man calls out to everybody. "Hey look! Larry's goin' for the piano."

A tall man takes a seat at a small keyboard at the right side of the room. Evelyn and Edwin return. Carol goes to stand by Edwin. Larry begins to sing Christmas carols while the room grows quiet and everybody listens. Carol rests her head against Edwin's arm. Evelyn massages her belly.

***

Somewhere in Chicago, a door closes in the control room. It's now early January of 1988. A cassette tape finishes rewinding. Two fingers pull it out. Jaime wears his sunglasses and peers at the item.

He tosses it back on the table and mutters quietly. "Piece of shit."

Rubbing his eyes underneath, he leans back with a sigh. The phone buzzes as an orange light appears. Picking it up, he returns to sitting up and taking his sunglasses off.

"Yeah? Put him through." Waiting for the pause, Jaime looks at something he wrote. The phone gets picked up on the other end. "Hey, Henry." Jaime says with a creeping smile. "It's great to hear your voice."

Henry says back, "That's unusual. Normally, you dread my calls."

Jaime frowns upon hearing this. "I've never said that."

"No, but I can tell."

Warmly, the producer says, "Okay. So, aside from giving me a guilt trip, what's goin' on?"

He grabs a Marlboro and a book of matches, listening to his longtime friend. Henry says in a prying tone, "I think the question is what's going on with you? I noticed a picture of you and Sandy Denell in the latest issue of US magazine."

Jaime says, "Mm hmm."

He sticks the cigarette in his mouth and leans toward the lit match in his left hand. With a quick jerk, the flame vanishes from the match.

"I don't suppose there's a caption underneath that reads, 'Sandy Denell, Pain In The Ass?'"

Henry replies, "Um, no,"

Jaime takes in a puff of his Marlboro.

With a slight amount of agitation he says, "She's a prima donna who knows shit about production demands. Her manager has me go to these goddamn press parties with no product in sight. It's not even finished by the time this stuff is made available to the press." He runs a hand through his ruffled hair, and then takes a hasty puff of the cigarette again. "Even worse is that she treats the whole studio like we're her go-fors."

"Wow! Sounds bad."

Jaime changes his tone. "Were you checking up on me?"

"Well...um, no. Okay. Sort of. I was just wanting to know if there was anything going on between you and Sandy?"

Jaime says in an exasperated tone, "God! Absolutely not! Now, what is your *real* reason for this call?"

"I was asking because I thought you had feelings for Evelyn."

Jaime puts his hand over his face, letting his long fingers spread out in an agonized fashion and mumbles, "Jesus." He takes a deep breath then says to Henry in a very deep tone, "Henry, you really enjoy drudging up things that really are none of your concern."

"I know, but I also know you happen to care for her...a great deal I might add."

"When did you become a psychiatrist? Listen, if I need help sorting things out, I'll find a therapist."

"Are you saying that she's the past?"

"I'm not saying anything."

A knock comes at the door. Jaime turns his attention to it. He says to Henry, "I have to go. I will talk to you again very soon."

"Okay," is Henry's response. "Bye."

"Bye."

Jaime puts the phone back on the hook and announces to whoever is at the door. "Come in."

Sandy, a blonde woman with a serious make-up job consisting of dark blue eyeliner is accompanied by a pout and her manager, Dennis. They enter the room.

"Why did you make me sound awful?" She demands.

Jaime says back in a matter-of-fact tone, "You told me to leave it that way."

Dennis, a small man with shoulder length brown hair and matching beard says to Jaime, "What are you going to do about this?"

The producer stands up, towering over his two tormentors. He says to Dennis, "We need to talk."

Sandy stands a foot away with her arms folded. Dennis strokes his beard, while he addresses the six-footer. "You were hired to produce Sandy's record."

"I know."

The manager smiles back, "So, why should there be a problem?"

Jaime puts out a beckoning finger. "Come here." The producer pulls the manager aside before looking at the perturbed singer who checks her nails. Jaime talks to Dennis in a cautious tone and speaks with many hand gestures. "Listen, Dennis. Your client has been down my throat enough times when she obviously has no idea what she's doing."

"That's *your* job."

Jaime smiles back. "My job is to make the production sound better. I can only do so much but she's making empty demands. She hasn't expressed anything other than having the crew or me fetch coffee for her. I don't have time for that."

Dennis states, "Weston, you're being paid to do this."

Jaime points a finger to the manager. "That's right. I do have another problem. You have me going to these media releases with you and your client to release information when nothing has been done yet. Not even half a track to critique and you expect me to form an opinion on it. I'm not good for these demands. Being under pressure is not my specialty."

Sandy grows impatient while she chews gum. "Hey, what's goin' on?"

Jaime turns to look back at the singer. He returns his attention back to the manager. "She needs an attitude adjustment."

Dennis says testily, "There's nothing wrong with Sandy's attitude, but possibly the problem is you. Maybe *you* just think you're above everybody else since you're called one of the best."

Jaime eyes the floor for a moment. The producer knows Sandy Denell isn't worth it or her weasel of a manager without a conscience. He reaches for the phone and makes a quick call within the studio. "Bobby. Dan. I need you both in the control room. Bring the black bag with you." He puts the phone down on the receiver. Jaime retrieves the still lit cigarette in the ashtray on the desk. He inhales deeply and releases a heavy ring of smoke.

"What are you going to do?" Dennis asks in a partially worried though demanding tone.

Jaime says back with quiet confidence and the knowledge that he's holding all of the cards, "You're going to have to look for another producer."

The manager's jaw drops. "You...you can't just walk away from *this*!"

Bobby and Dan enter the room. Bobby holds the black bag before turning it over to Jaime. He puts out the cigarette in the ashtray, then rummages through the bag and produces what looks to be a pad, which he tosses on the table and clicks on a pen. He writes something quickly and tears out a page that turns out to be a check. Handing it to Dennis, he says, "It should be more than enough."

Dennis looks down at the item in his hand. "Weston, what are you doing?"

Jaime tosses his checkbook and pen back in the bag, zipping it up. He fetches his dark tinted oval sunglasses and puts them on. Nodding to Bobby and Dan, they leave the room. Jaime walks past Sandy, who remains clueless.

The producer says to Dennis as he has his hand on the doorknob, "She needs direction and better representation."

The door slams shut behind Jaime Weston as he exits.

Sandy says, "I need some coffee."

Dennis turns to look at Sandy with a pathetic glance and nods in despair.

***

Carol puts the key in the keyhole. Evelyn looks ahead. Carol could tell her roommate had something on her mind. A month away from her due date, the singer begins to feel slightly depressed.

"What's the matter?" Carol asks, taking the key out.

"Oh. I was just thinking. Everything seems so wrong. I should openly be happy. Not hiding. I went about this completely wrong. At this stage, I should have a baby shower. A month left and I'm doing nothing. I just feel as though I have to keep on looking behind my back, hoping nobody recognizes me." Evelyn lets out a sigh and feels her large rounded out belly.

"But it's what you wanted, right?"

"I *thought* it's what I wanted. It's too late now. He doesn't even know. I made a mess of this."

Carol puts the key in the hole again. She reassures her. "We'll talk about this inside."

The door opens. Evelyn flips on the light switch.

"SURPRISE!"

She stiffens with a quick breath. A crowd of twenty women stand in a half circle in the living room. They consist of Carol's artist friends and other acquaintances. All around the TV set are fancily wrapped gifts in pastel colors and baby related images. Evelyn takes a step forward in awe. She turns in a complete circle. Mylar balloons are strewn about clinging to the ceiling with words like, 'Congratulations' and 'Baby' on them. Other regular balloons are tied in groups of pink, blue, yellow, and green with lavender streamers hung on the railing of the stairs.

"Oh my God!" She exclaims. "You knew about this!"

Carol laughs back and nods enthusiastically.

Evelyn gives her a big hug.

"You are incredibly sweet. Nobody has ever done anything like this for me!"

"This is your first child though."

"Yes. I know. But I've never had anyone go through these measures to pull off such a party for me. Not even my own friends back in England. Oh, this is... This is just beautiful!"

Carol says nonchalantly, "I was hoping you would like to have one."

A blonde woman in her late thirties announces, "You should see what's in the kitchen."

Evelyn looks at the guests then makes a dash for the kitchen. She flips up the top of a large box on the table. A cake in the shape of a baby bottle with the words, *Congrats Evelyn* is written out in blue frosting.

"Betsy made that." Another woman says as the lady across from her stands up and waves.

"Oh thank you, Betsy!" Evelyn shouts out with glee.

"No problem!"

The singer looks at the crowd. She puts her hand over her heart. Seemingly enough, Evelyn feels a little regretful with all of the unrecognizable faces paying attention to her.

"I feel so sorry I don't even know who all of you are. I do know who Betsy is now."

"Cake lady!" One voice shouts out.

They all laugh.

Evelyn sees a curly haired brunette who looks slightly familiar to her.

"I know I've seen you before."

The woman says back, "Lisa. From the Christmas party."

"Okay. That's right."

A guest with pink highlights in her hair informs the mother-to-be. "We did it for Carol. She wanted us to help... And a friend of Carol's is a friend of ours."

Evelyn wipes her eyes from becoming slightly emotional from the outpouring of compassion. "In that case, I thank all of you." She smiles joyfully and proudly.

Wrapping paper flies in the air as Evelyn tears through packages of a variety of sorts.

"Oh! It's beautiful!"

The crowd oohs and ahs as Evelyn holds up a handmade yellow ducky outfit. She looks at the hood. It's the face of a yellow rubber ducky.

A guest says, "It's for after bath time. Kind of like a towel. It's made of terry cloth. You know, if you have to hurry and take them out, just put it on and they'll get dry fast. I did it with my youngest."

"It's precious. I'll definitely use it!

While Evelyn places the outfit in a growing pile of opened gifts, a dark red headed woman asks her a question. "Any idea of what you might have?"

"No." Evelyn replies.

A longer haired brunette answers for her. "Usually, if you don't fill out, but it looks like you're carrying a basketball? Chances are it's a boy. If you're big and have gained a lot of weight and you have a hard time trying to locate your chest..."

They all snicker.

"...You better believe it's a girl."

Another woman says, "I know. Us girls look out for our vanity but our daughters insist we grow big for them. Guess it's roomy enough for them inside there."

Laughter is heard throughout the room.

Evelyn announces back, "I really don't care as long as they're healthy."

"That's the smart way to go."

"From the looks of things, they'll be wearing a lot of green and yellow."

A few women laugh at the suggestion.

"Any names picked out yet?"

"I have a few."

"Are you one of those that uses the name, Junior?"

"No. I wouldn't want to do that."

A blonde asks, "What does your husband think?"

Evelyn gives a blank look. The woman catches her glance. "Boyfriend?" She asks.

"Um. Sort of." The singer nods.

Carol watches the women carefully.

The pink haired one inquires. "What does he do?"

Evelyn thinks for a moment.

Photographer or record producer?

Since she admitted the father was not her husband, she would have to come clean. She takes a cautious look at Carol. "Um, record producer."

One of the women say, "Uh huh. And you're a singer."

The brunette raises her brows. "Mm hmm."

The redhead chimes in. "Interesting sessions!"

Evelyn quickly feels a bit uncomfortable. The line of questioning by virtual strangers wasn't something she anticipated. She gets up and goes to the kitchen.

Before she can say a word, her roommate speaks out. "Don't let them get to you. They're only trying to get to know you and your situation."

Evelyn shakes her head while standing by the sink. "It's not them. It's me. Why should I even have to think of who the father is when I know? Photographer or record producer? That's what I was thinking of. I know and I'm very happy about it. So, why don't I show it? I'm going to go back out there and have fun. No more hiding."

Evelyn walks away, proud as a peacock.

In the living room, she holds court once again. "You asked me what the father is. Yes, he's a record producer. Now, I didn't tell you but he's simply amazing!"

"I'll bet!" One of the women sharply replies.

"Oh, and he's beautiful. Incredibly handsome."

"Any chance of this little one looking anything like him?"

"Well, you never know." Evelyn laughs back.

From the kitchen, Carol's concern changes to a smile. Her roommate made good on her vow to have fun. More gifts are opened followed by everyone eating cake.

***

April 6th.

Evelyn and Carol attend a party in the Village. They walk up the steps of an unassuming building that is a converted meeting lodge. For this occasion, the place is turned into a premiere for one of Carol's painter friends. Evelyn is now nine months pregnant. It could be any day she would give birth. She waddles in to see all sorts of people dressed oddly. Wearing a white and polka dotted full-length dress, it makes her look more like an oversized Minnie Mouse. Carol is attired in a pink blouse with puffy sleeves, a bright blue vest and matching pants.

Non-alcoholic beverages are being served in wine glasses. Evelyn looks at the odd colored liquid and taps Carol on the arm. "What is this?"

Carol turns to her. "It's actually fruit cocktail juice. Fresh squeezed unlike the canned stuff."

"Oh." Evelyn takes a sip and is pleasantly surprised. "Hmm. Delicious!" She wanders over to a picture and studies it. Suddenly, there is an abrupt rupture from deep within her. Evelyn looks down and massages her oversized belly. "It's okay. You kick up a storm in there. Are you going to possibly become a drummer?" She smiles widely. Walking along, the rupturing grows stronger. Evelyn stops to feel something within split. A huge pain seizes her stomach like a flaming arrow torn straight through. She opens her mouth with nothing to come out in the form of sound. Leaning over, she grabs hold of a table. Squeezing her eyes shut, she says hoarsely aloud, "Oh God! Not now! Ow!"

A couple happens to see her. The glass she holds slips from her hand and crashes to the floor.

The gentleman in his fifties stoops down and asks, "Ma'am? Do you need help?"

Evelyn says between gasps, "I'm...going...to...have...a...baby."

His eyes go wide and he calls out to his wife or anybody around. "Call 9-1-1! Somebody! *Anybody!*"

The hostess, Cynthia, rushes to see the growing commotion.

"What's the matter?"

Someone from the crowd shouts out, "She's going to have a baby!"

Another voice calls out. "I called the paramedics! They're on their way!"

Carol bumps into people as she winds her way swiftly through the crowd. She stops short of running over a propped Evelyn against the wall.

Carol says, "Oh shit!"

Evelyn looks up. "It's time."

Stooping down on one leg, Carol takes Evelyn's hand attempting to ease the burden of her labor pains. She says apologetically, "I am *so* sorry. I should have just left you back... We shouldn't have even gone today. God, how stupid of me! How *asinine* of me to be walking around with a woman who's nine months pregnant. Stupid, stupid me!"

Evelyn says, "It's okay. I wanted to go."

Carol nods with understanding.

"Okay. I'll call Henry and see... Hopefully he's still at the hotel."

Carol runs away from the crowd and heads for the hallway where there is a pay phone.

Just then, a siren can be heard. Two paramedics arrive at the scene. One gallery patron points to Evelyn. The crowd disperses as the pregnant woman is lifted onto a flat gurney. She howls hoarsely in pain. Carol rushes back. As the medics place the gurney in the waiting ambulance, Carol calls out to her.

"Evelyn! Sweetie! I'll meet you at the hospital."

She calls out to one of the medics, "Hey, Roosevelt, right?"

Both paramedics nod in agreement.

At the hospital, Evelyn is wheeled into the maternity ward. She wears a hospital gown as the pain has ceased long enough for her to change.

The doctor says, "Ma'am? Do you know your name?"

She says back in a weary tone, "Evelyn Marie Winthrop."

A nurse says to the doctor, "She told the medics team she was forty-one and she wants drugs."

The doctor raises his brows behind glasses.

"Oh. Well, she's going to be a mother soon. Get her off the gurney and onto the bed." Evelyn is helped to her weakened feet. Then she feels a crushing pain. She holds her stomach. Squeezing her eyes shut she screams in a raspy, loud screech.

"Get it out! Get the *bloody* thing *out*! Ow! Ow! Ow!"

Evelyn plops down on the bed. She howls in more pain with raspy cries.

The doctor calls out to his assistants. "Let's do it."

Evelyn's eyes go super wide as she tremors from the excruciating pain.

He asks her to spread her legs.

Evelyn yells back. "How the bloody hell do you think I wound up this way?"   "Breathe!" One assistant tells her.

The doctor pulls up the sheet. "Oh my! A few more pushes and this baby will be out. There's a head already. This kid won't wait for an Epidural."

Evelyn tries to sit up, breathes then pushes.

The doctor says, "No drugs for you."

Evelyn shouts, "WHAT??? No *drugs*?"

"Come on. Almost there. One more push!"

Evelyn musters up all the strength and pushes. One of the assistants holds her hand as she squeezes. Evelyn lets out one deep agonized scream.

Carol looks through a small window in the maternity wing.

Henry says as he flips through a magazine, "Childbirth is so messy."

"Speak for yourself you goober. You're a man. You get off easy."

"Well, it's unpleasant."

"Yeah. Meanwhile the father of this child isn't around."

"She refused to tell him!"

Carol eyes Henry. "It doesn't help her. She has to squeeze out that life through a small opening."

Henry winces.

"Oh sorry. Did I gross you out?" She smirks.

They hear the muffled sound of a baby crying.

Henry asks, "What's goin' on?

Carol says with mischief, "You want a play-by-play?"

"Well..."

"Ah, you know what my favorite part is?"

"What's that?"

"The cutting of the umbilical cord. The vine of life." She grins.

Henry cringes. "Yuck!"

Carol laughs back. "Wimp!"

A doctor leaves through the swinging door. He asks if the two are related.

Henry puts the magazine down and answers quickly. "She's her roommate."

They get attired in hospital scrubs, and enter the maternity ward doors.

A nurse wraps up the baby and carries Evelyn's bundle of joy into the nursery to get weighed and checked. Along the way, both Carol and Henry rush up to her.

Carol says, "Can we see?"

The doctor arrives back to check on things. He says, "She fell asleep before we could tell her or show her the little girl she had. Evelyn needs her rest. We don't usually let older mothers go through natural childbirth without a little something to help ease the pain but this little one was coming out fast. We needed some sort of a verification name for her but like I said, her mom conked out. We labeled her as Winthrop. Or would she be under the father's name?"

Carol replies quickly. "Weston."

Henry matches her. "Winthrop."

They look at each other.

Henry begins to ask, "I thought... Never mind. Weston."

The doctor says, "Whatever the name, the formalities can wait."

Carol asks, "Can we see her?"

The doctor shows the two.

Henry takes one look at the baby. "Yep. Weston." He nods with a heavy breath.

Fifteen minutes later, Evelyn begins to slowly open her eyes to a cloudy vision. Two pale figures sit next to the wall. She opens her eyes to realize Carol and Henry are in hospital scrubs with her. Carol leans against Henry's arm and awakens herself.

Evelyn groggily calls out. "Carol? Henry?"

The two get up quickly.

Evelyn asks, "The baby?"

Henry smiles at her and squeezes her hand with his. "The baby's just fine."

Carol adds in, "You did great."

She goes to the door and tells Henry, "I'll be right back."

Carol leaves Henry with Evelyn.

He says, "You didn't see her yet?"

With a pleased tone, Evelyn says, "It's a girl?"

"Yeah."

Evelyn smiles back. "A girl."

Carol comes back.

A nurse soon follows holding the little bundle of joy. She says, "Apparently her Mommy wanted to meet her."

The nurse walks over to Evelyn who sits up. The little girl who is bundled in a blanket is gently placed in her mother's arms. The nurse steps away to leave them alone. Henry looks at Carol, wondering what Evelyn will think. The new mother unwraps her newborn slightly examining her face. What she sees makes her jaw drop.

Quietly she exclaims, "Oh my God. She's beautiful!" The reality was that the baby girl looked an awful lot like her father. Evelyn says, "I have a name for her. Amanda. Amanda Jean Weston. I read in a book of names how Amanda means 'beloved or adored,' and Jean is for 'God's gracious gift.'" Evelyn holds up the newborn, giving her a hug. "'Cause, that's what she is. My beautiful little gift." She gently pulls the covering away from the newborn's head, revealing Amanda's lightly covered dark brown hair.

With all of the happiness, Henry still has some questions in his mind. Carol smiles at both the mother and daughter. He slowly steps away.

Carol turns to him. "What's the matter with you?"

Henry gazes at Evelyn. He shakes his head in disbelief. "Why would you want to keep *his* name for her?"

In a defiant tone, Carol answers back. "Why not? She looks just like him."

Ignoring what the artist has just said, Henry grills Evelyn. "Up to this point, you didn't want anything to do with him. Now you're just going to take his name?"

Evelyn answers assertively. "Legitimately and biologically, Jaime *is* her father."

"Why didn't you just use Brockton? He's going to raise her anyway."

Evelyn's eyes go wide. She turns her head away as if taking in something bitter.

"No. I would never do that."

"What would you do if he...Ed, ever found out?"

"I would get a fake ID made for her."

"With her looks? Good luck!"

With confusion, Evelyn asks, "Why are you doing this? Why are you saying these things?"

"I just want to make sure you know what you are doing for the sake of your child."

For the moment, Evelyn feels as though she wants to cry. "I didn't intend for any of this to happen! You think I don't know how screwed up my life is? Henry, she is my second chance."

Henry looks at her. In defeat, he nods back. "All right. You're right. I just hope everything goes well for you."

By mid afternoon the following day, Henry returns to New Paltz in the pouring rain. He pulls his dark green Mazda up onto the unfinished driveway to the studio of I.C.E. Stopping his car, he examines the rain pelting down hard on his windshield. As the wipers move back and forth like a pendulum, Henry is left to wonder how he should present the news to the record producer.

"Jaime, Congratulations on having a daughter."

Picking up a box from the backseat, he places it on the passenger's side. The ignition is shut off. Henry buttons up his coat, checks his stash of cigars and grabs two. He dons his gray cap, grabs the box, and then leaves the car. He looks over at the black BMW parked on the other side.

Jaime is definitely there.

Henry dashes quickly through puddles and pebbles. Reaching the door and looking up at the extra ten inches of shelter above where it remains dry, he raps at the door. There comes the sound of a click and the door opens slightly. Henry pushes it open to let himself in. Nobody seems to be around. He turns a corner after the stairwell. He calls out.

"Jaime, you here?"

A voice comes from within. The door unlocks and there he stands. Wearing a black jersey-thin sweater that defines his tall slender figure, he puts his hand out in the gesture to come in. Henry immediately can see something has been troubling his friend. Jaime's normal seductive looking eyes have the glance of little to no sleep. Without words, Jaime goes back to the chair and picks up a half empty bottle of Corona, then fetches an almost finished cigarette leaning in an ashtray. No lights are on, only the gray skies from available windows project any source of brightness.

In a deep almost tired tone he says, "If you've come here to chastise me, don't. Please leave."

Jaime turns a wary eye to Henry.

"No. *None* of that." Henry says in agreement. To make small talk he asks, "So, how is it going?"

"It's not going well...let me tell you that."

The smile cancels from Henry's face. It would be a hard sell to somehow manage in getting the producer to be vaguely interested in what he has to say. Again, he tries to get Jaime to lighten up.

"Um, it's a *downpour* out there."

Jaime gets up, takes one last puff of the cigarette before snuffing it out in the ashtray.

"I know that already." He responds deeply. Slightly more agitated, he puts a hand to his fully slicked back hair and says with a voice a little on edge, "How do you think this mess happened?" Before Henry can say a word, Jaime continues. "Eight hours of cleaning up demos down the fuckin' toilet. No backup. I told Bobby he had to help me with the computer. Dan was supposed to get a component fixed for the mixing modular. It broke. Never got finished. Shit, man! Then it was raining." He plops back down on the chair and covers his face with both hands. Then, while squeezing his eyes shut and pinching the narrow bridge of his nose, he says aloud, "Fuck!"

Henry feels around in his coat pocket for the cigars. He listens some more to his flustered friend.

"I've had *no* sleep because I was trying to get some things fixed. The power went out earlier this morning, so everything that Bobby and I worked on is gone. On top of no sleep, I've been having beer and coffee to keep me going. Other than that? I'm dead to the world."

Henry digs in his jacket and brings out the rectangular box. He says cautiously, "I have something that might cheer you up."

"If it's any way to fix the eight hours lost, I'd be grateful. If not, then it's hard to tell."

"I went to the city and picked up a little something for you."

Jaime turns his sight directly at Henry who presents him with the box.

Looking at the picture on the cover he asks, "What is it?"

"If you open it, you'll find that they're posters printed as postcards."

Jaime opens the box and flips through the cards. A smile starts to show on his face.

Henry continues. "They're that early century German artwork you like."

Jaime looks down and smiles widely. "Where did you get these?"

"I went to MoMA."

"Museum of Modern Art?"

"Yeah."

Jaime nods but still smiles. "It was really sweet of you to do this for me and I thank you..."

Henry interrupts for a moment. "Ah, I have one more thing for you."

"Oh? What's that?"

Henry takes out the cigars. He hands one to the producer. Jaime angles in confusion while looking directly at Henry.

Henry says, "It's for a celebration. Somebody I know had a baby last night."

"Anybody I know?"

"No."

Henry takes out his lighter as he puts the cigar in his mouth. Jaime does the same.

Henry adds in. "I'm just really glad for them."

"What was it?"

"A girl."

Jaime smiles back with sincerity as he takes the cigar out of his mouth. "Well, hopefully they're doing okay?"

Henry inhales on his cigar as he smiles with contentment. "That they are my friend. That they are."

Henry notices that Jaime hasn't lit his cigar yet.

"Here you go." Henry flicks on his lighter again while his friend leans toward the small flame.

***

At Carol's, Evelyn feeds her daughter a bottle of formula. The newborn gorges down on the warm liquid. As a mom, Evelyn feels content. She thinks nothing more than the well-being of the baby she gave birth to only a few short weeks earlier. Amanda's eyes look directly at the bottle in front of her. She begins to get sleepy, as her stomach grows full. Evelyn gives her a kiss on the head. The newborn's eyes close heavily. Without noticing what is on the radio, Evelyn remains on a chair in the kitchen.

Downtown Manhattan, Bobby and Jaime visit a radio station to talk about some of their latest projects they have produced. If Evelyn Winthrop wasn't going to promote *Hero's Requiem,* then they would do it themselves. Syd Kurknow hosts the program on WGLH on 89.1, a college station. Both Bobby and Jaime walk in the room and take a seat. While placing their headphones on, Syd begins talking with them.

"How are you guys? I haven't seen you Bobby in what is it? Five years."

"Gee, Syd. It's been that long?"

"Afraid so, man. And next to me is Jaime Weston, who...um, well, I don't believe we've ever talked, but I'm a big fan of your production."

Jaime replies back. "Thanks."

"I must say the spelling of your name is a bit different than other people I know."

Bobby says back, "It's Spanish."

"But, it's pronounced *Jay-me*, right?"

"Wrong. It's pronounced as Hy-me." Bobby replies.

Jaime reassures Syd. "Yeah. He has a point."

Syd replies back. "Sounds Jewish."

Jaime laughs. "That it could."

"Are you yourself Spanish?"

"No. Actually I've got a bit of Indian blood in me."

"So, that could explain your name."

"Yeah. Well, I don't know how my mom came up with it, but what you see is what you get I suppose."

Bobby adds in, "Or... Or you have that other option."

Both Jaime and Syd look at Bobby curiously. "He could be called, Diego."

In anguish, Jaime puts his hand to his forehead. "Oh no." He groans.

"I found out that both Jaime and Diego have the same meaning." Bobby glances at his friend. "*Diego.*" He torments with a grin. "Doesn't it sound like a Spanish lover's name? Diego."

Jaime chuckles with embarrassment.

Bobby changes his tone. "Verdad que si, mi amigo?"

Jaime says back deeply, "His mind is on siesta."

They all laugh.

Syd says, "So tell everybody out there what you've been up to?"

Bobby says, "Uh, just the normal stuff. We've had a very busy year. Let's see, we had Matt Hattinger."

Syd asks, "The Project?"

Jaime responds. "No. Just Matt. He wanted to do something different for his solo album. A more organic approach than his normal New Age stuff he does with the band. Then we brought in, Pete Rosenbaum."

"Of Rose Deluxe?"

"Yeah. He wanted a lot of mixing on his project. Then there was uh, Evelyn Winthrop."

"Tell me fellas, what's it like for you when you get a good reception from an artist you've been working with."

Jaime answers readily. "If I may. It's really like a good..."

Bobby interrupts. "Uh, Jaime? We're on the radio."

Jaime in an agreeable fashion turns to Bobby. Then he finishes the answer with, "It's just a tremendous feeling. Lighter than air."

Syd picks up an album and tells the two, "I listened to Evelyn Winthrop's latest, *Hero's Requiem* and the production and sound is just fantastic."

Jaime utters, "Thanks."

Bobby says, "We didn't have much to go on."

Jaime picks up the story with more enthusiasm. Talking about Evelyn would get him started. "She gave us parts, initially."

"What do you mean?" Syd asks.

Jaime says, "She brought in a load of tapes. These were unlabeled parts. Like a...oh, a guitar fill here. A bass line there. We had to piece these things together like a puzzle. She told us that she had gone through other studios but wasn't thrilled with what she got."

Bobby chimes in. "I think she said about a dozen of the best studios."

"And she found that sound with you guys?" Syd remarks.

"Yes." Jaime answers.

Syd holds the album, taking out the inner sleeve.

"Now, what I'm most curious about is the title track. Can you tell us a little about this?"

Jaime answers again. "Yeah. Evelyn had a real difficult time with this track. She said the whole album was supposed to be somewhat jazz oriented. That didn't work. This track we're talking about, like I said only was in parts. So, we had the full vocals. Just her. And it was the first track we worked on and completed within three or four days."

Bobby adds in. "It took her two years but we were able to get it done in a few days only."

"Did she think it was impossible?" Syd questions with curiosity.

Jaime continues. "Yes. We began adding in things and there was a specific bass line I really liked, that I felt fit just right. So, we took that, and then we ran into sort of a snag. The percussion wasn't right. It didn't have the right feel to it. And the um...same night she presented us with the song, Bobby and I started putting our heads together and began thinking of what we might be able to replace that sound with."

Syd asks. "It's not cymbals? 'Cause it kind of sounds like that."

"No. Absolutely no drums on the track."

"Oh really?"

Bobby says, "Jaime came up with the idea of something with a deeper sound to it. He started looking in the kitchen down in the studio we have and then came up with an idea."

"Right. I started humming the tune she had."

Bobby grins. "He can pull off a nice falsetto!"

Jaime looks at him for a moment.

Syd looks at Jaime who says, "You do what you have to." He looks down. "Anyway, what you're actually hearing is a trash can."

"Isn't that something? Now, how did you come up with that?"

"Her voice is very low and the cymbals were too tinny sounding. Kind of bright where the song itself is that... It has a sense of mourning to it. *Very* dark. We needed something different that could match it. I came up with the idea of a trash can. It had a low timbre but also a fast cadence where a cymbal's note goes on for a few seconds longer and seems to echo. That wouldn't work. It had to be fast, clean, but *dark*. That's what we were shooting for and it worked wonderfully as you can tell. This is basically the way we've done things for twenty-three years now. Since then, Bobby and I have been like brothers. He's the closest thing to me aside from my own mom that I consider family. The way we work things is like a yin-yang effect. For the most part, I do a lot of the mental work, sorting out arrangements in my head and thinking of the over-all concept and Bobby does the physical. He transcribes my thoughts into reality."

Bobby states. "I can be very mental too...in more ways than one."

Jaime chuckles back. "Yeah. You've got that right."

Syd laughs with them.

Carol switches the dial on her boom box. She goes back to a sculpture sitting on the table in her workspace. The station comes in clear with Syd announcing.

"This is Syd Kurknow, and you're listening to WGLH. Serving all of lower New York State down to Trenton, New Jersey. We're in the studio with famed producers, Jaime Weston and Bob Whitfield."

Carol's eyes meet the radio sitting on the shelf. It occurs to her who is on the radio.

"WGLH? Oh shit! That's downtown. They're not that far from here at all."

Her gaze is fixated on the door up the steps. Just upstairs was Evelyn taking care of Amanda... baby Weston. What would she do if she heard?

The conversation resumes.

Jaime laughs back. "I had no idea who Bobby was at first. He didn't look very much different than what you see now. Always cracking jokes. Completely crazy. He made the engineers and producers break into hysterics to the point we would both get in trouble. Until finally we became so notorious between Ottawa down to Mississauga that people were a little suspicious of us."

"I was banned in a few L.A. studios!" Bobby pipes in.

Jaime continues. "That's true too. We got good enough that we decided to head to Buffalo and try things out there. Eventually we made it down here in Manhattan, specifically the Bronx. For a short while, we split up. I went to L.A. and Bobby stayed here to raise a family. It was a wonderful time but we missed each other badly and our work suffered a bit. Finally I came back and... *this* is home."

Syd says, "Jaime, you keep a low profile."

Bobby states. "Always a man of mystery."

Jaime concludes. "It's better that way."

Syd says, "But you did have a reputation."

"Yeah. I did. Truth be told, it was a product of the times. Everything seemed so fun then and I did get caught up. It was a good vibe, but just overindulgent. Things were done to the max. Luckily, it did not show up on the records I produced at the time."

Syd looks at the album again.

"I haven't heard much about this album, so I was a little surprised but very pleased when I heard it."

Jaime states. "That seems to be the consensus at the studio. She was really proud of this but for one reason or another, she hasn't done anything of a major magnitude for this record. Not that I've noticed."

Syd asks, "Does this life cause any problems for your family? Are you married?"

"No."

"Children?"

"No. Quite honestly, Syd, I'm just too busy to raise a family. I'm really dedicated to my line of work and it wouldn't be right to get loved ones involved in this crazy business. At least not now."

"How about you, Bobby?"

"I've got a wonderful wife and a great daughter who's twelve. She'll be thirteen in August. They know the way I live. Although, I keep my priorities straight and come home on time."

"How is it working with Dan Soren? He did some great work about eight years ago."

While Carol listens, she figures it's a good idea she not tell Evelyn that Jaime is on the radio. His answers summed up how he felt. She still couldn't help the thought that perhaps if he knew, he would change his mind. But, it wasn't up to her. Best to simply leave it alone and let Evelyn tell him on her own time, if ever.

"Carol!" Evelyn calls out.

Carol stands alerted, rushes over to the radio and shuts it off. She jogs up the stairs.

Once the conversation is over with, Jaime and Bobby walk out of the studio.

Bobby tells him, "Do you really think we should have mentioned that stuff about Evelyn? We really don't know what's going on with her."

Jaime lights up a cigarette, making the matchbook disappear like a switchblade under the palm of his hand.

"You know, Bobby, sometimes you start sounding like Dan and Vicki. What are the chances she'll even hear us? I don't think you can get the station in England." He puts on his sunglasses and nods with a smile. "Let's go catch a cab."

Both men walk away, disappearing down the street.

Bobby taps his fingers on the table. Jaime looks up. While removing his sunglasses, a waitress places two cups of coffee down. She then walks away.

Bobby tells Jaime, "I could distinctly tell while we were being interviewed that you might have been hinting at something I never knew."

Jaime stirs his coffee. "What's that?"

"While we were talking about your name."

"Syd brought it up. I don't know for what reason though?"

"No. No. I don't think either you or your mom has ever said anything. You're Jewish."

Jaime looks down at the table with a hint of a smile on his face.

"Portuguese?" Bobby guesses.

"You're reading too much into nothing."

"Something from the Spanish speaking culture."

"No."

"You're at least part."

Jaime continues to stir his coffee.

"I only agreed when Syd said my name could be that."

Bobby says, "Yeah, right. And elephants fly."

"Maybe they did on some past LSD trip of yours." Jaime laughs back.

Bobby turns his attention to a framed photo on the wall.

"Hey, they've got a picture of Jimi Hendrix. Feels like home, now."

Jaime corrects him. "Jimmie James."

"What?"

"Hendrix. That's what he was called before he hit it big. Chas Chandler from The Animals discovered him here."

"How do you know this?"

Jaime shrugs. "Been around here enough." He pulls out a Marlboro and lights it. Bobby stays quiet, listening to the music that's pumped throughout the cafe. A deep groove beat starts up, led by Bob Marley leading the way into "Could You Be Loved." He taps his fingers again, looking out the window.

Lenny Mead walks in the cafe. Bobby looks at him, immediately recognizing the face.

"Uh-oh. Don't look now. We've got company."

Jaime looks up in time to see the man standing next to their table.

Wearing a black leather jacket and printed shirt underneath, Lenny looks at both of them angling with his dark aviator sunglasses on. He puts a hand to his shortened curled hair with the beginnings of a mullet.

"Jaime and Bobby. Funny seeing you two here." He says humorless.

Bobby says back. "Lenny. How are you?"

"Fine."

Lenny looks right at Jaime, who still has his eyes on him.

"Jaime Weston. Well. Long time, no see. Still a lady killer after all these years?"

The producer smiles back.

"Yep. Jaime Weston. Bachelor extraordinaire. I've seen your style...at a thrift store."

Bobby furrows his brows. "Lenny, are you still trying to compete with Jaime? I thought you were cool too but, perhaps not enough. Face it, man. You just don't have it. Trying to read poetry on the streets of Yonge won't get you places."

"This is New York City, not Toronto, Bobby." Lenny gleans. "So, I heard you produced Evelyn Winthrop's latest album."

Bobby responds, as he can't wait to stick it to the self-absorbed Beat poet. "We're quite proud of that. That's our gal you're talkin' about."

Jaime sucks on his cigarette, and calmly asks Lenny, "Don't you have Kerouac to read or Ginsberg to meet?

Lenny ignores his cool rival. "Gals, huh? Why bother when you're other half is sitting next to you."

Bobby gets up quickly. The waitress looks at them from her unmade face. Jaime puts his hand up.

"Bobby. Cool it. He's not worth it."

Lenny cracks a smile then walks away.

Jaime dabs out the remnants of his cigarette in the ashtray on the table. With one final curl of smoke from his mouth, he tells his friend, "He's just trying to rile you. The guy obviously thinks he's hot shit."

Bobby glares in back of him.

"Turd is more like it. A cold piece of turd."

"Come on. We have a plane to catch for Chicago tomorrow." Jaime smiles.

Bobby responds. "Yeah, you're right."

They gather their money for the check. Jaime begins to think of his interview with Syd and the just mentioned Evelyn Winthrop by Lenny Mead. He plunks down his money while Bobby does the same. Both get up. Bobby goes outside while Jaime checks his matchbook. Another man heads them off just before they are about to leave.

Jaime announces. "Geoff."

"Jaime. I haven't seen you in a long time!"

"Same here."

"Hey, I just heard the interview you did with Syd on the way, while crossing over the bridge. You did a great job with Winthrop's album."

Jaime asks, "You know what's going on. Have you heard anything about her in general?"

"She's basically M.I.A. on promotion. No posters. No slicks. No press kit stuff in any way. Nada. She just disappeared. I went over to Bleecker St. Records and they said the same. It really shocks me, Jaime. It's such a good album and she's nowhere."

"What about her manager? Anything?"

"Her manager is in West Germany. Didn't you get the info when she recorded?"

Sheepishly, Jaime responds. "I didn't check."

Geoff tells the producer, "It's just baffling. You know every top-notch producer tried to help her and didn't get very far. Talk about a blow to the ego. She goes to you and the thing sounds like a friggin' masterpiece! How do you do it?"

"It's just the way it turned out, Geoff."

"Man, a trash can! They ought to put that in the Hard Rock Cafe! You are a pure genius.

"Well. I thank you. Um, I would really like to talk longer but we have to go to Chicago tomorrow."

"Is that at the big convention?"

"Yeah."

"Hey, well good luck. Maybe I'll see you televised on the Grammys if you win an award."

Jaime laughs back. "I'll see you later, Geoff."

***

A knock comes at Carol's door.

Evelyn shouts out, "I'll get it!"

She rushes towards the door. Upon opening it, she sees Edwin smiling big.

Cheerfully he announces, "Hello, luv!" He looks right at the baby in her arms. "May I?"

Evelyn says, "Why of course? I have some things I need to do anyway."

She's about to hand Amanda to Edwin when he suddenly says, "Oh, wait a minute."

He takes off his blue blazer, placing it on the arm of the couch. Then Evelyn finishes handing her daughter to him. He picks up Amanda. Holding her up for inspection, he says about the one month old, "Come to Uncle Edwin."

Placing her upward against his chest, his eyes widen at the sight of her.

"My! My! Just look at those eyes! My dear, you're looking like your daddy more and more."

Amanda's brown eyes wander with curiosity. Edwin then catches the scent of something cooking.

"Evelyn, what is that delightful smell?"

While tending to the oven, she says back, "Lasagna."

Edwin hears the sound of footsteps from the level below. The door in the right corner opens. Carol appears. She sees Edwin sitting on the couch holding Amanda.

"Edwin! I didn't know you were coming over." Walking over to the couch, she leans over to kiss him. Carol smiles then walks into the open kitchen. "How's dinner coming along?" She asks Evelyn.

"It should be ready very soon,"

Carol calls out. "Edwin, hon, did you eat yet?"

"No, and I'm starving!"

"Great! We'll have plenty to go around."

Edwin smiles at little Amanda. She looks up at him. Carol washes dishes while Evelyn sits at the table.

Carol says to her roommate, "My God, that little girl is an absolute magnet! Edwin is so attached to her. Anybody who sees her always asks questions."

Both women begin laughing.

Evelyn's eyes lock onto a magazine partially obscured by a small pile of papers.

"I didn't know you get these kind of magazines."

"Oh, Lisa left some of her stuff here. I should give her a call."

Just as Evelyn reaches for the magazine, the timer above the oven rings.

"Ready!"

Amanda lets out a cry. Edwin still remains on the couch, asking the baby, "What's the matter, Mandy? Are you hungry? Tired? Hopefully, not wet."

The concerned mother turns quickly and quietly asks of Carol, "Can you take out the lasagna?"

Carol mumbles back, "Mm hmm."

Walking back to the next room over, Evelyn reaches over Edwin and takes Amanda back into her arms.

"She's tired. Poor little thing has been up long enough."

She walks upstairs with Amanda.

After their meal, Carol, Edwin, and Evelyn sit back.

Edwin asks, "Got any dessert?"

Carol barks back jokingly, "You pig! You ate two helpings of lasagna and big ones at that. Now you want dessert?" A moment later she admits, "I got some great cheesecake from a bakery midtown."

While the two talk about pastries, Evelyn eyes the magazine that she was going to flip through just before the timer went off. Her fingers slide it over. It was one of those glossy celebrity type of publications. The kind that showed Hollywood people at parties, premieres, and all sorts of get-togethers mixed with the latest fashions. She picks it up and looks through it. There seemed to be no short abundance of women with puffy sleeves or over-sized shoulder pads. The men on the other hand must have carried twenty pounds of Aqua Net in their hair. Smirking at that, she wonders what ever happened to the day of shaved or spiked hair, or just plain old leaving it alone. The fashions used to be funky and fresh. It seemed that the '80s were now a newer decade with different indulgences, particularly hair products. Flipping the page while Edwin sits beside her laughing, she scans something with her eyes. It's disturbing enough to her that she feels the urge to cover her mouth. Losing focus among the blurred vision of tears, Evelyn drops the magazine back on the table.

Carol asks while her head is in the refrigerator, "Evelyn, did you want a slice?"

Evelyn doesn't respond. Edwin looks at her and sees she's a bit distressed and hears the muffled sobbing. Getting up from the kitchen table, she remains clasping her hand over her mouth while squeezing her eyes shut. She dashes out of the kitchen, fleeing up the stairs where the door to her room closes quickly.

Carol asks in a concerned tone, "Edwin, what happened?"

She places the big plate of cheesecake on the table.

Confused, he looks down shaking his head. "I don't know, darling." Then he says back, "She was looking through this magazine..." He picks up the item and flips through it. "...And found some..."

Edwin pauses when a page about a record company party is displayed. Looking at it, he sees a photo of Jaime Weston with his arm around a young, pretty brunette identified in the caption as Wendy

Marslich, an assistant for Janger Records. It looked like they were cozy and made a pleasant couple. The smile on the producer's face said it all.

Edwin says while still looking at the page, "I think I just found what upset her."

Carol puts her hand on his shoulder while leaning over to take a look. Right away, she catches sight of the picture. She snorts out, "Oh." She looks up at the stairs. "Poor girl. She's still in love with him."

Edwin shakes his head. "Very tough."

Carol returns to the other side of the table and is about to cut the cheesecake. Only her conscience gets in the way. Placing the knife down, she walks over to the phone. "You can help yourself. I have to call Lisa." Carol puts her hand out towards the table. "I just can't have stuff like *this* sitting around the house. Lisa is going to have to pick up her stuff."

Carol then dials the bright pink phone on the wall.

"Gentlemen, it's the Hudson Pro SRX600. It throws off reverb about fifty feet in diameter. You won't have to worry about mixing and remixing to get the right sound. This here baby does it all. Best of all, the connectors aren't a pain to wire through the motherboard. Any instrument and you've got instant gratification. Make a guitar explode on level ten and you can have a nice blend with a keyboard. You'll have state of the art and up to date sound long before the hotshots make knock-offs in three to four years. It's got a hefty price tag but it's worth the money for producers and engineers such as yourselves. Five fifty-eight for 'er."

That's what the man with the red badge says. He turns his eyes to see if anyone in the crowd of ten is interested in the product.

A producer in his early fifties leans toward Jaime Weston's ear. He whispers, "They'll be selling something else in nineteen-ninety with the same pitch."

With his sunglasses on, Jaime's lips turn to reveal a growing smile.

"Mm hmm."

After the explanation, Dan Soren slips away to talk with a distinguished looking man in his late fifties, who chats with a few females.

"Nice to see you again, Hal."

"Oh, Danny! How is it going?"

"I'm fine. Hey. I need a little favor from you. Jaime's been feeling a little lonely lately. He had it pretty bad for someone and… you know, I'd like to see him *happy*."

Hal perks up his ears. "Ah, well, I happen to have a double scoop." He elbows Dan, who grins.

Over in the lounge area, a few engineers and producers chat. With a plush bordeaux colored couch, a few chairs and a couple of bottles of wine, they all make themselves comfortable.

One person asks Jaime, "So, where is Bobby Whitfield, the funniest producer known nationally and notoriously?"

Jaime looks nervously around and sees Dan heading their way just in time. He didn't need to be stuck with something he couldn't answer. Quietly, Jaime eyes Dan and pulls him away before he can get to a seat.

"Where's Bobby? He was supposed to be here."

"Oh yeah. He and Andrea went to check out some amusement park."

In a low tone, Jaime asks, "An amusement park in Chicago? This is not Disney World and we didn't come here for fun and games. Did you tell him that? We were supposed to look at new equipment."

Dan says back, "I know that."

Jaime shakes his head in disgust while walking back to the lounge portion of the convention center. He addresses the room by saying, "Bobby won't be joining us. He's sort of under the weather."

Dan sheepishly looks in back of him to see Hal heading up the dark gray carpet with two women. Hal winks at Dan when he walks by him. Heading into the lounge, he steps right in back of Jaime who holds a glass of wine. A few of the people snicker. Jaime turns around to see the older man.

"Hi, Hal."

"Jaime, so nice to see you after all this time. Still taking New York by storm?"

"I'm doing fine."

"I heard there wasn't much in the form of fun over there for you. What is that, Albany?"

"New Paltz. You can rest assure Hal, I'm content."

"Well, I'd like you to meet two girls." Hal points to his right at a tall blonde with wavy hair, blue halter-top and black capris pants with heels. "This is Tiffany." Then he points to the girl on his left who is also tall and model-like, with light brown hair and cinnamon colored skin in a gold lamé dress with spaghetti straps. "This over here is Jasmine."

Before pulling off his sunglasses, Jaime gives Dan a hardened glance. Then with warmth he greets the women and smiles at them while shaking their hands. Dan grins. Hal goes to sit in a chair. The two women take Jaime by the hand on both sides, leading him to the couch. They keep him company like bookends, sidling next to him, smiling and looking over the producer.

One of the other engineers asks Jaime, "So, is there anything you've found of interest for I.C.E.?"

He nods back. "Some. There are a few microphones I was looking at."

Another producer asks, "Do you still have those recorders?"

A second producer chimes in. "Christ, Weston! You *still* have those dinosaurs?"

Jaime looks up for a minute with a curious glance. He says almost defensively, "I happen to like those."

With a laugh, he sees that Dan is a little nervous.

Jasmine slips her arm over the producer's shoulder. Tiffany sips on wine and giggles.

The same engineer says to Jaime, "You live in 1980."

Dan finally pipes in. "You'd be surprised at how much the artists like it though."

A different producer asks, "So, who has come through the famed walls of I.C.E.?"

Dan offers up. "Just this past year we had, Matt Hattinger, No Sweat, Jive Box, Gin & Tonic, and of course, *Evelyn Winthrop*." As he says Evelyn's name in a suggestive tone, Jaime darts his eyes at Dan.

Hal sees the producer's expression change to agitated. He intervenes on Jaime's soft spot by asking. "Ladies, are you having a good time?"

Both women nod their heads in agreement.

Hal says to Jaime, "You know, these girls are a lot of fun for a single guy like yourself."

Jaime darts his eyes in confusion, then looks up at Dan with an all-knowing stare while the engineer glances back guiltily.

Hal continues. "I'm willing to give them to you."

The other producers and engineers snicker some more. This was the last straw for Jaime Weston. He quickly makes up an excuse.

"Dan?"

Dan looks at the producer nervously.

Jaime says in an almost pleased tone, "We need to talk about that keyboard we saw. The GXC180."

"Where was that?" Dan's eyes wander.

Jaime gives Dan a smile belying an undertone.

The producer dislodges himself away from the two women. "Excuse me, but Dan and I need to talk."

He gives a tight-lipped smile to Jasmine and Tiffany. Hal smiles at the two women.

Tiffany says, "He's cute."

Jasmine adds in, "*Very cute.*"

Jaime pulls Dan aside next to the men's room some feet away from the lounge area. He takes Dan's arm. His pleasant smile disappears as he quietly asks, "Okay, what is going on?"

"What?"

"Did you talk to Hal about something that I'm not aware of?"

"No."

"Then why has he joined us? He doesn't care about music. Hal is the Hugh Heffner of the music industry with his...*women*. Everybody knows that. Only difference is he has no business sense... he's an industry wannabe. He has no real connection to what we do. Do you know what he would do back in the fifties? He would hang around hotels in Vegas trying to befriend every available entertainer of the time. Suddenly, I have the honor of him being nice and bringing these women over? I'm supposed to enjoy it?"

"Come on, man. He's just trying to be nice."

"These ladies look like something you would see on a game show. Do you think they really have any place in music? I know, I don't."

Dan grimaces.

Just as Jaime is about to say more, Dan speaks up quickly. "You need it! You've been moping around ever since..."

"Since what?"

Dan nods. "Ever since Evelyn left. Ginger was sweet but you all but ignored her. I was hoping you would get over *her* but I think it's worse than what I thought. I know. Maybe Bobby doesn't. I saw the way you acted with Winthrop. It was different than everybody else."

Jaime bows his head down as though he were ashamed of his behavior. He turns slowly with guilty admission just by body language.

Quietly, Dan responds. "Why don't you just admit that you're in love with her?"

Jaime runs a hand through his hair as he tells Dan in a soft though deepened voice filled with regret. "Tell the girls I won't be able to join them."

Walking into the men's room, the producer leaves Dan to think of his failed attempt to play matchmaker with either of Hal's lovely ladies. With a small amount of guilt, the engineer half smiles and half grimaces at his efforts. He felt sorry for his friend but was glad to get the reaction he did as it confirmed his suspicions.

Digging into soft beige clay with wet fingertips, Carol pinches the edges making pie-like indentations. She keeps her full attention on her latest project, eyeing it from every angle. Dipping her fingers in a small bowl filled with water, touches are added in quick succession like paint applied to a canvas. Moving all of her clay instruments and the bowl, Carol begins to pick up the cutting board containing her latest piece.

A knock comes at the door. Placing the board back on the table, Carol wipes her hands and goes to answer it.

She asks, "Who is it?"

The voice comes from outside. "Me. Lisa."

Carol opens the door. With almost black colored curls, the woman smiles at the artist.

"Hi, hon." The artist replies pleasantly.

"So, do you have the offensive material?" Lisa asks.

Carol grabs the magazine, handing it to Lisa.

"Page twenty-seven."

Lisa straightens the small scarf around her neck while she flips through pages quickly. She then finds it.

Carol says, "Bottom right hand corner."

Lisa says back, "The one with the brunette?"

"Yep. That's the stud muffin."

"Hmm. Well, he looks very attractive. That's for sure. Is he the one that you said your ex-boyfriend, Henry, knows?"

"Yep."

"I could have sworn I've seen him some years ago. One of those playboy types."

Carol answers with no hesitation, "He should be more like Playgirl material."

Lisa rolls her eyes and throws her head back in mock disgust. "Carol, there's a reason why you're still single."

"Hey, I can't help it."

"Tell me, Carol. How do you measure a man?"

"By his inseam."

Lisa groans.

Carol grins back while her friend continues to analyze the picture.

The artist says, "I just can't help it. Good looking guys make me think that way."

"So, *he's* Amanda's father." Lisa nods then takes a deep breath. "From what I can tell, this picture looks harmless."

"To you and me it does. Not for Evelyn."

"Let's face it. He is a magnet to people. My belief is that this man can charm people easily."

"That's what I said last night about his daughter. Whenever we're out and about town, people get attracted to her very quickly."

Lisa grows more serious. Carol sees her expression change.

"Uh oh. I *know* that look. Come on, Lisa. Give the guy some slack. It's not like Jaime's the scum of the earth. He doesn't even know about the baby."

Lisa's heavily eye shadowed purple accentuate her brown eyes as she turns them in Carol's direction.

Carol pleads. "I know you have the advice column, but don't treat him like one of your letters."

Lisa sucks in her teeth and states flatly, "Hon, I don't give advice based on someone's looks. Beautiful as he may be...he's still a man."

For a moment, Carol agrees with her. Hesitantly she says, "Yeah."

"You *know* how men are. Does this Jaime fellow have any feelings for Evelyn?"

"I don't know. I mean, I guess so."

"How do you think he would take the news that he had a child by this woman?"

"Oh, just talk to her...but be gentle with her."

"Where is she?"

"Upstairs. She's been in her room since last night."

Lisa begins climbing up the steps while still holding the magazine in her hands.

Carol shouts. "He's drop-dead gorgeous! A fox!"

Lisa calls out over the railing. "He's single."

"Jaime's a male babe!"

"Single!"

"Killjoy!"

"Thank you!"

Lisa disappears up the stairs.

Evelyn's reflection shows her making up her eyes in black mascara. She takes a deep breath while placing the applicator back in the bottle. Looking at her reflection, she sees the face of a forty-one year old woman who was feeling embarrassed by her emotional outburst the previous night. A knock comes at her door. She asks, "Yes?"

Lisa opens the door to a surprised and nervous Evelyn. Cautiously, Lisa tells her, "I want to talk to you about something."

Evelyn pulls out the applicator from a bottle of red lip-gloss. She keeps her concentration on getting made up, hoping to forget what she saw. Opening the magazine and folding it back, Lisa holds it in front of her. The singer, with her lips tightened for the brush's applicator turns her eyes. She places the item down and covers her freshly made face with her hands. Averting her glance, Evelyn says, "Have you come to rub it in my face?"

"No."

"Then what? I'm not as pretty nor am I in my twenties as...*her*."

Lisa sits on the edge of Evelyn's bed.

"I know what you're going through. I've gone through three marriages. I got two kids out of two of them. You don't think I've ever been hurt?" Evelyn looks at the mirror's reflection of Lisa looking at her. "Hon, I deal with people's problems all the time."

"I know. You're one of those magazine shrinks."

"Ah, advice columnist is better."

"Carol told me."

Evelyn turns around on the stool to face Lisa. "I could never compete with the women of today."

"That's right, because you're better than them." Looking back at the magazine, she tells her, "This picture doesn't look threatening at all. It just looks like two people posing for a picture. You're a singer. I'm sure you've been to dozens of parties like these."

Evelyn shakes her head. "I was never into those."

"Well, think of it this way, how many of those women at functions like that can claim they've had a child by him?"

"You're right about that."

"After all, I think that they would be the ones to say *you're* the lucky one."

Evelyn smiles.

"From a one-nighter, you sure made out well."

Evelyn corrects her. "Not a one night stand."

Lisa asks confused. "It wasn't? Then how many times..."

With a slight smile, Evelyn puts up her hand holding up three fingers. Lisa looks shocked. She hesitates. "Well, *almost* three. It didn't get that far."

In back of her, the columnist hears a small gurgle come from the crib.

Lisa asks, "That's Amanda in there?"

"Yes. That's my little baby."

Lisa smiles big. "I have yet to see her. When I came over the other day you weren't home and neither was the baby. I haven't seen you since the shower."

Evelyn admits, "She's right there."

Lisa turns around expecting to find a blonde haired, blue-eyed baby in the crib. Her eyes go wide at the sight of the tiny girl. Amanda wasn't what Lisa imagined her to be. The dark brown hair, and brown eyes, is her greeting. Amanda looks up ahead with her tiny hands flailing in the air.

Lisa laughs. "Is she waving?"

"Oh, she gets excited around company."

The columnist looks at the magazine photo again. She can't get over the resemblance to Jaime Weston.

Evelyn says at the same time, "Amanda Jean Weston."

Lisa looks over in the crib again at the excited and wiggly baby girl. Then she looks back at her mother, telling her, "Wow. She looks like *him*."

In a deep voice of pride Evelyn says back, "I know."

Lisa remains quiet, as she doesn't quite know what to say. It would be hard to try and give advice when the truth was evident. Trying to refocus her scholarly mind, the columnist says, "There is the *one* thing that makes the difference. It's that he's single. You might not want to hear it but you have no marital ties to this man. He belongs to *no one*. That is unless you're willing to tell him. Otherwise, he's not worth it. *No* man is worth it. Carol told me that there was somebody else in your life."

"Ed."

"Why not just have him, Ed, as Amanda's daddy?"

"Shit. I've made an absolute mess out of everything. Ed and I weren't getting along because I couldn't...I *thought* I couldn't have children. We wanted them very much. At least I did. Then I came here to New York to record, of course, that's when Jaime and I got along quite well, and then the pregnancy happened... And I just... Things are so complicated. I came to think over things about Ed and was going to tell him it was over." Evelyn folds her arms while looking down. "I don't know what to do."

Lisa advises, "Go back and see what you can do with Ed. Then if it doesn't work out, move on."

"I just could never tell Jaime. I would never want him to be weighed down by a responsibility that I wanted so badly. As it is, I must have looked foolish and stupid bawling and sniffling in front of Carol and Edwin the way I did last night. Why I must have carried on like a silly school girl over a boy." She begins to laugh and pulls out a tissue.

"We've all been down that road." Lisa giggles back.

Both women look at each other before breaking into gales of laughter.

Evelyn wipes her freshly mascara made eyes. Even with that ruined, she laughs even harder. Lisa throws her head up in a fit of laughter. Calming down between giggles, Evelyn says, "I really want to thank you."

Lisa says, "For what?"

"For helping me realize I need to reevaluate my needs."

The columnist turns serious. "Really, I want to see everything work out for you and your little girl."

Lisa gives Evelyn a hug.

Afterwards, Lisa closes the door and heads back down the stairs.

Carol hangs on to the railing. She asks, "How did it go?"

"Fine. Although I wish she would tell Weston."

"I'm telling you, hon, he's beyond beautiful."

"Single...and a daddy." Lisa turns to look upstairs for a moment. She tells Carol, "Boy, she's hooked on him but good."

"What do you expect? She was with him twice."

Lisa shakes her head before hesitantly holding three fingers up. "Nearly three. Something stopped them. Listen, hon, I have to go. But I'll call you to talk some more." The columnist opens the door, then closes it while holding onto her papers and magazines as she exits.

Carol fans herself with a hand.

***

Downstairs in the kitchen of I.C.E., Jaime sits in a contemplative manner. Bobby walks downstairs to join him.

"So, what happened?"

"Just a *miserable* fucking headache." Jaime says with regret.

"Hangover?"

"Yeah." Jaime replies deeply. He pushes up the sleeves to his elbows. "I don't even know what happened."

Bobby asks, "Did you at least have a good time?"

"I guess. There were a few women I was talking with. But that's pretty much all I remember. Although, one asked me if I needed a lift and I said, 'Sure.' So, I guess they dropped me off here. I don't think anymore than that happened. You found me on the couch in the office and that's where I've been since." He places a hand to his forehead. "What time is it?"

Bobby looks at his friend. "It's 2:33."

"AM?"

"PM. I wouldn't be here *that* early."

Bobby bites his bottom lip. "We had to postpone our trip to Miami for the Duggan sessions. I'll tell you right now. Danny's not happy about that. He's pissed. I don't know what's going on with you but you seriously need to take responsibility for missed sessions and cancellations. We've lost three artists already. And it's certainly not because of Danny or me. If you don't shape up, you're going to lose an engineer...and you'll have to find another producing partner. There's only so much of this that I can take. You haven't been the same since last year. We started to do all right with Gin & The Tonics but then she abruptly left and nobody is saying why. Denel was a catastrophe. You need to get your act together, man. You're seriously becoming a drag. I didn't even want to hang around with you at that convention in Chicago."

"Yeah." Jaime groans.

"No excuse. You're not in your twenties anymore. Not even your thirties. This is just being foolish and careless. Take a vacation."

"Are you implying that I don't go out enough? I do travel."

"Who are you kidding? Those are business trips. I'm talking about relaxing by a pool, soaking in the sun. Go to a spa. Drink Piña Coladas, not wine or champagne. Live. Don't let work get to you. Come back refreshed. Then we can do what we're good at. Rest your brain for God's sake. Just go *somewhere*. I don't care if it's Montana or Jamaica. The west coast. Whatever. Please, just get your battery recharged."

Jaime looks down. "I will be going down to the city in a couple of weeks."

"Go to Long Island while you're at it. Just do *something*."

Bobby leaves his friend to think.

Jaime walks up the stairs. He enters the office again.

An issue of Billboard sits on his desk. Noticing that it wasn't there before, he picks it up and flips through the pages. It's an issue from April. He stops flipping when he sees a recognizable picture on the right hand page along with a small caption underneath. It's a picture of himself, Bobby, Dan, and Evelyn. She was sandwiched between both producers. All of them with smiles on their faces.

The caption reads,

Evelyn Winthrop No-Shows Promotion. Manager Says She's Not Interested.

Jaime remembered the picture and the sessions fondly. Only, he's a little confused about what he reads. Evelyn was proud of *Hero's Requiem*. So, why wouldn't she promote it? It wasn't as if he were hoping he and the production staff would get awards. He only found it peculiar that an artist who truly liked their project would simply let it fall between the cracks of the music industry.

The producer walks over to a filing cabinet and pulls out the Winthrop file. There he finds her manager's phone number in West Germany like Geoff said. He looks at the clock. Hopefully it wasn't too late. He punches in the numbers waiting for the ring tone.

The other end picks up. In a distinct German tone, the gentleman answers. "Hello?"

Jaime responds. "Yeah. Hi. This is Jaime Weston from I.C.E. Studios in New Paltz...New York. I produced Ms. Winthrop's latest album."

"Oh yah, Weston. What would you like?"

"I'm wondering since I just saw a recent issue of *Billboard*... What happened to her? It says that you claim she's not interested in any kind of promotion."

"Yah."

"In all due respect, that sounds a little strange considering she showed that she was very pleased with this latest project."

Voorhaun answers back readily. "She never mentioned she was disappointed with the work. She expressed her pleasure with it same as you. It confused me too when she called and said she won't be doing any press for it. Something came up and that was it. I told her she should let whoever call her about this. Her record company is going to be furious if they aren't already. I take it she told you nothing either?"

"No. Do you have any idea where I might be able to reach her?"

"I thought she was back home in England but she never did say. I have tried to reach her and she's not there. Sometimes, in the past she's been known to take vacations or go somewhere else after ending sessions."

"Oh. I see."

"That might be the case. If I see her though, I'll let her know you called. Thanks for calling, Jaime."

"Yep. Thank you, Ben. Goodnight."

He hangs up the phone. Jaime looks back at the picture. He pulls out the page, folding it so that it is small enough to fit into his wallet. The producer shakes his head. In the middle of lighting a cigarette, he spots the latest mail hidden under the magazine. The return address immediately gets his attention.

"Weinderhof."

Grabbing the envelope, he leaves the office quickly.

***

Jaime arrives at Cosgrove Gallery in the further reaches of Greenwich Village, winding his way through the crowd. Wearing his sunglasses, he surveys the various odd works of art. A waiter comes by with a tray filled with glasses of champagne. Jaime picks one up and still studies a picture on the wall. A woman with a patterned babushka and flowing jersey adorned with a scarf, walks up from behind as he tries to figure out the meaning of the picture. It's a collage framed in black with pieces of newspaper from the 1940's, promptly displaying the words *World War II* in between and small red and purple swastikas finger painted around.

The woman says, "Nazi Party."

Jaime turns around. He gives her a hug and says warmly, "Wilhelmina. I figured it was you. I was quite surprised to receive an invitation."

She says back with her hand on his arm, "How are you, Jaime?"

He smiles back at her, telling the hostess, "I'm doing fine."

"I forgot. Now, are you a painter?" She asks with her German accent.

"No. I'm into music."

"Oh, how delightful. What do you play?"

"Oh. I'm a record producer."

"Okay. I see. Well...this has to be one of my greatest shows."

Jaime holds onto her shoulder and leans over slightly to talk above the loudness of U2's "Bullet The Blue Sky" blasting from a nearby boom box. He asks her, "Why is that?"

Wilhelmina says back, "It's a great response. I got everyone to come from my first show in '77." She looks him over in a pleased though surprised manner. "You, dear, haven't changed at all. You still look wonderful after eleven years."

Jaime gives her a boyish grin with his head down. Then he looks around hoping to find Evelyn.

Wilhelmina continues on. "Even Bernice came!"

Jaime looks over her shoulder as she surveys a list of guests. All are checked off.

He sees that Evelyn's name is checked off as well. He tells Wilhelmina, "Excuse me," as he puts his hand on her arm and walks past her.

Taking off his sunglasses, Jaime walks around as he places them in his jacket pocket. A woman steps up to him. Her boyfriend, a small man with dark hair and graying beard, joins her.

"Hey, Jaime! Remember me? Doug. From the Mueller gallery." The man calls out. He speaks in a rapid tongue. Then he continues with, "We just wanted to say you have a beautiful niece!"

Jaime looks at him and replies, "I think you must be mistaken, Doug. I don't have a niece."

He then continues his search for Evelyn. The couple looks on in shock. Doug's girlfriend says, "Thanks a lot! Once again, you've managed to embarrass me."

He says sheepishly, "I...I didn't know. I mean, I thought I was sure."

Jaime catches a glance of a blonde haired woman making her way out of the side entrance quickly. Before he can even reach the door, the female in a dark coat hustles into a cab and is whisked away down the rain-drenched street. Jaime just manages to step out of the building when the back of the cab can be seen rolling away. He watches as it disappears into the steam and blinking lights ahead. With the futile attempt to catch up, Jaime's only source of consolation is a Marlboro, which he removes from the pack he has in his front pocket of his jacket. He pulls out a book of matches along with it. Only the tip provides any light, as there are no streetlights lit. He takes a drag of the cigarette and momentarily closes his eyes. Jaime looks at the desolate, dark street ahead.

Again, he had lost her.

***

Evelyn looked around at the studio while holding Amanda. Bobby stepped up from behind her.

"Looking for somebody?" He asked.

She turned around.

Immediately, he saw her holding the baby. He responded with, "Oh."

"You see, Bobby, I came here to see Jaime...about his daughter."

"I understand." He offered.

Bobby led her by the arm downstairs into the recording room. While walking down, Evelyn noticed the smoke billowing around her feet as she found the large recording room converted into what looked like fun house mirrors. About a dozen or so were lined up like a wall. Slowly she walked by them and saw a pregnant woman dressed in a light blue smock. The woman smiled. Then the image turned to the right and another pregnant woman appeared. They looked to the left and yet another showed up. Eventually the numbers built as more ladies in the same condition appeared. Evelyn, with shock and confusion stepped back, watching the images grow closer to her.

In back, Bobby told her, "You're not the only one. You probably thought you were the first. But you see, there are more."

"More? What do you mean?"

"Honey, this is only the latest crop of gals to be acknowledged."

The swirl of smoke came up to her knees as she stepped back. Three more women that are pregnant approached her. This time, they didn't come from the mirror and were not simply images. All of them rubbed their protruding bellies at the same time.

In a shaky and bewildered tone, Evelyn asked, "W...w...what's going on here? Where is Jaime?"

Bobby responded with, "He's not here. He's not there. He's everywhere as you can tell."

He laughed hysterically.

All of the women laughed too.

Feeling trapped like a caged animal, Evelyn raspily announced, "I want to go home!"

She then heard a familiar voice.

Lisa stepped out from a curtain of smoke. "Why not just have him, Ed, as Amanda's daddy?" The columnist said. "Jaime belongs to no one. No one." Her voice repeated.

Evelyn swiftly turned to the mirrors again to see the images of the pregnant women laughing madly at her. The singer clutched her daughter closer to her in fear.

Amanda turned to her with Ed's face.

In the dark, Evelyn catapults to a seated position on the bed. She breathes hard. Closing her eyes, she realizes it's only a bad dream.

A nightmare!

She walks over to the crib to check up on Amanda. When she turns on the night-light, she sees the baby fast asleep. Evelyn is awaken by the reality that she must do the right thing, not only for herself but for her daughter as well.

Within his hotel suite overlooking Central Park, Jaime wakes up to the thoughts in his head. Could it have been Evelyn that he saw at the gallery? It sure did resemble her from the back, and by all accounts, he looked over Wilhelmina's shoulder to see every name checked off the list for the showing.

Slowly he sits up and reaches for his wallet that is about arm's length away on the nightstand next to the bed. Turning on the small lamp to the dimmest setting, he opens the wallet. He strokes back his hair and leans over to place his favorite blues tape in the portable radio he brought along and stuffed in his suitcase. He then smiles slightly at the sound of 'Mississippi' Fred McDowell crooning with the bleak starkness of a slide guitar on, "You Gotta Move."

Jaime pulls out a folded paper from his billfold. It's the cut out picture from Evelyn's sessions in *Billboard*. The picture shows him, her, Bobby, and Dan. Those were some sweet moments. Ones he couldn't deny. A smile creeps across his lips. He steps around to the end of the bed and sits in a contemplative manner, pondering. Placing a hand to his forehead he thinks. If only he told her. If only he had the guts to say how he really felt.

If only.

"I don't know what happened." Carol expresses to Edwin while pouring a steaming pot of freshly brewed coffee into a colorful cup.

It's morning, as Edwin has decided to drop by early.

Carol continues. "She got up and caught a cab. The only thing she told me was that she had to get a plane ticket to go back to England."

"Didn't you tell me she was a temporary guest anyway?" Edwin asks while watching the steam wave flourish into the air.

"I did, but I was hoping with the birth of Amanda she would change her mind and go back to Jaime instead. Henry told me that his wife, Karen, suggested she stay upstate, since she was thinking of possibly opening a gift shop in the near future. I think that would have been great. But, like I said, she wants to go back home."

"To Ed?"

"Yes. I don't know him but from what she's told me, I don't like the sound of him. He strikes me as a very cruel man."

"I've had the displeasure of talking with him on the phone." Cautiously he sips his coffee. "You're right. He's not a nice fellow to get along with. Very suspicious. He would question the motives of her wanting to record."

"For real?" Carol asks with shock.

"Mm hmm."

"No wonder I didn't like what she had to tell me about him in the first place. Jaime would be so much better for her. Do you know enough about him?" She asks while pouring a cup of coffee for herself.

"Not too much. Jaime is a man who keeps very much to himself, but I know that he does treat everybody around him very well. You'll get no complaints about that. Evelyn of course... Well, obviously you'll hear no complaints from her." He smiles.

Carol gives him a look.

"Still, it's weird that she wants to go home. Something must have happened and she's not saying anything."

Carol takes a sip of coffee.

In England, afternoon gives way to full sunshine. Joggers roam the park. Ed briskly makes his way up a bike path. Looking down, he takes the cigarette out of his mouth with a familiarity of remembrance. It was the same bike path that he and Evelyn had taken earlier on in their relationship. They would ride their 10-speeds past people, whizzing by without a care in the world. Just laughing and smiling as both would try to outride the other. Ed could still remember her laughter and her joy as he passed her by.

Just as he eyes the ground again, he sees a woman wheeling a baby carriage. He walks over to take a peek at the little one while the mother settles on a bench to read a book. The baby girl begins to open her eyes. Her mother doesn't even notice that Ed is close to the carriage. Ed looks in, only to hear the tiny scream.

Quickly, he rushes off mumbling, "Crybaby."

The woman turns to her daughter, dropping her book down. She tends to her crying baby.

The bell sounds off when Jaime steps inside Bleecker St. Records. As he gets in, he removes his sunglasses. A man in his early forties stands behind the register finishing off his conversation on the phone. He places the phone back on the hook. The man darts his eyes to see his potential customer.

In a coarse voice that might be described as a permanent sore throat he asks aloud, "Can I help you?"

Jaime looks at him just as the phone rings again. The man holds out his index finger clad with a large ring.

"Hold on." He picks up the phone. "Bleecker St. Records, Dale speaking. We've got everything from ABBA to Zappa, Conway Twitty and James Brown in between. What's that? Miles Davis' *Bitches Brew*? Yeah, we've got that. Well, come on down, man. Yeah!" He laughs hoarsely. "Okay. I'll see you around. Bye."

Again, Dale puts the phone back down. He sees Jaime looking through a column of records in the isle. The producer walks up to the register. He takes notice of the sales clerk.

Dale has nearly black hair that hangs a little over his shoulders. With full lips and the motion of him slowly chewing gum, he squints his small beady dark eyes.

Dale says, "You just missed her."

Jaime looks at him slightly perplexed. "Sorry?"

"Yeah. The blonde that was in here...no more than..." Dale picks up a sleeve of his shirt, sifting through bracelets and bangles. He finds his watch. "...Five minutes ago."

How would this Dale guy know Jaime was in search of the blonde, Evelyn?

"There's a bus stop at the end of the street. Maybe she's there?" Dale advises.

Jaime takes a long stride to the door and almost breaks into a run. He stops to glance to the left and right. Squinting from a harsh wind that bustles through, he sees nobody around except a couple walking across the street. The wind continues to blow fiercely, that his hair gets caught in the breeze. He attempts to push back the foppish mass of hair that flitters over his right brow. Lowering his head, Jaime steps back into the record store.

Momentarily, he looks down at the black and white checkered floor. He goes back to the register and asks, "What made you think she was with me?"

Dale says back as he chews gum, "I can tell these things. Also, you reacted quick enough."

"Can you describe her?"

"Sure! She was beautiful, what with blue eyes, heavily made in mascara. Prominent chest. I know when I see it! I'd say she was about chin level to you or me. She looked like she had a lot of moxy, in her early forties."

Jaime nods. "What was it though? Did she have a British accent?"

"I didn't hear her."

Dale tends to an inventory book. As he does this he says to Jaime, "Man, people tell me my daughters look like me, but that kid looked an awful lot like you. My wife's a blonde but that didn't stop all three of our daughters from looking like me." Dale looks up and says with no exaggeration, "That baby was a dead ringer for you. Dark hair...and same eyes."

Jaime eyes the floor, chuckles and shakes his head in disbelief.

"No. It couldn't have been her. She doesn't have kids. Neither do I."

Dale sits up surprised. "Could have fooled me!" Tapping the end of the pen to his large upper lip, he thinks for a minute. "You know, I think I've seen her before...but I can't remember where. Was it a restaurant? I don't think so."

"Well thanks, but it couldn't have been her." Jaime graciously smiles. "If I'm back up this way, I'll stop in here again." The record producer dons his sunglasses and walks out the door.

Five minutes later, Dale removes his tall, skinny body from the stool and takes the inventory book between the isles. Placing it down, he flips through albums as he talks to himself. "Deniece Williams, Jackie

Wilson, Edgar Winter, Johnny Winter, Evelyn Winthrop, Steve Winwood..."

He flips back to the Evelyn Winthrop album and looks over the cover, which shows a picture of a rose with its stem broken in half. Dale gets intrigued enough to look at the back.

"*Ravaged Beauty*. Hmm."

He flips the album over to see a buxom blonde with a noticeable amount of cleavage, wearing a skintight form fitting black leather jacket zipped halfway up. She was throwing rose petals in mid air. Dale stops chewing. Then it occurs to him.

"She looks like that chick a matter of fact."

He turns to look at the door for a moment.

Over on the Bowery, just off of Bleecker St., a man in his late forties with thinning brown hair walks over to a repair van. He takes a surreptitious glance through one of the windows at the man who approaches the door of the CBGB & OMFUG.

Jaime studies the brightly colored flyers, wondering if there is any sign of the singer he had grown to love. No names strike him, as they all seem to be either punk or new wave. Even the sprayed on graffiti has a different feel to it.

The man standing beside the van, curls a thick black wire, tosses it into the back, and shuts the double doors. He takes another look at the tall man with round sunglasses on.

In a booming Brooklyn voice, he calls out. "Hey man, don't I know you?"

Jaime turns quizzically as he pulls the lenses down to his nose. Then he begins to smile as he recognizes the man.

The Brooklyn native says, "Jaime! I thought that was you!"

"Davy. Haven't seen you in a long time."

He gives him a quick hug.

"Likewise. I thought you moved to L.A."

"It didn't work out."

"What happened to that redhead?"

"Megan?"

"Yeah. That's it!"

"Oh, she married the maintenance guy from the restaurant she worked at a few years ago."

"What about that weird artsy chick you were seeing for a little while, the auburn curls?"

"Shirley ran off with the keyboard player from a band we went to see at The Roxy. That's when I decided to come back to New York. I got homesick."

"You still a gormandizer?"

Jaime chuckles back. "Gee, Dave, I'd like to hope so. I still consume music on a regular basis."

"I quit engineering in '82. Came here. The boss took me in and now I help set up equipment and run through rehearsals. How about you?"

"Oh, I'm still producing...a lot."

"You still a party-goer? Mr. Charisma. Huh?"

Jaime replies back in a deeper tone. "No. I'd like to hope that I grew out of that."

"Come on man. No need to be Mr. Modest now. Jaime Randall Weston. The playboy *extraordinaire* of the late '70s. Pretty as a peacock."

Jaime leans an elbow against the garbage can outside the door. Placing a hand over his face, he agonizingly moans deeply. "Oh God. You *would* have to bring that up."

"Listen man, did you ever keep any of those outfits? From what I can tell they probably still fit you."

"I kept a few of the old relics...in a closet where they belong."

"I'm sure there's a missus in your life by now." Davy pries.

Jaime digs in his jacket pocket, pulling out a Marlboro.

"Well, not really. I *am* looking for somebody though." He picks up a matchbook from the opposite pocket. "Have you ever heard of a singer named, Evelyn Winthrop?" Jaime strikes a match, lighting the end of the cigarette then shakes the match out. The flame vanishes. He tosses the used match in the trash can. Inhaling heartily, Jaime can already tell he's having a hard time keeping the smoke down the right way as it tickles his throat.

Davy says, "The Dumpster Diva?"

Jaime doesn't fully catch Davy's response as he coughs a couple of times until he has the small problem fixed. He says quietly, "She was what?"

Davy repeats, "The Dumpster Diva. Yeah. She built a reputation back in the day. I used to see her hang out here enough times. While you were doin' up the party scene, she was at all the trashy clubs. Her dates were engineers, roadies, and technicians. All junkies from the punk scene. The boss collected a lot of pocketknives back then and one of her mates got pissed off. He pulled one out but got it taken away. He was mad because he wanted to open up a big bag of coke with it. Evelyn turned into the elder stateswoman for the girls at places like this. She was in her early thirties and her fan base of idol worshipers were in their late teens to early twenties."

"Do you think the boss might have seen her recently?"

"No. He can invite Joey Ramone or David Johansen to dinner or pick new bands from Boston. The truth is Evelyn Winthrop is old news. She took up jazz."

Jaime says as he has the Marlboro in his mouth, "You sure about that?"

"Yeah. Let's face it man. Evelyn had some really good records last decade, but she's not into the scene anymore. I saw her in '83. She told me she was happy and cleaned up her act. I'm not sure if she's still with the guy, she met a couple years before that. He was a stray. A photographer from Boston."

"She never said anything about him to me."

Davy gives Jaime an odd glance as the producer turns for a moment.

"Wait. What does this have to do with you? Are you tellin' me she's moved up the food chain? Like perhaps *record producers*?"

Raising a brow, Davy slaps his knee while laughing.

Jaime looks at him not amused. He grabs hold of the man's shoulder. With a slight lean, he glares into Davy's eyes.

The taller producer says firmly, "Don't tell anybody about this."

"You mean the Playboy Producer and the Dumpster Diva? Who would have ever thought?"

"I worked with her and it wasn't jazz."

Interested, Davy replies, "Oh? You know if she were around, she would have turned up here already."

Jaime nods back with a hint of a smile. "Thanks."

A male voice can be heard coming from inside the building. He sticks his head outside.

"Come on, Dave. We've gotta get this stuff ready for tonight's show."

Davy turns to the door, then Jaime. He tells him, "Gotta go. You know what they say. The show must go on."

"Okay. Hopefully I'll see you again soon." Jaime responds.

"Don't be such a stranger."

Jaime waves to him and begins to walk away.

Davy calls back. "Jaime!"

The producer turns around quickly.

Davy says, "When you see her the next time, let her know she's welcome anytime."

Jaime says back, "All right."

Davy steps in the club then sticks his head out the door as he sees Jaime walking away. With parting words, the technician shouts out, "Go on Romeo! Find your Juliette!"

Jaime puts on his sunglasses and gives a back handed wave while walking further down the street.

From the opposite way of the CBGB is a woman wearing a coat, shawl, and sunglasses. She approaches the front door of the club. The woman huddles her baby firmly against her chest. Leaning for a look at the schedule, she nods. Then she takes a step back looking over the building's facade as a piece of her past. She walks past the graffiti ridden building. Turning the street she came out of, Carol holds a large sack.

The two women walk away.

***

Carol steps out of the car into the July afternoon heat. She pulls up the sleeve of her jersey knit shirt, checking the time on her watch. 4:10. Less than an hour left until Evelyn's flight would depart.

Evelyn opens the passenger's side and slides out. Unbuckling the baby seat in back, she releases Amanda. Grabbing the baby carrier, Carol steps around placing it near Evelyn. The singer gently puts her baby in the center then pulls up the blanket to her waist level. Amanda's eyes immediately dart around, taking in the surroundings. Carol's hair flies in the coastal New York air. The roar of a jet's engine churns above as it takes off. Both women watch the underbelly of a plane glimmering in the sunlight, shading all in its path.

Amanda gurgles.

Evelyn turns to her.

"It must be loud for her." She tells her soon to be former roommate.

Carol squints as all three are caught in the shadow of a jet heading out west. Several more engines boom within the confines of the airport.

Evelyn says to Carol, "I thought Edwin would be coming along?"

Carol folds her arms. "No." She looks down. "I told him not to. I didn't want him to see me."

Wiping away a tear before it runs down her cheek, she pops open the trunk. The two slate gray colored suitcases sit inside. Carol pulls them out, dragging them with the weight of the four little wheels underneath. Her sight meets the gaze of Amanda's eyes. Her tiny little body wiggles within the covering of the light green blanket. Amanda's miniature hands wave as her fingers curl.

Carol immediately breaks down and cries.

Wiping away a steady stream of tears caused by knowing they were leaving, she reveals to Evelyn. "I didn't want Edwin to see me like this." She holds out her tear stained hands. Evelyn looks at her sympathetically.

"It's all right. Carol, if you do that, you're going to make *me* cry."

Even she starts to feel the tears well up. "Don't. Please don't." She insists of the sculptress.

Carol chokes back. "I can't help it!" Wiping and fighting off tears she says, "You know, you and Amanda taught me how to love. Not in a romantic way, but, how to be loved unconditionally. I learned how to look deep down inside myself and have real compassion. Under that toughness...I'm really a..." Her voice breaks. "...*Softy*." She informs her. "I hate goodbyes." She then hugs Evelyn good and tight. Letting go, she looks down at Amanda in the carrier. "I'm going to miss you little girl. An awful lot." Carol reaches inside the carrier, holding Amanda's little hand with a few fingers. "Bye, little cutie." Amanda breaks into a smile before her eyes wander around again.

Carol says as she checks her watch, "You've got to go. It's getting late."

"I'll send out for the stuff as soon as I get back." Evelyn tells her.

"Okay."

Carol gives Evelyn one last hug for good measure.

"Go!"

Evelyn picks up the carrier and drags the two suitcases attached to each other piggyback rigged. Carol gets inside her car and pulls out a Kleenex from the pack sitting in the glove compartment. She starts up the engine, moving into a legal parking space nearby to watch the planes take off.

Inside the airport, Evelyn waits in line to drop off her suitcases. She plops down her carry-on luggage from her shoulder. Placing the basket carrier containing Amanda in it, she tosses the luggage onto a conveyor belt once it's her turn. Both pieces get stickers and labeled. Evelyn takes out her passport and ticket. Allowed through, the singer makes her way to getting checked. She pulls out Amanda as her carrier is checked with the carry-on luggage. Above is the sign for British Airways. Putting Amanda back in the comforts of her basket, she takes out a shawl, placing it over her head so her blonde hair doesn't show. Then she dons a pair of large dark sunglasses. Bringing up the blanket a little higher to Amanda, she looks around.

The woman waiting by the gate to the terminal peers up from the fringes of her dark brown hair. Her round face brightens as she looks down at Amanda peeking from the blanket. Evelyn sees the woman's badge with her name, *Eloise*.

Eloise, a doll faced French-Canadian with virtually no makeup on is similar in height and age to the British singer. She leans over. Her full brown eyes change to upside-down crescent moons above her cheeks as she turns up a tight-lipped smile.

"How old is she?" Eloise inquires.

A man in his thirties comes barreling through the waiting room with a group of photographers racing after him. The sudden outburst startles a few patrons. They get let in through the gate as the time comes. The man continues racing past patrons, almost running into an old woman with a walker.

The man bellows in a British accent. "Leave me alone!"

Evelyn has already taken off with Amanda, sandwiching herself between a narrow wall and garbage can. One of the crowd members on the chase calls out.

"Jake DeShane! We just want a good picture of you!"

"Leave me the bloody hell alone!!"

He runs into a packed crowd waiting for another flight, hopping over seats.

Eloise looks at the commotion while trying to announce the sections, which are now open for people taking the flight. Too annoyed, she picks up the microphone attached to the desk.

"Security! Security!"

Her eyes catch sight of the British woman cowering next to the wall with her baby in the carrier.

Evelyn remains too frightened to move. Her worst fear is only some short distance away. The only thing standing between Evelyn and the truth about her child is the paparazzi. Her picture could be either in the New York Post on page six or The New York Times. Worse yet, The Ulster County Register. For sure, Jaime would find out then.

Eloise says with her accent firmly intact, "Good for nothin' sad excuse for security!"

She mumbles inaudibly in French.

Security rushes over. Two little vehicles pull over.

The woman shouts, "Gate C8! C8! They're over there!"

One security member ushers a cameraman out. Another argues, pointing out that it's his job.

A third cameraman shouts to the man being chased. "Got anything to say about your new movie, Jake?"

"Yeah! Get out of here!"

Jake begins trotting backwards as the man checks his camera while still going after the actor. Jake shouts out and points when he stops. "Hey! Hey! Tom Cruise is right there! Tom! Tom! Tom!"

The cameraman stops. Tom Cruise was worth more than Jake DeShane! He turns to look. Jake turns and runs past him.

He had been famed for eluding the paparazzi from the Madrid Film Festival to Cannes. He could never be caught. Jake had a bounty on his head all the time. Craftier than the Road Runner, he could dodge any camera or sprint like a gazelle. He had grown accustom to the unexpected exercise.

Evelyn remains stuck between the walls, holding Amanda in the carrier. She dislodges herself, carefully stepping forward as she takes a swallow. Peering from the rims of her sunglasses, Evelyn looks to see that the coast is clear. She feels that she's not alone though. Slowly she turns to face a three-inch flash bulb attached to a large camera. The big lens focuses on her face.

The cameraman smiles. "Evelyn Winthrop. What a pretty sight!"

Like a deer caught in the headlights of a car, the singer is left standing in fear. For sure Jaime Weston would then know Evelyn was in New York and had a child...his.

Eloise calls out over the speaker. "Last call for C2. British Airways flight 440. Flight 440 will be taking off in five minutes."

The singer turns her eyes. Would she miss her flight? The determined camera operator starts up his camera.

A red light flashes. It won't click. He mutters, "Dammit!"

Before being able to make a run for the gateway door, Evelyn feels herself almost taken off the ground. A hand grabs her arm and she's whisked into the gateway tunnel, pushed along the way. Without looking back, Evelyn gets in the narrow passageway of the plane. The pilot looks at her and the person behind her.

A stewardess smiles and says, "Just in time."

The pilot closes the door.

In the airport, Eloise checks to make sure nobody is left. Just as the few remaining camera people race towards the open passage, it closes. Eloise gives a tight-lipped smile to the men standing before her.

One cameraman says, "C'mon lady. Do you know how much Jake DeShane is worth? For one picture, it's fifty thousand dollars. Have a heart. Just let us get one and we'll be out of here."

Standing on firm ground, Eloise says, "Nope."

Another antsy photographer yells out, "Come on! Just one!"

The gateway lady feels her patience being pushed.

In an exasperated tone, she tells them her exact feelings. "This is not a red carpet affair. You come through here. Scare patrons. I don't even know how you got here!" Her eyes widen in fury. "Running around like it's a kindergarten is not permitted on these premises! I *never* had to deal with this when I was at Dorval!"

"Come on! Fifty thou, Ma'am!"

She snarls back. "Je m'en contre-calisse!"

"What?"

"Stupid, very *very* stupid! Rotten animals! Leave! Go! Go now before I call the cops on you!"

In the plane, Evelyn turns around seeing Jake DeShane in back of her. She removes her sunglasses.

"Thank you. Thank you so very much for helping me."

"I saw he almost had you there. The bulb not goin' off was a miracle."

"And how!"

"Luv, you got lucky. They're getting a little slow." Jake nervously laughs, as he knows it was a little too close for comfort. "Would you care to sit with me? I always buy up more space than I need."

"Where are you sitting?"

"First class of course."

Evelyn hesitates for a moment. "Oh, I couldn't."

"You're a rock star. Don't you prefer the best?"

"You know who I am?"

"Of course! I grew up on your music from the sixties. Your voice changed but you're still lovely." He looks down at Amanda. "And you have an equally lovely looking child."

"Why thank you. She gets that from her father. I'm sorry but I'll have to take a pass on your invitation. Thank you anyway."

Evelyn walks further into the belly of the plane. Looking at her number, she matches it with the seat. While she buckles herself and Amanda, a stewardess stands at the front of the isle while the pilot is giving a safety speech along with explaining emergency exits through the intercom for everybody to hear. Then he informs the passengers the flight will take six hours and forty-five minutes. Evelyn blows out a sigh. She looks over at Amanda. She checks to make sure the baby isn't shaken too badly from the run. The three month old contently stays bundled with her eyes wandering.

An engine starts up, escalating into a deeper roar. The plane starts to vibrate as it backs away from the terminal. Evelyn looks out the little window. Flight 440 waits for its turn to take to the skies. The plane barrels down the runway, slowly lifting its weight higher and higher. As the plane begins to soar, Amanda squirms more. She shuts her eyes and begins crying softly. Evelyn tries to lean over while buckled in her seat.

In the parking lot, Carol stands outside her car. A jet is heard. She checks her watch. The logo says British Airways on it. Carol watches the plane soar into the midday sky.

Wiping a tear from her eyes, she says, "Bye."

Returning back inside the car, Carol starts up the ignition and pulls away.

Passengers turn Evelyn's way as Amanda screams louder. She knew she had changed her before leaving Carol's. Maybe she was hungry? Tired? A couple in the next seat over looks her way. A man adjusts his seat while another tries to close his eyes. The teenager a few seats ahead lowers his headphones while glancing over at Evelyn with the crying child. No one wants to contend with an infant for the nearly seven-hour flight.

Evelyn looks at the various pairs of eyes and expressions thrown her way. What was she to do? The glances become overly uncomfortable to her. Then something pops. The growing distance in gravity becomes more apparent as her hearing goes muffled. It is only then she comes to the conclusion that that's what had been bothering her daughter so much. Evelyn would remain helpless for the time being.

Ten minutes later, the plane is at 35,000 feet. The overhead light turns on with an orange glow and beeping noise.

The pilot announces in a Cockney tinged voice. "You may now unbuckle your seats if you so wish to use the bathroom. Please be advised we may run into a little bit of turbulence. So, return to your seats as soon as possible. Leave the isles uncluttered. Thank you for flying British Airways, your top-flight agency serving all of the United Kingdom. Cheers."

As soon as the pilot finishes his speech, a woman talks aloud. "Finally!"

One of the men sitting near Evelyn turns to her. "Miss? Can you please do something about your child?"

The singer removes the belt from Amanda's carrier.

Amanda continues to bawl at a high pitch as her mother tries to sooth her. Evelyn picks up Amanda, holding her. The prying glances make Evelyn feel completely unwelcomed. Finally, she makes a decision she hadn't thought of until that point. Obviously, she was not welcome with Amanda in coach. There was only one thing she could do.

Quickly she takes out her carry-on bag from the overhead compartment. In one arm, she holds her baby. With the other hand, she jams her sunglasses and shawl into the bag. Heaving it waist level along with the carrier, she squeezes through the isle, making her way to the next section behind the curtain.

First class.

Maybe it was only fitting for her to sit in the better area.

Jake DeShane sits comfortably in a seat.

Evelyn asks, "Is that invitation still open?"

He opens his eyes and smiles. "Got a window seat for you."

The singer plops down in the seat closest to the small right side window. She gets situated with Amanda back in the carrier. She places her carry-on bag in the overhead compartment above, and then is able to relax. Looking out the window, her reflection appears murky. A vast desert of white, cotton candy-like wisps fill out the landscape below. In between are the empty patches, dark from the land and water. She gets to the point of pondering.

Where and what was home? Staying put in one area such as the state of New York for a whole year would certainly make one wonder. England had its own charm but it seemed distant in her memory. The characters, the feel, and the atmosphere won her over greatly in the Empire State. Bobby Whitfield, Andrea Whitfield, Dan Soren, Vicki Soren, Jaime Weston, Henry and Karen Winslow, Carol Mulligan, Edwin Muller, Lisa, Wilhelmina, all of the various people she came across at the galleries. All were embedded into her conscience. Every experience she had while being there was fresh and new. The studio itself was unlike any other. Jaime was completely different than what she expected. Her affair with him was hard for her to comprehend or believe. She looks at Amanda who is calm. It did happen and the little girl next to her was indeed the product of that affair. Everything about Jaime Weston had an extreme affect on her. Now she had his daughter. Evelyn couldn't think of it as a dream come true when it came to him. Amanda was. Jaime was only fleeting, she felt. Amanda was a different story. She had expected to have children with Ed but that did not happen. She closes her eyes and drifts to sleep.

Hours go by. Light turns to darkness.

The orange light blinks on as Evelyn feeds Amanda formula.

The pilot's voice is heard throughout the whole plane. "Good evening, people and hello once again. We will be landing at Heathrow in approximately thirteen minutes. Buckle up. We're heading for home. Cheerio!"

Amanda turns her head away from the bottle as she has had enough. Evelyn bundles her up once again, carefully placing her in the carrier. She buckles both herself and the baby. The plane begins to descend from the high altitude.

Once safely on the ground, the passengers are let off. Evelyn looks ahead trying to peek around or stand on her tiptoes seeing if she could spot Jake in the crowd. The passengers walk through the terminal. There is still no sign of Jake. She wanted to thank him again. Not only for helping her stay away from the photographers or even allowing her to sit up in first class with him. Simply she wanted to thank him for genuinely being a kind soul and wanted to wish him good luck.

Stepping out into the openness of Heathrow International Airport, the singer gives one last look. Jake DeShane was the British white rabbit. The photographers and paparazzi were his Alice. He remained untouched. He left no tracks. Jake was off on another great adventure. Somebody might spot him in a crowd but they would never catch him with their camera.

Evelyn finds herself wandering through various areas in search of the baggage claim. Just as she sees the sign for British Airways, her face lights up. She begins to head in the direction of the arrows.

"Evelyn Winthrop?"

The singer hears her name.

Spotted!

Was it a journalist or even a photographer? Evelyn spins around to see who had said her name. A woman with her mouth open speaks.

"Oh my God. As I live and breathe, Ms. Evelyn Winthrop."

Evelyn sees the woman walking toward her in astonishment. The woman quickly holds out her hand. She shakes Evelyn's.

Under nearly black fringed foppish hair, her darkly made eyes beam with joy. She pushes the hair that covers over most of her eyes.

"Wow! I am a huge fan of yours. I've been living here some dozen years but I never thought there would come a day... I mean, my husband has told me things about you but I just never imagined that I would meet you myself. My name is Jill Howard. I'm with the band Spectrafish. We're a little band out of Cambridge. I'm waiting here for my mom to arrive from Michigan. Anyway, you have influenced me plenty. Really, in so many ways. I have to take it so far as to say my life wouldn't be the same if I hadn't heard your records."

Evelyn looks down at the floor with a huge smile.

"That's terribly sweet. Thank you!"

Jill says, "*Ravaged Beauty* is my *absolute favorite* record of all time. I have your others but that album made me want to quit my dead-end waitressing job here in London and pursue my music full time. I got maybe eight copies of that freakin' album, *Beauty*. I wore out the needle on the record player. There is no other song like *Jack Off Of All Trades*. It's just so brutally honest about men in general...and that beat. I loved the bass in that. Funny enough, I married Neil."

Evelyn awakens from her flattered and blushing state.

"Neil? Do you mean, Neil Broden?"

"Yeah. We met when he came to check out my band. He thought we had what it took, got us in a great..." Jill happens to look down when she hears a baby cough. "A great studio. Then we fell for each other, lived together for two years." She looks down again at Amanda. "Then we got pregnant and decided to get married. My firstborn we named Electra Marie. I know that Marie is your middle name and it was my grandmother's name. So, we used it. Then our second daughter came along and we named her, Monica Evelyn. Anyway, I'm just thrilled I got the opportunity to meet you." Jill then figures she's talked enough. "You're probably in a hurry to go somewhere and I've taken up all your time just blabbing away."

"No. No. I enjoy hearing you talk about my apparent influence on you. It's truly gratifying. As a matter of fact, I just released a new album called *Hero's Requiem*. There's a long story that goes on with that record but I thoroughly enjoyed making it and I'm thinking of making another in the near future."

"That's fantastic! I'll have to look for that. What was it called again?"

"*Hero's Requiem.*"

Jill looks down again. There was that certain something when Jill saw Amanda.

"Before I forget, there's a studio you should check out. Yeah, it's uh, some seventy or eighty miles out of Manhattan. Really, cool folks there. There are three guys that run operations. It's called I.C.E. It doesn't mean anything really. About these guys, two are producers and one is an engineer. It's uh, Bobby, Jaime, and Dan. Bobby's a really fun guy. Neil and I had dinner with him and his gorgeous redheaded wife, Andrea. Those two are so much alike. Dan's super quiet, but he works well and gets the job done. And then there's Jaime. Handsome as hell. I think he's the bachelor of the bunch. He's a real flirt. You have to be careful with that one." Jill looks down at Amanda yet again. She utters, "Unbelievable."

Evelyn sees Jill shake her head in disbelief. She attempts to stop a growing smile, as she knows that the woman is heavily reminded about the studio just from looking at her daughter.

Evelyn asks, "What's the matter?"

Jill replies quickly. "Oh, nothing. I thought of something really..."

An older woman in her sixties starts to turn in place. Jill spots her. The woman looks around in confusion. Jill approaches her.

"Mom!" She calls out.

The woman turns and announces, "Jill!"

She rushes up and gives her daughter a big hug.

"Mom, I'm so glad you made it here all right. Is Dad okay?"

"Oh yes. Of course. Oh, but it was a long trip! I need to remind myself to bring more things on the plane to do."

Jill looks at Evelyn.

"Mom, I want you to meet someone." She smiles and holds her mother by the shoulder. "Mom, this is Evelyn Winthrop." Jill's mother puts her hand over her mouth. "Oh my word!" She shakes Evelyn's hand as if honored. "Nadine Howard. It's an honor to meet you! I truly would like to thank you for a delightful son in-law. Neil and the girls are an absolute joy. I know that Jill is a huge fan of yours. How unbelievable is that? My daughter would marry your bass player. I just think it's incredible."

Nadine looks down seeing the baby carrier next to Evelyn.

"I see you have a little one yourself. Is that a little girl you have there?"

"Yes it is. That is my pride and joy. Amanda Jean."

"I'm sure your husband is quite happy."

"Oh, well... I'm not married."

"I'm sorry. Well, I'm sure her father must be quite proud."

Evelyn smiles back. "Yes."

If he only knew.

Jill asks her mother. "Who does little Amanda make you think of?"

"Let me think." Nadine looks over the infant in her carrier looking up at her. "Come to think of it, why does a picture of you and some people enter my mind? It was from a couple of years ago. It's on the bookshelf near the dining room. Was it taken at a studio?"

"That's the one."

"The features are very similar to one of them in the photo. Only, I can't place a name. Wait. Did it start with a 'J'?

"Yep."

"Jake? Jerry? Jay? James?"

Jill looks at her. "Mom, his name is Jaime."

"That's a girl's name."

"Guys use it too. It's really a Spanish name."

"Oh. Is he Spanish? I thought you said he was something else."

"He's of Indian heritage."

"How odd." Nadine laughs.

Jill looks at her watch.

"We *really* should get going. I told Neil I'd be back quick with you." She turns to Evelyn. "It was a thrill meeting you... and your daughter." Jill turns to her mother, taking her purse and carry-on luggage.

Evelyn suggests, "Maybe we can work on something together in the near future."

Jill turns back to Evelyn in shock. Her jaw is slightly dropped.

"Yeah. I'd love that!"

Evelyn picks up the baby carrier. "Great. I'll let Jaime know."

Jill says back, without even thinking of what her idol has just said, "Okay."

She begins to walk with her mother. Then it strikes her.

Jaime?

Jill turns to look back. Only, Evelyn is gone.

Under her dark bangs, a slow smile creeps over Jill Howard-Broden's face.

Chapter 8

Under the dawn skies, Evelyn gets out of Phil Grumbach's car. He takes out her luggage. Amanda's carrier becomes unstrapped in the backseat as her mother tenderly picks her up. Amanda looks around with wandering eyes at the foreign surroundings.

Phil checks his watch. He yawns while informing Evelyn. "It's a little past 7 AM. I'll have to be at work in another two more hours. You'll be okay, right?"

"Yes." Evelyn responds.

"Okay. And if Ed doesn't like it, then you know you can stay with us."

"I know and I thank you for your lovely invitation, but I think everything will be fine."

Phil drags the two suitcases one at a time up the small steps to the front door of her house. Evelyn gives him a kiss to the cheek.

"Thank you." She smiles.

He smiles back at her.

"Okay. Goodbye."

She waves at him.

Picking up the carrier, she places it in back of her, careful to keep it out of sight when she rings the doorbell.

Inside the house, Ed rushes around with some contact sheet proofs and pulls out photos from a black folder. The doorbell rings. Ed strides as quickly as he can to get it. He announces, "Yep!" Checking his watch, he says to himself, "Kind of early." He opens the door with an unlit cigarette in his hand. He stares right at Evelyn. For a moment, he forgets his obsession with her as he looks as though he may be seeing the face of a stranger. She is familiar slightly, but different and removed than he could remember from seeing her the previous year. She looks at him the same way. Neither smile. They stay fixated on each other.

Ed says, "You're back."

Evelyn says in a deep tone, "Yes. I didn't want to use the key and scare you."

He looks down in hopes of gathering his words and thoughts. In a weary though surprised voice he quietly states, "I...I didn't think you were coming back."

Evelyn slightly nudges the carrier with the back of her foot. Ed puts the cigarette in his mouth, rummaging for the lighter in his pocket. "I was going to go and bring some pictures to a client."

"Ed. Darling, I have some news. Well, it's rather exciting news at that." The singer expresses hesitantly. She looks over in back of her. "I want you to see something...someone. More like, it's somebody I would like you to meet."

Ed furrows his brows in confusion. Just as he is about to light his Camel, Evelyn brings the carrier into full view for him. The photographer's jaw drops. His unlit cigarette slides out of his mouth into the doorway of the main entrance. He drops his lighter, where it spins on the hardwood floor.

Ed stares in shock.

Amanda's eyes dart up to see the man with the surprised expression on his face. The man she would call, Daddy.

Evelyn beams with pride. She asks, "Well?"

Ed is unable to speak, as his eyes are never removed from the little girl before him. As if turning white or seeing a ghost, Ed stumbles over his words. "H...h...how did this happen? You...you couldn't have..."

"I know darling. That's what I thought too. Then shortly after I arrived in New York, I found out I...*we* were going to have a baby finally. Isn't that wonderful? I found it a complete shock! After all this time. Why it turned out that timing was all we needed...and a little faith. I even had her through natural childbirth. No drugs! I thought you might be quite happy of that. I suffered in the delivery room without any substance. The doctor told me that she was coming out too fast for even an epidural. And it was all such hard work!" She laughs.

Ed turns away, letting her ramble on.

"But then, I got to look at this preciously perfect little person in my arms and felt it was all worth it."

The photographer darts his eyes and grits his teeth. Not being able to take any more, Ed lashes out.

"How did this happen?" He demands.

"Darling, the way it always happens. When a man and a woman love each other, things like this always happen. Both of us wanted this. I know how much it hurt you. It hurt me tremendously when I believed I couldn't bear children. Now darling, we have our own. A *Brockton child*."

"When was she born?"

"March 6th."

Ed thinks for a moment. That would make it June she was conceived but he couldn't remember when the last time he and Evelyn had sex. It was too long ago, perhaps even longer than June. He turns away, steadying a balance against the back of a chair. Without her noticing, he mouths, "Impossible."

With denial, he barks back. "You and I didn't..."

"Yes we did."

"No we didn't."

Calmly she coos. "Yes, we did. You just don't remember it."

"I would remember something like that."

"Not if you were drunk. Yes, darling. Drunk out of your skull after we went to a gallery showing. You consumed enough wine, that it's no wonder you can't remember that wonderful evening we shared when we got back home. It was so lovely."

Evelyn finds herself trying to substitute Ed for Jaime in her thoughts of when she was with the producer for the first time. Replacing Jaime with Ed?

Yuck!

Ed looks away with suspicion. He would have to try and play her game. He would have to try and play, Daddy. He thinks for a moment when looking back at Amanda. Then the thought occurs to him.

"Where did she get the dark hair from?"

"You had a dark haired aunt." She tells him.

"Yeah, but it was never *that* dark."

"Oh, I'm sure it might get a little lighter later on. You know generations sometimes skip."

He questions her. "I thought it's usually the opposite way."

"I'm sure it can happen." She reassures.

Ed shakes his head. Rubbing his chin, he proclaims, "Damn. Looks like I've got a daughter."

Evelyn pulls in her luggage, sighing heavily. She thinks for a moment.

That worked!

Only, Ed knew better.

The charade was about to begin.

While wheeling her suitcases to the bottom of the stairs, Evelyn turns to Ed. "I feel the need to lay down some ground rules, for Amanda's sake. First of all, no smoking in the house. She does not need that with her new pink lungs. Furthermore, I have no problem with this as I've learned to curb my own nicotine habit. Second of all, she stays in our bedroom for at least several months. I need to change one of the guest rooms into a nursery. Probably pink. Third of all…"

Ed ignores the rest, pushing his hair back, going into his own little world and watching it go topsy-turvy.

Shortly after Evelyn goes to her old haunts to show off Amanda, Ed invites Mac into the house.

"How are you? You sounded almost like you turned pale?" Mac remarks.

"Yeah well… I'll be damned." Ed says in a telltale sign that all is not right at the house.

"Evelyn's back I take it."

"Yep."

"So what is it?"

"She did something and I'm gonna get to the bottom of it if it's the last thing I do." Ed sips on brandy. He lights up a Camel and drops the lighter back in his pocket. "You know what she did? She brought home a child, a little girl. I asked her right off the bat. 'How did it happen,' and she's tryin' to say that the girl is mine. You know it and I know it can't be true. She said that she wound up pregnant before her trip to New York. Right! That's not all my friend." Ed goes into dramatic gestures. "This girl has dark eyes. Visibly brown. Dark as the night. Her hair. Her hair is brown. Not dirty blonde, or light brown. I'm talking, *dark chocolate* brown. If you were to wet it, it would turn jet black. This baby...Amanda... She's got low lids. Does any of this sound like the kid would be related to either Evelyn or me? Huh?"

Just about with a loss for words, Mac answers quickly though hesitantly. "Um, no. My guess, it was an adoption."

Ed turns his back as he thinks. "Evelyn was away for a whole year. That would give her plenty of time to hit the sack with someone and conceive. Nine months is what it would take."

"That would be correct."

Ed's voice crawls up a couple of octaves higher in a sense of amazement. "Naw. Conceived in June? Nine months." He repeats. In a more shaky tone he says, "Amanda could be Greek or Spanish. Hell, even French for all I know." He looks over at Mac with an all-knowing glance and a hint of sadness in his blue eyes. "She mentioned that my late aunt had brown hair. I don't buy it, and I sure as hell don't buy that kid being four months old." Ed growls. He picks up the glass of brandy and before lifting it to his lips he says quietly, "I'm gonna find the son of a bitch who did this to her."

Mac looks on with worry.

Ed stares ahead. "Yep." He gulps down the liquid. "I'm gonna find him. And when I do, Mac... There's gonna be hell to pay. Yes siree. Hell...to...pay."

Upon entering The Green Light with Amanda snuggled in her carrier, Evelyn hears the music blasting from the P.A. system. Anita Ward's "Ring My Bell" is everywhere. The man with a towel over his shoulder peeks over to see if Kelly is paying any attention.

"Tad, change that or I'm going to box your ears in!" Kelly yells out from the bar.

Yep. She was listening.

Tad, the busboy and sometime waiter grins while the bartender pours beverages in glasses. Evelyn looks to see Kelly shaking her head and eyeing the P.A. system at times. A couple of other workers wind around, cleaning and setting things up for the evening customers bound to walk through the door. Kelly sees the familiar face walking towards her with what looks to be a basket from her angle. She squints.

"Evelyn? Is that you?"

Evelyn announces, "I'm back!" Then she laughs hoarsely.

Kelly runs over to her for a moment, giving her a big hug almost completely forgetting about the large basket on the floor.

"Ooh me God! How are you?"

"Oh, I'm fine."

"Where have you been, Lass?"

"I was still in New York. I was there for a year."

The cracking sound of a snare drum awakens Kelly Gowan's senses as the beat begins and what turns out to be The Village People's "YMCA." The bartender darts her eyes over to the busboy next to the P.A. system. She arches up her shoulders defiantly and grits her teeth.

"Excuse me." She says in a very polite tone to the returning Evelyn. Then she turns her attention to Tad.

"You're pushin' me patience dear boy."

Tad stands by snickering.

"Okay. If I have to go over there, you will be in a heap of trouble."

Kelly takes a step forward. Immediately the music changes to something by The Ramones.

"That's better. Now leave it alone!" She barks.

Returning her attention back to Evelyn, she asks, "So, what have you been up to, missy?"

"I came home with a little something extra."

"Ooh, what might that be?"

Evelyn looks down, and then points in the same direction.

"If you look down, you'll see."

Amanda blurts out with a small sound.

Kelly immediately leans down over the bar counter. She accidentally drops a glass in the back. Her jaw drops. A fellow worker runs to get a dustpan and without Kelly even noticing, cleans up her mess.

"Holy shit! Oops! I mean... Ooh me God!"

She looks back up at Evelyn who smiles. Amanda gurgles looking up. Kelly looks at her again with shock.

"You...and he... The both of you... That creature... His? How did...? I'm speechless!" She laughs. "Where is that beaut? I'd like to congratulate the lucky man."

Kelly begins looking around.

Evelyn breaks it to her. "Kelly, he's not here. I didn't come back with him." In a more sheepish tone she reveals, "Um, he doesn't know."

"What?" Kelly says with eyes wide open. "He doesn't know?"

"No. It came as a complete shock to me."

"This is the same man I'm thinking of, right?"

"I don't know."

Kelly dashes away from the bar into the back room. Seconds later she reappears with an issue of *Billboard* in her hands. She flips through the pages quickly. Then she comes upon the image of Evelyn standing with Bobby, Dan, and Jaime. Kelly points to Jaime, turning the magazine so Evelyn can see it. The singer looks down at it, realizing this is the first time she ever saw the picture. There he was with a large smile on his face, looking his incredible handsome self. It was an image that made Evelyn feel sorry. She looks down at Amanda with a sense of guilt. The singer bows her head in shame. Kelly looks at her. She didn't need anything to be spelled out to her, the truth was right there.

Kelly says, "She looks just like him."

Evelyn looks back up. "Yes. I know."

"I hope this doesn't mean you're still with Ed."

Evelyn doesn't answer. Again, Kelly can tell.

In disgust, the bartender shakes her head.

"Aw, how can you stand to stay with that man? After all this? Jaime needs to know. He's probably the best thing for you and you go back to that disgusting brute. Tell me, is he anything like what the articles have made him sound?"

"He's *everything* and so much more." The singer says with pride.

"So? Why not tell him?"

"It's difficult. I never asked for this to happen but it did and I just didn't feel it was right in trapping him with a child."

"Trapping? Have you lost your marbles? This is a beauty of a man! I suppose he treated you so much better than that arse turd at home. Christ, woman! Trapping? Look what Ed does to you? He's trapped your mind into thinking you need him! "

"Well. Yes, Jaime did treat me well. But, it was only a fling. Short-lived, just like the sessions."

"Details?

"Oh. He was wonderful. Incredible. *Passionate*."

"Mm." Kelly says, imagining what it must have been like for Evelyn.

Evelyn blurts out, "I miss him." She looks back down at Amanda.

Amanda turns her eyes upward to meet the eyes of her mother.

***

The doorbell rings at I.C.E. Jaime strides over to the door. He opens it. Holding a lit cigarette between his fingers, he looks at the man in front of him. No more than 5'6" is Billy Montrose, a repair guy from the Bronx. His brown poodle haired mane flies in the summer breeze. Wearing a blue satin jacket with a tight fitting green fitness shirt on underneath, he sports tight faded blue jeans. Billy is the type that people wouldn't want to mess with. The attitude of a prizefighter, and a tough little shit at that. In his late thirties, Billy is a pro at fixing equipment. His van logo reads, *Montrose Equipment Services*. He speaks in his Bronx accent, which seems jittery and pissed off at times.

"Hey man, got your delivery." Billy says to the producer.

Jaime inquirers surprised. "Already?"

"Well, I do have a tight schedule. You know this prehistoric shit is gettin' harder and harder to find. While you're at it, get your fuckin' driveway paved, man. It's hell on my tires. It's one thing I have to go through potholes in the city but you're a major studio with major money. I'm sure you can afford it."

Jaime contently yet sarcastically admits, "Gee Billy, if we would have known you were coming by today, we would have laid out some tacks for you on the driveway." He puffs away at his Marlboro with raised brows.

"Ha ha. Funny, man. Must have missed your act at one of the comedy clubs." Billy dryly responds. "Got a girlfriend who's been driving me nuts. 'Billy, why are ya goin' upstate?' 'Cause I have a fuckin' job unlike you.' She nags me to no end. She moans at me for leaving my tools out in the basement. I tell her, 'what do you want with it? A beauty parlor? I do this to earn a living. What does my van say, honey?' I adore her to no end but she drives me nuts sometimes."

Billy hands over the fixed piece of equipment. It's one of Jaime's prized Derby recorders.

"I got her fixed but like I said, they're getting harder to find parts for. Eight years old for these things, man. DRB57s. You seriously need to update your equipment. Of course, your stuff isn't a pain in the ass like the last guy I had to deal with. Some hotshot out of Utica wanted a piece of his mixing console fixed by today. He brought it in *yesterday*. The thing is all wires. Hooked up like it's on life support. Stayed up 'til three fixing it for that lousy ungrateful sack of shit. Jaime, what do I look like, pizza delivery?"

Jaime shakes his head in disagreement.

Billy throws his hands out. "The guy wants me to bring it back all the way to Utica. He said there's no guarantee he'll like the job I do and he's unsure how much it'll cost. What the fuck, man? I don't wanna deal with any more of this guy's shit after this. Let him get someone else. That grease monkey over on 180th St. can fix his problem. Then he'll have to get a replacement. Serves him right." Billy grumbles. "No guarantee my ass. Anyway, here it is and…well, you know the drill."

"How much do I owe you?" Jaime asks.

"Aah, the normal." Montrose guiltily tells the producer. "It's not *that* bad yet."

"Well, I'm really grateful that you were able to fix her." Jaime says in a deep pleasing tone.

Billy hands over a clipboard. Jaime signs it.

"I do consider this as one of my children."

"Very cute. I suppose now you're gonna tell me you have more than one of these."

"Really, Billy, she's one of my seven."

"You have seven of these things? You wanted me to come back here and give you back one of these even though you had six more?"

Jaime looks at him.

Billy is reminded again. "I know. They're one of your children."

Jaime smiles at him as he hands back the clipboard. He digs in his pocket, pulling out a small wad of folded bills. Billy looks at the clipboard then thinks of something else. The producer hands him two bills firmly placing them in Montrose's hand. Billy looks at the folded V shapes in his palm.

"What are you doin', man? I said it was the normal. You gave me two Franklins."

Assuredly, the producer tells him. "I know and I'm grateful. I'm giving you major money to show my gratitude for the work you do."

"It's so nice to have somebody kiss my ass for once."

Jaime grins while looking down. He answers back readily while putting a hand on the repairman's shoulder. In a more hushed tone, he expresses. "Billy, use it to take your girlfriend out to see a Broadway show. Get her a new dress. Treat her to dinner. Do whatever makes you happy. 'Cause that's what you've made me."

Billy looks up with his blue eyes, blinking in a state of surprise.

Jaime gives him a tight-lipped smile.

Almost speechless, Billy utters. "Thanks. Really, thanks, man."

As Billy looks down at the money, the thought he had incubated in his mind is ready to hatch.

"Speakin' of kids. When did you have one?"

"What?" Jaime expresses with confusion and the smoke pouring out of his mouth.

"Yeah. Molly said she was visiting a friend in SoHo and saw a kid that looked a lot like you about a month ago. A girl with Pug."

Jaime smiles with a crooked grin. "How old are we talkin' about? Ten or eleven years old? It's *possible*, I suppose. Anything is...from *then*."

"Try more like two...three months tops."

The expression on the producer's thin lips changes to serious. "You're kidding me, right?"

"No. The next thing I was going to ask was, why mate with Pug?"

"Pug? Who..."

"Yeah, you're buddy, Henry's ex-girlfriend. Folks call her Pug because she's got a face like one."

Jaime blows out his smoke almost onto Billy. "Carol?"

"Yeah."

Taking a swallow and squinting at the idea, Jaime gets more curious.

"What is this about? Why would... Rest assured Billy, nothing has ever gone on between Carol Mulligan and me. Believe me."

"Well, that would be fine but Molly said that baby looked like you. All you have to do is look in a mirror. Her words were, 'If you know what the producer, Jaime Weston looks like, you have an idea of what he must have looked like when he was that young.' So, you want me to believe you because she's ugly? I can understand that." Billy shrugs.

Jaime corrects him as he laughs back. "I never considered Carol to be *ugly*. She's too eccentric for my taste. A little *too* wild. Other than that, she's fine. A pug? This coming from a guy whose hair could take first place at a dog show?"

Billy eyes Jaime unamused.

"Look man, all I know by Molly's account is that something's up with Pu...Carol and that she's got a kid now that just happens to look like you."

"I'll keep it in mind."

Bobby heads up the stairs from the first floor.

Jaime finishes telling Billy, "I really appreciate you fixing her for me."

Billy replies. "No problem. I'll see you around." The repairman walks down the steps, kicking a few granite pieces on the driveway, shrugging to himself with his hands in his jacket pockets. He drives away.

Bobby inquires. "Billy Montrose?"

Jaime looks down for a second. "Yep. I paid him extra so I wouldn't have to hear him treat me like I was his personal psychiatrist next time. He talks about everything. I couldn't tell him I wasn't interested. The guy fixes my recorders for pennies. The least thing I could do is listen to him talk about everything under the sun."

"Sounds fair enough." Bobby nods.

Jaime thinks for a moment.

"Bring her downstairs, will you?"

"Sure thing."

Bobby takes the recorder from Jaime.

The head producer mumbles deeply. "This is getting ridiculous."

His friend watches him leave the lobby only to shut the door to the office.

***

Carol unlocks the door to her loft. Carrying a few bags in her hands and one with her teeth, she drops them on the couch. Scurrying to the counter where her answering machine is, she presses rewind. Almost immediately, Carol pulls out groceries. As soon as the tape finishes, she pushes play. She opens the refrigerator door, placing the latest produce in drawers.

The first message begins.

"Hello, darling. We're still on for dinner, right? I was thinking of bringing a bottle of Cabernet if you think that's all right? I'll see you later on."

Carol smiles at the sound of Edwin's voice. As though answering him back she responds.

"Of course it is, honey."

The beep concludes Edwin Muller's message. Another one begins.

Carol begins eating a peach while putting things in the cupboards above the stove. An older female's voice is heard.

"Hello, Carol? This is Gladys. I just wanted to tell you I absolutely love the bowl. My daughter in-law came over and loved it too. Do you thing there's any way you might be able to make a similar one for her? Her name is Audrey. I'll leave a number with you. Okay? Bye!"

"Sure thing, Gladys." Carol says back to the machine.

She puts the partially eaten peach on the kitchen table. Carrying on, the sculptress transfers dirty dishes from the sink to the dishwasher.

The third message begins.

"Hi, Carol. This is Jaime Weston. You know, Henry's friend? Call me back when you get the chance. I know this may seem odd, me calling you, but I would really like to talk with you. So, if you can do that, it would be much appreciated. Thanks."

The beep finishes all of the latest calls. Carol stands up, staring at the answering machine. Her jaw is slightly unhinged.

"Oh shit."

That deep voice scares her for once. Certainly, Carol would be nervous. Jaime never called her. She could sense he was serious. There seemed to be a slight urgency mixed with a hint of nervousness. What did he want though?

Turning her eyes over to the phone on the wall, she picks up the receiver. Looking at the refrigerator door, she finds Evelyn's phone number. Her fingers begin jotting away at the buttons.

"Hi, Evelyn? This is Carol."

Evelyn answers back. "Hello, darling!"

Carol hears a baby noise in the background. The singer pursues to have a conversation with her in a pleasant tone.

"How are things going?"

"I'm fine." Carol looks at the machine, shaking her head. "Listen, there's a reason why I'm calling you. Your boyfriend called me last night. I didn't get to check the messages since yesterday morning but apparently he called me while I was out."

"Ed?"

"No. The *other* one."

"Jaime?"

"Yes. That one. He doesn't usually call me but I think I know why. Do you think he knows?"

"No."

"Well, why else would he call me? I think he knows. You know, I tried to tell you those photographers hang around the city, especially Central Park. Or...or maybe it was the theater or during shopping when we went to F.A.O. Schwartz."

"Does the press know who you are?" Evelyn asks.

"A little. When you've got a kid in tow and you normally don't, they catch on fast. I'm not John F. Kennedy Jr., but when someone like the New York Post wants gossip, they'll look anywhere. So, I don't think we were careful enough."

"Did he even say why he was calling?"

"No."

"Then maybe it's just to visit. Or, perhaps he found out about you and Edwin."

"Why would he care about that? No. I think he's onto us. I think he knows about Amanda. He either read about it or someone told him. You know she looks just like him. I wouldn't be surprised if others around his circle saw the resemblance."

Evelyn tries to reassure the jittery Carol. "Darling, there are tons of children in Manhattan. What makes her any different than the rest? I'm sure there are others who look like him as well."

This proved to be a tough situation for Carol. She knew she couldn't tell Evelyn that she knew Jaime too much through Henry. That was something Henry did not want either Evelyn or Jaime to know. He advised her not to interfere with them. Their relationship was something they had to figure out on their own without anyone's help or encouragement. As it was, Evelyn didn't want Jaime to know about Amanda either.

Carol answers back cautiously. "Yeah. But, it's still unusual for me to get a call from somebody I barely know."

"Do you suppose Bobby found out? He talks with Henry often enough."

Carol shakes her head. "I don't know but I think he's fishing for answers. Listen, hon. I've got to run. I have some pieces I need to finish. Then there's dinner over here with Edwin. I just got in the door. Complete chaos. You give Amanda lots of kisses from Auntie Carol."

She hears Evelyn cooing and talking softly to the baby.

"Okay. I'll talk to you later or if anything else should happen, let me know. Bye."

"Bye, hon."

Carol hangs up the phone as she nibbles on her bottom lip nervously.

"Hope that's done with." She thinks for a moment about the phone call from Jaime. "Gotta work on some more items."

Carol retreats downstairs into her basement-studio.

Several hours go by when Ed tries to calm down Amanda. She screams until Evelyn holds her. Ed knows that he is having a very hard time adjusting to having the baby around. Neither he nor Amanda are comfortable around each other. It could be nerves or just a dislike for one another. It drives Ed crazy. Not necessarily her distaste for him, but her screeching when she looks him in the eyes. That is murder to his ears. There is no warmth, as she would get from Uncle Edwin. Ed is never playful or full of smiles. No cooing or holding her, flying like a plane. Nothing fun and the little girl notices it. The only comfort is her mother. Ed still seems too much like a stranger for her.

Into the late afternoon, music pours out of Carol's basement. She's on the phone once again talking to a customer.

"Yeah, well I didn't have time to do any of it. I checked my messages earlier this morning. Then I went out for groceries. Last night I didn't get back home until about eleven. Yeah. I went to New Jersey. Passaic. Yep. Then I had to go across to Ewing, near Trenton and drop off some stuff for someone else. By the time I got home, I dropped onto the couch. Now I..."

The doorbell rings.

Carol's eyes turn in the direction of the door.

Over the phone, she says, "I'm going to have to let you go right now. I promise to get it done before next week. Yeah. Someone's at the door. I'll talk to you later. Bye."

Carol puts the phone down and runs over to the door. She figures it's a little early for Edwin to arrive. Then again, it could be one of her girlfriends.

She opens it. Her jaw slightly drops. Jaime smiles at her. He removes his sunglasses. "Hi, Carol. Hope you got my message." She looks at him half surprised and half disapprovingly. Wearing dark blue jeans with a black jacket and black T-shirt, the producer stands just outside her door. "May I?"

She answers back. "Yeah. Just remember that I'm very busy. We'll go downstairs in the basement."

They walk down the steps. Jaime takes in the surroundings. There were no signs of children's things. No toys or rattles even. He looks past the stairs and into the small studio space. Again nothing.

"Nice what you've done to the place."

"Have you ever been here before?"

"I came with Henry when you were just settling here. There was no furniture and you were painting the walls above the cement. Maybe you had the kiln there. I can't remember."

"Very good memory! You actually did remember all of it. I had just gotten the kiln." Carol saunters over to the boom box, turning it on. The music pours out of the speakers.

Curiously, Jaime asks her. "What do you listen to?"

"Whatever inspires me. Rock, reggae, jazz, blues, progressive, orchestra, country, R&B, some rap."

"Got any favorite artists?"

"Aretha Franklin for sure."

"Nice choice."

Carol begins thinking of ways to chase away the producer. She was unsure of what he wanted and was afraid if he had found out about Amanda. While changing the dial, she wonders if she can find some absolutely horrid music that will send him racing up the stairs and out of her home. She switches the station. Then she comes upon Marvin Gaye's "Sexual Healing." Maybe she could seduce the producer? That might make him high tail it out of there.

Carol turns to Jaime.

"Put me on spin cycle."

She sways in front of him with her tall willowy body. He holds his arm out and she spins right into him with her hand landing against his chest. He looks at her with a slight smile.

It doesn't work and he's not leaving.

Carol wanders over to an unfinished piece of sculpture. She shows him a few of her finished pieces. They look very peculiar to him, but that doesn't matter much. He's there for answers. If he has to engage in conversation to get what he wants, then his trip all the way from New Paltz is worth it. Although, he isn't much into small talk, Jaime observes her every move carefully. Carol walks over to the kiln, placing clay bowls, odd sculptures, and vases in it.

In the meantime, he walks over to the comfy magenta sofa chair. Plopping down, he still eying the surroundings.

Great.

Now he's going to really make himself comfortable and not show a chance of leaving. He continues to watch her with one hand propped to the side of his head.

Carol closes the kiln door and turns up the temperature. Walking back to her workspace and painting, she says as she stirs some paint, "The fun part is when it's done. Don't you think? I mean it must be a similar feeling as to when you've finished somebody's album."

Jaime takes a moment to think before answering.

"Yeah. It is rewarding sometimes, but only if the artist likes it. That's all I care about."

Okay. Next line of stalling tactics.

As she paints, she looks at him. He catches her glance. His low-lidded eyes show a slight hint of boredom. Still he remains gracious and patient. He has nothing else to do anyway. The sculptress smiles while looking over the six-footer on her chair. She knew just how to get rid of him. With her back turned she smiles slyly.

This might send him running.

"You know... Have you ever considered becoming an artist's model? I'm certain you have a *great* figure under there."

Jaime bows his head with a shy smile. Lightly biting his bottom lip, he responds quietly though deeply. "If it's the kind of modeling I *think* you're talking about. Then my answer would have to be, no. I'm not into that kind of stuff."

"Even if you were paid?"

"Even with all of the money in the world."

Carol snorts out. "Everyone says that. Then they do it and say it wasn't bad at all." She looks at him chuckling softly to himself. "Ah, you're shy."

Defending the humor he sees in it, the producer folds his hands and tells her. "Really. I respect people who do it but it's not something I would ever be tempted to do myself."

"Oh, too bad." Carol says with disappointment. She notices he isn't leaving. He wasn't even turned off or embarrassed by her suggestion. Jaime doesn't budge. This both surprises and annoys the lanky artist.

Carol checks her watch to see the time. She tells him, "I truly have to work on preparing dinner aside from working down here, so if you can bear with me." She grabs a small bowl from the shelf. The sculptress presents the producer with the little gift.

"You're a smoker, right?"

He nods his head, smiling slightly. "Yep."

"Here's a little something for you. Just a way of me saying, 'Thanks for stopping by.'"

She holds what looks like a small pink and plum colored bowl adorned by turquoise crystallized sequins with three wires coming out of it on the bottom.

He looks it over rather perplexed. Smiling, he asks, "What is it?"

"It's an ashtray."

"An ashtray? *That is*?"

"Yep. You can really use it too."

"I've never seen one that looks like this."

"It's an original."

Looking it over he admits. "I'm sure it is."

Quickly she walks up the steps, leaving Jaime just sitting on the chair.

He gets up and follows her.

Walking in the kitchen, Carol begins preparing dinner, pulling out various bags of vegetables. Jaime walks in to join her. While reaching for a pot she says, "You know I have to get dinner made. It was nice of you to stop by."

He watches her every move with growing agitation. She goes from the counter to the sink, to the refrigerator, to a drawer, so on and so forth. Jaime places the Mulligan made ashtray on the counter, and looks at Carol putting uncooked pasta in a pot. Again, she walks over to the refrigerator. This time Jaime stands in her way.

Jaime says back to her. "All right. I've been nice to you long enough. I came here for a reason and ever since I walked through that door, I've gotten the sense you don't really want to talk to me. I don't think you had any intention of calling me back when I left that message for you last night."

"Really, I'm busy. You came to my house, unannounced. I haven't seen you in who knows how many years. I get a call from you saying you need to talk to me.

Putting his finger up, he leans toward her and says in a serious restrained tone, "I don't like to be fucked with."

Carol looks at him equally as serious. She knows he means business.

With an exalted breath she says, "Okay. *Maybe* I know where this is coming from. She changes her tone to calm. "I'm sure people were asking about a kid."

Jaime rolls his eyes, then closes them in frustration as he leans his back against the refrigerator door.

"There's a little girl who I sometimes baby-sit for. It's a Portuguese family that moved a block away. I don't know if she *exactly* looks like you. That's tough to say. I know that you're half Indian. I guess the dark hair could be like yours. It's so hard to tell with little kids especially when they're so young. She's only four months old. A few others baby-sit her too. Maybe that's what you heard about. Like I said, Jaime, it's hard to tell. She could pass for Italian, Spanish, French, yes, American Indian like you, West Indies, anything that produces brown hair."

"Are you telling me the truth?"

"Yes."

He pushes his hair back in frustration.

"Several people have told me already."

"Isn't it a little naive of you to take their word for it? I'm guessing you haven't seen anyone like this yourself."

"No. But others have asked me if I had a daughter or niece."

Jaime looks down at the floor.

"You seem awfully concerned about this yourself."

Carol walks away from the blocked refrigerator to tend to the pasta. "I told you everything I know."

He starts to look up.

She glances right into his eyes. "Now are you satisfied?"

The doorbell rings.

Both look over. She goes to answer it.

Edwin stands before her with a bottle of Cabernet. Gleefully he announces, "Hope you got my message. I remember you said you would be a little bit busy so I decided to bring it in any case."

Edwin heads straight for the kitchen.

Jaime looks at him with surprise. "Edwin. How are you?"

Edwin responds. "Long time, no see. How are you, Jaime?"

"Fine. I was in the city and decided to drop by and visit Carol." He steps away from the refrigerator, picking up the homemade ashtray.

Carol looks down, then at Edwin.

Jaime gives a tight-lipped smile. He looks down and notices the bottle of wine Edwin holds.

"Are you two...?" He points a finger at them. "I think I'll be going now."

Carol suggests, "You're welcome to stay for dinner."

"That'll be all right. I have to go back to the studio."

Jaime begins to walk towards the door with his head partially bowed down.

Edwin calls out. "Jaime! I forgot to say you did a great job on Evelyn Winthrop's latest album."

Jaime turns around. "Thanks."

Edwin recalls, "I remember she had an extremely difficult time trying to get *Hero's Requiem* to sound the way she wanted it to. We had many arguments over it. But you did it wonderfully."

"There really wasn't much to it. It was a hit or miss thing. Well, I'll see you around, Edwin."

Jaime puts his hand on the doorknob then stops turning it. He says, "Carol. Some people might call you Pug. Just know that I don't." He smiles slightly and walks out.

The door closes behind him.

The sculptress gives out a sigh as though she were holding her breath, waiting to breathe again.

Edwin tells her, "I didn't know he was coming over."

"Neither did I."

He sees that she's very relieved.

"What did he ask you?"

"Too much."

***

The hapless photographer doesn't quite seem to grasp parenthood too well. He discovers that Amanda is a bundle to handle. More than he ever imagined. Ed goes through days of the baby spitting up on him, bringing suits to the dry cleaners, several hours of standing by the washing machine. Experiencing screams at ungodly hours in the morning. He won't even touch diapers. Every time he reaches in the crib to pick her up, she curls up, trying to avoid his hands on her. If that doesn't work, she cries very loudly. It's her only way of telling him to leave her alone. Ed can never hold her calmly. It could be from his drinking that would make his nerves twitch or he just felt that they could never get along, due to his resentment towards her. Every time he looks into her eyes, he feels he's looking into another man's. He knows that she does not like him.

Ed picks her up from her high chair, attempting to look her right in the eyes. He sees her overcome with worry.

"I know how you feel about me. I know I'm not your daddy."

She begins to whine before breaking into full-blown crying.

"Wah. Wah. Wah." Ed mocks. "Is that all you know how to do? Will you even try to let me understand you?"

Amanda screams.

"Guess not." Ed shrugs.

One particular morning, Evelyn has to go out and run some errands. She leaves Ed to take care of Amanda for a short amount of time. As soon as she leaves, both Ed and Amanda begin their duel of crying child versus annoyed parent. While Ed sits at the kitchen table, Amanda sits in her high chair overlooking him. She begins to whine. Ed's eyes snake over to where she sits from reading the newspaper. She looks right at him and whines an octave louder. Ed turns to her.

In an annoyed tone he tells her, "Shut up."

He tends to the dailies again.

Amanda sees this and bounces a little bit.

"Shut up you little brat." His eyes peer over to where she is. "Listen, if you have to go to the bathroom then do it in your diaper. I know your game and I'm not fallin' for it."

Amanda begins to scream.

Ed puts the newspaper down on the table. He grits his teeth and takes a deep breath.

"Listen you, if you want attention, then too bad! I can't smoke in my own damn house because of you. So, if either one of us is gonna whine then it'll be me. So, shut up." He mumbles. "Crowding my space. I never invited you here in the first place."

Amanda continues to scream. This time she waves her tiny hands. She wants someone to hold her, but Ed still refuses. He gets up from the chair and walks over to where she sits.

"Waaaaaaaaah!" Ed mocks disgracefully. "How would you like it if I did that to you all hours? Huh?" He looks right at her then gets an idea. "You hungry? Huh? Is that what the problem is?"

He wanders over to the refrigerator and pulls out a small jar of applesauce. Opening it, he puts it on the tray of the high chair, leaving it there.

"Here. Now eat up and leave me alone."

Ed goes back to reading the newspaper. Quickly, he notices Amanda. She's quiet, although, she digs her tiny fingers in the gooey fruit. The jar rolls on the tray, leaving a smattering of applesauce all over. With pure delight, the three-month-old swipes at the tray, patting it down like paté. Ed smiles back at her.

By the time Evelyn comes back home, she sees her daughter sitting in the high chair among a mess. Amanda raises her hands to her mother, all sticky and gooey. Evelyn inspects the girl.

"My God! What happened to you?"

Amanda has applesauce smeared on her face and on her clothes. Ed remains sitting at the table.

Evelyn turns to Ed. "What did you do?" She says in an accusing tone. "Why is she like this?"

"Me? I gave her the food. She was crying and wouldn't stop."

"Did you honestly think she could eat on her own?"

"Well..." Ed replies sheepishly.

"Ed, she's only four months old! And you didn't even give her a bib!"

Evelyn begins taking a wet paper towel to Amanda's hands and wipes her mouth. Quickly she removes the baby's top and pants until she's left with only her diaper on.

Ed barks back. "Listen, I did what I could. I'm trying. I'm really trying. I don't have the patience you do. I'm not equipped for this parenthood stuff. I need more time."

Evelyn holds Amanda. She says, "I don't know if you'll ever get the hang of it because I don't know if you even want to. Now if you excuse me, Amanda is going to have a bath. I do expect you to clean this up since you were so helpful in feeding her." Evelyn snarls with sarcasm before leaving the kitchen to go upstairs.

Amanda gurgles.

Ed turns back and begins to clean up the mess on the high chair.

On the phone, Evelyn speaks in a frustrated tone to Mildred.

"Millie, he's horrible with Mandy. Just horrible! Last week, I went out to do some shopping at the market. I left her with Ed. When I came back, she was smeared with applesauce. He told me that she was hungry. No spoon or anything. He simply left the jar on the tray of the high chair and let her fend for herself. What was he thinking? Treating her like some wild animal!"

Mildred replies. "That does sound bad."

"And when he goes to hold her, she cries terribly. It's as if she can't stand him. I know he's angry that I had this child but I thought everything would turn out all right."

"Dear, just because you have a baby doesn't mean everything will change. He needs to get used to her. I'm sure that having her around is tough on him."

"I just wish things would go smoother. We still argue. It seems like even though I hadn't seen him for a year, nothing changed. With Mandy, it almost seems worse. Oh, Millie, you don't know how much I just want to pack in my belongings and move back to New York."

"Seeing as though she's Ed's daughter too, I must say that it would not be fair."

Mildred has a hard time believing Amanda is Ed's at the same time. She had seen Amanda quite a few times and was not convinced the man was Amanda's biological father. She won't say anything to Evelyn about it though, for she might upset her with such an accusation.

She tells Evelyn, "Listen, sweetie, August is fast approaching. I'm sure Ed will be going somewhere to take pictures. Some of the landscapes are beautiful during this time of season. That way you'll have proper distance away from him for a short while. Like I said, it's completely new to him, caring for a baby."

Evelyn begins to completely regret not ever telling Jaime about his daughter. Maybe taking that chance wouldn't have been so bad after all? It would have given Evelyn closure, to know his feelings on having a child.

Chapter 9

"Do you think he'll be okay? Andrea asks her husband as she clutches his shoulder.

She quickly adjusts Bobby's bow tie.

"I don't know. I mean, hopefully."

"Is there anything we can do?"

"At this point? Just hope he finds a nice girl at this party."

They wait at the bottom of the steps in the dimly lit lobby. Andrea's silver sleeveless gown shimmers as she turns to face the stairs.

"He barely ever goes home."

"Where is home to him? Think about it, honey. Where is home if there's nobody there?"

Andrea looks at Bobby.

In the meantime, Jaime finishes getting ready. He gets done buttoning the second button and places the undone bow tie around his neck. Checking his look in the mirror as he ties it, his eyes peer down to the calendar sitting on the wall. It was now July 26th. Approximately one year since he and Evelyn started their brief affair. The singer made a profound impression on the producer who was used to being alone. Jaime picks up his black suit and puts it on. He shuts off the light as he leaves the room, then shuts the door. Straightening the bow tie, he looks at the door to the first room nearest the stairs on his left. That was Evelyn's room for a little over a month the previous year. He smiles slightly at the thought of how proud she was when he was able to make "Little Miss Independent" and "Hero's Requiem" sound the way she wanted it to. That was Ms. Evelyn Winthrop, the one who plopped down some two dozen cassettes on a table and managed to get a whole album's worth of material from scattered pieces.

Downstairs, Andrea talks to Bobby.

"He doesn't even flirt the way he used to."

Bobby clears his throat.

Jaime walks down the stairs. He addresses them quietly. "Bobby. Andi."

Andrea looks over Jaime.

"You're looking good."

"You're looking lovely as always, Andi."

She walks up to the handsome six-footer. "Your tie isn't right."

Quickly, although cautiously, Andrea fixes it. He says nothing back to her as he simply allows her to correct it.

Jaime utters. "I never liked them anyway."

"It *is* a black tie event. I don't think the head of Melville Records would want to see you *too* casual." She finishes doing the bow tie. "There. That's better."

Bobby announces. "All set?"

The other two both nod.

Andrea says, "We're taking the Camaro."

Bobby teasingly prods as he grins. "Aw, what's the matter, hon? You don't want to take the Bug?"

"I'd rather die before you bring me in your hippie mobile to any major event."

Jaime snickers. Bobby grins. The party of three leaves the studio.

Evelyn tends to Amanda as Ed takes off his slippers and slides into bed. He looks over at Evelyn who coos to the baby and tucks her in. Ed shakes his head in disgust and puts his head on the pillow, still watching her. Once Evelyn is content with Amanda sleeping, she retires to the bed and climbs in. She turns to face Ed and kisses him.

"Goodnight, darling."

Ed closes his eyes as he responds with, "Goodnight."

She turns over and turns off the lamp above the bed.

Looking at the crib near the wall, she smiles warmly as she begins to drift asleep. Amanda's presence makes Evelyn think back to her humble beginning existence a year earlier. She sinks into a deeper phase of sleep, which begins to become a dream-like haze of vivid recollections.

The mid July evening remains fresh in Evelyn's mind. Jaime was heavily in her thoughts. He treated her greatly with kindness, warmth, compassion, respect, and sensual passion, which she never felt with Ed. It wasn't simply lust, but an understanding for each other's feelings that couldn't be held back any longer. Jaime was genetically gifted with brooding good looks and charismatic charm. He had a way of making her feel completely at ease, enough to spend the night with him.

She thought of the long fingers. The way he held a cigarette. It was like those old black and white movies she had seen. Her thoughts turn to when she asked him which did he rather see burn. His eyes, mesmerizingly dark under low lids so seductive. The way he wore an unbuttoned shirt could send her temperature to one hundred and fifty degrees. Oh, and that voice, so deep and sexy, even when spoken in a hushed whisper. Deeper into sleep she thinks of the way she was kissed and touched.

On the fringes of reality, Ed shakes himself out of his sleep when he sees Evelyn moving around in her sleep. He props himself up and reaches to shake Evelyn out of whatever it is she's thinking about.

"Evelyn!" Ed says in a harsh whisper.

Finally, she awakens.

"What?"

"What's goin' on?"

"Huh?" She says in a sleepy tone.

Ed reaches for the light.

Half startled, Evelyn tells him, "Don't turn it on! You'll wake Mandy!" She turns to face Ed. "It was nothing. Will you please get some sleep?"

"Was it a nightmare?" He pries.

"No. Just get some sleep!"

Evelyn tosses the blanket close to her head. Ed grumbles and turns the opposite way, attempting to fluff his pillow. Evelyn smiles as her eyes close.

***

A couple of weeks go by. Dan arrives at the studio. He walks down the stairs after he sees nobody on the main floor. He finds Bobby curling up wires and extension cords. Dan looks around as Bobby wanders over to the topaz colored drum kit on the riser.

The engineer asks, "What's been goin' on?"

"I've been redoing the drum track for the last band that came through. Phil said his snare didn't sound right and there was no bottom to the bass drum." He unscrews the crash cymbal from its stand. "I'm no drum techie, but I thought it sounded fine. Then again, I'm not the one who's been playing for twenty-one years. So, I've been redoing the thing. How was the vacation to Virginia?"

"Oh, it was fine. We got to go to Busch Gardens. The boys had a blast." Dan then asks, "Where's Jaime?"

"I haven't seen him in the past two weeks. He called at the beginning of the time he's been missing and told me to just take care of business. No other explanation. He's been acting pretty weird lately."

"Wow. Got any idea where he might be?"

"No. Although he might be keeping company."

"Oh?"

"Andrea and I went to the Melville Records party two Thursdays ago. We brought him along with us. He met a pretty young brunette. You know, he came with us in Andi's car but he didn't go back with us the same way." Bobby raises his brows.

Dan asks. "So, he was still in that funk?"

"Yeah. Afraid so. Consider what time of the year it is."

"Summer."

"Yeah."

It starts to strike Dan. "Evelyn? One year ago this time."

Bobby points a bolt at Dan that he's just taken off the drum kit. With one eye squinting shut, he announces, "Bingo."

Dan looks at Bobby.

"So, you think his mind is off of her finally."

"Quite possibly. I'm not saying to look out for any wedding bells, but he's found somebody." He stacks the tom-toms in the corner, and then remembers. "Oh! I found out why Ginger Aldaire left so quickly from the sessions. I ran into Carter. The big black bass player built like a football player. You remember him?"

"Yeah."

"He told me that she said she kissed Jaime and things were going along fine. But then he called her the wrong name. I'll give you one guess what that name was."

"Evelyn."

"Yep."

Dan shakes his head.

Bobby says, "She took off right after that because she felt humiliated and she didn't feel she could work with him anymore."

"Poor girl. Casanova strikes again."

"All we can hope for now is that this gal he met takes his mind off the past."

Dan nods in agreement. "Boy, that's something'."

Within the light breeze against his gray suit, Henry closes his eyes and takes a sip of coffee as he reads a magazine. Ah, the beauty of upstate New York in the summer. He hears the clanking of dishes. The sounds of the morning crowd gather outside of the bistro. Among the noise and hustle bustle is the sound of shattering. It's bound to happen as pieces of a plate splash to the floor a little off in a distance. A tall, thin figure glides past the waitress who picks up pieces of the broken ceramic. Onlookers and patrons look her way. Henry is unaffected by the commotion. It's just part of the morning atmosphere.

Jaime Weston reemerges from two weeks of hiding. He's a bit disheveled. Attired in a green and black flannel shirt with the first three buttons undone and untucked under his lightweight black jacket with the sleeves rolled up to his elbows over black jeans. He holds an already half smoked Marlboro between his fingers. Jaime's seductive low-lidded eyes are caught between the state of little sleep and depression. He takes a seat quickly across from Henry. In turn, Henry slowly lowers the magazine he was reading and looks at the individual.

Half jokingly, he asks. "Do I know you?"

Jaime says back. "I called the house and Karen told me that I would probably find you here."

He takes a drag on the cigarette.

Henry replies with a smile. "You look like hell."

Jaime pushes back his hair from flopping over his right eye.

"I've had five hangovers in the past two weeks. I told Bobby to finish up a project with a band that was recording at the studio. It was something I didn't feel like doing. How *odd* is that? I don't feel like working? Normally, I can't *wait* for a challenge from an artist. This time, I just couldn't bring myself to do *anything*."

He looks down at the dark blue speckled surface of the tabletop.

Henry asks curiously. "Where have you been for the past two weeks if you haven't been in the studio at all?"

Jaime answers back as the smoke drifts out of his mouth. "Home."

Henry repeats. "Home?"

The producer smiles back. "Yeah. I know. I don't usually stick around the house." He takes a swallow as he remembers. "Um, I went with Bobby and Andi to a record company party in Albany. A black tie affair. I didn't really *feel* like going either. Andi persuaded me. You know, she's good at that. But, um...I went with them, met everybody ten times over. It was the usual thing, champagne, cocktails, pat on the back, speeches. I started talking with this young lady. I'm sure everybody who knew me thought, 'Jaime's found someone to take home.' Well, we talked and talked. Got in a cab and I paid her fare. I let her go like *that*. She was sweet but a little too young for me. After that, I went to a bar. Met up with one of the guys from the party and he drove me all the way back to the studio. I picked up my car and went home. I haven't been to the studio or almost anywhere since."

"So what's on your mind?" Henry inquires.

Jaime sucks on the Marlboro.

"It's been a year since my life *changed*. I feel that a lot happened after my birthday last year."

"Oh, you're talking about *her*."

Jaime becomes hesitant, choosing his words carefully.

"I just can't understand why I couldn't say what was on my mind."

"It's easier not to. Hey, it wasn't easy for me to tell Karen how I felt about her."

"Maybe if I would have said *something*, things would be different and we wouldn't be having this conversation. I guess I was just unsure about the whole thing at first. Telling her it was a mistake or something that simply happened was the *worst* thing I could have said. Not for her sake but mine. How could I have been in complete denial? It was a full-blown affair, or liaison. However way you want to put it. It's not like it was a one-night stand. She just..." He puts the cigarette in the ashtray on the table. He then pulls out a fresh Marlboro and lights the end with the previous one. The producer continues. "When we made love, it had meaning. She just made me feel really...*content*. It felt *right* and really good." He smiles.

Henry then says, "Sleeping with someone is how you gauge a relationship?"

"No. No. My comfort level with her is...*was*... I was able to let my guard down with her. I felt like I could just talk with her like what we're doing right now. We went out one night to dinner and talked about our pasts. How we were, our feelings about the last decade. We came out of it alive. How we felt about the present. Just anything. She fascinated me. I can't forget that." Jaime takes a drag from the newly lit Marlboro. "You remember how the air conditioning went out last year and you asked how I was feeling? What did I say?"

"You told me you were comfortable."

"Strangely comfortable."

"Yeah."

"What I realize now is it wasn't because of the physical circumstance. It had *something* to do with it but not completely. At that point, I was actually comfortable in my own skin, that so much being exposed didn't bother me. Quite honestly Henry, it felt liberating. Even when Andi and Vicki came over, it didn't really bother me. Everything then in my life felt fine. I was truly happy. Then, once Evelyn left, I didn't know how much it would affect me."

"Has it?" Henry squints.

"Tremendously. Profoundly. It has affected every other encounter I've had with other women. Just talking to them, I couldn't even think of an intimate relationship with anybody right now. I went out with this other singer in October. Uh, Ginger. She kissed me. Well, everything was going along fine. Then I said something that she caught. I called her the wrong name and she left the studio the next morning. What I didn't realize was that I was still *raw* inside. I couldn't just forget about *her*. Here I found her ten years later and it would be preposterous for me to let it go after I allowed for it to go that far. You know?"

As Jaime takes a drag from his cigarette, Henry looks at his friend out of concern. He takes a sip of coffee and sees how much it bothers Jaime, but he can't do anything. He listens some more, only more helplessly.

The producer smiles back. "I went down to the city a couple of months ago. This is how crazy it gets. It seemed as though wherever I went, I had the reminder of her. Evelyn."

"And did you see her there?"

"No. But, others might have. At least I thought. I told you about Cosgrove. The gallery I went to where I first saw her. Well, I went back because the woman who ran that show sent me an invitation. She was coming back for another showing, this Wilhelmina Weinderhof. So, I was there checking it out." He squints his eyes. "I *thought* I might have seen her there." Jaime holds up the lit cigarette in his fashionable style. He looks down. "Although, I could have been wrong. I checked out the list that Wilhelmina told me about as she said it was a huge success this time around. She said that everybody from eleven years ago was back this time. So, I don't know."

Henry looks at Jaime with pity. "It's tough."

Jaime snorts out. "You're tellin' me."

As the smoke streams out of his mouth, he relays another tale.

"The next day I went to Bleecker St. Records to see if there were any interesting albums. The sales guy said to me that I missed her by five minutes. I thought that was rather *odd*." He chuckles. "So, I asked him what she looked like. He practically described her perfectly. The blue eyes in mascara. Um, prominent...chest. Her height was at about chin level to me. Then he told me the real clincher. This guy said, 'People tell me my daughters look like me but that baby was a dead ringer for you.' I told him it couldn't be, even when he said his wife was a blonde. It's not like I don't *believe* a child can take on the looks of one parent more than another. Just that in Evelyn's case it's different. One of the times when she first arrived at the studio she told us, uh, myself, Bobby and Danny how she couldn't have kids. It was truly *heartbreaking* the way she explained it. I know it hit Bobby and Danny pretty hard just by seeing their expressions. So, anyway it was terribly sweet of this guy to assume I had kids. He said, 'You could have fooled me.' What else could I say?"

He chuckles again.

"Um, but I'm pretty sure if she were able to, we probably would have had one by now."

Henry looks at Jaime peculiarly after taking a sip of coffee.

"That's a strange thing to say." He replies while looking at the tiny pack of sugar.

Jaime answers hesitantly. "It wouldn't seem so strange..."

Henry understands right away. "Unprotected?"

"Yep."

"I'm sure she didn't care since she knew nothing would happen."

"It was never mentioned."

"Oh, well of course not." Henry becomes a little annoyed by his friend's cavalier attitude. "What would have happened if she did have your kid? Really, think about it. Would you be able to be a father to anybody or would you just be like, 'Oh, okay. So it's mine but I don't need to be part of their life'?"

"No."

"Or would you just want to visit them once in a while, when it's convenient for you?"

"No."

"You know, having a child takes up a lot of time, love, and patience."

"I know. It has occurred to me as I've taken care of Becky enough times since she was born. And I'm not saying that because she's invited me to virtually all of her tea parties either." Jaime says with a laugh. "Seriously, there comes a time when one needs to grow up and think of others. I think I'm old enough. Jeez, at least I hope." He smiles at the thought. "It would be wonderful to have a little girl like Becky around, or a little boy. But I guess I have more of an affinity towards girls since I've taken care of Becky and she's like a niece to me."

Then he thinks for a moment realizing nothing could come of it.

"Why are we even having this conversation? It's not like it will happen. Not with Evelyn. I've come to the realization that children of our own would play no part in our relationship or future. Adoption isn't out of the question but..." He shakes his head at the absurdity of it all. "What am I saying? She's probably better off in England. I'm a complete workaholic. I'm forty-five and look what I have...a very fucked up life. My priorities are so backwards. Vicki was right when she said I hide behind sunglasses so nobody can tell how I truly feel. I don't do much outside of the studio. So, really what woman would want to deal with me on a daily basis?"

Jaime holds out his hands in a giving up manner. Leaning back against the chair, he lets out a groan. Regretfully he says while sunk down, "Shit. She's better off without me."

With his hand to his forehead, Henry sees the pain of his friend. He thinks of what he would love to say to the forlorn producer.

"Evelyn's in love with you too and you have a four month old daughter who looks like you. Quit feeling sorry for yourself!"

He takes out his wallet. Rummaging through it, he finds a small folded paper among receipts next to his billfold. It was Evelyn's address in Oxford. Picking out the paper he knew was in his possession, he considers a good cover-up.

Bobby!

While Jaime still looks glumly at the floor under sullen eyes, Henry slides the paper across the table.

"Obviously, this is killing you. Go to her."

Jaime's eyes slowly lift to meet his friend's straightforward glance.

In a quiet though confused tone he answers back. "What?"

"Just go to her."

"I wouldn't have the slightest idea on how to find her."

Henry slides the paper a little closer to the producer. Jaime catches sight of the item.

"What's this?"

"Possibly your future."

Confused, the producer puts the cigarette in his mouth while unfolding the piece. His eyes dart up.

Henry explains. "Bobby gave this to me a little while ago. He figured I talk to you enough."

***

While Ed is downstairs, Evelyn gives Amanda a bath. When she returns, the baby is left clad only in a diaper. The rushed mother hands her daughter to Ed.

With quickness, she states, "Hold her for a few minutes. I have to prepare what clothes she'll wear." With no way to escape, Ed is left holding the four month old.

Bonding time.

That's all he needs to slow him down. Amanda would struggle and whine normally, but this time is different. She doesn't seem to squirm or scream. Rather, she is oddly calm. Maybe the bath soothed her.

Ed takes a look at her. He positions the baby up in the air like holding a puppy. Her feet leave him and her little hands dangle in mid air as she's held under her arms. The baby's eyes bounce upward to meet his. Ed closes in on her face leaving his sight targeted directly on her eyes.

Those eyes.

Full black pupils with the brown irises, no sign anywhere of blue not even hazel. Amanda doesn't even crack a smile. Ed has an obsession of wondering who she is. Where she came from and why Evelyn lied to him by saying he was the daddy. He grumbles to the little girl.

"I'm not your daddy."

Amanda's eyes wander elsewhere. Ed positions her with more authority, in hopes that he'll get her attention and she'll understand what he has to say. She turns her head. Amanda's slightly arched brows get his attention instead. No way were they shaped like his or Evelyn's. How could two blondes create a brunette? Genetically, Ed feels it's impossible. Every feature betrays his and Evelyn's features. "What are you?" He muses. "I'm gonna find out who your real daddy is and we're gonna talk. Yeah. A nice little chat. You know Amanda, I knew Mommy was up to something, but this...you take the cake. She went to see three doctors to make sure someone like you couldn't happen."

Just then, Amanda begins to cry. Evelyn rushes downstairs. Ed quickly holds the baby against his chest.

The concerned mother asks, "What happened?"

"I don't know. We were just having a nice little chat when she started crying."

Evelyn reaches to pull her daughter away. She holds the baby, stroking her hair back and giving kisses to her head.

"Shhhhhhhhhh. What's the matter?" She coos. Holding her closer against herself, she feels the sagging diaper. "I just changed you. Back upstairs we go." She walks up the stairs as she tells the baby, "You're going to look nice and pretty in your flowered shirt and matching pants."

Ed looks up at the balcony. He had successfully scared the shit out of Amanda.

***

The doorbell rings at the Whitfield's residence. Becky peeks out of the curtains.

She calls out. "Mom! Dad! It's Uncle Jaime!"

Bobby runs up to the door to answer it. He sees his longtime friend with a slight grin and smiling eyes. Jaime has since cleaned up his act. He says, "Bobby."

"It's great to see you, but where have you been?"

"It doesn't matter. Hey. I need a favor from you."

"What?"

"I need you to drop me off at the airport."

Bobby says, "Are you talkin' about JFK? Jaime, that's over an hour away, almost two. And the traffic is going to be hell getting through the city. The five o' clock jam you know is gonna be one big pain in the ass. Do you have reservations even?"

"Yeah. I got them yesterday."

"This must be pretty important."

Andrea steps up from behind her husband. Becky remains nearby.

Jaime answers. "It is. I'm going to London."

Bobby turns around as he senses Andrea right nearby. He gives her a glance. She looks back at him.

Bobby asks Jaime, "What time do you have to be there by?"

"Eight at the latest."

"Well, okay. It's about four-thirty right now. If we're gonna go, we should get going...this minute."

Jaime digs out of his pants pocket a ring of several keys. "Catch!" He tosses the jangling item at his friend who catches them. Bobby nods his head as he sees one that he's surprised by.

"Jaime, this is the key to the BMW."

"I know. I'm not going to leave my car in the parking lot at the airport for two weeks."

"Two weeks? That's how long you'll be there for?"

Bobby walks out the door, following Jaime to his car. Jaime pulls out a suitcase from the trunk then takes his carry-on bag from the backseat.

He pats Bobby on the shoulder. "Relax Bobby. You don't even have to feed her unless you drive her. Unleaded. Premium. Then again, I know she's not your style. Take Andi's car."

"Wait a minute. You demand I take you to the airport. During rush hour, I might add. You insult my beetle. Then you automatically say, 'Let's take the Camaro.' Anymore demands Mr. Weston?"

Jaime stands looking at his friend.

Bobby turns to see his Volkswagen beetle. Rust spots. Ugly light shade of blue. Tan interior. Small. He smirks at it.

"Aah, we'll take Andi's Camaro."

Jaime lets out a laugh. Bobby takes the suitcase, placing it in the trunk of the car.

From inside the house, Andrea watches out the door.

Becky gets on the couch. Looking out the front drapes, she asks her mother. "Mom? Why is Uncle Jaime going to England? He said it was important."

"Yeah. He's hoping to get you an aunt."

Andrea smiles at her daughter.

Becky smiles back widely. She giggles. "You mean he finally has a girlfriend?"

"Well, um...sort of. I don't know the whole story, but he's determined enough to seek her out in England."

Inside the car, Bobby starts up the ignition. Jaime looks out the window on the passenger's side. He spots Andrea and Becky waving. He smiles and waves back. They back out of the driveway. Bobby turns on the radio. Guns N' Roses, a new hard rock band is heard. Lead singer, Axl

Rose screams out the lyrics to "Welcome To The Jungle." Jaime induces a cringe, placing his hand against his forehead.

"What is that?"

"Some new band. They're not *that* bad."

"Metal?" Jaime replies in an exasperated tone.

Bobby corrects him. "Hard rock."

Jaime tells Bobby in a deep tone, "Change it, please."

Bobby grins at his passenger. "Not a fan of that kind of music?"

"What music?"

"So, if we ever get a hard rock...or metal band, you won't want to produce their album?"

Jaime turns to him. "That's right. I'll let you handle it."

Bobby laughs. "Good thing I do the same you do. Huh?"

"Yep." Jaime says back tight-lipped.

Bobby turns the conversation around while shutting off the radio.

"Why England?"

Jaime says back. "I think you know."

"Come on man. I've known you far too long for guessing games. This is about Evelyn Winthrop and don't you deny it. Come clean with me. *Something* happened. I just *know* it, but you won't say anything." Bobby answers. He looks over at Jaime who is glaring at him with intensity.

Jaime says back huffily. "You think you know everything. You don't know me."

"No. I don't. I guess that's what happens when you've only hung around somebody for twenty-three years. Since then, you've acted the same way."

Jaime gets defensive. "What way is that?"

"You know."

"No. I don't know. Why don't you remind me?"

"Distant! You're always *distant*!"

Jaime runs his hand through his hair. He closes his eyes. In disgust he says, "Shit, man. I'm tired of people getting in my business no matter what their intentions are. I just don't need it. Look, I'll tell you when I feel like it. When I'm not so *distant*." He says with edginess and sarcasm.

Bobby nods. He turns on the radio once again. This time, not to upset his passenger he switches the station right away from the usual fare of metal and hard rock. Turning the knob, he leaves it on a pop station playing Bobby McFerrin's jovial and hopeful if not annoying, "Don't Worry, Be Happy." Jaime remains silent. Bobby says nothing. He simply pays attention to the New York State Thruway. The Camaro passes by Newburgh.

Onward they go past Rockland County to Yonkers. It's only then Jaime makes any move to look Bobby's way. Bobby simply listens to the music to keep him company. If his friend was going to have a pissy attitude then why should he bother trying to talk to him? "Missing You," by John Waite starts up. The song of denial makes Bobby smirk slightly. He wasn't going to change the station either. If anything, it was amusing for him to listen to the lyrics of songs that were on par with what was going on at that moment in time. Jaime still sits silently. Looking down, he hears the lyrics that seem to speak right to his inner soul. He closes his eyes. It was a bad reminder. Still he wasn't going to tell Bobby to change it. That would give the driver too much satisfaction. Anguished, Jaime shakes his head.

Disgusted at himself, he says, "Ah, fuck. I slept with her. Is that what you wanted to hear?"

Bobby turns his head in time to see his flustered friend staring back at him. He looks back at the highway ahead of him. "Of course. Jeez, Jaime. You're forty-five, not twenty-five. We've been through this before. What was it, five years ago you said you were serious about that one? It's always the same with you. You put up these walls. You're more guarded than the Berlin Wall, my friend. You won't let anybody inside, but your heart wanders off and gets trampled on. You went in too deep."

Jaime's eyes dart over to Bobby with his curt response.

Bobby realizes and glances back quickly, without taking his sight away from driving.

"With your feelings."

Jaime closes his eyes.

"I wouldn't be surprised if you have a residency at one of the five motels in town."

"You don't know shit." Jaime answers, turning towards the window.

Bobby looks in the rearview mirror as he changes lanes. "Just what exactly did happen after Danny and I left the studio?"

Jaime turns to him without saying a word.

Bobby reacts to the revelation in his mind. "You're not telling me *there*." He looks at his friend. "Upstairs?" Glancing at Jaime again, he can see the guilt starting to show through. A curled palm hides the right eye in shame. The left eye keeps a steady gaze on the driver. Bobby shakes his head. "Jeez, Jaime. That explains the temper tantrum halfway into sessions with her."

Jaime finally feels more comfortable in explaining.

"I knew her when she first arrived at the studio. I remembered seeing her ten years before then, at an art gallery in the city. I didn't know her name or know she was a singer. So, when I saw her last year, it all came rushing to me. There was a certain something that I repeatedly tried to deny. When she was recording or just walking by, I felt a huge pressure to do something about it. I don't know. Pursue it? It was just there unlike any other time. A surge of energy. I guess it eventually wound up more serious by the second week. Even for her. It wound up being a full blown affair. Look, I made the mistake of calling it a mistake. She asked me after the first time it happened and I was very nonchalant about it. What was I supposed to say? 'I had a fantastic time?' It was something where I had to digest the notion that a serious relationship could happen from it. It wasn't something romantic ideally. There wasn't any candy or flowers. It wasn't one sided either. It's just that I didn't have the guts to tell her how I felt."

"Ah, fear of commitment." Bobby answers back wistfully. "That'll get a guy every time. Remember, I used to be wild and free like you. I had a life of uncertainty before I met Andrea. She's a hell of a woman and I'm glad she's in my life. I've had to make compromises but I'm still the same old Robert Alan Whitfield as the day I was born. Even though I got married, I didn't really change. If anything, I'm actually better now. I'm content. I love my wife still. That spitfire redhead." He grins. "Becky, who I adore with every fiber of my being. My friends who I still drive crazy."

Jaime smiles back. "That's true."

"Do you remember we made a pact when we became producers in our own right? We agreed that we would never compromise the music for our egos. We would never have our sound on every album we made but that we would make the artists sound better. That right there is how I think of relationships. So, if anything should really happen between you and Evelyn, nothing will change. If it does, then something is wrong."

Moments later, Bobby announces. "Shit."

Jaime looks up.

Bobby then says, "Traffic. Just like I thought." He switches lanes. "We'll go through 233rd St. and wind up catching exit 10 on the Bronx River Parkway."

Slowly they make their way into the exit lane.

Forty-five minutes later, they arrive at Interstate 678.

"Toll bridge." Bobby announces as he holds out his hand. Jaime looks down with confusion.

Bobby says, "Come on. Do you have the money on you? I'm not paying. The least thing you can do is pay for the toll."

Jaime reaches inside his pocket begrudgingly pulling out change.

"This ain't no free ride. I'm not your cab service." Bobby demands.

Jaime dumps the coins into the palm of his friend's hand.

"Here."

Again, they pick up speed. This time they cruise down the Van Wyck Expressway.

Bobby checks his watch as he sees the large sign for John F. Kennedy International Airport.

"You've got about an hour left. Which service?"

"TWA." Jaime answers back.

They drive around until they find the proper doorway. Bobby drops him off.

"Two weeks?"

"Yes."

"All right then."

Just before leaving the car, Jaime says, "Thanks."

He reaches in the trunk for his luggage, and then pulls out the carry-on bag from the backseat. Returning back to the passenger's door, he smiles at Bobby while placing his sunglasses on. "I'm really sorry for being a pain in the ass."

Bobby shrugs it off and smiles. "Nah. What are friends for?"

Jaime begins to pick up his luggage.

Bobby calls out. "Jaime!"

Jaime turns around. "Yeah?"

Bobby hands his friend a cassette of Evelyn Winthrop's *Ravaged Beauty*. "Here. Try taking a listen to what your girlfriend recorded earlier in her career."

Jaime bows his head down shyly. He takes the cassette from Bobby. They shake hands.

Bobby tells him, "Happy trails my friend and good luck!"

He then revs up the Camaro and drives away.

The producer looks around. Just outside the door, he lights a Marlboro while thinking.

Was it all really worth it?

There was nothing to lose.

He steps into the airport. A utopia or city with people as traffic. It's similar to a mall. Only, folks wheel around luggage like a mobile home. In reality, most would be living off of whatever they brought from their trip to and from wherever they were. The long line winds itself around by the front desk where each ticket is taken and luggage would be deposited onto a conveyor belt headed to the proper flight.

Jaime finds himself doing the same as all the rest. He's checked for his passport, and then makes his way to get scanned through the metal detectors. His carry-on bag goes through the scanner and the change in his pocket gets dumped into a bowl as he gets checked through. Various flights are called from the speakers above in specified seating sections. There is the low roar of a plane taking off over the airport. Ahead are numbers and letters marked off in the waiting area. Jaime walks a little past D4.

A little girl with dark blonde hair roams around. Then she crosses his path. Her blue eyes meet her own reflection shown on the record producer's darkened lenses. She smiles. A slow smile creeps across his face as he looks down.

An upset woman's voice booms from across the way.

"Samantha Lee Jervin! Come here right now!"

The little girl turns quickly, but as she backs away, she still looks at him. She sprints away to her mother.

Kids were weighing heavily on Jaime Weston's mind. More than he could have imagined. He admitted to himself now more than ever, children would be a must one way or another if he were to wind up getting Evelyn back.

He looks up to see D5. There aren't too many seats left in the waiting area. Who would be the least annoying to sit next to? He didn't like to converse much with strangers. His eyes scan the area from where he stands. Then he spots an empty seat.

An old lady sits crocheting a knitted cap. She looks to be the sweet grandmotherly type with a head full of white and gray hair pulled into a bun. She seems pleasant enough for Jaime to sit next to. His foot lightly knocks at something on the floor. He reaches to feel for it. Picking it up, he sees that it is a black patent leather pocketbook.

"Excuse me, Ma'am? Is this yours?" The producer asks.

The old woman stops her knitting and looks over.

"Why thank you, young man. I'm sorry about that. I keep dropping it from my lap." She says in a rather fragile tone. "I'm trying to knit this for my granddaughter and this thing wants to scurry away." The old woman laughs as she jams the purse between herself and the seat. "Stay there!" She scolds the item.

Jaime removes his sunglasses and looks around. The old woman packs in her sewing material.

"Goin' to England?" She asks.

He answers back. "Yep."

For a moment he pauses before asking, "Was anybody sitting here?"

"Oh. No. Just me here. I'm doing this trip alone. My husband's too sick this time around. Rotten cold. Rotten shame. We don't get to see our granddaughter, Rachel very often. My son is in the Air Force. He was stationed to London eight years ago. Got himself a lovely girl to marry and they have a beautiful daughter."

Jaime leans over slightly as she talks some more.

"Oh yes. I have five other grandchildren. They're spread all over the place. Montana, Tennessee, Michigan. Four grandsons and two granddaughters. I was disappointed to see my youngest want to live so far away. But, it was his choice. Cambridge is lovely but so far. Where are you headed to?"

"Me? Uh, Oxford."

"Now that's a lovely place too. Your wife didn't come with you?"

Jaime chuckles back slightly. "I'm not married."

"What a shame. A good looking lad like you unattached?"

"Yes, Ma'am."

"No children even?"

"No. None that I know of."

"Bigger shame."

"Why is that?" He says with a slight smile.

"With your looks, you would have *gorgeous* children."

Jaime bows his head down with a big boyish grin then chuckles deeply. "I get that a lot. I don't know where it comes from. Really, I should blame my mom for that. The looks department."

"No. No. *Never* blame anybody. If I were forty or fifty years younger I'd ask you if you would like to go out for coffee sometime. You're not from England, are you?"

He smiles. "I'm actually from Canada."

"Oh! She says joyfully. "How long have you been in the States?"

"Twenty-two years. My mom and aunt live up near Buffalo. More like Rochester."

Jaime then remembers a special item he had tucked away.

The old woman says, "Any siblings?"

"No. It's just me. My mom had enough to deal with just one."

He pulls out his wallet from his back pocket.

Quickly the producer flips through the billfold, releasing a folded paper that is printed. He unfolds the picture from *Billboard's* April issue. Showing it to her, he says with a sense of pride, "This is why I'm going to London in the first place."

It was the picture of himself, Bobby, Dan, and Evelyn. The old woman's face lights up as she smiles.

"She's a pretty young thing!"

"Well, I don't know if either of us are *young*."

"When you get to my age, everybody seems a whole lot younger." She giggles back. "But she's precious. British?"

"Mm hmm."

"I couldn't think of a better reason why you should go. That's just incredibly sweet."

With uncertainty, Jaime says back, "Well, I just hope she'll agree to come back here with me. Then we can see how things would go from there." He smiles.

"Oh, but there's always hope. For any man to travel across the ocean to send for his sweetheart shows a lot of dedication. Before we got married, my husband couldn't afford a ring right away. He was working at a metal factory. I came by to visit him one day and just outside the building, he presented me with a sheet of metal. 'Marry me' was etched onto it. Of course, I said, 'Yes.' The sheet means more to me than any piece of jewelry I own."

The producer listens intently to her.

A voice comes over the loud speaker.

"Now boarding for TWA. Flight 1080. Rows 1 through 10. 1 through 10, now boarding."

Both Jaime and the old lady are alerted to the speaker. He picks up his carry-on bag.

She says, "By the way, my name is Rosie. It was so nice talking with you."

"Mine's Jaime. It was my pleasure."

He reaches to shake her fragile bony hand with a smile. Then he gets up to walk a few steps away to join the line.

Rosie calls out. "Oh Jaime!"

He turns around.

She says with a smile and the wave of her hand. "Good luck on finding her!"

With a tight-lipped smile, he waves back to her as he disappears into the terminal doorway.

Aboard the plane, Jaime pulls out the tape Bobby had let him borrow, *Ravaged Beauty*. He thinks of what Bobby told him.

"You should at least listen to your girlfriend's music."

Girlfriend?

The producer smiles at the thought. He picks out the Walkman from his bag and places the headphones around his head. Looking at the cover, he finds it somewhat odd. Most artists had a reason to choose the artwork for their albums. This was no different. A broken stemmed rose. Soon he would find out the meaning. The inside picture of the flap was a bit intriguing to him. There she was, Evelyn in captivating glory with a tight-fitting black leather jacket on, zipped halfway. A titillating image at that.

Once the music starts, Jaime gets a quick crash course on Evelyn's thoughts and feelings on love gone bad, lascivious poetry, and body parts of desire. She delivered in a bawdy, raunchy, cigarette soaked voice with a beat every punk drummer wished for. The blending of the rhythm section over her voice matched. Little sharp stabs of guitar accented to give a dirtier feeling. He smiles deeply to himself.

Evelyn. Sweet Evy.

He likes what he hears.

The producer gets pulled back into thinking of his month long affair with the singer. Her voice provides a time warp from the past year. He closes his eyes.

Vicki Soren put her foot against the bottom step, extremely close to him. He remembered wanting to look past the rims of his sunglasses.

Vicki remarked. "He thinks it's your new guest, Evelyn."

"You know Vicki, Danny's suspicious about everybody." Jaime eyed her. "Apparently, you are too."

"We just want to look out for your happiness. Me and Andi wouldn't mind a third party on our shopping excursions."

With a slight smile, he told her, "There is *nobody*."

Vicki leaned in closer to him. She folded her arms in an accusing manner. "You're hidin'."

He thinks of what had happened after his first night with Evelyn, and how they weren't on speaking terms for a few days. She had enough and wanted to put an end to the silent treatment. Evelyn took a step back. He was still flustered at himself and showed it in mannerism.

"Evelyn." He finally said.

With that, he snuffed out the Marlboro in the ashtray. Her eyes adjusted. He had just said her name. There was either hope or failure in trying to reach out to the producer. Walking over to her very closely he said in a deeper than average tone, "Don't leave on the count of me. Do it only if you don't believe in this project anymore. What went on with us should not affect our progress with recording. I'm as much to blame for letting things get to the point that they are now. We can't turn back time, since the past is the past. Do you understand?" He asked with his hands out.

They couldn't turn back time, and nothing was going to change their feelings for one another. It was that hot night in late July, he was left with previous thoughts of Evelyn and her words that were oh so captivating.

"Which do you rather see burn?"

That evening heat which would drive any human being crazy. It was a desire for something far more potent than a simple smoke. A feeling no man could deny. In the middle of those thoughts came a knock at the door.

There she was.

Leaning a hand against the doorframe, in a sexy strapped black nightgown. She looked him over. He still held the lit cigarette.

Evelyn said, "You're still awake."

He replied in a deep tone. "Couldn't sleep."

Cautiously she told him, "I was thinking about the *other* night."

He turned away for a brief moment, closing his eyes. With his back turned he told her. "It shouldn't have happened."

She went over to face him. "So, what are you going to do now? I mean, now that you are awake."

He said, "I don't know. Do you have any ideas?"

She replied with, "I might." Her finger lightly glided down the open portion of his fully unbuttoned shirt. "But only if you're up to it."

Evelyn had teased with words, seduced with her touch, and flourished him with kisses. It was time to act on it. He responded in a soft gravelly tone. "Oh, what you're thinking of is a reprise."

That was the beginning of their second night together.

He switches thoughts to the year before *Ravaged Beauty* was made. 1977. It was the first time he saw Evelyn Winthrop. An auburn haired lady was talking to him when he spotted the blonde clutching a glass of wine and looking down. She didn't look too happy. Alone was more like it. Her eyes were a soft blue but filled with the confusion of wondering what she was doing there. He was able to see past some of the crowd. Then she disappeared. He asked a woman by the door.

"Excuse me? Did you happen to have a blonde on your list?"

The woman said back. "There are a lot of blondes."

"She had noticeable blonde hair; maybe she was 5'4" or 5'5", heavily made eyes. Black leather jacket."

"Oh, I think I know which one." She looked down at her list. "Eve Marie? I can't be sure. Is that her?"

The woman had looked up just as Evelyn was walking out the door. Jaime looked up and tried to catch up with her outside. A cab sped away into the night.

She was gone.

He sits listening more to the music in a contemplative manner. Would Evelyn even want him back? Would she ever truly learn to love him or had she thought differently of their affair? He wondered what it meant to her. Obviously, she hadn't returned to New York as she said she would. He just had to know what happened to her. Were the circumstances different now after a year? Had she found someone else? Either way, he had no idea what truly awaited him.

The tape stops.

Only, he has the urge to listen again to fully take in Evelyn's style. He notices the second time around that the music never seemed to drown out her deep vocals. The work he had done for *Hero's Requiem* was in the same range as her older material without him even knowing it. Those bawdy lyrics brought out a smile. She wasn't quite bawdy with him. Bold was more like it. The latest album seemed less harsh than her escapade into cheap tawdry affairs and love gone awry. All that he learned about her once she was gone didn't turn him off in the least bit. Evelyn was an intriguing woman to him. She was passionate about what she wanted with her recordings. She didn't hold in her feelings or leave it to him or the other guys in the studio to do whatever they wanted to. Evelyn gave them enough room but specified what she was looking for that couldn't be fulfilled with other producers. Her sense of adventure to him included taking a cigarette out of his mouth, kissing him, and then putting it back. A true tease of his affection for her.

Ah, Evy.

Jaime was one not to look out the window of any plane. It was simply too high for him. With the lineage of past ancestors who took to building skyscrapers in New York City, he knew he could never think of himself the same way. Back then they were crazy or brave. It was in their blood but not his. He decides to keep his focus on all that surrounds him aboard the plane. He relaxes comfortably, reclining back a little while taking in the sounds of Evelyn Winthrop.

Once the plane lands at Heathrow, all the passengers file out into the terminal. Jaime grabs his carry-on bag heading out with the flow of traffic. It seems all so foreign to him. The people, the voices, the whole atmosphere. He looks around. Luckily, the signs aren't in another language. Putting on his sunglasses, he goes out to greet England's daylight. He checks on a small slip of paper in his jacket pocket. This was the only way he knew how to remember what hotel he was staying at. Cabs pull up in front of the airport just outside the glass doors. Just like everybody else, he's whisked away to his destination…closer to finding Evelyn.

Chapter 10

Ed pulls into the parking lot of Dowd's Pub. The green neon sign descends upon the beige sedan. Ed hurriedly takes out his cigarette, gives one last puff before tossing it down to the freshly wet pavement and snuffs it with half of his foot. He gathers his jacket while walking to the door.

Once he's inside, the pub reeks of alcohol, and cigarettes. It displays the effervescent glow of the neon lit beer signs among a smoky haze. The Clash's "London's Calling" is heard throughout the entire place.

Ed takes a seat at the bar and orders from the bartender. In his deep and rusted vocals, he says, "Yeah. Gimmie a Scotch on the rocks."

Ed takes a glance around the room, seeing if there is an empty table. His eyes fall upon the dark haired man dressed similarly as him, in a suit jacket and buttoned up shirt. Jaime remains at one of the tables alone, clutching a glass of beer while wearing his sunglasses. Ed takes his Scotch and saunters over to where Jaime sits.

Right from the start, Ed feels comfortable enough to approach the stranger. He looks from across the table and says, "Mind if I join you?"

Jaime, who is lost in thought due to any number of things, sits in silence. He then peers up from the rims, answering Ed.

"Sure."

Jaime removes his sunglasses and places them on the table. Ed sits across from him. Jaime glances up for a moment before looking back down. He rubs his heavy lids and says to Ed, "Sorry if I'm not exactly the best of company."

Ed pipes up. "Problems?"

Jaime responds with, "Yeah. Yeah, you can say that."

"Women?" Ed implies as he pulls out a Camel from his tweed jacket pocket.

"It's really a variety of things. I came here to England to find answers."

"Ah, find any clues yet?"

"No."

Both men stay silent for a moment. Ed reaches for the small silver lighter engraved with *E.B.,* putting the tip of his cigarette to the flame. Jaime takes particular notice of the item, which ignites his memory. He had seen plenty of lighters in his lifetime even though he was mostly used to matchbooks. Still, he couldn't get Evelyn's lighter off of his mind. Ed's was nearly identical. It was very much like the one that she had propositioned him with the first time they had made love.

Ed sees Jaime looking down at the lighter and says, "Something wrong?"

Jaime slightly chuckles, before he too grabs out a cigarette and lights it with a match. He steadies his fingers with a matchbook from one of the cafes in New York. Ed sees that the logo is from the States.

Jaime takes a puff of his Marlboro and asks Ed, "So, what about you? What brings you here?"

Ed smiles and replies in a gruff tone of confidence. "Me? Aw, I just come here usually." Ed pauses before inhaling a breath from his Camel. "Women."

Jaime chuckles back at his remark.

Ed launches into his story.

"The woman that I love has been driving me nuts. I don't know what it is about the female species. I mean she's captivating and beautiful, but also really hard to figure out. I don't know what it is, but I feel like I'm losing her to a greater force. I love her like crazy. I met her about eight years ago and she's the greatest thing that has happened to me." Ed takes a gulp of Scotch and watches the ice cubes sink to the bottom, and then resurface to the top again. The curious Ed Brockton glances up at Jaime and asks, "How about you? Got anybody?"

Jaime looks back at the stranger across from him then replies. "No. Can't say that I do."

"Well then, what is love to you?"

The record producer looks down at the table and holds his glass of beer while replying, "Fleeting." He lets out a slight nervous laugh.

"Yeah. That can happen." Ed says before he takes another drag from his Camel.

There is a moment of silence.

Something strikes Ed rather odd. He says, "Have I ever seen you before? You look awfully familiar to me."

Jaime sits back in the chair, a bit surprised. In a deep tone, he answers back. "I don't think so."

Ed's cigarette gets smaller and his glass of Scotch begins to empty. He stops taking a swig of his drink and puts the glass down as he suddenly remembers where he had seen the dark haired stranger. "Now I know where I've seen you." Jaime takes a sip of beer while Ed continues. "Well, not necessarily you, but someone who looks like you."

Jaime responds with, "Oh, really?" He chuckles and takes another sip of beer.

Ed replies. "Yeah. My daughter looks just like you."

Jaime nearly chokes back his beer and his normal heavy lidded glance turns into wide-eyed bewilderment. He gives out a few coughs and manages to sputter out the word, "What?"

Ed who practically remains oblivious to the stranger's reaction explains with little joy. "It's the damnedest thing." Right when he looks back up, he sees that Jaime is shocked at his statement. In an assuring manner, Ed asks, "Are you okay?"

Jaime snuffs out what little is left of his Marlboro. He answers quickly to save face, "Yeah. It went down the wrong way. What were you saying?"

"My daughter doesn't look anything like me or her mother. She's a few months old but she has dark hair and dark eyes. Sort of like yours. She's not exactly the most bright-eyed kid either. My girlfriend says that the girl is actually mine. She said to me she got pregnant before her trip and we now have a daughter." Ed swigs down the last of his Scotch as he continues. "The only one in my family with considerable dark hair was my aunt, but not *that* dark." Ed stares off in a distance, away from Jaime and everything else. He ends his line by saying, "I know better."

His intense far off glare makes the music producer a bit uncomfortable. Ed was a bit burly and rough looking and he swigged down his Scotch like he really wasn't in the mood for anything nearly amusing. Jaime thinks better of it and stays quiet.

The long, awkward moment of silence is broken swiftly when four men at another table and one sitting on the stool at the bar, break into a cheerful yet drunken chorus to Elvis Costello's "Alison." Jaime turns his head to see where the raucous revelers are.

Ed comments. "The steel factory workers just punched out. Overtime."

"Oh."

Ed puts out his cigarette in the ashtray.

"Do you have the time?" Jaime asks.

Ed returns his attention back to the stranger. "Yeah. Yeah." He replies gruffly. Ed turns up a cuff and slides it to reveal a silver watch. "It's about half past nine."

Jaime gets up, puts his sunglasses in his pocket, and grabs out a wad of cash while trying to figure something out. Turning to Ed, he asks, "You wouldn't happen to know the exchange rate...would you?"

Ed says back as Jaime fiddles with change, "Nah. Don't worry. I'll take care of it."

The record producer stops to look up and says, "You really don't have to," in his deep resonating tone.

Ed shrugs it off. "Ah, one beer isn't gonna bleed me dry. Just think of it as a welcome...on me." Ed begins to turn. He stops to say, "After talkin' to you all this time, I never did get your name."

Jaime puts the money back in his pocket, and then holds out a hand for a firm handshake. "Jaime." He says back with a slight smile.

"Edward, although folks just call me, Ed."

Jaime says, "Nice to meet you, Ed."

"Same here, Jaime. Maybe I'll see you around town sometime."

"Maybe. Thanks."

Jaime walks away.

Ed walks back to the crowded bar area and calls out to the bartender. "Hit me with another Scotch."

Before the producer leaves the pub, he shakes his head in disbelief thinking of how Ed said that his daughter looked like him. He thought it was odd in New York, but now the comparisons were coming in England.

***

A week has passed. Evelyn looks down on the floor. There standing up next to the railing is a suitcase. Ed walks by her.

She asks. "Ed, darling, what is this for?"

Without Ed looking back at her, he replies. "I'm going out."

"Out where?"

He turns around slowly to her.

"I need time, plus I want to get some pictures done in Exeter."

"Exeter? Why there?"

A little more agitated he answers yet again. "Because I want to catch the summer spirit before it changes into fall. Any more you feel a need to ask?"

"No. It's just that I was hoping to go out shopping for a little bit during the week and…"

Ed cuts her off.

"You wanted *me* to watch after her while you went out with your girlfriends. So, you can buy your little frilly frocks, and flowery shoes. Ooh and ah over baby stuff. Go to the cafés and stuff your faces with croissants and lattés. My answer to you is, find somebody else who's willing. I've had enough for now. It's about time I get to do what I want, what I need to do. I'm a photographer, not a maid or a babysitter. You wanted this kid so badly, so you take care of her."

"Darling, she's yours too."

Ed grimaces at the thought. He almost wants to tell her she's wrong, but that would never work. She would become suspicious and ask why. Without any words, Ed holds back. Instead, he snarls. "Get one of your friends, Millie or Liz to do that. I'm not cut out for diaper duty." He stops zipping a bag. "It's always something I've done wrong with her. I try to feed her. She knocks it off the table. I try to bring her upstairs to sleep and she winds up fighting me until she gets tired. I try to talk to her. She screams in my ear. Face it, Evelyn, she doesn't like me, which is fine by me. I wouldn't want somebody handling me either and trying to be nice."

"Ed, she's just a baby. Babies do that all the time. She has a will all her own."

"I'm not cut out for any of it. You know that and she knows that. You manipulated this pregnancy just so you could get your own way. Now you have it. Be satisfied. I need to do my job."

Ed begins to walk up the stairs.

Evelyn calls out. "How long will you be gone for?"

"Five days."

She waits for him when he walks back down.

He walks down the steps with a small sack of extra film. Ed tosses it in the suitcase and zips it up. Picking up his luggage, he walks to the front door.

"When are you leaving?" She asks.

"Now."

Ed lights up a Camel, jamming it in his mouth. He turns to her, being both flustered and angered at the same time. He tells her before leaving the house, "I don't care what you do. You could turn the house into a childcare center. You can go and do that weird naked sunbathing thing even. Or run up and down the street in your pajamas. I just don't give a damn right now. I'm leaving."

He plops the suitcase in the trunk of his car, gets inside and starts the ignition.

Evelyn shouts out, "We have neighbors!"

Ed leaves the driveway, leaving Evelyn in the doorway.

She mutters underneath her breath. "Sunbathing? What would I need with sunbathing? You need a few ice cubes down your shorts, darling."

Evelyn walks back in the house disgusted at her boyfriend's attitude.

Some father!

In his hotel room, Jaime sits in a comfy chair, thinking. It had already been one week since his arrival to England. He hadn't even made an effort to look for Evelyn. Instead, he took in the sights. It was a time he needed to himself.

Children were heavily on his mind.

It was these thoughts that kept him wondering what was going on. His mission was to find Evelyn, but then he was thinking of what he had told Henry the day before he left. If he were to get Evelyn back, then adoption of children was probably part of the deal. Still it baffled him that other people had mistaken little girls as his. He had known Doug around the art circles, so when he ran into him at Cosgrove, it came as quite a shock the guy would assume Jaime had a niece since he knew the producer had no children.

Then there was Dale, the guy that worked at Bleecker St. Records.

The memory sticks out in his mind.

Dale had said, "Man, people tell me my daughters look like me, but that kid looked an awful lot like you. My wife's a blonde but that didn't stop all three of our daughters from looking like me. That baby was a dead ringer for you. Dark hair...and same eyes."

Billy Montrose had said that Carol Mulligan was seen around the city with a baby who looked a lot like him.

He remembered being pushed too far by Carol while visiting her. He stood right in her way of getting something out of the refrigerator. It was that determination he had in getting to the truth until finally fed up.

She answered back, "Okay. *Maybe* I know where this is coming from. She changed her tone to calm. "I'm sure Henry told you that people were asking about a kid. There's a little girl who I sometimes baby-sit for.

It's a Portuguese family that moved a block away. I don't know if she *exactly* looks like you. That's tough to say. I know that you're half Indian. I guess the dark hair could be like yours. It's so hard to tell with little kids especially when they're so young. She's only four months old. A few others baby-sit her too. Maybe that's what you heard about. Like I said, Jaime, it's hard to tell. She could pass for Italian, Spanish, French, yes, American Indian like you, West Indies, anything that produces brown hair."

"Are you telling me the truth?"

"Yes."

He answered her in frustration.

"Several people have told me already."

"Isn't it a little naive of you to take their word for it? I'm guessing you haven't seen anyone like this yourself."

"No. But others have asked me if I had a daughter or niece."

"You seem awfully concerned about this yourself."

Carol walked away from him to get dinner prepared. "I told you everything I know."

He considers that Carol could have been right. Portuguese. Carol wasn't the motherly type so he had good reason to believe her. Why would she lie? He didn't visit her alone before. It was only the second time he had been to her loft. It was a little nervy of him to confront her when he didn't exactly know what to believe and then unload on her. Her answer should have satisfied him. It did until nearly a week earlier, a day after he had arrived in England that he came across the blond haired gentleman named Ed who bluntly asked.

"Have I ever seen you before? I mean you look awfully familiar to me." Ed's suspicious glance made the light bulb in his mind turn on. "Now I know where I've seen you." He stated, "Well, not necessarily you, but someone who looks like you."

Jaime responded with, "Oh, really?" He chuckled.

Ed replied back, "Yeah. My daughter looks just like you."

Jaime gets up from the chair, and walks over to the adjacent side of the room.

Thousands of miles away from New York and it had been the same thing. Different place, same comments. Maybe it was merely a coincidence this time but it ate away at the producer more. The voices then echo through his mind. He closes his eyes and leans his back against the wall.

Doug: "We just wanted to say you have a beautiful niece!"

Dale: "That baby was a dead ringer for you."

Billy: "Molly said she was visiting a friend in SoHo and saw a kid that looked a lot like you about a month ago."

Carol: "I don't know if she *exactly* looks like you. It's so hard to tell with little kids especially when they're so young."

Ed: "My daughter looks just like you."

The voice echoes.

Just like you.

Just like you.

Just like you.

Jaime contemplates the words. He goes to the window, looking out past the street a level below.

Dale's words grab him.

"Dark hair...and same eyes."

The timing and the age of the child Carol said lined up with the last female companion he had been intimate with. There was only one since that time. Evelyn was it. But he knew that couldn't be possible.

She couldn't have children.

He then thinks of Evelyn. She exuded passion that he felt was definitely real and even blurted out the words, '*I love you*,' as she sunk into sleep after being satisfied by her new lover for the first time. She opened up to him about the tumultuous part in her life as he had too. It's not what he would normally talk about. If anything, he dreaded drudging up the past. So many mistakes. Evelyn had managed to put the producer at ease. He teased her. Serenaded her. Took her to the mountainous peaks of passion, but let her down hard. No wonder she might not want to come back to him. What would she want with a scuzzy street kid from North York?

Then it strikes him in a different way. One week left. He looks at the phone sitting on the small table. Quickly, he steps away from the window.

Jaime goes to the couch at the other end of the room where he picks up the phone.

Immediately, his fingers dial. Karen picks up at the other end. Then he hears a slight scuffle.

Henry's voice is heard. "I'll talk to him!" He says, "Hey, Jaime. How's life treating you in jolly old England?"

"Fine. I need to know if anybody has heard from Evelyn at the studio by any chance."

"Isn't that what you're there for? You're the one who's probably closest to where she is since her address is in England."

"I know but..."

"Are you getting cold feet now?"

"No. I was just wondering."

"And?"

"There's something going on here. Something that has been bothering me but every time I try to put it out of my mind, it comes creeping back into my subconscious."

"What does it have to deal with? Her?"

"No. Not exactly her. Children. Ever since I went to Manhattan back in May, it's always been happening."

"You mean the guy that worked at the record store you told me about?"

"Not just him. There have been others. I didn't tell you before I left that somebody told me they saw Carol Mulligan with a kid. She said people were probably asking me."

Oh shit! Carol nearly spilled the beans. Henry thinks.

Jaime says, "I confronted her and she assured me it was a kid she was babysitting. Portuguese she said."

"So? What's the problem?"

"Well, I was at this bar a little a ways from here and I met this guy. Just a regular. He didn't have an English accent though. So, maybe he's a transplant or something? He said the most peculiar thing to me. I took off my sunglasses and he looked at me as if he had seen me before. He says to me, 'Have I ever seen you before? You look awfully familiar to me.' And then I thought, maybe he saw me at the studio, possibly a party or at a gallery. Instead, he said that, maybe it wasn't *me* after all but someone who looked *like* me. He comes out and says 'I know now. My daughter looks just like you.' I couldn't believe it. I thought this all stopped in New York with this supposed Portuguese kid. It's the same damn thing." Jaime chuckles back in astonishment. He pushes back his hair. "Then I started thinking about Evelyn and I really messed that up. I couldn't blame her if she didn't want anything to do with me. After the way I treated her... I wouldn't doubt for a second that she decided not to come back to New York. It almost seems like a waste being here. I just don't know..."

Henry asks out of confusion. "What have you been doing there for the past week?"

"Thinking."

"You've come this far, opened your heart up to me. Bobby told me you just about begged him to bring you to the airport during the rush hour, and now you want to call this off? Jaime, you're right there. Finish the mission. How do you know she won't take you back? Isn't it possible she might be waiting for you?"

Jaime reacts confused to what he hears Henry say.

"You're almost making it sound as if you know this first-hand. If I didn't know any better."

"It's *obvious*. You make it that obvious around others. You've come this far, why not just go and see her? You owe it to yourself to find out the truth...the whole truth. Go!"

Sometime in the late afternoon, Mildred Grumbach and Elizabeth Rinalti sit on the couch while sipping tea. Both women chat about anything and everything while Evelyn is in the kitchen.

Mildred calls out. "Evelyn, dear? Where's Ed?"

Elizabeth snickers back quietly with her slight Scottish accent. "Probably taking pictures of weeds."

Evelyn shouts back from behind the kitchen door. "On assignment for a few days!"

Elizabeth asks Mildred, "Have you seen the way Ed handles the baby? He's so nervous around her."

Mildred says back, "That's what a pint of Scotch will do to you."

Elizabeth turns to her with perplexity on her face.

"He drinks like a fish?"

"Ever since Evelyn came back home with Mandy."

"Do you think he knows about not being her father?"

"Well, she doesn't look anything like *him*...thankfully." Mildred says before taking another sip of tea.

Elizabeth says in mock disgust, "I'd shudder to think!"

Mildred looks at Elizabeth in a state of mock shock with her jaw dropped, "Do you?"

Both women turn to each other and laugh.

Meanwhile, Evelyn is in the kitchen, trying to feed her five month old daughter baby food. She puts the spoon up to her, which Amanda has to examine before taking in a mouthful of mushed carrots. The little girl looks up, signifying that she'll go for another bite. Evelyn smiles at Amanda.

"My beautiful girl."

Back in the living room, Mildred picks up a magazine and flips through it. She and Elizabeth look through the pages to find the fashion section. Mildred examines one page with disdain.

"Oh, that's bloody awful."

Elizabeth points to one with a cup of tea in her hand.

The doorbell rings. The women look up. Who could that be? Ed was away for the time being. He certainly wouldn't need to ring the doorbell.

Evelyn calls from inside the kitchen. "Liz or Millie, can either of you get that?"

Mildred gets up and tells Elizabeth, "Finish your tea. I'll get that."

Elizabeth looks up and puts her cup down on the coffee table in front of her.

Mildred opens the door to find a tall man nicely dressed in a red and black shirt over black jeans wearing round sunglasses. Her eyes go wide at the sight of him.

He asks, "Is Evelyn Winthrop here?"

Mildred gets lost, between Evelyn having a gentleman caller and her own shock at how attractive the stranger looks. She returns to her senses and in a delayed reaction tells him, "Yes. Yes. She's here. Please, come inside."

Jaime says back, "Thanks."

He steps inside.

Mildred puts her hand over her heart and mouths the word, *"Gorgeous!"* She then leads him into the living room. Jaime looks around to see what kind of house Evelyn lives in. He spots one of the many large prints on the wall by Edward Brockton, not knowing it.

"Please, sit down and make yourself comfortable." Mildred says while pointing to the chair across from the couch where Elizabeth stands. The Scottish blonde introduces herself, "Hi. My name's Liz."

Warmly, Jaime smiles. "Nice to meet you, Liz."

Mildred who still stands adds in, "And I'm Mildred, but everyone calls me Millie."

Jaime takes her hand for a firm handshake, then Liz's.

"I'm Jaime Weston."

Mildred pipes up. "Ah, lovely name!"

They all sit down. Jaime looks down at the tan and various red hued Oriental rug on the floor. He takes another look around and tells the ladies, "Nice place."

Mildred inquires with interest. "So, Jaime, how do you know Evelyn?"

He responds with, "I'm a record producer from New York. Um, I'm really from Canada though. I produced her latest album."

Mildred leans to whisper to Elizabeth, "She and her North American gents."

Elizabeth asks, "How long have you known her?"

Thinking about it, Jaime knew it wasn't for very long and hesitantly reveals, "Since last summer."

Right away, the two women look at each other.

Mildred says back with ease, "How interesting."

Evelyn calls out from the kitchen. "Who was at the door?"

Liz says back, "It's for you!"

Evelyn says again, "Give me a few minutes."

The sound of a spoon dropping on the floor can be heard. All three people turn to look at the kitchen door. They hear Evelyn scold somebody from within.

Jaime turns his attention to the two women.

"Are you…her sisters?" He asks.

Mildred answers. "Us? No. No. We're all just friends."

Elizabeth suggests to her friend, "I think it's the blonde hair."

Mildred mumbles to Liz. "He can think whatever he wants. Stunning creature he is."

The producer gives a tight-lipped smile, oblivious to Mildred's remark. Finally, Jaime removes his sunglasses revealing his heavy-lidded eyes. The two women suck in a breath from their shock. Immediately their jaws drop.

Same eyes!

Mildred suddenly says, "Oh my God."

He looks directly at them in a concerned manner.

Mildred says quickly to Elizabeth, "Look at the time. I have to be at the shop. Can't let down customers. We have to go now." She gets up from the couch quickly and grabs Liz's right arm. "It was nice meeting you, Jaime." Mildred tells him as she grabs two handbags and heads for the door with Liz in tow. She turns to Liz and demands, "Say good-bye, Liz."

Liz says, "Bye!"

Both women hurriedly leave.

The heavy door shuts behind with a thud. Jaime looks at the door, and then raises his brows as he stands up for a moment and a possible move to the more comfortable couch.

Just then, the kitchen door swings open.

Evelyn appears with her sight solely on the front door for a moment. "Millie? Liz?" She then turns, not realizing who remains in her living room. Her eyes catch sight of the tall figure. She holds back a breath. Her jaw drops as she says, "Jaime."

He smiles at her as he says in his rich, deep quiet tone, "Hi, Evy." She gets lost in the moment.

Suddenly, the sound of a kitchen utensil hitting the floor again can be heard. This time it's followed by the sound of a small, deep, hollow item rolling, then a thud, and a crash that gives way to breaking.

Evelyn shakes herself out of her trance like state and says, "Wait a minute. I have to do something." A small whine is heard from behind the kitchen door. "The cat is making trouble again. Such a mischievous creature she is."

Jaime says back to her calmly but almost urgently, "We *really* need to talk."

Evelyn hears a little more commotion and dashes through the swinging door.

Feeling a little fed up with putting off his feelings for Evelyn, Jaime decides to follow her. He starts to get in the kitchen and say, "Evy..."

Suddenly he stops as the sound quickly grabs his attention. He looks over where the lower cupboards are. Jaime blinks and takes a big swallow as his mouth begins to slightly open. He draws in a breath before slowly approaching the sense of wonderment. Ignoring the sweeping sound coming from a short distance away, he stoops down and stares at a small pair of eyes watching him. There is no more than silence and a drawn breath. He stares intently as if at his own reflection from years gone by. The baby in the high chair has an uncanny resemblance to the producer himself. She has practically the same features as him, the same dark hair and eyes.

Amanda gurgles, holding her tiny hands out. She spreads her fingers in mid air. Jaime reaches over and picks up the hand with two fingers. He takes another large swallow, as he gets a little glassy eyed. She grips tightly and looks down.

Evelyn reappears at the top of the basement steps. Drawing in a breath, she quietly steps around Jaime and puts her hand over her mouth to stop herself from a creeping emotion fighting to get out. Surprised by what she sees, she's careful not to disturb the father and daughter union. She goes to the left side of Jaime as a smile and tears of joy fill her eyes. He looks at the baby with a creeping smile. Looking down with a shy look, he chuckles softly, nodding at the thought of her existence.

Jaime senses Evelyn's presence right next to him. As he watches Amanda he says, "So, this is what everybody was talking about. I was constantly asked if I had a daughter or niece because someone looked a lot like me...or so I was told." He blinks in a bit of wonderment as he asks Evelyn, "When was she born?"

Evelyn moves to the kitchen table and replies. "April sixth."

Jaime sucks in a breath before saying, "Well, I think it's obvious. I don't think you need tests to prove anything." He begins to laugh slightly, then grows quiet and in a contemplative position, turns to Evelyn for a moment and says in a deep, warm tone, "So, April..." Jaime gets to his feet from stooping on the floor. Running a hand through his hair, he says to Evelyn, "God. The first time."

Evelyn wipes her eyes. "I didn't know how to tell you. The third night... I should say *nearly*. When I was experiencing cramps and strange sensations, I didn't know what was happening to me. Before I was to leave for home, I felt it again. A friend of mine suggested I see a doctor. It was supposed to be about medication for anxiety or flight. He came back with the results. I told him, it must be a joke." She sits down, with thoughts rewound in her head. "I saw my results three times. "Each one explained to me in full detail. I heard every heartbreaking word." Her voice trembles. "I saw the empty sonograms." She recomposes herself. "I figured I had destroyed my body from all the drug abuse. I had no one else to blame but myself. When the doctor… When *this* doctor told me I was… I felt I couldn't tell you. After my sad tale of what I told you, Bobby, and Dan. It would have been vicious of me, a lie. When I first laid eyes on her, I knew she was a miracle. I had beaten the odds." Her voice trails as she looks at her baby girl. "A surprise."

"It's certainly a surprise." He says with a slight smile. Turning to look at the five month old, he addresses her mother. "What's her name?"

Evelyn says, "Amanda Jean…*Weston*. That's what's on her birth certificate."

Jaime chuckles softly. "Well, that says it all." Continuing on, he expresses to the baby in a soft tone, "You probably don't have any idea who I am, but you and I have a lot of catching up to do. He closes his eyes, feeling a lump in his throat as he smiles back tight-lipped.

Evelyn holds back the tears starting to well up in her eyes. She wipes them quickly.

He does the same.

Now, Jaime has something important to tell Evelyn. With a nod and exhalation of disgust at himself, he says, "Listen, we really need to talk." He says this with the gesture of his right hand out.

She looks up at him and says, "Okay."

Quietly, he says, "What I have to say, I don't want to in front of her for obvious reasons. She doesn't need to hear it, not that young."

Understanding, Evelyn gets up says, "The living room."

The two of them step out of the kitchen. Evelyn responds to the location they are in. "What's on your mind?"

Jaime starts by explaining with a slight hint of nervousness. "This is really hard for me to verbalize to anyone, especially to you. I've been a complete fuckin' jerk for a long time, towards you for sure. The fact is I've *always* hid away from people in general. That's why I'm a record producer, aside from actually liking the work I do. It's never been easy. I don't wear my feelings on my sleeve. When you first arrived at the studio and I saw you, I knew there was something special because it's extremely rare for me to feel that way towards someone. I acted like it was no big deal…when it actually was."

He raises his brows at the thoughts racing through his mind. Looking down at the floor, he admits to Evelyn, "The day after the first night we spent together, I was totally fucked up in the mind." He stops explaining and sits in the chair while Evelyn remains on the couch. Holding his curled hand with the other, he grazes his thin lips against them in a contemplative state. Looking up at her, he continues. "I treated everyone poorly in the studio mainly because I just didn't know how to handle what I was going through."

Evelyn interrupts by adding in, "It threw you for a loop."

Looking at the floor, his brows go up. He says back in a deep tone, "Yes, it certainly did."

Evelyn remembers. "What about what you said in regards to Wilhelmina's?"

He turns his head away for a second. "That was eleven years ago. It's basically saying 'I saw you across a crowded room.' It's clearly not the same as it is now."

Her eyes search him for answers. "What are you saying?"

Jaime takes a harsh swallow before telling Evelyn, "That um... I'm crazy about you and I want you to come back to New York with me."

Evelyn's jaw begins to drop. She never saw this coming. There were complications to the handsome producer's request, namely one. That was Ed. It would be so easy for her to leave England and run off with the father of her daughter. Only, it would be cold and cruel for her to just forget about Ed, even though there was nothing left between them. Even with Amanda, things were no better.

Evelyn gets up from the couch, staring at the large framed photo on the wall. She tells Jaime, "I need some time."

He looks up and asks, "How much?"

"About four days. I need time to digest this."

He nods in agreement, "Okay," then gets up from the chair.

"Jaime, can you do something for me?" She asks.

"What's that?"

Evelyn steps up to the six-footer, saying, "I want you to move in for the time being. That is, only if it's not a problem for you."

"I came a long ways to find you. So, I think I could manage." He smiles down at her.

Evelyn's blue eyes get lost within his brown-eyed gaze. She gets on her toes to reach up to him. Jaime leans forward, putting his right hand between a blonde tress of hair and the side of her neck. Slowly, their mouths connect and they embrace.

Jaime pulls away from Evelyn.

They sit back down as he tells her, "Even with this moving in thing... If it doesn't work out, don't shut me out of her life. I missed out on five months already and I really don't like being kept in the dark. I know the circumstances haven't been the easiest and I do have myself to blame for that. I wish things could have been different."

Evelyn looks into his eyes. "What would have that done? My whole reason for not telling you was because I had no desire in trapping you. I felt as though this is what I wanted. I didn't have the heart to burden you with a child. I had planned a big promotional extravaganza for *Hero's Requiem* and a tour of Europe once the record was finished."

As she explains, the producer bows his head down in shame.

"I talked with a few people who told me I should go back to England, raise my child, and that would be it. But, I knew in my heart that I had to tell you sometime. I had wanted to return to New York once I settled something here but that didn't happen. Instead, I stayed there and had Amanda. I stayed with a friend of a friend of mine in Manhattan throughout my pregnancy. Henry told me he would help me in finding..."

"Wait. Henry who?" Jaime asks.

"Bobby knows him and I have too."

"Henry? Are we talking about Henry Winslow?"

"I've known him for twelve years. He helped me out when I used to live in Manhattan. He was working for the newspaper over there. I knew I should fear anybody from the press but he told me our friendship wasn't based on me being a singer. He said it was because I was a decent person. I've come to know him as a sort of confidant."

Evelyn turns to look at Jaime who stares off into another direction. She continues with, "He told me he never..."

They say it at the same time. "...Mixed business with pleasure."

Evelyn looks in shock. "You know?"

"I'll be damned. Henry. I know. Yeah. I've known Henry for ten years now. We've had *many* of the same types of talks as well. He's a trusted friend of mine. Um, I was supposed to go to his and Karen's wedding but couldn't make it."

"I was invited but I couldn't make it either." Evelyn's lips part in awe. "Our paths could have crossed then but never did."

"Yeah. He knew all along. Henry knew." He then turns to her. "Strange twist of fate. You. Me. Amanda. Nine years later." With curiosity he asks, "What did you do? Where did you go with the baby?"

"Henry told me I should stay with a friend of his. Really, more like an ex-girlfriend."

"Carol." He answers deeply.

"Yes. I stayed with her in SoHo."

Jaime nods his head while mumbling. "Portuguese, right."

Evelyn says, "Hmm?"

He responds quickly. "Just thinking about something."

Jaime thought of the conversation he had with Carol a little over a month earlier at her loft.

Evelyn says, "I stuck around long enough after Amanda was born before coming back here. During that time I had come across a producer I had worked with early on for the first sessions of *Hero's Requiem*. I don't know if you would know him, but he surely knew who you were. Edwin Muller."

Jaime looks down. "Yeah. I do know him."

At that moment, Jaime feels like smacking Edwin if he were there in person for being in on the secret.

"He and Carol acted as an aunt and uncle to Amanda."

"April. April." He utters in a form of remembering something from the past. Jaime takes in a deep breath and turns his head. In an agonized fashion, he looks down with a hand through his hair. "I'm guessing it was you then."

Evelyn looks at him not able to understand.

"Um. Henry came by the studio in early April. I was in the middle of having a *really* bad day. He came by and told me he was in the city and that a couple he knew just had a baby. A girl. He asked me to celebrate with him by having a cigar, which I thought was a little odd. It's not like him to come out to the studio and celebrate about somebody *I* don't even know." He chuckles back before getting serious again. "What I didn't know was that he and I were truly celebrating *us*. Our daughter. Amanda."

"I told him not to say anything."

"He did a good job of that. While I was in the city, sometime in May, I kept on getting people telling me how lovely of a niece or daughter I had. I tried to tell them, it wasn't possible because I remembered what you told me. So, I dismissed it and carried on. Then there were others that I knew and I checked into it and was told that it wasn't or I was mistaken. I had no idea. Then July rolled around. Another birthday. More of the same stuff in my life. I had a hard time functioning because I was thinking about the previous year and what it meant to me. I realized that what we had was very special and I nearly threw it away. Probably the best thing. I don't reveal this part of my life very often, if ever to anyone but... I don't want to be like my father. I don't want to just *walk* away from something special. My mom dealt with it okay but I'm determined not to repeat the cycle. I *want* to have the responsibility for my daughter. Like I said, just don't shut me out. I've missed too much and I don't want to miss anymore." He adds in, "My priorities have been *completely*..." He lightly grazes his top teeth against his bottom lip in a contemplative manner, and then finishes his sentence. "...*Disorganized* to a fault. I've always put myself ahead of anything and anyone else. It's a very selfish way to be, but I got pretty used to it. Then one day I woke up and got sick of it. So, I came out here."

He looks directly at her. She looks back at him with wonderment.

"The deal with this business gets really weird sometimes. It's a long merry-go-round ride. Produce somebody's album, celebrate it, possibly get awards for it or a pat on the back, then do another one. Week in. Week out.

It's the same thing repeatedly. I've never thought about personal happiness for myself. I figured at this point, why should I even think about it. Being over forty and a complete workaholic doesn't match up with a day of taking kids to school and taking the wife out for lunch or dinner. I got used to it. But now I'm looking forward to living like a normal functioning human being. I welcome the opportunity to sit back and watch what my daughter does. What kind of mischief she'll get into." Jaime smiles at the thought. "I just never knew it would happen to me. At least not now." He says back in a deep tone. "I spent about a week here in England trying to come up with the words I wanted to say to you but it wasn't happening. I talked with Henry on the phone and he set me straight."

Jaime chuckles warmly.

Evelyn responds joyously. "He definitely knows how to do that!"

"Yeah. He does."

They pause for a brief moment.

He then says, "So?"

"So, do you want me to call a cab to bring you back to wherever you were staying, so you can pack your stuff and come here?"

He hesitates. "I guess."

"I do need an actual answer. Will it be yes or no?"

Jaime takes a deep breath. "Yes."

He looks at her seriously with a nod of the head.

Soon a cab arrives, whisking the record producer away. Evelyn shuts the door and furtively gathers photos on the shelves that have anything to do with Ed. Small frames get turned face down with potted plants on top of them. She rushes around upstairs in the bedroom doing the same. As long as Edward Brockton's face was nowhere to be seen, that would be fine by her, although there weren't too many. If she were to have Jaime as a houseguest then she was going to cover all of the bases until she was ready to tell him about Ed. Only two 24x36 inch pictures remain left on the wall bearing anything to do with her photographer boyfriend.

About ten o'clock in the morning the next day, a knock is heard at the door.

Evelyn shouts out, "Come in!"

The door opens and Mildred walks in as though she's in a hurry. She steps through the swinging kitchen door and is overcome by shock at what she sees. Her eyes go wide and she puts her hand over her chest.

It's the look of shear-domesticated tranquility. A family.

Evelyn stands by the stove with practically a half undone black shirt and tight black jeans. At the table is Jaime, his hair is combed back in front, and the last two buttons of his beige shirt is the only thing left closed over brown slacks. Amanda remains in her high chair with a pink outfit on. Mildred can't help but see everybody is very comfortable and casual. She addresses Evelyn.

"I need to see you for a few."

Evelyn holds an egg over a pan. Instead of breaking the item, she places it on the counter nearby.

The women step out of the kitchen.

Mildred asks Evelyn, "Are you crazy? Have you lost your bloody mind?"

Evelyn remains oblivious to Mildred's questioning. She answers back, "No."

Mildred shakes her head. "What are you doing...with *him*?"

Evelyn holds her hand over her heart. "I'm in *love* with him. Millie, I have to tell you something about Mandy. Jaime is her father."

"Well, it doesn't take a rocket scientist to figure that out. Ed is going to kill you when he finds out. And I'm not going to your funeral! It's insane the risk you're taking on this man, whether he's Mandy's daddy or not."

Evelyn takes a deep breath and holds the shoulders of her frazzled friend.

"Look, you don't have to worry. I will tell Ed as soon as he gets back. My risk on this man may not be so bad either. He wants Mandy and I to go back to New York with him."

Mildred shakes her head in despair. With the air of defeat, she says, "If you're happy and sincerely mean it, then I can't say anything else."

Assuredly, Evelyn says, "Please, Millie. Everything will be fine."

Mildred looks at the kitchen door, knowing there are two very good things behind it. She hesitates in what she wants to bring up to her friend. "I think you need to hear this. Now, I've never been Ed's greatest fan. I don't want to make this sound like I'm kicking him while he's down, but Phil saw him at Marky's Tavern while playing pool. Ed was downing about a pint of Scotch. Phil said that Ed's been doing that since you came back with Mandy. He's there every Friday."

Evelyn turns away as Mildred continues, "It's not like I shouldn't trust my husband. You know this might be the reason why Ed is so uptight and edgy all the time."

All the while, Evelyn listens, figuring it's time to make the break away from him once and for all.

"Sometimes he acts like he's hiding something," Mildred tells her.

Evelyn turns abruptly to her and asks, "Do you think he knows?"

Mildred looks down, shaking her head. "I think it goes deeper than that. I don't know, but it seems that way."

Evelyn gives Mildred a look and buttons up her blouse a little more.

The two women return to the kitchen.

Amanda begins to whimper. Jaime gets up quickly from the table and fetches Amanda's bottle. He surveys her for a few minutes in hopes she'll calm down. The whimpers get louder. She breaks into full-blown crying mode.

In a hushed husky whisper he asks, "What's the matter, huh?"

Evelyn hears Amanda's cries and tells both Jaime and Mildred, "I know *that* sound. Breakfast has arrived."

Jaime puts the bottle down and quickly steps away from the crying baby. Evelyn reaches to take Amanda out of the high chair. Jaime goes back to sit at the table and begins to pull at the pack of Marlboros in his shirt pocket. Evelyn turns to Mildred while holding Amanda. She sees the now dangling cigarette hanging out of Jaime's mouth and he's about to strike a match. Evelyn hands Amanda abruptly to Mildred and waves her finger at the perplexed producer.

He says, "What?"

She states, "I'm not going to permit anybody to smoke in the house with my daughter here. Do we have an understanding? Outside."

Jaime takes a look up at her with a telling glance, and then takes out the Marlboro. He chuckles and removes his tall body from the chair.

Mildred breaks into a small smile without the other two knowing it.

Evelyn takes back Amanda who has a few fingers in her mouth, remaining with a pained expression. Mildred looks at Evelyn then Jaime who is about to head out of the kitchen to the back door patio.

Evelyn says to her, "Make sure he doesn't light up in the house."

Mildred nods.

Evelyn disappears through the swinging door.

Outside, Jaime exhales a puff of smoke when Mildred appears. He studies her motionless, stout expression while holding his cigarette with everything but a pinky finger. The gaze of her eyes makes him slightly uncomfortable, although he remains friendly towards her.

Mildred expresses boldly. "I want to make sure that you treat Evelyn well. Not simply because you feel some obligation to her and the baby, but to truly mean it in your heart. She's had her heart broken many times before. I've known her for fifteen years. I know she's fragile. A one-nighter is not what she needs. Nor some short time lover."

Jaime nods then smiles.

Mildred continues seriously with, "I don't know the whole story aside from the result of that beautiful little girl. I'm sure there's more to it. I don't enjoy hearing about her sad lyrics or the way men treat her simply because she is a singer. Underneath that tough exterior is a badly damaged woman. She has feelings you know?"

Jaime says back, "I know," as the smoke unfurls into the air. "Do you think this hasn't occurred to me? I'm serious about this whether you want to believe me or not." He puts his hand to his chest for greater emphasis. "Quite frankly, I'm rather sick and tired of my life with the way it's been going."

Mildred interrupts by saying, "So, you're saying this is an easy way out of whatever you're going through."

"I didn't say that. You're trying to put words in my mouth."

Mildred puts her hand over her mouth in mock awe. "Oh, I'm so sorry!"

Jaime pushes back his hair as a few strands topple over his brows.

"Did she tell you that I wanted to take her back to New York with me?"

"Yes."

Jaime puts his hands out in a giving up motion. "Doesn't that convince you?"

Stoutly, Mildred reprimands quickly, "I'm not the one to convince. When all is said and done, it's Evelyn you have to impress. I myself... I mean you are a *very* attractive man..."

Jaime looks down and softly chuckles to himself.

"Don't sell yourself short." Mildred says. "It's hard not to see you have some redeeming qualities, aside from physical traits...which are quite nice."

He looks back directly at her and breaks into a smile.

"She's obviously the one who sees something in you. Just remember, I'm on your side, luv."

Mildred breaks into a growing smile.

Jaime says, "Let's go back inside."

He snuffs out his cigarette and they walk back in the house.

Evelyn, who is at the stove again, turns to see Jaime and Mildred are back in the house. She begins to wonder what was said outside, as she knew her good friend couldn't leave things alone. She didn't need to look for approval from her friends but it was nice to see how they felt.

While scrambling eggs, Evelyn's eyes meet Mildred's without talking. Evelyn looks toward Jaime, then back to Mildred. Her friend exchanges looks and breaks into a closed mouth smile, then slyly darts her eyes to him. She mouths the word, "*Lucky.*"

Jaime turns to her as he senses something going on behind his back. Mildred returns to her normal somber look, only to fidget with a dangling earring. He looks at the now calm Amanda in her high chair, buttons up his shirt, and then goes over to her. He picks her up, returning to the chair and holds her on his lap. Quietly he talks to her.

Evelyn says to Mildred, "Have you had breakfast yet?"

"No."

"Well, please stay."

"Okay."

Mildred goes to make some coffee and passes by Jaime and Amanda on the way, stopping to watch the father and daughter interact.

Later on the same day, Evelyn gives Jaime a tour of her home. His eyes wander around the spacious and roomy cottage-like house. She takes him down to the basement where she explains it is where she has the washer and dryer.

He asks her. "Do you have help here?"

"You mean like a butler or maid?"

He nods his head.

She says back. "No."

Evelyn knew that Ed absolutely hated the idea of having hired help for things they could do themselves. It would make them look too rich and glamorous.

They walk back up where she shows him the various rooms off to the left of the kitchen. She stops short of the door to her sanctuary. Unable to bring herself to show him her getaway, she opts to skip it.

"That's just a spare closet." She informs him.

They continue to walk around. Evelyn steps in front of him suddenly as they near a door. She notices the sunglasses in his shirt pocket. Teasingly, she places a finger to his chest, sliding it down the unbuttoned portion of his shirt.

In an ever so seductive voice, she asks him. "How would you like to take a ride?"

Jaime notices her tone. It was a sort of innuendo and he sees where her finger rests. He looks down, grinding his teeth against the bottom lip in his usual contemplative though sometime nervous style. In his deep tone, he replies. "Didn't we already?"

Evelyn leans her head against him. It takes a minute for what he just said to sink in. She feels his body shake as he chuckles warmly. Realizing now that it was a very suggestive answer, she pulls away.

"Oh! Not *that* kind of ride! I'm talking about a real one."

In a sly tone, the producer tells her, "So was I."

He laughs harder.

She edges him further against the door. Leaning over him, close enough for a kiss, she suggests. "Why don't you open that door and see what's on the other side?"

"What's there?"

"What if I said the garage?"

Evelyn removes the sunglasses from his shirt pocket. He looks at her peculiarly then chuckles again, this time while opening the door.

"I'm not going to judge you by the car you drive." With astonishment, the producer stops in his tracks. He lets out a loud and raspy, "Whoa!!" As though someone has hit him with something hard, his jaw drops.

There it is.

She notices that his sight isn't exactly on the Austin Rover. He stands shell-shocked, staring at the white Alfa Romeo. Jaime adjusts his sight. Evelyn sidles up to him. Blindly he puts his arm around the back of her shoulder. Holding his sunglasses, Evelyn places them on him.

He asks. "Where did you get this?"

"You know what it is?"

"Yeah. It's an Alfa Romeo. Possibly later 70's model."

"A '78 Spider Veloce."

Jaime marvels at the plush dark red interior. He pulls up his sunglasses so they sit on top of his head.

"I just never thought you had such a fine automobile. When you said to look in the garage, I thought you had something like...." He looks at the Rover. "... Like this."

She smiles at him. "I bought that car from the money I got for one of my first punk related albums I made."

"*Ravaged Beauty?*"

"No. The one before that. *Kiss Kiss, Bang Bang*. I used to have a '67 Aston Martin GT. I called her Baby Blue. She was light blue. That car I got from a record company called Anlan. They wanted me so badly on their roster that they gave me that one. I had to give her away though, some seven years ago. It was something I had to do."

Jaime looks at her carefully. He could see in her eyes that she didn't really want to part with that Aston Martin. Something deep down told him that whatever it was, it had to have been major. He eyes down, noticing the melancholy tone in her voice.

She changes gears. "But really darling, that was a long time ago. I still have the Alfa. So, do you want a ride?"

He smiles back at her. "Yeah. Sure!"

"Well, hop in!"

Evelyn rushes over to the garage control panel, pressing in a few buttons. She then hops in the driver's seat. Both watch as the garage door opens. He puts on his sunglasses. Evelyn starts up the Alfa and they glide out of the driveway.

"Wheeeeeeeeeeeeeeee!" She squeals with joy.

Away in Exeter, Ed fumbles with a stubborn tripod. One of the legs won't stay balanced. Already, the photographer is wrestling with thoughts of Evelyn and the baby. Why did Evelyn have to bring home a child after a whole year? They argued about it and here she claimed to have his child. No. That couldn't be. Ed tries to put it behind him. He was supposed to take pictures and tend to business like he normally would. Although, that tripod stand was getting more and more frustrating. He grimaces and grinds his teeth together. Grabbing a Camel, he jams it in his mouth. The smoke comes out in puffs as he tries to straighten out the troubling item. Finally, like throwing a spear into the ground, he sticks the leg into the hardened soil. Now, all he would have to do is have the right setting and he could take pictures. But that wouldn't be easy. The film advance lever won't push forward.

Jammed!

"Goddammit!" Ed blurts out.

His fingers forcefully try to drag the lever. A third into it, the action stops as it remains stuck.

"Come on! Come on!"

He grits his teeth, bearing down on the Camel in his mouth.

"Advance! You no good son of a bitch. Come on!"

With his blood boiling, Ed stares at the camera knowing he can do no more. He yanks up the camera from the tripod and lets his anger spill over. Taking it off, he undoes the hinged door to the camera and pulls out the film. The sound clicks as the roll of exposed film unravels. He throws it with might. It bounces over little patches of grass where it stays. Then he takes the camera itself and throws it up in the air. The piece of photo equipment takes to the sky before landing on some hard ground with a crash. Ed sees a tiny piece of glass fly off of the camera. With his camera bag nearby, he kicks it like a soccer ball.

Wham!

Another crunch.

Ed checks the bag. A few lenses take the brunt of his punishment, either broken or shattered. He runs over to retrieve his flung camera. Kneeling down next to it, he checks it.

"Shhhhhhit!" He quietly remarks.

The telephoto lens is shattered. The rim basically keeps it from completely falling apart. Ed stomps out his cigarette. Noticing the damage he's done to his precious equipment, he runs over to the tripod and picks it up by one leg, brutally whacking it into the ground. Dirt and grass fly. One of the legs gives way. When Ed has had enough, he views the item and tosses it down on the ground. Ed Brockton's anger had gotten the best of him. Pricey equipment destroyed and he didn't seem to care.

Chapter 11

The following day, Jaime steps out onto the back patio and lights a cigarette. There was something extremely comforting that afternoon. He savors a puff of the Marlboro as the smoke floats in the air. Life had definitely treated Jaime Randall Weston very well as of recent. He had no calls on wait, no annoying managers to deal with, no deadlines, no broken expensive equipment, or even Bobby and Dan telling him what they thought of some production. None of that seemed to matter to the forty-five year old record producer who found solace and a sense of stability with a woman from London. Along with that, he was now the father of a beautiful baby girl.

Evelyn walks outside to join him.

"It's lovely today." She says.

He turns around with a slight smile on his face. "It is."

Getting close enough to the lady he had fallen for, Jaime puts his arm over her shoulder. She reaches for it, placing his arm around further while she snuggles within the soft material of his black shirt. Evelyn wraps herself within his warmth. She looks up into his eyes.

He asks, "Is Amanda asleep?"

"I just put her down for a nap."

He lightly nuzzles her hair and asks in a breathy tone, "How long?"

"A few hours at least." Evelyn lightly bites her bottom lip as she has an idea on her mind. She says with a sly smile, "How would you like to go somewhere and do something?"

He sees the big smile creeping on her face.

"Oh? Where's that?"

Evelyn says with the same expression though a seductive tone, "Upstairs."

Jaime raises his brows as his reply is, "*Really?*" He chuckles at the mere thought. There's a lot of risk-taking upstairs. He looks down at her and says, "Which room? Yours or mine?"

Evelyn looks down as she replies with, "How about the bathroom?"

Looking at her slightly perplexed, he says, "Oh. That's not what I had in mind."

Evelyn breaks away from snuggling.

"How would you feel about some squeaky clean fun?"

"Is this another one of your trick questions?"

She says back in a deep tone while placing a hand on his right side, "No. Come upstairs and you'll see what I'm talking about."

Evelyn walks back in the house. She undoes the second button of her white blouse.

Outside, Jaime finishes his cigarette and smiles deeply with a big boyish grin.

Curiosity gets the better of him.

As soon as she hears him come back inside the house, she calls out. "There's a robe in the closet to your left of the guest room. You won't be disappointed!"

That sounded intriguing enough.

Jaime nods and walks up the steps to the second floor.

No more than ten minutes later, he arrives at the bathroom door attired in a dark green robe. Jaime is about to knock, when he notices it slightly ajar. Slowly he opens it and looks around before entering. The sound of running water piques his curiosity to walk in. He pushes back his hair. In back of the bathroom door, he spots a white robe hung on a hook. It's smaller in size. Jaime raises a brow and eyes the shower. A hand suddenly appears from the slightly opened door. The sound of rushing water grows louder. Steam pours from the ice matte finish, making it nearly impossible to know where the hand comes from.

A finger beckons the producer. He steps close enough for the finger to lightly feel the soft robe. Jaime stifles a full smile. Again, the finger beckons, as the touch entices, waving faster. Then it disappears through the door, opening slightly more. He chuckles back.

Quickly, he's grabbed by the front collar of the robe and drawn into a lengthy, succulent kiss. Evelyn's mouth finds his again for a demanding kiss. This time, her wet hand reaches around the back collar. Her fingers scrape against the back of his neck, underneath the dampening waves of dark hair. Their mouths remain connected as her other hand runs down the opened portion of the robe. Lightly, she feels her way down his carpeted chest. He leans closer, balancing his tall body with one hand gripping the shower door panel and the other against the tiled wall. Evelyn's hand makes its way down to the tied knot of the dark green material. There, she fumbles to get it untied as she gives it a pull, loosening the nuisance. With one more tug, she unleashes the terrycloth-cotton material like undrawn drapes. Her hand goes back to his hair, where she takes hold of the now loose collar, attempting to draw it down to his shoulders. He wraps one arm over her shoulder, but retracts it at the feel of his sleeved arm getting soaked. It's then Jaime decides to fully disrobe and let the garment pool down to his feet.

Immediately, he steps inside the shower, closing the door behind him. The soft spray of hot water hits his whole backside. Evelyn runs her hand through his flattening hair, which is growing blacker by the second. Jaime pins her against the tiled wall, kissing her with feverish passion. Evelyn's once flaxen blonde hair changes to a flat mass of light brown. She draws a sponge over his right shoulder, drizzling it lightly over him. He releases her from the tiled wall and looks her in the eyes. Instead, he takes the sponge away from her and gestures for her to turn around, facing the wall. With a leading hand, he looks up at the faucet and turns up the pressure a little further. He gets her to stand a little off center. Then he braces himself for the feel of the water to hit him full force. Fully soaked, he wipes back his drenched hair. Jaime draws the sponge over Evelyn's shoulder. Pushing her hair aside, he squeezes a generous amount of hot water across her back. Evelyn turns her head to the side. She kisses him, then gives him a look.

Both break into giddy laughs, before kissing again.

Some time later, the two are still giggling and chuckling. Only, the water in the shower has stopped. Evelyn's robe remains hung on the door while the dark green one lies on the floor.

Off to the other side is the large bathtub with an arm sticking out. Evelyn's leg rises from beneath the soapy water. Jaime let's out a ghoulish laugh. She giggles. The producer sits propped up in the tub, submerged a little under chest level in water. His left arm is draped over the tub as he's leaning back. Evelyn leans partially on her side against his right. Her fingers curl around a few blackened strands of his hair.

She asks him. "What has been your worst and best production?"

He looks up at the ceiling.

"Oh jeez. Um, there have been a few truly bad ones simply because they were a nightmare to work with."

Jaime reaches over with his right hand to grab the sponge. He draws it over Evelyn's exposed knee as he continues to answer her. "I had one really bad experience at the beginning of the year. I don't like to talk about clients in a bad way, but she's an exception. Sandy Denell." He groans. "Oh God...her manager was a pain in the ass to deal with. There are others, but that was the worst." Jaime smiles at the thought. "My picture was in a magazine with her and that was set up by her manager. He was promoting her before the record was even halfway completed. I guess it goes with the territory. It was so bad that I quit before it was done." He laughs.

Evelyn grabs the sponge from his fingers, dipping it in the water and pouring it over his left shoulder. After all, he was starting to look a little too dry for her taste. Evelyn leans to reach over around her much larger companion.

He says while ignoring her pouring water over him, "My best production is Amanda Jean." Jaime looks down with a smile on his face and with his deep tone says with pride, "No doubt about it."

Evelyn stops drizzling the sponge over his chest. She blinks for a moment of disbelief over his answer. Her lips slightly part. Evelyn leans up a little more, staring right into Jaime's eyes, ignoring everything else about him or their surroundings. She leans up further with a shocked expression that leaves her face frozen. Underneath a few blackened strands of hair, his eyes study hers as she moves upward, looking down at him. The answer and truth shows in the fact he says nothing more. She places a hand on his cheek.

Evelyn slowly shakes her head in disbelief. She says to Jaime, "God, I love you. You are amazing."

Then she drapes her arm around his shoulder, leaning against him. With her mouth against his, she gives him a long kiss. He props up a little more to get comfortable with her practically draped over his lap.

Evelyn starts to feel numbness in her fingertips that are underwater. She lifts her hand to find that the skin has shriveled up a bit. She begins to use his shoulder to get her balance to sit up. He holds her hand to help her out. She gets to her feet. He looks up peering at her from the tub, crossing arms under chin.

"Sure you won't stay?" He says angling to her.

"I don't wish to look like a Shar-Pei."

Jaime furrows his brows in perplexity. Looking down in thought, he looks back up innocently. "Funny. I never heard you bark."

A tossed towel to his face is her response.

Dripping wet, she fetches her robe.

He pulls the towel away with a mischievous smile.

While tying the knot, she turns to him and replies, "I've had enough." She walks over to the tub and leans over to kiss him. Then she pulls away and says to him, "Aren't you going to come out of there now?"

Sliding back to his comfortable leaning position, the producer takes a deep breath, then darts his eyes her way with the slightest smile of stubbornness. He places his right arm on the side of the tub, next to the wall. His left remains draped over the other side.

Evelyn nods in disbelief. "Darling, you're going to shrivel up like a prune in there."

Without saying a word, he gestures 'goodbye' with his left hand.

"All right. Have it your way." Evelyn giggles and shuts the door behind her.

Feeling a little too dry, Jaime sits up then leans forward to soak his hair a bit. Returning back to his comfortable position, he wipes back his hair. Looking up at the ceiling, he let's out a quick breath. Closing his eyes, he feels himself slipping. Finally, letting out a moan of contentment he slides further in. No longer able to keep his arms out, he brings them in and submerges himself into comfortable bliss.

No care in the world for Jaime Weston.

About two towns over, Ed's mind swarms like flies on something repulsive. The deepening blue of the United Kingdom skies does nothing to dull his pain or calm his senses. Evelyn and Amanda are the only two things on his mind. Ed unravels fast. He had hid his true feelings of despise towards the baby girl. Every time he looked into Amanda's dark brown eyes, he saw emptiness. If she could talk at six months, as he was to believe, he was sure she would say, "*I hate you too.*" Ed had already acknowledged to himself that he felt no love for Amanda. She was a painful reminder of what he never could have. He felt with his binge drinking she was to blame. If his liver would suffer, then it was all Amanda Jean's fault.

The busted tripod lay on the backseat of Ed's car, along with his camera and bag of equipment. Items roll around with every sharp corner Ed makes. He knows he has to pay a visit to Dowd's. It's one of the only places Ed could feel comfortable at. Plus, he feels a growing need to use a pay phone. Time slips away as the skies grow darker. He looks in the mirror, narrowing a search for anything remotely of similarity to Amanda's eyes. He can find none. Beyond the dark buildings and desolate transit benches is Dowd's Pub. There is something more vibrant there than Marky's Tavern. Turning the wheel, he pulls to the side of the building, along with other automobiles.

Stepping out of the car, he unwrinkles his gray jacket and jams two fingers into the front pocket to make sure he has a fresh pack of Camels with him. He picks up a small metal flask from the backseat and unscrews the cap. With a tight squint, Ed swigs an alcohol concoction consisting of

Whiskey, Scotch, and a dash of Vodka. It's a true eye-opener that dulls his pain but loosens him up. Before leaving the car, he inspects his visage in the reflection of the side-view mirror. Sliding a hand over his foppish blond bangs, he strides away with confidence, yet insecurity on his mind.

He opens the door.

Music comes pouring from every speaker. Loud cheers and jeers are heard within the dart players area. The harsh wah-wah tone of Eric Clapton's guitar and Jack Bruce's falsetto break into the air in the form of Cream's "White Room." Glasses are heard clanking or sliding on the tables.

Ed walks away from the commotion into a small corridor of restrooms and a pay phone on the wall. With a harsh sigh and the taste of his eye-opening sip, he digs into his back pants pocket. He pulls out his wallet, ruffling through some folded papers. Unfolding one, he reaches for the phone receiver and turns the dials carefully while every looking at the number he wrote. The phone rings twice, then someone picks up.

Ed says in his normal gruff tone, "Yeah. Can I speak to Nigel Watkins? I'll hold. Yeah? Good thing I caught him when I did. Okay."

He gives a grin waiting to be put through. While tucking his wallet back, the voice comes through the other end.

Ed answers. "Hey, Nigel? It's me, Edward Brockton. Yeah, well I've gotta ask you something. Sorry to call you so late. It's about Evelyn...Yeah, yeah... Well, we've got a kid now... That's what I've asked...Impossible? Right...Yeah. I know. Did you ever tell her there was a remote chance? The girl doesn't look like either of us." He takes a deep breath while looking up at the ceiling. His voice starts to change to disappointment. Closing his eyes and rubbing his forehead, he lets out a defeated, "Yeah...Thanks...Bye."

He slowly puts the phone back on the receiver then walks away with contemplative disgust. Gritting his teeth, he blends back within the noisy portion of the bar.

The photographer takes a seat on the stool and orders his drink of choice.

Just then, two men walk in. A patron from a far off corner calls out to one man. "Hey Barney!"

Barney is attired in a grubby shirt and baggy pants. For a man of thirty-six, he has a strongly receding hairline. He's slightly full in his gray face from working the steel mill factory, but he sports a childlike demeanor. In one hand, he holds work gloves two sizes too big.

Barney calls out. "Hey!"

Then he shakes a hand. Right behind him is his co-worker and drinking buddy, Steve.

Steve is close to ten years younger than Barney and a bit trendier with his blond mullet that makes him appear more like an English rock star than a blue-collar worker.

They step through the crowd. Ed ignores all that surrounds him. His contemplation is a cauldron of pain, insult, confusion, and growing anger unbeknownst to anybody at Dowd's. He takes out his fresh pack of Camels and unpeels the cellophane in deliberate strokes. His eyes stare coldly across the bar mirror behind glasses and bottles of alcohol beverages by the liter. Pulling out the lighter, he leans toward the flame, and then tosses the item in his jacket pocket. The bartender places the glass of Scotch in front of Ed. He pays no attention, still choosing to investigate his unclouded blue eyes that hide any twinkle. Instead, is the steady gaze of a man burnt by his own lies and deceit. The machismo and feeling of male virility was stripped for the fact Amanda could not be his. He takes a deep breath, running his hand down his face, and then taking in a puff of smoke.

Behind him, he feels a strong slap on the back. The Scotch inside the glass seesaws from his elbow hitting it in a chain reaction. With gritted teeth, his eyes dart to the right as he flares his nostrils.

Barney announces, "Hey, Ed! How ya doin' ole buddy?"

He steps to the left side of the seething photographer with a humorous smile, partly tight-lipped. Ed's eyes swing to the left to meet Barney's happy squint. Ed's body coils with his shoulders up in a hunched position.

He says back with his throat tightened, "Barney."

Ed takes a sip of Scotch.

Steve appears to his right. Slapping down his work gloves, he hops onto the stool, drumming his fingers on the surface of the bar. He sucks in his teeth with a flick of the tongue. Immediately he says to Ed in a thick Birmingham accent, "What's the matter Ed?"

Without glancing Steve's way, Ed replies. "Steve."

The blues tinged song "I Drink Alone" by George Thorogood begins in an odd coincidence of place and circumstances. Ed rubs his forehead under the blond bangs that hang. Steve requests a bottle of beer to the bartender. Barney looks around.

Steve says, "Whatcha doin' here, Ed? Ain't it a bit early for you to come here?" He snickers at his own words. A bottle of beer is slid in front of him. Looking at Barney, he says confused, "What's got his goat, man?"

Ed remains silent, pulling the cigarette to his mouth. Steve inspects Ed's posture and asks, "What's with this?"

Steve mimics the coiled up photographer on the stool and laughs.

Barney shakes his head and reaches for the bottle of beer placed in front of him. "House problems, Ed? Or maybe diaper duty isn't fitting into your schedule?"

Steve says, "If I had a girlfriend like Miss Winthrop, I wouldn't be here, man." He chugs a sip of beer. "She's a hot broad, ain't she Barn?"

Barney says back, "She's a fine lady."

Steve then says, "She deserves better attention."

Ed stares down at the bar surface, seeing a very hazy reflection. The most obvious is the bobbing that appears too often as Steve laughs at Ed's troubles. It angers him more.

Ed finally says with a low growl, "You don't know shit about me."

Barney looks around again, telling Steve, "I'm gonna find us a table. In the meantime, ease up on the man."

Barney walks away. Steve watches as Barney disappears among the crowd. He goes back to goading the seething Ed.

"You probably make more love to your Scotch than anything else."

Ed begins to breathe harder, while his hand balls up into a fist. He grits his teeth, takes a puff of the Camel, and then snuffs out the rest in an ashtray. He goes for a large swig of Scotch and closes his eyes.

Again, in a low growl, he states to the steel worker, "Son of a bitch. Mullet head."

Ed takes a deep breath as he feels himself growing enraged. He pulls back his bangs in frustration.

Steve looks ahead, oblivious to Ed's blood boiling. He holds the bottle of beer and says, "Ah, probably getting no action at home."

Ed's eyes dart to Steve's face.

Continuing on, the brash Steve sucks in a mouthful of beer and says, "I know I'd be ballin' 'er night and d..."

Before he can finish his sentence, Ed speedily uncoils his body; wheels around knocking over the bar stool and slam his empty Scotch glass against the table as though making a touchdown. The glass shatters in such a manner that shards fly off to the right, past other patrons who scamper from their stools. Other pieces slide off the bar surface, scattering in the barkeeper's area. Ed's foppish bangs fly to one side as his coattails take to the wind.

"That's it!" Ed unwinds a raspy yell.

With a burning glare at the taunting steel worker, he slams Steve's face against the bar's glossy wooden surface, knocking off the beer bottle that rolls down the edge, joining shards of glass broken previously by Ed. A large hand covers over most of Steve's left side of his face. The steel worker's eyes go wide with fright at the sight of a shard of rippled glass dangerously close to his right eye. He's able to see the spidery cracks and rainbow slivers in a blurred capacity. Ed leans his weight, further squishing Steve's face against the counter top and sliding a large finger to push away the offending shard. With gritted and the harsh smell of Scotch and Camels on his breath, he closes in on Steve's ear with a deep, demonic growl.

"Stevie boy. You think you're so fucking funny. I wonder how many people would laugh if I turned you inside out?"

Ed's breathing is unsteady.

Barney runs up to the bar. "He's bloody mad!" Let 'em up, Ed! He didn't mean no trouble!"

Everybody watches in shock. The games stop. Laughter and talking is stilted.

Steve breathes uneasy as Ed slowly pulls away from his face, letting up his hand. Steve looks down with both eyes at the bar surface, trying to regain a semblance of normal breaths. He takes a big gulp. Ed edges away further, blowing out a breath and strokes back his hair. He picks up and straightens out his collar. The frazzled photographer pulls out some bills in his pocket, plunking then down on the bar.

The barkeeper looks at Ed in such a manner that it makes Ed quietly say, "It's enough to cover for the mess."

Steve touches the right side of his face, placing his two gloves up to the hurting sensation. He says quietly yet angered, "He's fuckin' nuts."

Ed walks away with his head hung low as he slouches over his own misgivings and display of unabashed violence. Barney watches, shaking his head. The only sound is the song's ending with a crash cymbal's crescendo ridden with guitars hot on the heels in typical blues fashion.

Ed walks out the door.

A half an hour later, back at Ed and Evelyn's stately cottage, all is quiet. Jaime appears in the darkened hallway, stepping out of the guest room. He finally had his fill of well-deserved relaxation and didn't shrivel up like a prune as Evelyn had exaggerated. Again, he's back to wearing a dark shirt with black jeans. His hair looks jet black among the darkness inside the house. The wetness has all but disappeared from his slicked back look. Jaime catches sight of the half closed door leading to Evelyn's room. He takes a peek and sees Evelyn partially curled on the bed, still attired in her white robe. She rests on her right side. Half of her hair is dry while the side she rests on remains damp and flattened. The lamp above is still turned on. He walks in very quietly, moving towards her. Leaning over to turn it off, he looks at Evelyn who has the hint of a smile on her pink lips. His eyes move down to the blanket and sheet at the bottom of the mattress. With both hands, he gently pulls them up over Evelyn's body. He leans his face close to hers, and edges away very slowly. Looking up, he reaches to turn off the lamp, leaving the room in darkness. From the light wispy curtains emanates a warm glow from the moon and lampposts lining the streets.

Jaime walks over to the other side of the room where Amanda's crib is. On her back is the cherub faced five month old with the look of tranquility on her thin lips. The lean six-footer arches his body down, placing a hand on the railing of the wooden crib. In the shadows, caught between the moonlit luminescence and darkness, Jaime slowly breaks into a smile. Amanda is fascinating to watch as she sleeps. He remains silent while leaning over the wonderment below for a few more extra minutes. Then he stands back up, and steps away.

The door closes quietly.

***

Evelyn and Mildred sit at a bistro. Mildred stirs her tea. Evelyn lights up a Marlboro, savoring it. She lets out a sigh of contentment. Mildred picks up the pack of cigarettes investigating the small red and white box.

"Hmm. Marlboro? Since when? I thought you were strictly for Camel." Then it hits her. "Oh, I should have known. I don't have to ask."

Evelyn raises her brows with darkened lashes underneath. She says, "Things can change. And no, Ed does not know. I just went back to my nicotine cravings as of this week." A smile creeps across her face.

Mildred replies. "Yes. They can change. Same with men." She takes a sip of tea. Then she says as she places the cup back on the saucer, "Does this mean you've made a decision?"

Evelyn replies wistfully as she puckers her upper lip. "Ah. I think you need to hear this, Millie."

Picking up her cup of hot tea, she sips it lightly.

Mildred says, "Is this about Jaime?"

Evelyn slides a basket of sliced bread in front of herself. Her concentration on eating for the time being is disrupted by the single name. She goes into her dream-like state as she utters the name fondly.

"Jaime."

Closing her eyes, she relishes in splendor. Evelyn makes direct eye contact with her friend at the same time she picks up a piece of bread.

"Well, he's truly wonderful. He's even taken to feeding and changing Mandy."

Mildred looks at Evelyn with a surprised expression.

"Really?"

Evelyn reaches for a small butter dish and buttering knife. Cautiously, she says, "Something happened last night."

"Please tell me not in the bedroom." Mildred pleads.

Evelyn begins to spread butter on her bread. She takes a bite and says with a mouthful, "No. The bathroom."

Mildred eyes Evelyn with puzzlement.

Evelyn continues to talk. "Okay. So, it was the bathtub."

Mildred turns her head slightly with indignation. Dryly she speculates. "Let me guess. No clothes."

In defense, Evelyn responds, "Oh, but it was completely innocent."

Mildred puts her head in her hands, repeating the word. "Innocent."

Evelyn reaches across with her hand to pry Mildred's away.

"Do you want me to finish?"

Mildred slightly gets over the shock and dismay but props up with fingertips to her forehead. "I'm certain Jaime thought it was all so *innocent* as well." She looks Evelyn directly eye to eye. "What would happen if Ed came home and found you *innocent*?"

Evelyn becomes a little disappointed and dismayed at her friend's attitude toward her happiness. "What? Are you going to treat me like you're my mother? I thought you were happy for me?"

Mildred informs her. "I am, but I care!"

"Haven't you ever done something exciting and fun...while being in love?"

Mildred leans more against the chair she sits in. She lets out a sigh and rolls her eyes. "Phil and I are content. We don't exactly have your kind of fun. You on the other hand have always been a wild child. I don't have to remind you of your antics in New Orleans that time."

Shocked, Evelyn retorts, "That was eight and half years ago!"

"You created a bit of a stir with your exposure."

"Everybody was doing it. So, I got a lot of beads for it. It's not like I was attached at the time. Ed was two months later."

Mildred says testily, "I was trying to make a point. You're actions of recent have not changed. You act like a silly little schoolgirl. Our excitement...Phil's and mine is having our son go to University. Or, when Phil gets a raise in salary, I'm excited. As much as I envy you for your fun with that attractive and endearing man, I have to say the thing that makes it wrong is...you are not married to him. Maybe not that even. It's the reality that you have two men in your life. One is away and will be back soon and another is in your home and you're doing all of these...these...*things* with him."

"It's not that big of a deal. I can handle it. I swear. I've told you this repeatedly since you found out about Jaime." Evelyn takes a bite of buttered bread and munches with pride.

Mildred looks at her with astonished eyes. She's unable to fathom the cavalier attitude of her friend, in love or not. With a resentment of being mocked, Mildred says back in a serious yet almost angered tone, "Evelyn, you have a boyfriend and you're having an affair while he's away. I'm not going to sit here and have an argument with you or have you pretend that I'm stupid. I'm no fan of Ed's either. But, what you're doing is wrong."

Evelyn looks at her in an understanding way. She begins to figure that her friend is right. "I'll tell Ed when he comes back that I need to go away for a little while. Then I'll call him from New York and..."

Mildred interrupts quickly. "You'll call to dump him?"

Evelyn looks up with lost eyes. "I...I don't know. I just happened to say it that way."

Mildred grows rigid with her response. "Whatever way it is, it won't be pleasant. Did you ever think about the possibility of both men running into each other? Ed drinks a lot now. Who knows what can set him off? He loves you deeply whether you like it or not."

"He hasn't shown it well." Evelyn offers back unapologetically.

Mildred continues. "That's beside the point. You probably don't even know Jaime's breaking point either. He would fight for you. I have no doubt. He's in love with you. Physically, Jaime's about Ed's height, and this whole thing of you in the middle of this... It can be very messy."

Evelyn quickly fetches the still burning Marlboro from the ashtray. She puts it in her mouth, and then blows out a hasty curl of smoke.

Her gaze falls to the table as she says in a solemn deep voice, "I asked him last night as a joke, what his worst and best productions were. He told me about a singer he worked with recently was his worst." Taking another puff, Evelyn cradles her face with a hand as she reveals while still looking down, "He told me that Amanda Jean was his best."

Mildred slowly looks up with her mouth slightly open. Her resentment of hurt feelings had disappeared upon hearing the news. She stops stirring her tea. Evelyn sheepishly returns the look. With no words, Mildred lets out a sigh, sinking back in the chair while eyeing down. Again, she looks up at Evelyn and shakes her head in a form of giving up and being left speechless.

Evelyn looks at the passersby. A couple walk arm in arm. The sight brings back a memory for her.

"He was able to do what no producer had done for me in those two years of recording. So much money spent. So many hours wasted on sessions left incomplete. I went there, and he knew." Evelyn's eyes meet the table as she says. "He was able to satisfy me like no other. I let him know it. I told him he was a fine... you know."

Mildred covers her eyes. "Shag?"

"Not the four letter word I said," Evelyn says with a growing smile.

Mildred shakes her head. "You have never been at a loss for words. As I recall, you let me listen to that foul little tune of yours. Jack-something."

Evelyn says, "Jack-Off Of All Trades."

"Yes. That's the one. A song you lamented about your experiences with men, in words that bear no repeating. It's no wonder Jaime traveled halfway around the world in search of you after your words. A compliment in your universe. Beautiful creature he is…" Mildred leans over. "You must tell Ed."

At the house, Jaime sits at the kitchen table talking on the phone with Henry. In his sights is Amanda, who grabs at his light blue shirt. The swinging door to the kitchen is fully open with a small wood block firmly jammed underneath to avoid closure.

He says to Henry while looking down at the baby, "Yeah. She told me everything, including the fact that you knew already and helped her."

Henry asks, "So, you do know about everything?" He was certain though confused Evelyn mentioned Ed, not thinking Jaime was talking about Amanda and how he, along with Carol had helped Evelyn during her pregnancy.

Jaime says back with pride, "This little girl is something else. When I first saw her, it reminded me of the baby pictures my mom had of me. The resemblance is unbelievable. She's taken pretty well to me so far, but I do sometimes wonder what she's thinking."

Henry closes his eyes and pushes his hair back with one hand.

Apparently, Evelyn said nothing to Jaime about Ed at this point. When would she mention this? Better yet, where the hell was Ed?

Returning back to the conversation with Jaime, Henry continues on where he left off.

"Now you know how others feel about you. Only, she doesn't hide behind sunglasses."

Jaime looks down at his daughter. Amanda looks up with every bit of her father's eyes, then looks to her right.

In a more animated tone, Jaime tells Henry, "I'm looking forward to having her and her mother around. I can't possibly tell you how my time has been spent here. Lovely as it has been, work needs to be done back at the studio."

He pulls the receiver away for a moment and reaches for the baby bottle sitting on the table. Amanda lets out a gargle before speaking her occasional baby babble.

Getting back to the phone conversation at hand, Henry asks, "When are you coming back?"

"Soon enough. My plane ticket is set for tomorrow. I'm sure I'll be setting aside reservations for three in…" Before he can finish his sentence, Jaime is interrupted by the loud shriek of Amanda. She looks up at her father again. Then she studies the floor below. His eyes turn to Amanda, seeing her hands reaching downward. He catches her before she can drop. Noticing her interest, he gently places her on the floor. She shrieks again.

Still on the phone, the producer exhales deeply and puts his hand to his forehead. He groans. "God, don't tell me I have to change her again."

Henry at the other end busts out laughing.

With an agonized look while closing his eyes, Jaime says in a deep tone, "Henry, I really don't need this from you right now."

Ignoring what the hapless and confused parent has said, Henry shouts in the phone. "Welcome to parenthood!" He then laughs more.

An unamused Jaime replies back again in the same tone as before. "You would." He leans over to feel her diaper. "No. She's dry…thank God."

Again, Henry laughs.

Jaime says back to him. "Anything been happening while I've been gone?"

Henry answers with, "Oh, you know. Bobby's been hosting parties."

"Very funny."

"Well, Andi now knows what was going on. Dan and Vicki can't wait for your return."

"Let me guess. So they could say, 'I told you so.'" Jaime shakes his head. He watches as Amanda looks around.

"Tomorrow you'll be coming back, right?"

"Yeah. She said she needed until tomorrow to do something. I don't know what that is." He pays attention to the conversation instead of Amanda. When he turns, the little girl shuffles off on her forearms in a crawling motion, sliding her body across the floor, into the living room. Jaime watches her in shock. "Shit. I didn't know she could do that already."

Henry giggles back, "I'll let you go now. You've got your hands full with her. We'll talk later. Bye."

Jaime says, "Goodbye Henry."

He goes into the living room in search of his little girl. Instead, he finds her at the beginning of the hallway. "There you are."

She looks up.

He picks her up from the floor. "I didn't know you could move that quick."

Amanda's little body stretches, as she gets fidgety. Jaime angles to her when she stretches her hands out. "What?" He asks her confused.

Gargling with delight instead, Amanda continues to stretch her fingers towards the hall.

He asks her, "Are you sure you're not half compass?"

Looking over at the door at the end, Jaime looks back at the little girl. He walks into the hallway. Amanda stretches further as he steps closer to the door at the end. He decides to satisfy his daughter's curiosity. Opening it without seeing what he's doing, he turns to Amanda and asks, "Okay. Now are you satisfied? It's just a closet."

His eyes turn to the open door. It's no closet as he was told. Instead, it's a room plunged into darkness. He scans the darkened room and feels around for a light switch. Once he finds it, he flicks it on.

The room becomes alive. Amanda lets out a small squeal.

Framed pictures adorn the walls. It carries the same look and vibe as the living room, although a little dimmer. Towards the adjacent wall is a beautiful upright Steinway grand piano with the top down. While still holding Amanda in one arm, he leans over the black piano bench. Then he takes a better look at the scripture, which looks to be lyrics. He takes a seat on the bench with Amanda sitting on his lap. The lyrics seem different in mood and tone than what they had worked on in the studio. They were seemingly happier, instead of a yearning for something more.

"Toxic Passion." He reads, shaking his head with a growing smile.

The tiny hands land on two keys. Amanda gives out what sounds like a joyous giggle. After all, it would be no surprise if she herself got into music when a little older. Seeing as though her mom is a singer and her father is a record producer. Not to mention she had been conceived at a music studio, it would be fitting. In truth, Amanda had grown accustomed to the room Evelyn had brought her there after feedings. The little girl had warmed to the sound of the tinkering and melodies of her mother, which soothed her. Most often, the tunes had a way of lulling her to sleep. Her mother didn't pay much attention to music accompaniment of music boxes or fancy musical baby mobiles. She preferred her own vocal chords, which to Amanda sounded like milk and honey. The baby knew and recognized her mother's voice in any tone. She knew Ed's too. That was the harsh, gruff, sandpaper-like, nervous intonation that made her squirm. Luckily, she didn't have to worry about Big Bad Ed. No. She instead felt comforted by the man who was her true father. A hushed husky voice that was sweet and full of compassion.

He gets up and places Amanda on the floor next to the bench. She looks up but doesn't let out a sound. Changing his mind as soon as he sees his little daughter's inquisitive expression, he scoops her up and holds her while touring the room. The pictures on the wall are all framed and are varied in content.

Off to his left at the corner is a large print of a woman in a screen print styled painting that resembled art deco from the first half of the century. Or it could have been Marlene Dietrich herself with a tall thin cigarette and the curvaceous swirls of smoke surrounding her. It was almost in the German cabaret style he was so fond of. Beyond the large window with heavy gold colored patterned curtains is another picture. The painting is a single child's handprint in red with blue and yellow smudges.

A piece of writing is scrawled in a small child's handwriting that reads, "*To Evlin... Love, Harris Grumbach.*"

A smile comes across his face. Little did he know that Harris is Mildred and Phil's son who was only six years old at the time? On the wall nearest the piano is a set of photos encapsulating Evelyn's beauty and charming innocence. Jaime takes a closer look at a very young Evelyn Winthrop. She looked to be no more than in her late teens to early twenties. Her long flowing hair shone like gold with big blue doe eyes. Lips that drew into a smile of delight framed the visage of natural beauty. Next is a second photo. It's of the woman he first laid eyes on eleven years ago. This time she was shown with maturity and a punkish rebellion one might exude in 1977. The blonde hair was practically in her eyes, same as he'd remembered. The black leather jacket clung tight around her body. She was holding onto the arm of a British music engineer with long dark hair, whom she had been going out with at the time. Evelyn kept the picture to remind herself of how she once was. Wild, free, and rebellious.

As he moves along, Amanda rests comfortably against his shirt. The most playful of the photos is of an exuberant Evelyn with two other women who Jaime quickly recognizes as Liz and Mildred. At the bottom is the line, *New Orleans Mardi Gras '81.* Evelyn had on a very revealing hot pink scoop-neck shirt that plunged down to some very noticeable cleavage. She wore long metallic beads of different colors around her neck. Both Liz and Mildred were in the middle of laughing and were attired in t-shirts more conservative than their friend. The last photo in the visual timeline shows a more recent image of Evelyn with her arm over the shoulder of a black woman with what looks like a gold and copper babushka wrapped around her head. The woman looks a little older. Evelyn's expression shows of deep respect for her. Zula Mansoon was an artist that Evelyn had worked with and was a huge fan of. She was from the jazz side of music. Jaime wasn't familiar with jazz as he mostly settled on rock and roll, contemporary, world beat, and a strong love for the blues. With all of the images viewed, he sees a couple of gold record awards hanging on the other wall. Looking back lower towards the window, Jaime spots the record player on the wooden table.

At last!

He knew Evelyn must have a stereo system somewhere. Throughout the tour of the house, there had been no sign of music equipment anywhere. Only now, he discovers a treasure full of albums. It would be extremely odd for a singer not to own any piece of stereo equipment, but it's all in there. A couple of tapes are strewn around in a pile, demos mostly and unfinished pieces. Stacked next to the table are records including Dusty Springfield. Beyond that, are an eclectic variety of jazz, rock, and punk. Some others come up from other genres, but very few.

Amanda who is firmly clutching Jaime's arm looks down when he stoops to the floor and investigates Evelyn's record collection. He flips through the order of John Coltrane, Iggy Pop, Thelonius Monk, Blondie, Sex Pistols, Miles Davis, The Clash, New York Dolls, Charles Mingus, The Pretty Things, and one he finds of particular interest, Gil Evans.

A smile creeps across his thin lips. He nods then gets to his feet slowly as he doesn't want to startle the baby resting comfortably on him.

Returning back to the piano bench, Jaime lets out a soft sigh. Everything in the room for sure reminded the producer he just didn't know Evelyn well at all. Then again the old saying of, 'You don't know somebody until you've slept with them' came into play. Jaime thinks for a moment and realizes that for the most part he knew Evelyn on a very physical and most intimate level. He's almost certain he knows what drives her crazy, pressure points, and overall feel. Only there was now the yearning to want to know Evelyn Winthrop on all levels including her spiritual, mental, and sometimes crazy and daring sides. She had told him about her past a little bit but not much.

Amanda breaks his concentration by pressing a key with her whole hand. Jaime looks down and gets an idea. Not only was he interested in producing records for others, he did sometimes dabble with the piano. His large hands reach around Amanda's small body to sit her up a little more so she won't slip off of his lap. She leans herself back with just the beginning chords. Jaime begins to sing softly a sweet little song at the spur of the moment. His normal deep voice surprisingly is affective with the smoky rasp of his cigarette worn vocals. Amanda once again leans her head against her father's chest. She begins to feel the effects of his singing and the sound of the piano. Her already heavy lids begin to close, and then flutter open by sheer force. Amanda's head begins to lower. Again, her eyes begin to close as she looks up in almost a rolled eyed fashion before her lids close and she drifts off to sleep. Her head remains against the partially exposed white tank top underneath Jaime's light blue shirt. He finishes the ending note unknowing the affect it would have on the little girl. Looking down, Jaime sees Amanda's head tilted against his chest. Her right arm drapes partially over the other side while her left arm is tucked close to her side. She breathes softly. Jaime leans down, placing a kiss on top of his daughter's soft and dark haired head. Carefully, he holds onto the sleeping baby as he gets up from the bench. Jaime places her against his shoulder. She gets even more comfortable as he feels her go limp. He smiles widely as he places a hand over her back and flicks off the light switch and closes the door.

About ten miles away in a motorway inn parking lot, Ed surveys the evening sky. Leaning against the hood of his car, Ed pulls out a cigarette from the pack of Camels he had stuffed in the pocket of his suit. He then yanks out the lighter and flashes the flame to the tip of the cigarette before dropping it back in his pocket. With squinted eyes, Ed thinks of his latest behavior and violent outbursts. What did he have to show for it? Barney probably would never want to speak to him again. Steve would never forgive him for almost busting his head open against the bar counter at Dowd's. About £800 in camera equipment sits broken and trashed in the backseat of his car. Ed knew he made a mess of things. He gets up and walks around to the driver's side. Ed unlocks the back door and reaches among broken lenses along with nuts and bolts until his hand finds the item he was in search of. His hand pulls out the small flask consisting of the alcohol beverage he made some days before.

"Aah!" He says out loud.

Shutting the door, he then returns to the hood of his car. He unscrews the cap of his eye opening concoction, tips the bottle ready for a sip. His mind then slips into brief images of his previous behavior towards everybody including Evelyn and Amanda. The bar scene. The throwing around of photographic equipment. Not making Evelyn feel comfortable at various functions. His refusal to be intimate at various times with her. Scolding Amanda for simply doing things babies do. They all run through like a bad movie for him. Ed stops himself from getting a single drop. Lifting the container eye level, he stares at it for a moment.

A change was needed.

If he didn't want to lose Evelyn then something would need to happen for him. Drinking would not bring him closer to the woman he loved. He also figured it was time to try and be an actual father to Amanda even if she wasn't his. He, Evelyn, and Amanda would live as one happy family. The fairytale would be complete. They would live happily ever after.

Ed laughs to himself over the notion and pulls back his bangs. He looks at the bottle once more and hops off the hood again.

"Yep. Time."

With that, Ed faces the bushes, trees, and darkness that lay ahead. He flings the container with all of his might. The further away, the better. Its metallic finish shines brightly for a fraction of a second as it sails past a lit lamppost, disappearing into the thick of the night with a light thud some feet away. Ed lumbers back to the driver's side of his car, starts up the ignition and turns on the headlights. He drives the opposite direction from the motorway, choosing to go through dark desolate streets instead.

The door unlocks to the house. Evelyn steps inside, placing her pocketbook in the closet. All of the lights are turned off but one. The lamp near the couch illuminates the room enough for her to see. She looks around. Her eyes stop to turn towards the couch. Only the top of a head can be seen from where she stands. Slowly she walks closer. The singer sucks in a breath. Her hand covers her mouth.

On the couch is Jaime, asleep and outstretched. Draped over him is Amanda who is asleep too. Her head rests against her father's chest, comforted by his heartbeat. His large hands rest against her back as if they had fallen asleep in a warm embrace.

Evelyn looks down at them. It's so sweet and touching. She never thought she would ever meet someone quite like Jaime Weston, so warm and caring, acceptable of having a child right off. Her focus rests on his closed eyes. She remembers looking deep into them after he had made the most beautiful comment while they were in the bath.

"What is your best and worst production?"

"My best production is Amanda Jean. No doubt about it."

It was the most amazing compliment Evelyn had ever heard. Not a put-on. He was completely sincere. She thought he might answer her about an actual recording session of some sort. This was personal though. This was special.

She begins to think of how poorly Ed had treated her. There was no love, warmth, or compassion. He had no interest in her musical ambitions. She could care less about his photography. Jaime on the other hand was into music like her on a serious level. Another small difference was that Ed was older than Jaime by two years. Not that it should matter. Any comparison between the two men would be likening apples to oranges. Now, it was time for her to make a final decision.

Had she wanted Ed or Jaime?

Just as she looks down at the sleeping two again, Jaime awakens. He begins to slowly stretch. His lids flutter open. He looks down at what is weighing him down.

Jaime asks in an awakening tone. "What time is it?"

She smiles at him.

"A little after nine."

"I guess we fell asleep." He replies rather sheepishly.

Jaime slowly sits up, still holding his little daughter. He gets up and notices Evelyn looking at him with fondness. He adjusts the sleeping five month old, propping her up to his shoulder. She remains leaning limply against his chest.

"I'll bring her back up." He says in a hushed tone.

Quietly he walks up the stairs. He approaches Evelyn's bedroom. Then he looks back at Amanda.

Downstairs, Evelyn thinks of how to tell Jaime her decision and how to explain about the other man in her life.

Within a few minutes more, Jaime returns.

She says, "Darling, I have to tell you something."

The producer reaches into his shirt pocket, pulling out a Marlboro.

With urgency, she tells him, "Really, Jaime. It's important."

He nods back in agreement but also savoring the taste of a cigarette.

"I'll be right back in a few minutes. Then we'll talk about whatever you want."

Evelyn can say no more. He walks through the swinging door to the kitchen and out the back door to the patio.

Under the porch light, a match flickers. He takes a drag and contently exhales. It was something he had wanted to do for hours, but was unable since he was doing chores and taking care of Amanda.

Inside, Evelyn waits with bated breath to tell her producer lover whether she will or won't go back with him to New York. Nervously she tries to come up with the words.

"Oh, how do I tell you, Jaime? Is there any easy way to say this? I haven't been completely truthful about something. I made things much more complicated than I ever imagined. You see..."

The lock on the front door jangles, stopping Evelyn from her thoughts.

It couldn't be!

He was supposed to come back the following evening. Not now!

"Did you ever think about the possibility of both guys running into each other? ...And this whole thing of you in the middle of this...can be very messy." Those were Mildred's exact words coming back to haunt Evelyn.

She knew there was nobody else who had another set of keys. Looking at the doorknob turn back and forth, she quickly turns to the kitchen door. Jaime was outside. If it were Ed unlocking that front door, which was a one hundred percent chance, how would she handle both men at the same time?

Finally, the door opens and in walks Ed.

"Hi, honey."

"You're back early." Evelyn says with surprise and concern.

"Just a day shorter. What?"

"N... Nothing."

"You're acting a little funny. Somethin' wrong?"

"No. Nothing wrong. I'm just a little surprised you cut your trip short."

Ed turns his head away from her for a moment. Evelyn finds herself looking at the kitchen door.

He says to her, "Yeah. Well, I had a lot of time to think. We have to talk about it."

He sees Evelyn's mind is elsewhere. Ed clears his throat.

She turns to him. "So, how did the shoot go?"

"It went..." He tries to clear his throat again. "Gettin' dry."

Ed begins to walk to the kitchen door.

Evelyn can feel her insides rattle with fear.

She calls out. "Ed! Darling? Let's sit here and talk. Better yet, let's go upstairs."

Jaime finishes his cigarette, snuffing it out and throws it in the garbage once he returns inside the house. Evelyn remains in the living room with Ed. She tries to dissuade him from going inside the kitchen.

"Please tell me how the shoot went?"

"I'll tell you once I get something to drink. My throat is really dry. Okay?"

He heads for the kitchen door.

She calls back as her heart beats faster. "Ed, I really think we..."

Ed puts his hand against the door about to open it. Jaime, from inside the kitchen opens it instead. Looking down, the record producer's eyes dart up as he's about to walk in the living room.

Evelyn turns her attention to the kitchen. Already seeing the two men nearly colliding into each other, she sucks in a breath. Worried that something might happen, she stays still on the couch. Ed lets his hand drop to his side. Jaime's eyes become wider as he's caught off-guard by the unexpected. His mouth slightly opens with surprise. He inhales a breath, stiffening his whole body at the sight of the man before him.

Jaime utters the name quietly, but enough for Evelyn to hear him.

"Ed."

Ed Brockton's eyes never leave Jaime Weston as he too stiffens with confidence.

In a gruff tone, he replies equally as shocked.

"Jaime."

Ed's mouth opens slightly. He squints, knowing full well he had met the dark haired stranger before. Both men stand eye to eye in height. Ed remains slightly larger in build than the slender Weston.

Ed quietly asks, "Found what you're lookin' for, Jaime?"

The producer's glance calmly settles on the blond haired, blue-eyed man in front of his path. Jaime says nothing. Ed looks deep into his brown eyes. The white flecks in his pupils from the reflection of light goes black as Ed narrows his shadow upon him. Ed's noticeable sea blue eyes steady a glance.

Those brown eyes, the windows of this man's soul. His look is of calmness and grace, majestic yet romantic. Ed takes a slight measured step back. His nostrils flare as his apparent smile slightly shows. In an almost disturbed glance as though he wants to dissect every inch of those eyes, Ed snorts back some air. His voice is a quiet growl at the discovery.

"Same eyes."

Ed slightly moves to the right, but Jaime's sight stays fixated on him. Ed takes another glance, preoccupied by the uncanny resemblance to Amanda's. The eyes, slightly arched brows, the thin lips, the dark brown hair, and the nose were the same traits as the nearly six month old, asleep upstairs.

Evelyn looks on in shock. Hesitantly, she remarks. "You know each other?"

Ed slowly turns back her way. Jaime's eyes look in her direction too. Then the two six footers face off again.

Ed says back, "Not as good as you do." He snorts out some air before directing his full attention to the record producer. "Now I know." His tongue rolls around in his mouth providing a bit of preoccupation since he wasn't sucking on a Camel.

Evelyn says, "I think we need to talk. The three of us."

Ed's voice vaults back. "There's nothing to talk about. It's all there. Everything I need to know is in front of me and I'm lookin' at it."

With a sharp flick of his tongue moving in his mouth from one side to another, he asks Jaime. "So, what are you? Portuguese? Italian? French? Spanish? Middle Eastern?"

Evelyn states sharply, "Native."

With interest, Ed says, "Oh, Indian...North American Indian."

Evelyn says back, "Half."

Ed lifts up his head in utter defiance and confidence.

Jaime slightly bows his head down while still looking at Ed with his lips flat of emotion.

Ed growls. "You're gonna be Sitting Bullshit when I get through with you, half-breed."

The producer looks back up narrowing his low-lidded glance at the taunting boyfriend of the woman he loved. Jaime closes his eyes, slightly shaking his head at the preposterousness of the confrontation and the way Ed wants to handle it.

Jaime mutters half amusingly to either himself or Evelyn. "He never finished school."

Ed says back quickly. "Anything you want to say to me, Indian boy?"

Jaime just looks at him. He knew how to handle somebody like Ed Brockton. His confidence had always shown in his coolness of how to handle a tough situation. It had been the comfortableness in his own skin, which allowed him to take on a rival who was trying to be hurtful. Jaime had heard all of the insults before. It was no different that Ed was pulling punches with his words.

Putting out his index finger, Ed says, "That accent of yours. Canadian, eh?"

Evelyn says, "Knock it off, Ed."

Evelyn intervenes, trying to get between the two men who are not even a foot apart. She says, "Why don't you ask me how it happened Ed? Why don't you ask me how I feel about all of this? You could never give me enough credit for anything."

Ed slowly turns her way. She backs away slightly towards the couch. The photographer raises his brows.

"It was something that happened unexpectedly." She explains. "There was a mutual attraction and really I wasn't sure about *us* anymore. But, I'm glad it did happen."

Jaime looks at her with concern. He quickly offers up. "Don't do it. Don't say any more."

Evelyn turns to Jaime who pleads with her.

She looks Ed right in the eyes.

"I want you to know I had the best time with him than anybody I know. That's including *you*. There were times we made love *long* into the morning. *Passionate* love." She hisses.

Jaime looks down at the floor in anguish. He closes his eyes along with taking an unsteady breath. Now he was feeling very uncomfortable. It may have been Evelyn's way to get even with Ed, but it sure didn't feel very good.

Evelyn needles Ed some more.

"You never could understand passion, could you Ed? You could never fully understand how it feels to be held, fondled, kissed unlike any other. No. You always thought of sex as a gas station. Stick 'er in, fill 'er up, and roll away! Funny enough, you never even *enjoyed* it. Why didn't you just become a priest? Maybe nuns would have been your pleasure. They would be like you, celibate!"

Ed's eyes become filled with enraged fury.

How dare she say these things in front of another man!

Ed feels his pent up rage boil deep down inside from a different and dark place, much like he felt when he smashed Steve's face against the bar counter at Dowd's.

She continues. "He made me feel *real*. He made me feel *loved*. One night turned into a whole affair which I don't regret for one second."

The photographer stops himself from doing anything irrational at the moment. He had no need for Evelyn's sarcasm. She sees that Ed is more interested in trying to push her lover's buttons instead.

Ed moves closer to Jaime who has his arms folded. He squints his eyes. "So lover boy, what do you see so fascinating about that broad? Is it the way she bats her fake eyelashes? How about the way she lures men like a black widow spider, devours it and spits out the remains? That's what she does, you know? She'll take out your heart. Stomp on it and leave it to fester and shrivel up. She's no better than a streetwalker in stiletto heels." Ed growls out. "Cheap whore."

Jaime gets slightly fed up with Ed's insults. He breathes harder. "Do you want to take this outside?" This time the record producer shows a little more disgust. In a much edgier tone he says, "You have no right insulting her that way. Show some respect."

Ed takes a slight step closer to Jaime. "Well, Don Juan. Didn't anybody ever tell you you're supposed to *earn* respect, not just figure you deserve it? You could learn a little something about respect yourself. Like for instance, to have enough respect to stay away from *my* woman!"

Ed steps back with a slight laugh.

"Jaime my man, you never did tell me what you did for a living."

Jaime answers back quickly. "What's it to you?"

Evelyn says, "He's a record producer."

Jaime turns toward her. "Evy, don't say anything else."

Ed raises his brows while his pale lips open. "Evy? Excuse me? Are we now calling each other pet names?" He looks at the both of them.

Jaime bows his head down slightly.

Ed cranes his neck toward him. "Was it in the contract?" He looks specifically at Jaime. "Seeing as though she had to buy up time to record in the studio, was it included?" He turns away, then moment's later lets out a laugh. "I just thought of something. Maybe I should eat my words. Maybe just maybe I was right. She can be bought...like a cheap whore." Ed's antagonizing remarks infuriate Jaime who has one fist already tightened, slowly retracting it.

"You son of a b..."

Evelyn rushes towards him and places her hand over his clenched fist.

Jaime looks right at her, partly worried and part nerves shot.

She barks out. "*Nobody* is going to start any fights in *my* house! Do you understand me? The both of you. I want you to stop this, Ed. This instant!"

Ed with profound confusion mutters. "*Your* house? I've been here for eight years, including the one where you were bed-hopping. Oh, so now you're gonna get technical with me?"

"I let you stay here. This was my grandmother's house, which she left to *me*. Not *you!*"

"The next thing you're going to tell me is that I meant nothin' to you!"

Evelyn says nothing.

The photographer interjects, "That's right. Seven years meant nothin' to you. Do you remember all of the good times together? How we would go to Boston and watch the sun set. How you would shop at Quincy's Market and have a ball? Fishing trips, we'd take and you would be so proud of a fish you caught. Those are the memories I have."

Evelyn states, "I remember the times you would be so cruel towards my friends. Belongings I'd had, you would throw away. How you would laugh at my expense when I wanted to talk to you about serious issues."

"Babies."

"Yes!"

"You know, Evelyn...Evy...whatever your *boyfriend* calls you... You know, you're a bit of a hypocrite. You said to me on more than one occasion that you didn't want to live like a rock star. When in truth, you're a *diva*! Everything has to go *your* way. You cry and get all melodramatic when things don't go in *your* favor. I never did like your friends. They never liked me. I suppose now you've found somebody of your own kind.

Do you know what your so-called friends would call me? *Stray*! Do you think I'm stupid? Like I don't know what that means. An outsider who doesn't belong? Is that how you thought of me? I saved your soul! I saved you from the bowels of Hell. Your career was down the toilet! The little Punk Princess had nowhere to go! You were a nobody. And this? This is the way you choose to treat somebody who saved you?"

Jaime says, "You have a hell of a nerve. First, you say you saved her soul. Then you say she's a nobody. Something doesn't sound right with this."

"*Shut up*." Ed replies.

Jaime turns to Evelyn. He talks to her in a low tone. "I'm going to go back in the kitchen. I'll let you sort out this mess." He shakes his head disgustedly. "I'm sorry this is happening." Jaime puts his hand against the door about to open it.

"Not so fast, Chief Uptight. You're not goin' anywhere."

Jaime takes his hand away from the door while getting tight-lipped. He turns around. Still pained and aggravated by Ed's words, he offers. "What? So I can hear more of your shit?" He grinds his front top teeth to his bottom lip.

Evelyn bitterly looks at Ed. "You just won't let up, will you? You never liked my friends. You never liked my job or my music. So, what was it then, Ed? Did you enjoy seeing me miserable? Keeping me in a cage was a good idea to you? I could never truly be myself around you. Never! Funny enough I came back to you because I wondered if anything was left between us."

Ed says back, "With Amanda. Amanda. Yeah. Now here's an interesting subject."

Jaime stands stiffly looking directly at Ed. His head is lifted a little higher as he pays specific attention. If there was any doubt about it, Jaime was observant. He always had his eyes on something. The producer keeps a close watch of the conversation about his daughter.

Evelyn says, "What about her? I don't think you ever liked her. You never could hold her calmly. I don't know if that's because you were so bitter or half drunk all the time."

Ed tightens his voice again. "You knew she wasn't mine. You lied your way even when I could see it. The thing is...I knew it all along. Come on Evelyn! You were seriously going to pass off a dark haired, brown-eyed baby as mine? As ours? Seeing as though she's not mine, how old is she really? Three months? Four?"

Evelyn replies. "Five."

"So, the first thing you do when you get to New York is sleep with someone."

"It's not like that. I..."

"Let's talk about the logistics of me having this little girl, which is impossible."

Jaime's eyes dart to Evelyn who is already seething with contempt.

"Amanda. Now what was it again? That meant something like, *loved*?" Ed mocks.

Evelyn corrects him. "Beloved and adored."

"Right. Right. And uh, what's that other name. Jane?"

"Jean."

"Yeah. Wasn't that having to do with oh, something like a miracle? She was your *miracle* child."

"God's gracious gift."

"Some miracle." Ed snorts out.

Jaime nods before looking at Evelyn. He exhales deeply. Quickly, taking a step forward he addresses Ed. "I've had enough of this shit, man. It's one thing for you to say things about Evelyn and myself to a certain point. What's done is done. There is a third party now. I didn't know anything about your past situation until now which I've learned within the amount of time you've gone off on her..."

Ed says as Jaime turns to Evelyn, "Did I strike some nerve in you, Jaime boy? Did I say something against your precious little bastard?"

The producer quickly turns with his eyes glaring. Incredulously he responds. "Where the *fuck* do you get off?"

"Shut up, Casanova! I've heard enough of you."

Fed up, Jaime takes another step up to Ed. He puts his right index finger up. "That's it. I've had it. You don't fuck with me." Jaime rolls up his sleeves a little more than what they had been. His left hand remains clench-fisted. "I asked you before if you wanted to take this outside. I'm not going to be pleasant about it any more. You're gonna get what's comin' to you."

Evelyn rushes in front of Jaime, holding him off by the chest. "Jaime, no!"

Ed smiles. "That's right Evelyn. Hold back your knight in shining armor. What's the matter Jaime? Need a girl to fight for you?"

Jaime breathes heavy and puts out his long middle finger. His voice resonates sharply. "Fuck you, man!"

Ed lets out a laugh. "Temper. Temper. Jaime."

Evelyn shoots back. "Ed, I want you to leave now."

"Oh, not so fast. We have to talk about *Amanda*."

The producer says quickly, "If you have *one word* to say against her, you're going to have to answer to me!"

Evelyn still has her hand against his chest. She knows she can't stop him even if he decided to charge forward.

Ed taunts back. "Hey pretty boy. Wanna hear the rest about your daughter? I'll tell you." Ed's eyes dart to Evelyn as he points a finger at her. He pushes back his flopped hair leaving his hand there. "She has to hear it too." He swishes his tongue in his mouth. "Now, where was I?" He rasps. "Oh yeah. The miracle child, Amanda Jean. Well, it would be nice if it were true."

Evelyn begins to feel Jaime's heavy breathing calm down. The two look at each other out of confusion.

If it were true.

What was that supposed to mean?

Ed circles them.

"You wanted kids so badly, didn't you? I just never knew how desperate you were. It was all your idea in the first place to want to start a family. I never wanted any, not even adopted. I was content with just the two of us. You rattled on and cried at the sight of just about every child.

Hell, you even cried at some parties. Turning forty, isn't that what you said it was all about, Evelyn? You were afraid of your biological clock stopping? It wouldn't. You had no need to worry."

Evelyn squints at Ed, trying to comprehend what he's saying.

"Three doctors told me..."

"Yeah. Yeah. Three doctors told you that you couldn't have any."

"Yes."

"Brandon Hawthorne, Nigel Watkins, and Gerry Johansen."

"Yes."

"I know because I recommended them all to you."

"I know. I saw the films, the sonograms. I heard what they told me." Evelyn looks confused.

Jaime takes a step back and folds his arms while keeping his eyes on Ed and Evelyn when they speak.

"Gerry's on the cricket tournaments with me, he's a trusted friend. Brandon I met at the gallery. He's a big fan of my work. Nigel worked with a friend of mine from years ago. Those weren't even your own test results. Did you honestly think I would tell you who *my* doctor really was to verify?" Ed asks.

Bitterly, Evelyn shoots back. "So? What are you telling me? These three aren't reputable doctors? Am I supposed to believe they're not even real and that they're all fakes?"

"No. They're all fine gynecologists. I don't go to them. I'm not a woman. What I'm telling *you* is that, Amanda was no miracle."

Evelyn angles her head directly to Ed. Her jaw slightly drops.

Ed looks down for a moment.

"You see Gerry, Nigel, and Brandon were all in on it. There was never any problem with you."

Jaime studies Ed's actions. Then it hits him. He puts two and two together. If Evelyn had no problems and if Amanda wasn't truly conceived out of some true miracle, it could only mean one thing.

The producer utters deeply while eyeing down. "Opposite."

Ed takes a step up to Jaime who gives him a cold glance.

"Why don't you tell her the truth?" The producer asks.

Ed points a finger very close to the wary Jaime.

"You need to shut your mouth."

The eyes of both men fall upon a very hurt and confused Evelyn. Both know what the real deal is.

Ed says back to Evelyn. "You never had problems with having kids. It all depended on the father."

Jaime nods before closing his eyes.

Ed smiles back sheepishly to Evelyn.

"You see...I can't have any."

For a moment, his eyes show a sign of psychotic rage delving into manic laughter. With her jaw lightly hinged to the rest of her skull, Evelyn feels herself grow completely ice cold numb. There was the repressed pain akin to being bodily thrown off a horse or falling down the stairs. She felt like someone punched her in the stomach with all of their might. Evelyn slowly seeps in a breath resembling a gasp. Her eyes remain frozen as if time stands still.

Jaime remains unmoved, trying to grasp the severity of the situation. Trying to soak up all that's being said, He feels caught with Amanda in the crossfire. The whole thing seems too surreal.

The revelation spins in Evelyn's mind. Ed turns and walks away a little from the other two.

Evelyn begins to feel hatred run through her veins.

Rage.

She shoots daggers with her eyes and her mouth becomes a snarl.

Icily she admits to Ed, "You're a liar."

She trembles with the anger seething inside. No more confusion. No more shock. Bitterness had taken place. Evelyn walks up to Jaime shaking her head. She looks up into his eyes. The only thing he can do is blink back.

Enraged, she yells at the photographer in a heavy rasp. "You're a liar, Ed!"

Jaime holds her back, blocking her from attempting to run after the man and start beating on him. He has a firm grip on the ball of fury. In anguished rage, she yells out with a voice that grates while she strains over Jaime's arm that contains her.

"You're a liar! You're a fucking liar!" Her voice begins to merely croak hoarsely, straining her vocal chords while she chokes back cries. Fuming, she yells back. "If you thought I was such a slut...a cheap whore, then why didn't you let me go?" Evelyn cries bitterly, unable to control her stilted breaths that almost resemble wheezing. "You low-life *bastard*!"

Able to push away Jaime's arm, she grits her teeth and snaps back in her deeper tone. "I wish I *never* had met you! I'd rather be driven down six feet under than have to meet a hideous, insecure, *little* man. Little in *every* way. Down to your tiny prick!"

Ed turns her way. His boiling point had been reached just like it had at Dowd's. Words could only set him off. His unclouded blue eyes glare with a fit of rage. In a demonic tone he utters, "Seven years." He coils up in his manic rage prepared to strike at anything.

Jaime looks on in fear of what Ed might do. He remains frozen near the kitchen door.

Ed's shoulders go up. His breathing goes unsteady as he walks over to the poster size framed photo he took of a vase of flowers some time ago in Scotland.

"I meant nothing to you!!!"

He yanks it off the wall and throws it down with fury. The glass encasing booms then shatters. Pieces skitter across the wooden floor. Evelyn lets out a hoarse shrilled scream. Jaime watches her run for the table by the window to the left side of the room. She quickly curls up her small body underneath the oak furnishing as protection. Ed throws a potted plant. Dirt and flowers flitter out while the pot itself smashes into the wall near the kitchen. Pink ceramic sprays around, hitting Jaime's right shoe.

He says aloud, "Shit!"

Then he takes cover. Tucking himself between the couch and the coffee table, he ducks down. Another item, a small picture frame gets thrown. The producer watches it glide past, hitting the kitchen door. A small splinter falls along with it. Ed takes away another large framed picture, the same size as the previous one shattered and does the same to it. This was of a scene from Cape Cod. Smashed! More glass flies and spills on the floor. He quickly walks over to the curio cabinet containing statues. Ed unhinges the glass door and flings it across the room. Evelyn cowers further as the shower of glass nearly hits her. Jaime turns around quickly knowing she's only inches away from the sharp carnage. He ducks down again as Ed flings China figures like baseballs at a dunking booth. Ed surely hits another target, this being the small shelf at the front of the room. Small plates that were left undisturbed shatter, exploding into tiny pieces. Ed breaks off what's left of the shelf and wails it into the hallway. More frames whiz by. One hits a part of the ceiling fan. A chunk of that drops like a dead bird in back of the couch. Ed trounces his way up the stairs. Jaime peers over to see if there's any more damage. He breathes heavy. Turning quickly, he crawls over towards the side of the couch where he sees Evelyn in his sight. Running but stooping down so he won't touch the broken glass on the floor, Jaime makes his way to where she is. He attempts to crouch down with her under the table but it's too small for the six-footer. Still leaning down, his hair flops down over his right eye as he tends to Evelyn. He chokes back as he feels his heart racing at a rapid speed.

"I think the worst of the storm is over."

Evelyn feels the urge to cry but she's too scared and numb to even summon up any tears. She shakes. Then with fright, she remembers that Amanda is upstairs. Ed is upstairs! Startled, her eyes dart forward towards the staircase.

"Amanda! My baby! My baby's up there with that maniac!" She rasps. "I don't want him to hurt her." She pleads with the father of her daughter. "Please. Please Jaime. I don't know what he's going to do!" Evelyn nearly cries as her voice croaks.

Jaime nods. Looking towards the stairway, he takes in a large breath and still ducks down.

He feels he doesn't have to worry too much about Amanda. Ed wouldn't find her in her crib.

More small frames are thrown, this time from the balcony. Jaime leans against the wall near the staircase. He looks up. Just then, a small glass elephant statue gets hurled, crushing against the wall above the main door's entrance to the house.

Upstairs in the bedroom, Ed takes out two large black suitcases and fills them up with as much of his belongings as he can stuff.

"Get in there you son of a bitch! Good for nothing pieces of shit!"

He zips one up and sends it on its way down the stairs.

Jaime quickly sucks in as it whizzes right by him.

Close call!

Ed goes inside the bathroom, grabs his toothbrush and cans of anything belonging to him. He brings those back into the bedroom and tosses them inside the one remaining suitcase. When he's done, he zips it up and sends it down the stairs same as the last one. Jaime figured Ed was done with his thunderous fury...but not for long. A small shelf with more statues in the bedroom gets tossed next to the main door joining the pieces of the glass elephant that was smashed previously. Ed was going to destroy every item he ever gave to Evelyn. That included, rare art deco plates, statues, ceramic figures and pots for plants, photos he took during their holidays together in picture frames. Anything and everything that represented Ed and Evelyn. Jaime couldn't be too sure if there was anything in the guest room, which he had taken up temporary residence in. He hears Ed walk further into the hallway upstairs. This makes him dash for the stairs. Now he feared for his daughter.

Evelyn looks on in a state of fright and confusion. She couldn't quite understand why Jaime wasn't too worried about Amanda being in the bedroom. Just as he makes it up a few steps...WHAM! A small picture frame hits him on the right shoulder.

"Ow!" Jaime holds his shoulder while ducking and clenching his teeth as more items shatter. Another frame flies by his head, narrowly missing the producer. In a worried tone, he says aloud, "Goddammit!"

Jaime makes a quick dash away from the stairs just in time as Ed hurls a small curio cabinet into the front wall.

Evelyn lets out a scream.

Pieces of glass shower over the door like rain. Splinters drop in front of the main entrance. The resounding thunder of Ed's footsteps down the stairs is heard. He picks up the two suitcases, flings them outside as he crushes through broken glass and debris scattered on the floor. Quickly, he pulls the doorknob and walks outside. The door gives a tremendous yet ominous thud that echoes throughout the house. Whatever pieces were hanging on the edge, break off. Both Evelyn and Jaime cringe from the sound. They hear more noise outside, then the loud screeching of tires. The only sound left is silence. No noise could be heard, not even the sharpened breath of two people.

Slowly, Jaime gets to his feet, stepping on crushed glass. Cautiously, he surveys the living room. Crunching his way through debris, he sees broken glass, pieces of statues, shattered plates, potted plants, splinters of wood. His jaw drops as he attempts to regain his composure of breathing normal. He feels a sharp pain from his shoulder and holds it again. His eyes are somewhat wider opened. He closes them as he shuffles through. It looked like a hurricane had hit the house. Jaime looks around. Debris everywhere. He looks up at the ceiling fan with a piece missing from it.

The sight of all that is broken gives him a sick feeling to his stomach. His half disgruntled, half worried expression explains it all as he grinds his front teeth to his lower lip out of habit. He finally breaks the silence by swearing aloud.

"Son of a bitch! That crazy fuck!"

He pushes back his hair from falling in his eyes. With his hand still in his hair, the producer exhales deeply. Jaime turns when he hears Evelyn's soft cries coming from beneath the table. He walks over to her and stoops down. She gasps back while looking in his eyes. With no words, she uncontrollably sobs in his arms as he leans over her with a consoling hug. He gently rubs her back. They remain in each other's arms.

Once composure is regained, Jaime and Evelyn wind up in the guest room on the bed, fully dressed. Amanda is sandwiched between them both. Jaime leans his head down, giving his sleeping daughter a kiss on the head.

Evelyn wipes her eyes from what had happened. The room remains untouched. No broken items are around as a painful and frightful reminder as there are throughout the living room and Evelyn's own bedroom. Jaime breathes back a little unsteadily from still being nervous about the whole incident. Evelyn looks at him with wary eyes.

"You knew Amanda was in here all along when all of that happened. Why did you bring her in here? Were you able to tell something was going to happen?" She lies on her side with her hand propped up to the side of her head facing him.

"No. Something did happen unfortunately. Or really I should say *fortunately* as the time couldn't have been better. Amanda had a slight accident. So, I did what I had to do and got her lining and sheets in the wash. When you came back, I completely forgot I still had them in the dryer. Plus I wasn't fully awake. Amanda was already asleep and I had to remind myself when I brought her upstairs here that her crib wasn't made yet. Then I decided I would put her on the bed in the meantime while I went to bring back the sheets. Of course, I didn't get to finish. So, it was really more of Mother Nature's doing that saved her in the nick of time."

Jaime cuddles closely to the sleeping baby. Evelyn lightly touches Amanda's face. She then looks over at Jaime.

"I feel extremely guilty of what happened. I should have been more truthful earlier. Only, I didn't know how to tell you that there was someone else. Of all the times I've been in love, I'm not quite sure if I was with Ed. It may sound cold but I don't think he was ever passionate. He took care of me but it's not the same. I thought I owed him. Then I find he betrayed me for seven years. That '67 Aston Martin I told you about? It wasn't me who wanted to get rid of it. Ed sold it off as soon as he moved into the house. I was crushed by the thoughtlessness and raged at him. Thankfully, he did nothing with the Alfa Romeo. He told me at the time that a fourteen-year-old car was useless and parts would be hard to find. Even if it was in supreme shape."

Jaime looks down at Amanda then back at Evelyn.

"He treated my friends poorly and would laugh behind their backs. Ed would be foolish. Sometimes he would use me as the victim for his amusement. Ed found me in a very bad state. Very strung out. He nursed me back to health but slowly wanted to change me. The more he thought he could remove what he felt were the bad things, the better I would be in the long run. My music is sacred to me, Jaime. It's like a diary of my thoughts and feelings, just put into melody. Ed *hated* the music I had made at the time. *Ravaged Beauty* is my best work I feel because it's *honest* and it's where I was at, at the time. He could never understand this. It was as if he had blinders on. He couldn't see the beauty in the music. The way the arrangements were constructed with volatile guitar playing and merciless drumming. The way my lyrics cried out for what everybody else possibly wants...love. He just couldn't stand punk or rock even. He felt that jazz was more stable and safe. The others he felt drew me to heroin and cocaine. He couldn't have been more wrong. It's what drew me out that made me fight for life. As you now know about the room you found, thanks to Mandy, my sanctuary, I created that room once I found out how Ed felt. It was my own getaway from his negativity. Since he had no understanding, I would go in there and write my music. When I came back here with Amanda, she began getting into a routine where I would sing to her on the piano and she would go to sleep."

Jaime turns slightly. "I know that feeling." He chuckles back with raised brows. "Just know that you're in a better place in your life. I know I am." He smiles half down on himself and the other half on the little girl between him and Evelyn. "I also know that it must have been tough on you. To be lied to for that amount of time. Seven years. That's just *mind-blowing* that someone could be...like that. It's one thing to be devoted even *passionately* but that's...I don't know. Obsession? There's no other word I can think of to describe the situation. It's a completely thoughtless and selfish way of thinking...being. Because this person helped you, it gives them the right to run your life. I don't get it." Jaime's voice drops lower. "I couldn't do it. That's all I know." He takes a deep breath, looking at the ceiling. "I take off tomorrow." He looks back at her.

She says in a weary voice, "I know. I'm thinking of selling off this house no matter what I do. There are too many bad memories here and it's about time I make a change, even if it means leaving England."

His eyes meet hers.

Jaime never had to ask her if she would go back with him. It was obvious by her statement that it meant, '*yes.*'

She begins to edge away from Amanda before giving her a little kiss on the forehead as she faces her father. "I'll need to clean up now if I want Phil to check on the damages before we leave." Evelyn answers back to the notion that a broom and dustpan await her.

He later goes to join her.

The next morning, attired in a fully buttoned yellow ochre shirt with a black suite and black pants, Jaime jogs down the stairs when he hears the doorbell ring. Evelyn waits to watch by the balcony. He puts a hand through his fully slicked back hair just before answering it.

Phil and Mildred Grumbach wait to enter. Jaime lets them in.

As soon as Mildred sees Evelyn looking over the balcony, she rushes up the stairs. She asks with concern. "Are you all right?" She gives her friend a hug. "When you called and told me what happened I was terrified for you!"

"I'm fine." Evelyn replies. "Please, let's go inside the room."

Jaime looks up at the balcony as the two women disappear. He returns his attention back to Phil.

"We never formally met, even though you have met my wife. I'm Phil."

"Nice to meet you, Phil. I'm Jaime."

"As Evelyn knows, I handle insurance."

"I know. That's why you're here."

"Shall we?"

"Fine by me."

Phil begins to check out the damage Ed had caused. "I take it you cleaned up the place a bit?"

"There was a lot of debris on the floor."

"Tell me, what did he destroy?"

Jaime folds his arms as he says, "A *lot*." His eyes turn to various sections of the living room. "Uh, picture frames, ceramic pieces, lots of statues, potted plants, vases..."

Phil takes immediate notice that the shelf in the living room is missing. He guesses, "Plates?"

"Those too."

"A shame. Well, he got all of those for her."

With surprise, the producer mentions, "He threw a curio cabinet above the front door."

Phil raises his eyebrows to Jaime when he sees a nasty gash on the door to the kitchen."

Jaime sees his reaction and tells him, "The guy went on a blind rampage. Like a human tornado. I've never seen anything like it before. I mean he was *furious*. It truly scared the shit out of me." He chuckles back nervously.

The insurance agent looks up at the ceiling. "Holy shit. He even took out some of the fan." Immediately Phil takes out a small note pad from his jacket pocket and clicks on a pen, writing down the estimates. As he jots things down, he informs the producer. "She...um... Evelyn got this ceiling fan shortly after her grandmother passed away. I think she got it in India in '73 or '74. It was one of those things she cherished as she spiffed up the place a bit. That right there has liability written all over it."

Jaime looks up and nods for a fraction of a second. Disgusted, he carries on with Phil. They walk along, checking out damaged items.

Phil asks, "How much needed to be cleaned up?"

"Two trash can loads of glass, pieces of wood, smashed stuff. All sorts of shit, man."

Evelyn and Mildred return down the stairs still chatting away.

Mildred remarks, "I was in complete shock when you told me that Ed said it was all a lie. That's unfathomable. Bloody awful!"

Jaime and Phil head into the kitchen. The producer peeks out of the doorway before walking in. Phil waits for him. Jaime follows. He turns to look back at the door. Returning his attention back to Phil, he asks, "So?"

Phil looks back at him with a slight sense of loss. "So, if we want to get Ed for any damage, it won't be much. Property damage won't be that much since he mostly destroyed non deductible items."

"Shit." Jaime mutters deeply, looking down.

"I can get him on the ceiling fan, the doors, the scratches on the wall from the stuff he threw, but the rest is just material things that don't belong to the house. It won't even make a dent in his expenditure." Phil sees that Jaime is unhappy at the news. "I know you want to get him in an act of vengeance. We can't do anything about him paying any bit of money for the house since he never signed a joint contract as a homeowner. This is purely Evelyn's house. There's no claim. Without a claim comes no liability. Ed is virtually untouchable and he knows it."

"How about what happened with his lie, like what Mildred was talking to Evelyn about?"

"The baby thing?"

"Yes."

Jaime puts his hands in his pockets as he listens to more disappointing news from the insurance agent.

"Unless Ed physically made these doctors lie, again there is nothing. You can't get the man on malpractice. He's not a doctor. Even if any of the three tried to contest it in a court of law, there would still be no proof. They could snitch on him all they want but if there's no physical evidence then they themselves are the ones that will become jailbirds and get their licenses revoked...*permanently*.

In a disappointed low tone, Jaime says, "So, what you're telling me is he can get away with this scot-free.

"Jaime, he's a damaged man. Ed *is* and *has* been an insecure buffoon as long as I've known him. I think the one thing that would destroy him is seeing Evelyn truly happy. She left here last year to go to New York to get away from him. It was becoming a bit of a mess. Then she became pregnant with your child and she was ecstatic. What with all of the phone calls she was making to us about how the baby kicked and whatnot. She was terrified to come home and of course, we didn't know why. Unfortunately, we thought the baby was his He's a cruel man. What with him selling off her car. Making her friends wonder what she saw in him. Being non-appreciative of her career. And of course, making light of what she thought was infertility. I can only imagine how she felt when Ed told her it was all a lie. I have a twenty-year-old son and his mother and I love him dearly. Our lives changed for the better. There's no doubt in my mind that Ed did save Evelyn, but she sacrificed her own happiness for it."

The producer looks down ashamed of his behavior when Evelyn was at the studio. He begins to think of how Evelyn uttered the words, '*I love you,*' the first night they had spent together. He's able to draw to a conclusion what Henry told him. How there might have been something going on with her that made her say it. That combination of sharing her feelings and feeling comfortable begins to make sense. Without answering Phil exactly, Jaime gets lost in thought while looking down at the floor. He utters, "Yeah," at the thought.

Inside the living room, Evelyn and Mildred continue to talk. Mildred answers while a tear rolls from her eye, "Well, that about does it. Fifteen years we've done so many things together. New Orleans, Miami, Nassau."

"Evelyn corrects her. "Nassau was with Liz."

"That's right. I would take no part in running around naked on the island.

Both women begin laughing.

"Oh, I'm going to miss our Three Musketeer days or even when it just used to be you and me. Picnics with Phil and Harris." Mildred sighs.

Evelyn says, "Oh, but I'll be back enough. I surely can never forget my roots."

"You can say that now, dear, but if you were to come back, it would only bring back bad memories. Home is going to become a painful remembrance. Eight years, or well, seven would spoil it. I know you loved New York the first time around when you were living there and now you'll enjoy it more. I'm just going to miss you...*a lot*." She smiles then gives her friend a big hug.

Jaime and Phil walk out of the kitchen. Jaime heads up the stairs while Phil steps up to the women.

"All set. I checked it out."

Mildred turns to her husband. "And?"

"A lot of material damage but not much was done to the house. You can't collect on gifts and added accessories. Like I was telling Jaime, there's not much that can be done about what...Ed did."

Evelyn eyes the floor.

Jaime returns downstairs, holding Amanda who is fully dressed in a blue jacket and bonnet on her head.

Mildred laughs and smiles looking at the baby. She says, "Jaime, you're already dressing her like you're going back to Canada! A jacket and hat? Dear, it's still August!"

"I know, but you would be surprised at how cold those planes can get."

Evelyn turns to Jaime. "Are we all set?"

He looks down at the four packed suitcases. Then utters, "Mm hmm."

"Okay then." She tells him.

A cab pulls up in front of the house.

"Ah, our limo awaits." Jaime chuckles back.

Evelyn gives both Mildred and Phil hugs.

Jaime then shakes Phil's hand and gives Mildred a hug.

He says to her quietly, "Thanks. For everything."

"Oh, you just see to it that she and Mandy get properly cared for."

Phil holds Amanda for a few minutes and gives her a kiss on the forehead, just below her bonnet. He hands her to Evelyn.

The cab driver picks up their luggage and puts it away in back of the car. Jaime and Evelyn wave goodbye to the Grumbach's. Evelyn picks up Amanda's hand and waves it too. They get in the cab and are ushered off to Heathrow International Airport.

Late in the afternoon, Henry pulls up into the Whitfield's driveway.

On the side of the house, Dan is flipping burgers with Bobby helping in getting the picnic tables set up. Andrea and Vicki chat on the front porch steps with Becky and Evan paying attention to the beagle, Joey. Karen busily serves Jake and Josh iced tea while they're the first to sit at the table.

Karen notices her husband's dark green Mazda sitting in the driveway alongside Jaime's virtually untouched black BMW. She still chats with the Soren twins. Andrea looks over while sitting on the steps.

Vicki tells her, "Hmm. Looks like Jaime's back."

Andrea stands up, wondering what happened for the past two weeks. She looks on with anxious eyes.

Bobby and Dan look over for a brief moment before returning to their cookout ordeal.

Bobby tells Dan, "Okay, now turn it over."

"Man, it's not fully cooked yet."

"Yeah. Just the way I like it. Take it off the grill."

Dan holds the spatula with one hand as he testily says, "You are such a backseat driver."

"That's right. I'm a producer and you're an engineer. Ha!"

Dan shakes his head.

Henry steps out from the driver's side. Jaime emerges from the passenger's side. They give each other a look as they stand by the backseat passenger's side. Henry unlocks it with his key. Jaime opens it with a tight-lipped smile. Andrea and Vicki notice he's dressed up and looks quite good.

Evelyn steps out, holding the bundled little girl in her arms. Andrea squeals with joy, alerting everyone else. Off to the side of the house, Bobby and Dan run over to see what's gotten into Andrea. Vicki's jaw drops. Becky and Evan look up. Joey rolls over from getting a tummy rub. Jake and Josh stand side by side with Karen right behind them. Andrea practically freaks out with joy as her eyes go wide and she holds her hand over her mouth, stifling her excitement.

Vicki shouts out. "Oh my God!"

Karen smiles widely knowing exactly what the bundle is that Evelyn holds.

Evelyn holds Amanda front ways so everybody can get a good look at her.

Andrea rushes over. She squeals again in a higher pitched voice. "Oh my God! Oh my God! You have...a baby!" She opens her mouth wide, taking in little Amanda's features. She gives Jaime a strong nudge. He gives her a tight squeeze and smiles down at her, leaning his head against hers.

Vicki says, "See? And nobody wanted to believe me when I said somethin' was goin' on."

Bobby grins wildly with his arms crossed in astonishment, shaking his head.

Dan smiles back just as big.

Jaime turns to them with a huge smile of pride and happiness. He picks up Amanda when Evelyn lets him hold her. Placing her in his arms, he gives her a kiss to her forehead while closing his eyes with contentment.

Chapter 12

In mid November, Thanksgiving fast approaches and at a pricey restaurant, the patrons dine on pastas, meats, and fish. The omnipresent sound of clattering dishes and silverware fills the restaurant. Italian music lightly plays in the background. Seated at one large round table are Jaime, Evelyn, Carol, Edwin, Henry, Karen, Mildred and Phil. They chat about anything and everything that's going on with them. Karen has disappeared into the ladies room. A waiter comes around pouring wine in each of the glasses. Karen returns to her seat. Henry watches her. When the waiter comes to Karen, she rejects the offering of wine. Instead, she asks for some ice tea.

Carol says, "Karen, I thought you liked wine?"

Karen replies. "I do, it's just that..."

She's interrupted as another group begin a sing-a-long of Happy Birthday. A waitress presents slices of cake.

Jaime remains a bit quiet as Carol tells Henry something fairly amusing but the producer is preoccupied in his thoughts. Edwin looks over at Jaime.

Mildred says, "Evelyn, I have some news to tell you. I hope you'll be all right in hearing this. It's about the gynecologists who were investigated."

Jaime looks at Evelyn concerned. Quietly he says, "Are you all right with this?"

Evelyn sips on her wine and nods her head. "Yes."

He holds her hand underneath the table, bracing himself more than her for the news.

Mildred looks at the couple diagonally from her. "Brandon Hawthorne, Nigel Watkins, and Gerry Johansen all had their licenses revoked. They were on suspension for a time while the case was being investigated. They discovered whose medical records were copied from Johansen's files and then found the same thing and other illegal practices were done by Hawthorne and Watkins relating to the same case."

Jaime closes his eyes with relief. He takes a sip from the glass in front of him before saying deeply, "Jeez. Glad that's done."

Phil adds in. "The house is looking good and there are some potential buyers. It's been fixed up more so than before and property value went up."

Evelyn tells him. "That doesn't bother me. I just needed to get out of there."

Edwin asks Jaime, "I never did ask. How did it go with Ed?"

In a very deep voice, the producer utters. "*Harrowing.*" His dark lashes flutter as he tries to push the memory out of his mind. "It was probably the most *frightening* experience I've ever had in my entire life. Unbelievable. I'm just glad that we were able to make it out of there alive. There were moments where I thought we wouldn't." Upon further reflection, his eyes drift down while he runs a hand through his hair. He snorts back. "Jesus."

Evelyn quickly gives him a consoling rub on the back.

The table goes quiet for a moment.

Carol breaks the silence. "I have some news of my own. Well, really Edwin and I do."

Edwin smiles back with an excited grin. "And it's delightful."

She announces. "We're moving to Westchester...together! I'm putting up the loft for sale. Oh, you should all come over and see it. It's beautiful. A colonial. They built it earlier this year. The original owners didn't want it because they preferred to move to the *Hamptons*. Ya know?"

Karen lets out a laugh at the way Carol emphasizes *Hamptons*.

Carol continues. "Best of all, it has a fantastic basement. There's a few rooms upstairs and Edwin would love to use one as his office."

Edwin pipes in. "It's absolutely smashing!"

"So, I said, 'Sure thing, honey.' And... *And*, there's enough room for another addition if that should happen." She nods at Edwin.

He takes Carol's hand, looking deep into her eyes. "Darling, all I need is one eye to see your beauty. You've made me so happy."

Most of the table sighs with oohing and ahhing. Jaime looks down at the table.

Carol announces to everybody, "Oh, he's such a romantic!"

Karen and Henry look at each other as if they have their own thoughts going on between themselves.

With interest in the conversation, Phil begins to open up. "Speaking of property and whatnot, Mildred and I are leaving England."

Evelyn repeats back in shock. "Leaving England?"

Mildred smiles broadly and contently. "We're moving here to New York. Phil got an offer a little before you left in August."

Phil continues the story. "They have better benefits."

Henry asks. "Where would this be?"

"In Albany." Phil rubs the fuzziness of his lightly grown in beard. His dark eyes peer over to his wife. "Millie wants to stick with shops."

Evelyn asks with interest. "Millie, what will you do with the antique store? I thought that was your life."

"I'm in the process of selling the shop. It doesn't mean I'm going to quit the retail market. Far from it!"

Mildred turns to Karen. "Should I say it, or will you?"

Karen replies. "I'll do it." Looking at everybody at the table she says, "Mildred is going into business with *me*. We're going to have a shop combining what we do. So, it'll be a gift shop and antique store.

Jaime looks up from his preoccupation of whatever seems to be on his mind. He smiles then looks back down at the table.

Evelyn looks at him for a moment before saying to both Mildred and Carol, "That's great!" She smiles widely.

Karen addresses Carol. "Carol dear, Mildred and I were talking and we were wondering if you'd like to put any of your art pieces on consignment at the shop."

Carol's jaw drops. "Really? Me? You would want *my* stuff?"

Karen takes a sip of ice tea. "Mm hmm."

Carol reacts quickly. "That is so sweet of you. Sure! Yeah! Yeah, I'll gather some pieces."

Phil looks around the table. "With all of this good news. Have our appetites been stirred up?"

Carol says, "Sure!"

"I'll second that." Edwin smiles gleefully.

Henry goes, "Here! Here!"

All at the table make their selections. Each couple confers over what to have. A lot of nodding and shaking heads along with quiet chatter goes on. The waiter reappears and takes everyone's order. He disappears afterwards. Carol looks at Jaime who still remains a bit preoccupied.

"Jaime, you're the one that insisted we be here and you haven't said much. Is anything wrong?"

The record producer looks back up. Lightly he runs his index finger under his chin. "I was just thinking about something."

Henry admits with some surprise. "You've been thinking a lot."

"Sorry about that." Jaime says with a little bit of guilt.

Edwin looks around the table, then at Jaime. The waiter returns with a large bowl of salad and a basket of bread.

Mildred prepares her plate, and then takes some bread. She butters it and takes a bite. "Oh! This is delicious!" Turning to her husband, she gives him a bite.

With a full mouth, Phil speaks. "Mm. That *is* good!"

Carol digs into a large bowl of salad, spooning out the leafy greens in a small ceramic bowl. Evelyn goes right for the basket. Edwin turns to Jaime who sits one seat away from him as Evelyn is in between the two men.

Carol begins scooping out salad for Edwin as he talks. "Jaime? I'm wondering if there's any way I can possibly borrow Bobby for a project."

"That's not a problem."

"Good. I'm thinking of the masterful work you produced for Evelyn with him. I would like to try something similar with a client."

Jaime cautions Edwin after taking a sip of wine. "A word of advice. Watch out. He can do some *crazy* things to you." Jaime chuckles warmly. "He's um...well, he's a bit unpredictable sometimes. The reason I have him working with me is because nobody else wants to put up with this guy." Jaime laughs back. "He gets *me* in trouble instead."

"Oh, come now, man. He can't be *that* bad."

Henry and Jaime exchange looks.

Henry offers. "Halloween of '84."

Jaime replies back. "Exactly. Do you want to tell it?"

"No. No. You can."

"Bobby is known to do strange things and anybody and *everybody* is at the mercy of his idea of fun. He goes to extremes on some of his plans. Halloween, four years ago he did just that. Bobby bought these bats. They were either battery operated or mechanical in some way, about six or eight of them. You could hang them on string and attach them to ceilings. He asked me if I knew where the additional light bulbs were. We had some different colored bulbs when the photographers would come by and want a dramatic shot of the studio or any one of us. So, Halloween evening we had a band that was staying upstairs in the guest's quarters and I think...I think there were...oh, I'd say about six people up there." Jaime breaks into a big smile and chuckles. "The bassist told us they wanted the place quiet because they wanted to sleep early. We thought, *fair enough*." He looks at Henry who begins to giggle.

Jaime continues with the story. "Bobby and Andi's daughter Becky was nine at the time. Andi and some other mothers brought their girls to have their hair permed. I take it they're not cheap."

Carol and Mildred shake their heads 'no.'

"So, Bobby was remixing something repeatedly. I didn't know what it was. Dan wasn't at the studio at the time either." He looks at Henry. "Then, *you* came by because you wanted to hang around and you knew we were serving Tootsie Rolls. I was downstairs fixing a mix this band had just made and then something happened. I noticed the lights were shut off upstairs. Somebody came to the door. Normally, we don't have trick-ortreaters come by the studio. The door was unlocked because apparently Bobby was expecting some sort of company. I heard these girls, about eight to ten years old. There were four of them, I think. Henry starts walking down the stairs and suddenly the lights are red past the lobby area. All of a sudden, we hear these girls *screaming* at the top of their lungs. And there's this commotion and sounds of bats...*many* of them. I rush upstairs. Henry's in shock. We look ahead and we see the silhouettes of these mechanized bats hung on the ceiling with transparent wire and this remixed version of a ton of bats piped through the speaker system."

Mildred says, "Oh no!" and giggles.

Evelyn breaks into a hoarse laugh.

"Becky and her friends couldn't leave the studio fast enough. They were holding their heads thinking these bats were going to ruin their new perms. Henry and I look at each other."

Both men exchange glances.

"We say, 'Bobby did this. He had to have.' So, now we have to find Bobby. He was in the dark sitting under the control room panel laughing himself sick. Just *uncontrollably* giggling like crazy. We ask him why he did it. He said he was waiting because Becky and her friends kept on talking about their new hairdos and he got sick of it. So, he scared his own kid and he later told me she didn't talk to him for a week."

Henry adds in, "Becky never did mention the perm again."

All at the table erupt into laughter.

Jaime chuckles back. "If you mention the word, *perm* to Bobby he'll lose it and crack up laughing. He was proud of that moment!"

Edwin asks while grinning. "What happened to that band?"

"Oh, we had to apologize for what happened. Bobby had to become their personal assistant for the last two weeks of their stay to make up for what he did."

Mildred and Phil turn to each other and giggle.

"That is too funny!" Carol points out.

Jaime says back. "With all honesty, I've had complaints from other producers who have said, '*What did you do?*' With Bobby, we couldn't get any work done because we were laughing too much. The only thing I could say was, 'you asked for it!'"

Henry asks. "Didn't he have live mice running around a studio one time?"

"Yes. And the assistants freaked out. To this very day there are some studios in L.A. where Bobby is banned."

The entire table erupts into laughter again.

Mildred grimaces. "Blech! Mice!"

The waiter comes back with a few main courses. Carol looks over at Edwin's meal.

"That's the Linguine ala Pescatore? That looks so good!"

The waiter places a plate of gnocchi on the table.

Phil announces. "That would be mine!"

A third plate is shown containing what looks like ravioli.

Mildred waves a finger. The plate is placed in front of her.

Phil cranes his neck. "Ooh. What is that?"

"Ravioli with mushrooms and asparagus."

"Looks quite good."

Slyly she responds back. "Why? You want some?"

The waiter then tells them a couple more dishes will be coming up.

Once again, Jaime feels uneasiness. Edwin looks down at his steaming hot linguine. He looks over at Jaime again.

"Jaime, I need to talk to you about something."

Jaime quickly becomes detached from his thoughts and gets up.

Edwin then looks back at everybody else. "We'll be right back."

The two men walk over to the restroom area.

Evelyn and Carol look at each other.

Mildred asks Evelyn. "Is he okay?"

Evelyn responds back. "He's been rather quiet and acting a little odd since we came here. Even when we were dropping off Amanda for Bobby and Andi to baby-sit, he was the same way. I think he and Bobby had a little talk but it doesn't look like whatever was on his mind is off." Evelyn looks back. "I'm sure he'll be okay."

Karen admits. "He's looked nervous ever since we arrived."

"Perhaps it has something to do with the studio?" Phil guesses.

Mildred turns to her husband.

Carol tells them. "Maybe Edwin can figure it out."

Evelyn then remembers. "Do you know what Andi calls Amanda? Junior!"

Mildred laughs. "Gee, I wonder how come?"

Everybody laughs again.

Away from the table, Edwin confers with Jaime quietly. "What's going on with you, man? You're incredibly reserved today."

Jaime offers up. "Nothing. I just have had something on my mind. Something I'm going through."

"Well, you've been very nervous, almost shaking from the get-go."

"God, I can just about go for a cigarette right now."

"Do you want to talk about it?"

Adamantly, Jaime answers back. "Really, I'm fine. I'm just wondering how I should handle something. I was talking to Bobby about it before we left and I just have to find a way to do this myself. That's all I'm saying."

The two men look back at the table.

More dishes arrive. Karen digs into the salad bowl. A bowl of steaming hot minestrone is served.

Karen looks at what her husband has. "What is that stuff?"

"Zuppa di tortellini. Cheese tortellini in chicken broth."

"Oh." She responds with her tongue sticking out. "Yuck."

"Why, what did you get?"

"Rigatoni and mussels."

"Ah, I see."

Evelyn eyes her veal scallops on the plate. The final dish gets placed.

The waiter announces. "And here is the Dentice Livornese."

Evelyn points to where he should place it.

While Henry stirs his broth, he squints. "Let me guess. Fish, right?"

"That would be correct, sir." Evelyn giggles back.

"I know him far too well." Henry laughs.

Jaime and Edwin return to their seats. Carol then converses with Edwin quietly. Phil gives Mildred a piece of gnocchi. She in turn swaps, giving him a bite of her dinner. As the Grumbach's feed each other, Karen gives Henry a look, as if wondering should she reveal something. He nods.

Quietly he tells her, "Whenever you want to, honey."

Jaime closes his eyes, trying to find some contentment within the uneasiness and nervousness.

"Um, Karen and I would like to announce some news of our own." Henry says.

Phil and Mildred with their mouths full look across from them. Carol and Edwin sense something as they smile. Evelyn places her glass down while Jaime attentively listens.

Henry then tells them, "Karen and I... Well, what I mean to say is that Evan is going to have a little brother or sister."

Carol wipes her mouth with a napkin, uttering. "Oh my God! That is *so* great!" Putting down her fork, she points to Karen. "*That's* why you didn't want any wine! I should have figured that out. Pregnancy!"

Edwin answers. "That'll make you stay away from alcohol for a time."

Karen cracks up laughing with glee. "We talked about the possibility and *boom*! There you have it! So, that's another reason I'm glad to have Mildred aboard. She can handle the store while I'm on maternity leave."

Mildred says back with astonishment. "Why, *I* didn't even know that. Congratulations!"

As they eat, Carol asks Evelyn. "How about you two? Do you think you'll have a second? A little brother or sister for Amanda?"

With an impish grin, Evelyn looks at Jaime who reaches for a fork. "Well. I know *I* have no problem with it. It's *him* that you would need to talk to about that."

Jaime peers up from preparing to finally eat his dinner.

Mildred adds in. "Wouldn't that be something, Evelyn. From having none with that scoundrel to having a brood with this splendid man."

Mildred and Evelyn laugh.

Jaime closes his eyes as if something is about to erupt from deep within him. He drops the fork down and gets up, tossing the napkin on the table next to his untouched dish of red snapper. Taking a harsh swallow, he bends down while removing something from his jacket pocket that is tossed over the seat. He says, "If we're going to have any more kids, we're going to do it the right way."

Phil asks. "What is he doing?"

Henry and Karen look with confusion.

Evelyn says to Jaime without even looking down at what he's doing, "Drop something, luv?"

Carol accidentally drops a piece of chicken on the floor. Edwin offers to pick it up. While he leans, she gets a full view. "Oh my God." Almost a whole mouthful of chicken drops to the floor by Carol. Her mouth freezes in shock.

Mildred stands up to get a better view.

Evelyn freezes. No words are spoken. Her eyes go wide.

On one bended knee, the singer's record producer lover, the father of their daughter holds out a small dark red velvet box. Shakily, with his fingers he opens it. Evelyn covers her mouth with both of her hands. She sucks in a deep breath. Her mascara made eyes change into half slits of merriment like two horizontal crescent moons. Her lips quiver from becoming shaky herself. Mildred grows to have a smile just as big as her longtime friend.

Jaime says with nervousness. "I've been *trying* to find the words to say this *all* night and it's something I've never done because I've never felt this way before. So, this is all so new to me." He places a hand over his heart.

Evelyn looks down at the small diamond ring sitting in the velvet jewelry box. Slowly, she extends her hand as he places the ring on her finger. With dark content eyes, Jaime looks around the table from where he is. "I will have news if it's agreed upon." With his gaze pleasantly drawn to Evelyn, he asks, "Will you marry me, Evelyn Winthrop?"

Evelyn's smile can no longer be contained. She squeals back with much enthusiasm. "YES! Yes! Of *course* I'll marry you!" She reaches over and grabs him for a long passionate kiss. She hugs him tightly while looking in his eyes lovingly.

He says deeply and ever so seductively. "I do love you."

"And I love you."

Mildred, who has since sat back in her seat, leans against her husband's shoulder with a smile of pride. He puts an arm around her, rubbing the back of her shoulder. Phil smiles largely. Henry and Karen nod in disbelief, laughing. Edwin and Carol smile widely.

Carol grins back while wiping tears from her eyes. "That is *so* awesome!"

Jaime gets back in his chair.

Henry asks him, "How do you feel?"

Jaime says back with a very large smile. "*Really good*, like I can breathe again. A weight has been lifted." He laughs while feeling his heartbeat.

Edwin announces, "I think it's time for a toast."

Evelyn gets lost in thought with the ring on her finger.

"Here's to friends, old, new, recent, past."

They pick up their glasses.

"Here's to the delightful news of Henry and Karen having a baby. Mildred and Phil on their move to New York, along with the store. To us, getting a new house. And of course, I would be utterly stupid to forget after what we all just saw... To whom will soon become Mr. and *Mrs*. Weston."

They all smile gleefully and toast their glasses.

"All right!" Exclaims Carol.

"Here! Here!" Phil pipes up.

"Yeah!" Henry says back with a smile.

They all return to eating their meals and talk some more. Evelyn leans against the shoulder of her soon to be husband. Again, she looks down at the ring.

***

Ed sits on a stool at Marky's Tavern. He had destroyed any chance of returning to Dowd's Pub after his violent outburst during the summer. It didn't bother him too much. There were enough different places he could slog down a brew or his favorite, Scotch.

The bartender eyes Ed. He slides the daily newspaper to him. "Your gal's in there."

"Who? Haley?"

Quietly, the bartender answers, "No. Not that one."

Ed had taken up with another female over the past few months. This time it was a photographer like himself. The Welsh woman had found Ed irresistible. Now he was happy. That was until he opened up the entertainment section. Inside the paper, he feels the stinging slap of disgrace. There is a decent size photograph from the Associated Press. A head and shoulders shot of Jaime and Evelyn smiling proudly for the camera. The title is even more distressing to Ed.

Punk's Elder Stateswoman Marries Premiere Record Producer

London's own, Evelyn Marie Winthrop; 42, known for biting songs such as "Pretty Pinks" and "Jack Off of All Trades," the Punk Princess of the late 70s scene married rock's renowned record producer, Jaime Randall Weston; 45, in an undisclosed location in upper state New York on March 18th. The bride and groom's friends attended the event, including Weston's longtime friend and associate producing partner, Robert Whitfield who served as best man. Other guests included sculptress, Carol Mulligan and her fiancé, record producer Edwin Muller. Ulster County writer, Henry Winslow attended with his pregnant wife. When asked about the nuptials, he responded. "It's been a long time coming. Only, who knew it was for each other?" Weston's mother, Anne, wept back tears of joy. "Finally! I never thought this would happen in my lifetime."

Jaime Weston had been known as a free-living bachelor, connected to a host of beauties and a partygoer in the '70s himself. For a long time, folks had given up on what one magazine called him, The Warren Beatty of the recording industry. "Where that came from, I have no idea. But, does this make Evelyn my Julie Christie? God, I hope not! I hope it lasts a lot longer than that." Weston replied with a laugh.

Evelyn on the other hand practically gave up on marriage altogether. Prior to this, she had been in a seven-year relationship with a photographer from Massachusetts. "It's not something she even likes to talk about. It ended badly." A friend of hers confided.

Weston produced Winthrop's latest album, 'Hero's Requiem' which was released last spring. Slowly it climbed the charts to a respectable #17 position on the Billboard charts. "I was very content with this album and had the most fun with it that I've had in a long time. In a sense, it was getting back to my roots." She admits. Jaime on the other hand had this to say about meeting her. "I knew there was something to her even when I first saw her eleven or twelve years ago. It's just that our paths didn't cross for another ten years. Now, you see the result." Their result is also the shared production of Amanda Jean Weston, eleven-months-old. "She was an unplanned production." Weston smiles, "But a very satisfying one."

Winthrop-Weston also says she won't quit the business now that she's married. "I'm far from over my musical journey and obsession. I'm planning a new album to finish off the contract I have. I'll also get my feet wet by putting on a few live performances around the New York City area. I've wanted to do that for a long time. Right now, we're going on our honeymoon." She laughs.

Tickets will be on sale shortly for her performance at the Hammerstein Ballroom in mid May.

Ed scrunches the newspaper while his eyes peer frenetically at the picture. He utters in a deep growl. "So, you don't like to talk about it, huh? Ended badly, my ass." Ed breathes back unsteadily. In a fast stroke, he slams the paper down on the counter. Taking a gulp, he tosses some bills down. With his bulk, the photographer stumbles off the stool, making the door his mission. He lights up a Camel quickly.

Others see the wire story about Jaime and Evelyn Weston. At the Green Light, Kelly looks through a music magazine, finding the story and a few photos with it. She smiles proudly at her friend.

"Yes! Victory, at long last! Ha ha! No more of that dirty ol' bastard, Ed. You snooze, you lose buddy." She says back while cackling with delight.

In Cambridge, Jill Howard-Broden smiles while looking down at a newspaper. "Yep. I knew it had to be Jaime. That little girl looked too much like him.

She calls out to her husband. "Neil, hon! Evelyn 'Ms. Ravaged Beauty' herself got hitched. Do you know to whom? Jaime Weston. The guy who did our album two years ago. Isn't that cool?"

"Bloody, yeah!" He yells back.

Somewhere in a quiet location of a lobby, Jake DeShane smiles at the sight in the newspaper of the woman he helped at the airport during the summer.

"Cool."

A voice calls out. "There he is!"

A man holding a large camera begins to scurry towards the actor. Jake dashes away in an instant with the newspaper fluttering in the air, landing on the marble floor.

Over in New York, it's more of the same reaction. Dale looks through the New York Post, finding the story. He gives a large smile with his wide lips. While chewing gum he says aloud, "Oh yeah! Too cool, man.

The Punk Princess and Record Producer. That's them. I knew that baby had to be his!

Sitting on the stool, he analyzes more of the story. "I guess happy endings do happen, not only in the movies." Quickly he puts on *Ravaged Beauty,* piping it through the speakers in the store. He begins nodding his head and air drumming along.

"Yeah! All right, Evelyn baby!"

In another part of New York, Rosie looks at a newspaper, smiling at the photo and its caption.

"You found her." She says.

It was one of those pleasing moments that made her feel special to have talked with Jaime. He had found his ladylove and brought her back with him just like he had told her he wanted to do.

"Mission accomplished, young man. Mission accomplished." She beams.

Everybody seems to be quite pleased to hear the news of the Weston-Winthrop union. Those who had thought Amanda looked an awful lot like Jaime were right. Not one person thinks ill of them. Smiles are felt throughout the music industry.

Everyone feels good about them, except for Edward James Brockton.

***

In the middle of June, yellow police tape lines the outer edge of the banks of the lake on a foggy, drizzly night. Under the bridge, uniformed police in raincoats study the area. One turns on a flashlight. Another inspects a darkened tan car removed from the lake.

"Poor bloke didn't have a chance."

Upon further inspection, the light shining on the automobile proves to be lighter than thought. A coroner's truck pulls up at the scene.

One officer says to the other, "You got to see what we found."

The heavier officer rushes over, stomping through mud. Once he reaches the car, the tall thin officer who called him over holds up a soggy ticket.

"Found it while looking for registration. Also, gun permit."

The heavy officer snorts back. "Practice shooting somewhere else? Check it when it gets dry. In the meantime, the only place this fella is flying to is the local morgue."

An officer on the bridge calls down. "Roger! Me thinks we got a sleeper!"

"A what?"

"You know, the feller probably fell asleep at the wheel and dropped off the bridge without even knowing. In the gully with a busted neck. Tire tracks show no sign of braking."

"Yeah. The backseat's got enough Jack Daniels, Vodka, and Scotch to fill up the bellies of a dozen bar folk."

The coroner gets help by the policemen in loading up the truck. The officer shuts off his flashlight.

Roger tells the rest. "We'll inspect more in the morning when it's daybreak. Can't do much right now. He's not going anywhere either. Let's catch some winks, then finish up tomorrow."

Eventually, all of the police vehicles leave, including the coroner's truck.

Crickets are heard echoing in the darkness.

***

At the Weston residence, on the right hand corner wall are record plaques along with various awards. On an end table close to the front entrance are photos. One is an image of Evelyn side by side with Jaime, who holds Amanda on the beach. They both have beaming smiles of pride. Amanda was in a bonnet and little bathing suit. Another image shows the Weston's with their friends and family at the wedding. A small framed snapshot depicts Anne Weston with her granddaughter. On the shelf is a clear plastic frame with the image from Billboard with Jaime, Evelyn,

Bobby, and Dan. Evelyn's Gold RIAA plaque for *Ravaged Beauty* is on the left hand side next to the stairway to the rooms upstairs. The art deco painting, which Evelyn had in her sanctuary sits on the wall next to the bathroom.

Evelyn calls out from the bathroom. "Darling, almost ready?"

Jaime calls from upstairs. "Yeah. I don't know. This just doesn't look right."

"No need to get cold feet now! It's probably not even that bad."

Fifteen-month old Amanda, sits on the couch looking all around.

Jaime mumbles deeply as he begins to descend down the steps. "I don't know how I get myself into these things." He walks down, attired much like his '70s look. The outfit is complete with half undone shirt, dark brown leather jacket and long dark red scarf draped over his shoulders. "Ready?" He calls out.

"Just about!"

The producer suddenly remembers something. He strides over to the turntable, slipping a record on. Placing the needle down, he turns to look back at Amanda with a smile. The record starts with a lulling string arrangement.

Evelyn calls out as she opens the door. "I'm not so sure if this looks right. I love this jacket but I feel like it doesn't fit me the way it used to."

She steps out while adjusting the sleeves. In the background, Etta James croons, "At Last." Looking back up, Evelyn clasps her hands over her mouth. She tries desperately to hide a very large smile. Jaime bows his head down grinning with shyness. She breaks into giggles.

He tells her. "I knew this would be a bad idea."

"No. No! It looks great. God, that really does take me back."

Jaime remains slender and svelte, barely a pound had been gained. He looks her over. She's attired like she had been for the back cover of *Ravaged Beauty*. Her hair is slightly puffier but she still fills that same black leather jacket nicely. The zipper is pulled up a little higher though. Jaime chuckles back, studying her with amazement.

"Wow. You look great. Not exactly the same way I first saw you but..." He lowers his tone to a deep seductive growl. "...Probably better." Jaime leans toward the side of his wife's neck as she laughs.

"Across a crowded room at Cosgrove." She begins. "I saw someone who looked positively breathtaking but I didn't have the nerve to say anything."

He pulls her toward him. Quietly he interjects. "You didn't have to."

Slowly he closes his eyes, clasping his mouth against her lips. She lightly pulls at the scarf. As Etta plays on, they begin to sway to the music.

Pulling away from her husband's mouth Evelyn says quietly, "You know, pretty soon I won't be able to fit into this."

"Next year you will."

"At the rate we're going with one a year, I'm not so sure."

"One thing is."

"Uh-huh?" She looks up.

With a smile, he responds warmly. "You're no hollow pumpkin."

Evelyn throws her head back and laughs. She leans her head against his chest. Her finger tips land on the scarf. His fingers brush against the bottom of her chin urging her to look up to his face. She smiles back. Again, he buries his mouth against her lips. She drapes her arms around his shoulders as he leans down to take in her kiss.

Amanda simply stays silent, playing with a toy in her hands. She could care less about her parents getting romantic with music playing in the background. Evelyn drops her head against Jaime's chest. Softly she kisses his throat making her way down the opened portion of his shirt. His fingers stroke the back of her hair, taking in the sensation. Again, she kisses against his mouth, only a little stronger. He breathes in sharply.

The phone rings. They stop. Jaime's eyes dart over to the phone. Amanda does the same. Evelyn looks over.

"The phone again. You do remember when it happened before."

Embarrassed, her husband looks down. "Never-ending."

"Wouldn't it be something if it were Henry again?"

"Dejá vu." He smiles. Walking over to the phone, he tells his wife, "I'll get it."

Amanda watches. He leans down, picking up the receiver. "Hello? Yeah. She's right here. Okay. I'll get her." Turning to Evelyn he says, "It's for you."

"Me?" She puts a hand to her chest.

He holds the phone for her. She takes it.

"Hello? Liz! I haven't talked to you for a little while. We're fine. Uh-huh. Uh-huh. I wanted to..." She gets quiet. "No. I haven't seen him since then."

Jaime notices his wife's tone changed to serious. He turns down the volume of the record player. Eyeing her cautiously, he awaits to notice if she has a happy tone once again. Whatever it was, it seemed incredibly important. Evelyn draws in a breath. Jaime reaches over and picks up Amanda. She makes a slight sound. He tenderly kisses her forehead, still looking at Evelyn.

On the phone, Evelyn remains still as she listens. "When did this happen? ...No. It's just that...I don't know... What else, luv?" Evelyn feels a cold chill rush through her body. She covers her mouth with fright. "My God... Did anybody have anything to say? Yes. Thank God. No. No, that will be fine darling. Yes. I'll talk to you later. Bye."

Slowly Evelyn places the receiver back down. She goes to sit on the couch where Amanda was. In a contemplative position, she thinks. Jaime cautiously walks over to her as he holds Amanda who toys with his scarf. He looks at her. She looks up at him.

"Uh, that was Liz as you know. She called to tell me that...Ed is...dead. His car slammed into a bridge and fell into a lake near London. It was three weeks ago. They just got the autopsy reports in. He'd been drinking quite heavily. The police guessed he had passed out from bingeing."

Jaime closes his eyes in disgust. He looks down, shaking his head. With his expression, Evelyn informs him.

"There is more."

Amanda tugs at his scarf while he tries to pull it back. She has a stubborn streak. He eyes his fifteen-month old daughter.

His wife continues as she numbly says, "While searching for his registration, a policeman who was looking discovered two very soggy pieces of paper. One was a gun permit. The other was...a two way ticket to New York." Remaining silent for the moment, Evelyn drops her sight to the floor, then darts her eyes back to Jaime. "He was going to kill me."

Jaime looks up from leaning against Amanda. His low-lidded dark eyes open wider with alarm and shock.

"Liz asked me how I felt. After everything we had been through for seven years, I have to honestly say, I don't know if I feel anything for him. After what he had done to me and what he probably had plans on doing... He's better off dead. He would have gone through and done it." She looks down at the floor again, rubbing her stomach.

Jaime walks over to the side of the couch, placing Amanda in her playpen.

Evelyn stands up. She walks over to the middle of the floor again. Jaime turns up the volume again on the turntable. She rests her head against his chest once again. She asks of him. "Make me forget any of this ever happened." With her hands around his leather clad back, she looks up. Etta soothes with a bluesy croon. Jaime's fingers pull the zipper of his wife's jacket down lower, displaying a larger amount of cleavage. He runs a hand through her hair, kissing her.

***

A six month pregnant, Evelyn Winthrop-Weston gives daughter, Amanda a push on the swing in the backyard. The little girl squeals with delight as she's whisked back and forth. Things seem to be so calm on a balmy August afternoon. Jaime on the other hand has been quite busy with something. Evelyn hadn't even bothered asking as she simply enjoys the time with Amanda. Then comes the sound of something resembling a car. The beeping noise is familiar to her, but then again it could be anything.

On the other side of the house, in the driveway Jaime exclaims, "I didn't pay you to drop them!"

Two tow trucks leave the area. He gets in one dropped off car, slowly backing it in the driveway, then the second one. It proves not as bad as he thought. Ah, but he certainly likes the feel of them. His own BMW sits in the garage. There is definitely more room for more than one car. His wife had figured he was collecting cars now, which was fine by her.

While on the swing, Amanda let's out a big yawn.

Evelyn says, "Tired?"

The little girl rubs her eyes of sleep.

"Okay. I'll put you upstairs for now so you can have some beddy-bye. Okay?"

Amanda nods in agreement. "Muh Ma. Muh Ma." The little girl speaks out.

Evelyn pulls her off of the swing and holds her while walking back into the house.

Just then, Jaime dashes up the stairs as Evelyn tucks in the little girl. He says, "Honey, you've got to see something."

She could tell by her husband's enthusiasm that this had to be good. Both wait until their daughter falls asleep. Then they head downstairs where he opens the front door.

With a little nod, he replies. "Check it out!"

Evelyn begins to step outside, but is greeted with the sight of shrubs first. Then she stops with her heart skipping a beat. Her eyes grow wide with shock. Her jaw begins to drop.

There on the driveway is her prized white 1978 Alfa Romeo Spider Veloce. Right next to it is a light blue Aston Martin seemingly enough looking like a 1967 model with the top up. Jaime stands between the two cars.

Evelyn gasps. "Oh my God!! How did you...? How? Where..." She shakes her head in disbelief.

He smiles widely. "So? What do you think?"

"I *think* you're *incredible*!" She laughs merrily.

In a sly manner, he replies back. "Oh really?"

"Mm hmm. *For sure.*" Evelyn edges up to him with the bulge of her stomach getting between them.

They both look down after a hug.

"How did you ever find one?" She asks as she pulls away to walk next to the Aston Martin."

"It wasn't easy." He picks out his matchbook and begins to pull out a Marlboro but looking at her makes him change his mind quickly. He shoves the matchbook back in his pocket as he explains. "It comes with a long story."

She leans against the Alfa Romeo. "Okay, I'm waiting to hear it." Evelyn rubs her belly contently.

"You remember we went to San Remo in May after you got done touring."

"Mm hmm."

"Well, this... This was something I had planned since we got back from England last August. Now, we knew you were going to sell the house but nobody thought about the cars. I wound up talking with Liz and Marco and they offered to help when I told them I wanted to bring back the Alfa. But with everything going on, Amanda, the new baby, your tour in the boroughs... I didn't think much of it. Then I remembered that Phil told me how before he and Mildred left England that they stored the two cars at a rented facility. Marco told me over the phone, 'I'll help you get the Alfa back to the States.' I thought it was a very kind gesture. The Rover got sold quickly to some kid who wanted his first car. Then, when I talked with Liz, she told me it would be great if we could find an Aston Martin to go with it. I thought, 'Great. How do you even begin to *look* for one?' And they said that they would look around and told me to just tend to business as usual. I got the call when we were on vacation in Italy that they found one, but it was red. The owner wanted to sell it but explained that it needed a bit of work. I thought this is probably as close as we'll get to one. Then Liz called back a day later telling me the guy sold it."

Evelyn smiles as she looks at the car. She couldn't quite get over the fact how much it looked like her Baby Blue.

"I remember how you didn't appreciate me getting calls in the middle of our vacation." He chuckles back. Jaime grinds his top teeth to his bottom lip. "But, business was business. And you thought it was Bobby or Dan. I had you fooled." He rolls up his sleeves more as he continues the story. "So, time went on and then Marco called me at the studio in June. He said, 'Jaime, you're never going to believe this. Liz and I searched high and low and we found something unbelievable. You seriously need to come back to England and see this thing for yourself.' I told him it was a bit rough for me due to all of the circumstances in our lives. And he said to me, 'All right then. We tried.'" His voice drops low. "I felt incredibly *guilty* after a while and thought, *'I have to do this.'* I just knew it was something you didn't want to part with. What you had gone through... I don't know? I just felt you deserved some form of happiness and maybe a little piece of home. You know, in case you got a little homesick?"

"Darling, you don't have to worry about that. I'm not. Not at all."

"Well." Being tight-lipped, her husband thinks for a moment. "I told you I had some studio work to do in L.A. It really wasn't L.A. I went to for the week. It was actually back to England. I met up with Liz and Marco. I felt badly that I had to leave that fast, but I think you were in good hands. Even though, I know that Henry and Karen had their hands full with their new daughter. But I'm sure Andi and Vicki handled things okay...along with Mom."

"Oh, she was delighted to spend time with her granddaughter. It gave us some time to talk as well."

He laughs back. "I'm sure that went well!"

"It did."

Jaime breathes back. "To continue what happened... The three of us went to this car dealership. They didn't have the best, but they were decent. This older guy originally told Marco he knew somebody who was looking for a '67 Aston Martin, he actually had one...in his garage. And it's like, 'Yeah, but what shape is it in?' The guy reassured Marco that it was in amazing condition, virtually untouched and no restoration. He didn't say what color. Or at least Marco and Liz never told me. So, we went there and

I told this guy..." Jaime pauses for a moment looking up to the sky for some answer for help on the name. "I think...um, it was Benson? No, wait. Benton."

Evelyn perks up more taking in the story. A little light bulb goes on in her head, but she can't convey her thoughts just yet. She needed to be sure about it.

"This Benton guy brought us over to this garage of some sort. He had at least ten cars. Supreme shape. He claimed he adopted them. I saw this light blue one and not knowing it, he said that was a '67 Aston Martin. Now, this is exactly what we were looking for and we found one. He told me how he couldn't sell it because the guy wanting to get rid of it some eight years ago did not have any papers. He said he just wanted to trade it in for something practical. So, Benton gave him this deal on a newer little car and some money back."

Evelyn begins thinking.

It couldn't be!

Jaime says, "The guy was in such a hurry that he didn't explain anything. He just left this car in terrific shape. Then, I started thinking about something you told me and I thought, there's no way in hell this could be the same, but the coincidences and everything matched up...*perfectly*, I might add. I said, 'How much?' He gave me this long look and then he suddenly said to me, 'You're wife is a singer, right? You were in the paper. I read about that guy she used to be with. That Ed fellow. I recognized the name because he did have to sign for the new car.' I told him that, 'Yes, I am married to a singer.' I didn't know if that meant he wanted more money for it or what. I was like, name you're price! He said, 'Listen, buddy, I can't sell you this car. I have to give it to you. The only person I could ever do this for is its rightful owner. The couple you came with told me the whole thing.' I said that she was devastated by it. Benton said, 'That guy, Ed, must have been crazy.' I said, 'Actually, he was.' So, we had the good fortune of...getting it back over..."

Evelyn looks at him with shock. She gets up immediately from sitting on the Alfa. Her jaw remains unhinged. "My Baby Blue!!!" She squeals with delight.

After a moment of staring at the Aston, she runs up to him. He leans against the driver's side.

That smile of his, Jaime was simply unbelievable. He truly wanted to make Evelyn happy.

She leans over him, giving a long and powerful kiss. She says in a deep, hushed tone, "I love you, darling."

He whispers in her hair, "I love you too, Evy."

Both close their eyes, taking in the moment.

She then feels a small jolt in her stomach, making her laugh. He chuckles back while holding her.

***

Sometime in the middle of September, I.C.E. is busy with studio musicians in the recording room downstairs. A guitarist straps on his guitar, checking the tuning. A bassist goes through lines. On the drum riser, a blue set of TAMA drums are quickly tested. In the control room, Bobby is writing something down on a recording chart. Andrea stands behind, against the wall with folded arms. In front of her is Dan, then Jaime who holds Amanda on his lap. Next to him are six year-old, Electra and her four year-old sister, Monica Broden who sit looking over the control panel at their mother.

Bobby looks into the recording room. He announces as his voice gets piped into the next room over. "Okay, we have "Toxic Passion."

Andrea begins laughing hysterically. "Oh my God!"

Everybody turns to her, including the Broden sisters.

With confusion Dan asks, "What?"

Andrea quiets down. She looks at all the eyes upon her. "Sorry." She says in a rather subdued tone. Moving next to Monica, Andrea stays tight-lipped. Even the four year-old has a hard time figuring out what is so funny. Andrea knows all too well, where the title of the name comes from.

"Ready?" Jaime asks.

Evelyn Winthrop-Weston and Jill Howard-Broden place on their headphones. Jill stands a little further away from Evelyn at a nearby microphone.

Bobby announces. "We're gonna see if we can get this in one take."

Jill turns to her husband and bassist, Neil. He smiles back at her while lightly stroking the strings of the fretless instrument.

In the control room, Jaime points for them to start.

Neil Broden begins a simple bass line. The drummer's bass drum thumps along. Evelyn steps up to the microphone giving a lengthy breath at the start of the song. She smiles, delivering her lines with no melody. It's only her and the drummer's backbeat which is heard. Occasionally, Neil's deep bass groove comes through. Jill steps in on Evelyn's chorus refrain.

Toxic Passion
Your love never goes out of fashion
You drive in the fast lane of life.

Cocaine and champagne used to be for dinner
Until you spotted her that fateful day.
Doleful eyes, wandering lost steps.
No need to wear rose colored glasses.
It will hit you like a ton of bricks.

Toxic Passion
(Toxic Passion)
Your love never goes out of fashion
(Never out of fashion)
You drive in the fast lane of life
(You drive in the fast lane of life)

A touch like soft petals
Lips so sweet that runs down to the core
Body like silk sheets covering a bed
Eyes like black diamonds, rich and rare

I know that face oh so well.

You give me that, Toxic Passion
(Toxic Passion)
Your love never goes out of fashion
(Never out of fashion)
You drive in the fast lane of life
(You drive in the fast lane of life)

Your moves are a touch of first class
Debonair to the tips of your fingers.
That velvet voice that sends up shivers
Street smart but your a romantic at heart.
I like the way you hold your cigarette... Marlboro I presume?

Tell me, which do you rather see burn?

See burn.
See burn.

Ooh, I feel the heat from your flame.

Toxic Passion
(Toxic Passion)
Our love never goes out of fashion
(Never out of fashion)
You drive in the fast lane of life
(You drive in the fast lane of life)

As the music ends, Jaime bows his head over to the side of Amanda. He looks as though he's about to change five shades of pink.

Andrea has her hands firmly clasped over her mouth as she holds back tears of laughter. She looks down at a very embarrassed yet flattered Jaime.

Bobby looks over, as does Dan.

Electra eyes the man next to her with slight confusion.

Hardly anybody understood.

It finally sinks into Bobby's head as he grins mercilessly towards Jaime.

In turn, the head record producer sits with a huge grin on his face chuckling away. Finally able to calm down he says, "Oh God."

He returns to laughing when Bobby announces. "Well now, I think we know what that's about!"

Andrea busts out laughing.

Dan joins in.

Evelyn takes off her headphones.

Jaime lets Andrea hold his daughter. He stands up then taps on the control room window. She turns around to see. With a very large smile on his face, he tries to stay serious. He points to her. As soon as he sees he has her attention, the resonation in his voice grows stronger. "You're gonna get it!"

She laughs back. He's unable to keep a straight face and throws her a kiss while he nods and looks back down.

With her stomach now in the seventh month of pregnancy, she smiles, takes a bow and gives the thumbs up.

Evelyn Winthrop-Weston's second album, *Lovesick* recorded at I.C.E. Studios in New Paltz, New York, is released on December 2, 1989.

***

Catrina Anne Weston is born on December 12, 1989.

www.ingramcontent.com/pod-product-compliance
Lightning Source LLC
Chambersburg PA
CBHW051936020726
47501CB00001B/141